D1499264

Random Survival 4

A Trip To Normal

Ray Wenck

A Trip to Normal (previously published as Hanging On)
© 2017 by Ray Wenck

ISBN-13: 978-1-7335290-3-7
ISBN-10: 1733529039

Book and cover design by *Caryatid Design*

To all the fans of this series and for your continued support, this one's for you. Thanks.

One

"Fishing?" Lincoln said. "Ah, yeah, no. Not me. I'll eat the hell out of some fish, but sit still for that long, waiting for the slimy things to jump on my hook, and pretend I'm enjoying myself is not me, man. Sorry." The muscular black former pro-football player raised his hands and shook them to emphasize his rejection of the notion.

"Well, maybe you should come if only to get away for a while," Mark said, with a laugh. He swept his long brown hair back with his hand. He stood several inches shorter than Lincoln.

"What, you mean like male bonding? I think we bonded enough just right here, safe, on the ground."

Mark gave him a disappointed look and Lincoln reacted. "Oh, come on now. Don't be going there. I get those same looks from Jenny when she wants me to do something I don't want to do. It's called pouting, man, and it's beneath you. Not to mention not very manly."

Mark laughed again. "I can't believe you're not interested in exploring new worlds."

Lincoln frowned. "New worlds? What's wrong with this world? Wait, don't answer that." He scratched his head. "Who else is going?"

"Caleb, Bobby, Becca."

"So, yeah, male bonding."

"Hey, easy now."

"I'm just saying. No offense, but Becca's more man than most of the men here."

"And if you're smart you won't say that anywhere within earshot of her."

"Got that right. I faced linebackers who didn't hit as hard as she does."

"So, I can't entice you, huh?"

"Aw, man! Let me think about it. When you going?"

"Early in the morning."

"When you say early, what are we talking, eight, nine?"

Mark laughed. "No, you lazy-ass, like five."

"Oh, hell no! Why we gotta get up that early? We gotta catch the damn worms too?"

"Hey, I'm offering you a chance for a relaxing day on the water and in the sun."

"Except you can't drink the water and lord knows I'm done working on my tan."

"We'll catch some fish we can store for the fast-approaching winter."

Lincoln shivered. "Don't remind me. Now, if we were taking a trip south, that might make me want to get up at five in the freaking morning."

"Okay. Okay. I won't beg. If you change your mind, we'll meet here at five."

"I ain't got no fishing gear."

"Don't worry. I've got plenty."

"I was afraid you'd say that."

"Well?"

"Stop pushing. I said I'd think about it. If I'm here, I'll be going. If not, I'll reserve a special place in my dreams for you."

Becca and Bobby came out of the farmhouse carrying bags full of gear and supplies. "So," Becca said to her father, "did you talk him into it?"

Mark dropped the tailgate on the SUV and the sibs slid their gear inside. "I don't think I made a good enough case for him to want to get up early and spend the day with us." She turned to her brother, a sparkle in her green eyes. "Huh! Told you. Pay up."

"Lincoln!" Bobby whined. "I had faith in you. You let me down." He opened his duffel bag and rummaged through it before pulling out his hand. "I was saving this for a special occasion." He displayed a candy bar. "Was gonna eat it to celebrate catching my first fish."

Becca snatched it from his hand. "Better I have it. It'd melt before you caught a fish."

"Bet you that bar I'll catch one before you do."

Becca looked from the chocolate bar back to Bobby and back to her prize. "As tempting as that bet is, I think I'll just enjoy this now."

Bobby reached into his bag again and pulled out a second bar. "You might win this one."

Her eyes lit with delight. "Oh, that's my favorite."

She reached to grab it but he pulled it away. "I don't think so."

"Aw, Bobby. Sweet baby brother. Trade me."

"No. Is it a bet or not."

Becca blew out a breath and held out her hand. "Bet."

Bobby shook her hand and replaced the candy in the bag. He looked at his sister and thought better of it, taking the candy back out and putting it in his pocket.

"Bobby!" She said in mock indignation. "Don't you trust me?"

"Hell, no." He walked to the back of the SUV and tossed in the bag.

"Daddy, did you hear what your son just said to me?"

He raised his hands in defense. "Oh no, you don't. Don't try to drag me into this."

"Yeah, I can see this would be a fun trip," Lincoln said.

"Give it some thought. It might be more fun than you

think. Certainly more fun than hanging around here. We'll even let you sleep on the way there."

"Like I said, I'll let you know." He waved and started off across the street.

Mark watched him go and then shifted his gaze to his children. They had changed so much since the deadly Event that altered the world. Not that they'd had a choice if they were to survive, and it wasn't what he would've wanted for them, but they'd adapted well. Both were tall and lean and fortunately, resembled their mother, Sandra, a victim of the Event, along with his youngest son, Ben. But it was Becca who'd changed the most. Her mental state was a constant source of concern for him.

Gone was the spoiled, blonde-haired young socialite, as if that person had perished with all the rest of humanity. That sweet, but pretentious young woman had been replaced by one far more dangerous. Her temper switch could be triggered in an instant. The sparkle in her eyes now, transformed to fire, and her playful banter to venom. In truth, when that persona manifested, he barely recognized her as his daughter.

He listened as she tried to persuade her brother into giving up the treasured candy bar. Shaking his head, Mark went inside the old farmhouse they'd called home for the past four months and through the kitchen. Two teenaged girls and a trim blonde woman stood at the sink, washing the dinner dishes. "Hey, ladies, how's it going?"

"Okay," the woman said, "but we can always use an extra set of hands."

"As tempting as that sounds, Caryn, I think I'll pass this time."

"I think he's afraid of getting his hands wet," the taller of the two young girls said.

The second girl added, "Yeah, the soap might actually hurt him." They laughed.

Caryn tried to hide her smile. "Girls," she mock-scolded,

4

"be nice to poor Mark. You wouldn't want his hands to shrivel. How would he fish?"

"He'd come home with minnows," one said and they laughed again.

Mark smiled too. It was good to see Caryn smiling and fitting in so well, after her ordeal just three weeks ago, kidnapped by a rival community. At the time, Mark feared the woman's mental state would be too damaged to rebound, but with Lynn's help, she'd made great strides. "Oh, you think that's funny, eh, young ladies?" He stepped to the sink, scooped up a handful of suds and dropped them on the girls' heads. "Now, that's funny," he said and hurried from the kitchen, their squeals following him.

He entered the first-floor bedroom he shared with Lynn and went to the closet. He bent and reached toward the back, his hand touching a canvas bag. The door opened, and Lynn entered. He released the bag, grabbed a pair of boots and stood abruptly.

"Hi," he said as cheerfully as possible.

She stopped, looked down at the boots, flashed a smile that didn't last and said, "Hi, yourself."

Lynn was attractive. Standing about five-five, her brown hair had grown long over the past few months. She wore it pulled back in a ponytail. Tiny scars marked her face, tokens of the battles and hardships they'd faced since the Event that changed their world. He always thought of the apocalypse they'd faced in those terms since they still didn't know the cause. The community had discussed it at length since then. They all agreed it was some sort of disease or bio-engineered agent, but no one knew exactly what it was or who had set it loose.

"You should come with us. It's not too late to change your mind. You might actually relax and have some fun."

"We've been over this. With you gone, I need to be here. We can't both be away. There's too much that needs to be done before the winter hits."

5

He sighed. "We won't be gone long. I promise I'll get all the tasks done before the cold comes. I just need a break."

"Since when do you need hiking boots on a fishing trip?"

He looked down at the boots and knew he'd been busted.

"You don't have to hide that you're taking extra weapons. I'm not happy about your trip, but I'd rather you be prepared than not."

Mark sighed, set the boots down and stepped forward.

Lynn dodged his attempt to take her in his arms. "I'm not some prissy little housewife you have to coddle and try to appease. You know how I feel about this excursion of yours, but you've made up your mind. End of story." She brushed past him and moved to her side of the bed.

"Lynn, come on."

"Don't, Mark." She held up her hands and looked out of the window.

"Lynn, can't you understand? It's just a need to do something from the world we used to know. To believe things can be that way again; to live a normal life."

"Huh! Normal!" she almost spat out the words as if they were a bad taste. "Like that will ever happen again. You're fooling yourself, your kids … and me, if you believe there's a chance of normal ever returning."

"I have to at least try, Lynn. Isn't that what we're trying to do here? To create some sense of normality for everyone? Isn't that what we all want? A return to the way things were before, if only for a few precious moments?"

She crossed her arms and stared at him. He knew he'd scored with that last remark, after all, it was the truth, but that wasn't the real reason she was angry and he knew it.

"I understand why you say you're going. I understand the rationale, or at least what you tell me, but if you are really honest with me, with yourself, you know the real reason you're going is because you need the excitement.

You thrive on the danger, as though you're addicted to it. Don't try to cover it by saying you're doing something good for the community, because we both know better."

"So, what? You think my whole purpose for going is to find a fight? Is that how you see me? Some warmonger who can't get enough of death?"

She frowned and pursed her lips as if trying to decide how best to phrase her next sentence. "You're a good man, Mark, and I do love you, but the emotional toll you exact each time you leave here, never knowing if you're going to come back, is more than I can take. Isn't it bad enough that danger seems to find us? Why go out looking for more?"

The words hit him like a fist. He reeled and took a step back. "Lynn, what are you saying?"

She turned her head and averted her eyes. She swallowed hard.

Mark stepped forward and she turned back, her eyes full of tears. "I'm saying that you should go. Catch your fish so we'll have food for the winter. Have fun and be safe."

"No, that's not what you're saying." He moved closer, but she backed away, so he stopped. "I don't know what to say to you now. I certainly don't have to go. If I'd known you felt this strongly, I would've dropped the trip right away."

"You knew, Mark. You just weren't listening. After everything we've been through in the past few months, I'm not emotionally strong enough to deal with another crisis. It's bad enough when trouble finds us, but making yourself a target for more makes no sense to me. You do what you want to do, you usually do anyway. I think it's best for me, for the time being, that I find someplace else to sleep, perhaps to live."

"What? Lynn, no!"

"I've been giving this a lot of thought. We're too crowded here already. Caleb and Ruth and I will find another house. Don't worry, we'll stay close. I won't abandon the family."

"No, just me," he spat bitterly.

"I just think it will be better for me to have some distance for a while." Tears streamed down her face. She wiped at them.

His anger softened. He wanted to take her in his arms and hold her, to reassure her that everything would be all right, but he found he couldn't move. Whether from the shock, or the fear that she would reject him, he stood crushed and staring. Anger rose up again. He stomped to the closet, reached in for the bag that held his weapons and pulled it out. In a hard voice, he said, "Don't bother. You want to be free of me, I'll go." He stormed from the room and out of the house.

Mark reached the SUV and climbed into the driver's seat, tossing the bag to the other side. He started the engine then noticed Bobby approaching with two sleeping bags. Bobby leaned in the driver's side window. "What's up? Where you going?"

Mark tried to hide his anger, but he'd never been very good at it. "I'm going to do a sweep of the area. I'll be back late. We can load anything else we need in the morning. I'll see you then."

"Ah, okay. Can I put these in the back, since I've got them?"

Mark tried to smile. The effort strained his face. "Yeah, sure. Go ahead."

The bags deposited, Bobby walked by. "All set. See you bright and early in the morning."

"Yep." Mark put the vehicle in reverse, but before he could move, he saw Lynn, arms wrapped around her body, standing on the back porch. Their eyes held for the briefest of moments; he turned his head and backed down the driveway. He drove off with no real plan in mind. Mark just knew he needed to drive, and far away from there.

The farther he drove, the more his speed increased. The

faster he went, the angrier he got. How could she do this to him? How could she say or think those things about him? Ten minutes. Fifteen. The miles flew by in a blur of trees, long empty farmhouses and overgrown, unharvested crops. The rage was too intense to allow sensible thought.

As the distance from the house increased, he calmed down. He looked around to get his bearings. He had no idea of how far he'd gone, the area around him unfamiliar. He slowed to get his bearings. The drive had been straight, no turns, other than those in the road. The sun had created a beautiful sunset when he left the house, but it had long given way to darkness.

In the dark, finding a landmark was not easy. He flicked on the headlights to get an idea of his whereabouts, but didn't want to leave them on too long, for fear they'd draw predators like moths to a flame. Much of the surrounding countryside and farmland looked alike. Mark speculated he'd crossed the state line into Michigan, which meant he'd gone more than twenty miles. More like fifty.

Recognizing the futility of trying to out-drive his problems, Mark pulled to the side of the road and turned off the lights. He sat in the dark listening to the night sounds. Other than insects and a distant owl, there weren't many. The silence was both calming and eerie.

Mark slid down in his seat and tried to relax, but replaying the bedroom scene only made him more tense. It was clear Lynn was upset with his plan to go fishing. It was equally clear that she'd been thinking about leaving him for a long time. How long, he wondered, and when had things changed? She certainly couldn't blame him for their last traumatic encounter, could she? It hadn't been his fault. Besides, he was the one who risked his life to rescue her.

He focused on her words. Did she really think he was 'addicted to danger'? How could she – this was nothing more than a simple fishing trip, wasn't it? He turned the thought inward, performing a self-examination. Maybe he did have an ulterior motive. No! The idea was ridiculous. How could she think anyone would rather be in a fight for their lives instead of living in peace? That wasn't him. Couldn't be him.

Sure they would do some exploring on the trip and in this new world the possibility of danger lurked around every turn in the road, but that didn't mean the purpose of their excursion was to find it and get involved. That was ludicrous.

An image of Lynn's face drifted before his eyes. A lump formed in his throat. He didn't want to lose her: he loved her and didn't want to live without her. How had everything gone so wrong so fast – had he really changed that much?

Mark lowered the seat and lay back. What was he going to do?

Two

He smacked his cheek, squashing the mosquito. The buzzing had awakened him. It took a moment to remember where he was. He sat up and worked his right shoulder. It had cramped, pinned beneath him on the seat. In fact, his entire body ached from the awkward position he'd slept in. Darkness still surrounded him, but the eastern sky was somewhat lighter. Panic assailed him. What time was it? He thought about the grief he would get from the kids if he were late. He started the engine, with no recollection of shutting it off. Insects flew around the interior. He rolled up the windows and wondered how many times he'd been bitten during the night.

Turning around the SUV, he started back. The kids would be disappointed, but he'd decided to cancel their fishing trip. They could take a day trip to the river instead. They would just have to understand. The idea of losing Lynn had swayed him, breaking down the wall of anger he'd constructed. Lynn was more important to him than any expedition.

He pressed the pedal down further, anxious to see her. To hold her and to apologize. Mark vowed to make amends somehow. He would convince her he wasn't as she envisioned him and was still the man she had fallen in love with. He had to. His speed increased.

With the farmhouse still a half mile away, he slowed, not wanting to squeal the tires into a high-speed turn and wake everyone. Bobby and Becca sat on two large coolers, waiting, when the driveway came into view.

He parked and hopped out. Excited, adrenaline pumping, he tossed the keys to Bobby and said, "Slight change of plans. Load up and I'll explain on the road."

"Dad," Bobby said.

"Get Caleb. We should be ready to go in a few minutes."

"Dad," he repeated.

"Just a minute, Bobby. I have to tell Lynn something." He jumped up on the porch two steps at a time.

"Daddy, listen," Becca said with more force.

Something in her tone made him stop and turn.

"She's gone, Daddy. They're all gone. Lynn, Caleb, Ruth and Alyssa. They packed up after you left and drove off. She wouldn't talk to me. She just gave me a hug and told me to be safe and tell you she was sorry."

Stunned, he sat down on the top step and tried to wrap his head around what his daughter had just said.

"What's going on, Daddy? Why did she leave? Did you guys have a fight?"

Mark was too devastated to respond.

Bobby walked closer. "Dad. What should we do?"

Becca came over and stood next to her brother. "She said she left a note for you."

"Dad," Bobby said. "Talk to us. Do you want to go find her?"

Mark drew in a long breath and let it out slowly. He shook his head. "No, I think we should go fishing." He stood.

"What?" said Bobby. "Are you sure?"

"No, Daddy. You need to go after her."

Again, he shook his head. "No. This is what she wants. She wants her space from me. Load up the SUV. I'll be ready in a minute." He stood and went inside. In the bedroom he found the envelope lying on the dresser, his name printed on the outside. He picked it up, fearful of what lay within, placed a finger under the flap, hesitated, and set it back down where he'd found it.

So be it.

He left the room and closed the door behind him.

His dark mood made for a long, silent and strained drive. They were a good ten miles down the road before Mark remembered his children were in the car. He glanced over. Bobby sat in the back, his head rested on the seat, eyes closed. Becca stared out of the passenger side window. Guilt helped him shake free of the depression. They'd been excited about this trip for days. Now, they looked as if they'd rather be anywhere else. He couldn't blame them. Ironic that the very trip that had enlivened them for more than a week was also responsible for the dark cloud that shrouded the vehicle now.

Determined to bring the fun back, he cleared his throat and said, "So, I've been thinking. I had a friend who owned a boat he used to keep docked at this marina. He took me out on it several times. I think it's a twenty-seven footer and ..." he turned and forced a smile to his face. Both kids' faces remained expressionless. "... I know where he keeps, or at least kept, the key."

Neither one spoke.

"Come on guys. I'm sorry for my bad mood. We've been looking forward to this trip for days. Let's not ruin it now."

Becca was first to speak. "It's not that we're not excited, Daddy, it's just that, at the moment, there're more important things that need to be dealt with. We could go fishing any time."

"We could. And I was going to suggest that this morning. But, when I found she ... well, anyway, that changed, and I for one am gonna have some fun. So, before we get too far away, let me know if you'd rather go back."

"That's not what we're saying, Dad," said Bobby. "Lynn's important, not just to you, but to all of us. You should've talked to her before we left."

"Leaving without settling the problem is a big mistake, Daddy. Trust me, as a woman, I'd be more hurt that you left without talking about the situation."

Mark felt anger surfacing again. That had been his intent. How was he to know Lynn would pack up and leave in the middle of the night? "There was nothing I could do. I wanted to talk to her, but she was already gone. I have no idea where she went or even where to start looking for her. Besides, she said she needed time to think. I'm respecting her wishes."

He pulled to the side of the road. "By the time we get back we'll both have had time to think and cool down. We'll be able to discuss the situation without saying things that will hurt each other. I understand what you're saying and appreciate your concern, but had she wanted to talk, she would've still been there. The fact that she couldn't wait to leave tells me she had no interest in talking. When she's ready, I'll listen. Now, do we go back, or do we go fishing?"

"Seems to me, you're the one who left first," Becca said.

Bobby leaned forward and placed a hand on her shoulder. "You're really not helping."

"Hey, just saying—"

"Let them figure it out for themselves."

Becca looked at Bobby, who shrugged. Looking back at his father, Bobby said, "You think those keys will still be there?"

Mark smiled. "Won't know till we look."

Becca shrugged and said, "Drive on, oh clueless one." She slid down in the seat and put her feet up on the dash.

Mark didn't move, feeling unsure of his decision.

"Well, what are we waiting for?" Becca said. "The longer we sit here, the longer Bobo has to think about how bad I'm going to kick his butt catching fish. That's just too cruel, even for me."

Mark laughed. Bobby gave a derisive snort. "You must be dreaming again." He made a sound with his mouth. "Hmm! I can already taste that candy bar."

"Yeah, about that. I think the best you're going to be able to do is smell it on my breath."

"What? Are you serious?"

"What can I say? Give a girl chocolate, it's going to get eaten."

"Unbelievable." Bobby shook his head.

Mark drove back on the road laughing to himself. This trip and being with his children was the best therapy he could have for Lynn leaving him, or what his dark thoughts now termed, her betrayal of him and the family.

Three

Mark estimated the drive would take about an hour and a half to reach the marina and channels that lead to Lake Erie. He hadn't been fishing for many years, but he knew it might be too late in the season for a great haul. On the other hand, there wouldn't have been many fishermen depleting the numbers this year either. Anyway, there was never a guarantee when you went fishing. They were either hitting or not. This was just as much about the adventure as the fishing.

That thought gave him pause. Wasn't that exactly what Lynn had said? *No!* He shut down the replay of her voice in his head. Looking for adventure and searching for trouble were two entirely different things. Not necessarily exclusive, but definitely separate.

They reached the expressway and went south on US-23. North was the faster route, but it would bring them too close to the city and the potential for danger. The thought leaped to his mind, *See Lynn, I'm going out of my way to avoid trouble.*

The sun had risen and as the road curved east, shone straight in their faces. A multitude of various vehicles dotted the road, and Mark slowed to maneuver around them. Several times, the abandoned vehicles were so prolific he had to drive along the shoulder to continue.

Mark swung north onto I-75 then took the off-ramp for 795, east. The sound of his children's excited voices as they chided each other kept negative thoughts from his mind. The morning was shaping up nicely. For late October the weather had been remarkably warm; more late spring than fall. The majority of trees still retained their green canvas. He relaxed and slid an old Keith Urban CD into the player. The first song's upbeat tempo quieted Bobby and Becca and soon had them all tapping in rhythm.

Becca started to sing along and Mark turned to watch her. Gone was the intense, hard-edged woman he'd come to accept as his daughter, who had replaced the young lady he'd sent off to college, what seemed so many years ago. She looked at him and winked. The sight warmed his heart and brought back an instant flood of memories.

The song ended, snapping the moment.

"Not bad, sis," said Bobby.

"Thanks, Bobo."

"I mean, if you enjoy the sound of a bullfrog croaking."

The next sound was a smack.

"Ow!"

"Serves you right, asshole."

The peace was nice while it lasted, thought Mark.

At the end of 795, Mark took I-280 north until he hit Route 2. There he continued east. It would've been faster taking the turnpike, but Mark wanted to take the narrower and more residential path and explore. Most of the foraging they'd done, for food and essential goods, had been on the western outskirts of the big city. After witnessing the death and destruction of the survivors inhabiting the suburban city of Sylvania, he thought it best to avoid the more populated areas. Now, six months after the event, he hoped the Wild West attitude had died down enough to make passage and exploration safer.

Maneuvering the two-lane road was more difficult than

17

the expressway. It left little room when blocked by abandoned vehicles. Steep drainage ditches often lined the roadsides. Several times, Mark had to reverse and find an alternate path around. In the end, they were forced to double back and take the turnpike.

They stayed alert for deliberate roadblocks. If the path looked too cluttered, as if arranged purposely, they stopped a distance away while Bobby and Becca scanned the area with binoculars.

Eight miles down Interstate 80/90 they found just such a blockade. Mark braked less than a quarter mile away, staring at a semi that stretched across the entire road. That was not in itself suspicious – the road was narrow enough that one truck could do the job – but the two smaller cars driven underneath the semi, between the wheels, made Mark leery about advancing.

"There," Becca pointed without lowering the glasses. "I just saw a head pop up and drop out of sight."

She pointed to the interior of the semi's cab. "I think it was a woman. She looked out of the window." Becca turned and looked at her father. "It's definitely a trap."

Mark nodded. He'd been watching in the side mirror to see if anyone came up behind them.

Bobby's excited voice brought his attention back to the front. "Dad, they're using the drainage ditches to flank us."

Without hesitation, Mark threw the gear into reverse and punched the pedal. He draped his arm over the seat and turned and guided the SUV straight back. A mistake now could put them in a ditch. Seconds after he reversed, gunshots sounded. "Stay down! Grab your guns and get ready to run if they disable the car."

A bullet punched through the windshield. Several others impacted the body. Mark outdistanced the shooters, but the bullets still followed. Fifty yards down the road was a driveway leading to a large storage building once used by the Ohio Department of Transportation. Mark steered the

SUV up the drive, slowed and spun the wheel hard. Shifting into drive he shot back on the turnpike heading west.

"Bobby, open the map and find us a way around."

Paper rustled in the back seat. A minute later he heard, "Ah, okay, looks like we need to go back to the next exit, ah, probably ten miles."

Mark followed his son's directions, exiting at the next ramp. "Okay, now turn right here. About three or four miles on, turn right again. We'll have to make a few more turns to get on Route 2, but I don't see any other way, unless we go all the way to the way to the next turnpike entry."

"We'll keep that option open if we need it. Let's try this way first. Keep your eyes moving. Bobby, you take the left, Becca the right."

They wound their way along a more residential road. At one point, Becca saw a young girl jumping rope in the back yard of a small house. The child stopped to watch them go, but did not react to alert anyone, nor did anyone else make an appearance. In other circumstances, Mark might have stopped to make contact, but now, their senses heightened and checking for danger, he kept moving.

Mark made the next few turns with caution. Twenty minutes later, they arrived at the junction with Route 2. They drove east about six miles and found another roadblock, this one two pickup trucks, nose-to-nose, across the two lanes. They stopped well short of it and managed to find a route around it without much difficulty.

Back on Route 2, they arrived at a place where the turnpike was in view. Mark eased the vehicle forward to a point they could see down the road. Through the binoculars, the roadblock on the turnpike, now to the west, was a dark line across the western horizon.

"I definitely see movement," Bobby said, "but it's hard to determine how many people are there. My guess is at least six, most likely more if they're bold enough to block the road."

Becca said, "I think the one on Route 2 had more people, but it looked a lot less organized."

Mark agreed. He sped away east. "Bobby, keep watch behind us. I don't want them sneaking up on us." He knew there would be some survivors out here. After all, it stood to reason that if he could draw fifty people around him, others could as well. One of his goals for the trip was to establish contact with at least one other community like theirs.

He thought about Lynn. If she believed he was out looking for trouble, she really didn't know him very well. Making more connections with other like-minded civilized groups was a way to join forces when needed, to trade and develop a new sense of community. He had no desire to fight anyone. He would respond with force only if force were aimed at him, or members of their family. What did she expect? He had to defend them. Maybe it was for the best they were no longer together. He pushed the thought aside to focus on the road.

They wound past the old defunct Davis-Bessie Nuclear power plant. The sight made him wonder about the safety of the fuel. Had it been shut down properly or would there be a meltdown at some point? It had been six months, wouldn't a nuclear event have occurred by now? The grounds were deserted and looked abandoned. Regardless, he had no interest in exploring there. He turned the SUV down the road that led to the marina and Lake Erie.

Four

"Great! Now, who's this?" Kentae said aloud. He watched the SUV pass from his vantage point inside the copse of trees on the side of the dirt-and-gravel road leading into the marina. It looked like three people inside. A shard of fear pierced his heart as he thought of his new family on board one of the larger boats docked at the pier. He had to get to them before they were discovered.

He waited for the SUV to go around the bend before breaking cover. He raced across the street and crashed wildly through the overgrown weeds and small trees. Emerging on the opposite side, he caught a glimpse of the SUV, as it turned to the right. He bolted left. Whatever they were searching for they had gone away from Shavonne and the kids.

He ran hard, his arms pumping like a sprinter, one hand wrapped around a Ruger 9mm he'd found on one of his forays in a house not far from there. He didn't have enough bullets left though; not to deal with more intruders. He'd used most of them when he ran into two men who'd tried to relieve him of the food he'd collected. That hadn't gone well for them.

He hadn't told Vonne about that. She worried enough as it was about his constant trips away from them, without knowing all the details of his encounters. But what was he supposed to do? They had to eat, and the fishing wasn't consistent enough to feed them for long. Besides, as much as he liked fish, there were only so many days in a row he could eat it.

Kentae stopped behind a dumpster and scanned the assorted docks. His slight frame was coated with sweat. A wide variety of boats, large and small, pleasure and commercial, were still berthed there. On the far side of the channel to the right, he saw the SUV crawl along, as if searching for a particular craft. It stopped. He glanced down the pier in front of him all the way to the end. The large sailboat bobbed in a gentle roll. He caught sight of Kendra darting past a window. A shudder ran up his spine. What if the girl ran up on deck in full view of the intruders? He had to get to them before they gave themselves away.

The ground in front of him was wide open. If any of the occupants of the SUV so much as glanced his way they couldn't help but see him. He looked right. To his relief the vehicle continued on, evidently not finding whatever they were looking for. He took the opportunity to make a break for the pier. There, he dropped to all fours and peered around a twenty-seven foot Criss Craft. The SUV was still moving. Kentae bear-crawled past two more small crafts, before stopping behind a much larger boat. There he stood and walked to the end, watching the SUV's progress without fear of being seen.

The vehicle inched forward and stopped. Evidently, it had found what it was looking for; it turned into a parking spot in front of a cabin cruiser. Three people, two men and a woman, got out. While the older of the two men walked toward the dock, the other two stretched and looked around. Their excited voices carried over the channel, but the words were lost in the breeze.

Kentae gave a nervous look at the vessel he'd called

home for the last few months. To his horror, Kendra had come outside and was now playing with something on the aft deck. Whatever it was had her standing, up swinging around, then dropping down. He sent a glance toward the people on the far channel bank. Neither of the men faced in Kendra's direction, but the woman appeared to look directly at her.

As Kendra popped up again, he prayed she would look his way. He gesticulated wildly with his hands in a downward motion, but the girl did not see. Kentae's nerves felt on fire. He weighed the chances of advancing further unseen, but the next two berths were unoccupied. Even a peripheral glance would catch him in the open.

He swept his gaze along the dock to find a safe path to the boat. His only real option was to drop into the water on the far side of the dock and swim. Kentae looked up and, at that moment, Kendra caught his eye. A bolt of mixed relief and panic hit him. She waved. He feared she would shout out, or at the very least, draw attention to herself with her hand movements.

Using both hands, he motioned with a downward sweeping wave. She waved back with both hands, evidently thinking he was playing a game with her. Frustrated, he shook his head, lifted his arms over his head and slower this time brought his arms down, dropping to his knees at the same time. To his relief, Kendra followed suit, ducking below the gunwale. He blew out a big breath and sneaked a furtive glance at the trio across the water.

His heart sank when he stood again, Kendra stood up and giggled. His heart skipped a beat and threatened not to restart. Though soft, the sound of her laugh reached him with ease. How much farther did it carry? In answer, the woman on the far bank froze and scanned the marina. Ready to defend his new family, Kentae raised the gun and aimed. It was a long shot from there with a handgun and he wasn't all that proficient with the weapon, but if they became a threat, his shots would at least serve to keep their heads down until he could reach the boat.

In a slow sweep, the woman's head moved from left to right, first taking in the shore, then across the first rows of boats. If the silly girl didn't get down fast, she'd be discovered and the fight would be on.

Again, more frantic now, he waved for her to get down. She did, but less than five seconds later she was back up. This time, however, as soon as she stood, she was hauled down by some unseen force and did not rise again. Concerned, yet thankful, Kentae wondered what happened. He hadn't heard a shot, nor had he seen anyone else on deck. A dark glistening face appeared in the cabin window. Shavonne. She had one hand wrapped around Kendra's mouth. With the other, she waved that she had everything under control.

Kentae dropped to his haunches, hugged his knees tight to his chest and rocked gently. Once again, Shavonne had come through. He sat for a long moment before snapping from his tension-initiated fugue. The danger still existed.

Seconds later, an engine sputtered to life across the water. He risked a peek. The woman was no longer in view. That gave him pause. Afraid she was on the move and sneaking up behind him, Kentae stood and let his gaze sweep the far bank. She was nowhere in sight. Panic raced through him and constricted his chest; he gripped the gun hard, as if choking the life from it.

Where were the others? He focused on the boat. The older man was at the controls. The younger man emerged from the cabin, stepped over the side and walked up the dock toward the SUV. But where was the woman?

Again he looked back down the pier expecting at any moment to see her advancing toward him. Could he shoot her? Hell, yeah, he told himself. If he had to, he would put her down, but even as the thought hardened in his mind, his hands shook. He'd had to shoot someone before. He'd shot at several people, but only once that he knew of, did he actually hit someone, and even though choice hadn't been an option, he was sickened by the act. He stood over the man and watched helplessly as his life ebbed away.

Kentae swung his gaze back to the boat. Shavonne would have the kids down and hiding, no doubt with the small .38 he'd given her, held in a far less shaky hand than his. He took in the far bank again. From behind the SUV, the young man and the woman appeared, carrying fishing gear in one hand and a large cooler between them. Kentae's heart lightened, the release of tension powerful enough to hurt.

As they boarded the smaller boat, Kentae raced up the dock for the sailboat. Reaching it, he placed one hand on the gunwale and vaulted. He landed in a crouch, rolled and bounced against the far wall. He came to rest on his back staring up at an endless blue sky. He took stock of his body, making sure all parts still worked, and crawled toward the cabin. Inside, he pressed his face to the nearest window and watched as the intruders cast off and moved slowly away from the dock and through the channel, amazingly obeying the 'no wake' rule.

Kentae did not take his eyes off the smaller craft until it was but a dot on the horizon. Only then did he turn and notice Shavonne, Kendra, and Toriano huddled on the floor. The skin color contrast made them look like a pre-apocalypse advertisement for diversity: Shavonne with her smooth black skin, wild hair and crooked smile; little red-haired and fair-skinned Kendra, who looked like the model for a China doll; and light-brown Toriano, the product of a Cuban father and Greek mother. Kentae's own chocolate color rounded the picture out.

He gave them a reassuring smile, though inside his pulse still raced. It had been a long time since anyone had ventured into the marina to explore and search for food or anything else of value. He'd long ago stripped each of the boats of anything useful. Other than canned foods, there hadn't been much.

"I think they've gone fishing," he said, trying to keep his voice soft and steady.

Shavonne nodded but offered no response. Her black eyes displaying the cold hard steel that had been constant since they'd first met.

Ten-year-old Toriano said, "Why don't we go fishing?"

Kentae chuckled and tousled the boy's curly brown hair. "We can go fishing if you want."

"Cool."

"What about you," he said to eight-year-old Kendra. "Would you like to go fishing too?"

The little girl scrunched up her face. "Yuk!"

He smiled at her, then looked up at Shavonne. Her stoic features had a sobering effect. He knew she was worried. She never took to the idea of living on the boat. To Kentae it was a logical choice. If trouble came, they could shove off and find safety on the water. On land, all they could do was run.

Maybe he was wrong, but he felt good knowing he could escape to where others might not be able to give chase. Even if an intruder followed on a boat, defending would be easier and boarding more difficult. The sailboat not only offered size but the ability to move without the engines running, thus conserving their limited supply of gas. None of that mattered if they didn't see the enemy coming soon enough to shove off. This had been a close call.

"We'll be all right," he said to her. She turned her head to avoid looking at him. Yep, they would surely revisit their previous discussions sometime after the kids went to sleep.

Five

Mark closed his eyes and allowed the warm, mist-filled breeze to slap lovingly at his face. He throttled up, changing the angle of the deck. His hair blew straight back and reminded him to ask Lynn to trim him up. Instant sadness overwhelmed him. He stared out over the windshield without seeing.

"Daddy, this is so awesome," Becca said, snapping him from his dark thoughts. The smile on her face beamed like a lighthouse. Her hair streamed in all directions. She wiped strands from her face, grabbed the window frame, and hoisted herself up to absorb the full effects of the view and the breeze. Her laughter lightened his mood.

Becca found a secure perch and released her hold on the frame, her weight well balanced above the protective glass, she extended her arm to the sides. "I saw this in a movie once. Yeehaw! This is amazing."

Mark laughed at her exuberance before his fatherly instincts took over. "Be careful. We're already a long way from shore."

Becca looked around. Land was an uneven line on the horizon behind them and to the right. Ahead lay nothing but open water. She let out another shout and jumped down. The deck rose to meet her, throwing her off balance and on to her butt. Mark laughed again.

"Nice landing, sis," said Bobby, as he came up the steps. "If you're practicing your diving I think the objective is to hit the water."

"Funny, Bobo."

He extended a hand and hauled her to her feet. She flung her arms around her brother's neck. "Isn't this great? The wind, the smell of the water, the warmth of the sun. It all makes me feel so ... free." She squeezed his face between her hands and planted a kiss on his forehead. "Did you bring my candy bar? 'Cause I'm sure as hell going to catch more fish than you."

"Dream on, fish face."

Mark shouted back over the wind. "Why don't you start getting the poles ready, I'm gonna stop in a minute or so."

The sibs went to work on the six poles they'd brought. As he glanced back watching them work, Mark was aware of warmth spreading through him: when was the last time he'd taken them fishing? It had to be quite a while. Rebecca was still in junior high. The images came back in a rush. His dead wife and youngest son were with them. He'd rented a pontoon boat because his wife had been afraid for Ben's safety. They hadn't gone out very far; Sandra wanted to stay in sight of land. Still, they'd caught fish and had a great day.

As the memory faded, he looked out over the water and smiled. Out here, away from the daily reminders, the world was unchanged and at peace. Coming here had been a good idea, despite Lynn's objections. Lynn. No, he wasn't going to allow anything to ruin this trip. He needed this, and if she didn't see that or understand his need, well, then ... he smothered the rest of the thought. As much as he wanted to come here, he didn't want the cost to be losing her.

"Ha!" Becca cried out. "Beat you."

"The heck you did. Look how you have the sinkers and

hooks attached. The first cast you make they're gonna come flying off and you'll have to do it all over."

"You're just jealous."

"Hey, don't listen. I'll have half a dozen fish caught by the time you get your lines reset."

"You're just messing with me 'cause I beat you."

"Whatever, fish bait."

Listening to the banter restored Mark's good mood. Yes, he needed this, regardless of what he went home to.

It was mid-morning by the time the first fish was caught. Mark was the winner, to the groans and jeers of his kids. He'd settled on a spot about a half mile to the east of the old water intake. They'd been fishing for almost an hour.

"I'm gonna move to the north a bit and try a new spot. One of you hoist the anchor."

"I've got it," Becca said. "I think Bobby's too tired from hauling up garbage from the bottom of the lake."

Bobby had caught an old pop can, a small plastic cooler and the scariest thing, a boot with the bones of a foot still inside.

"Hey, at least I caught something."

"Yeah, nice come back there, bro-ster."

Mark fired the engines and throttled up. Twenty minutes later he backed off to idle and scanned the area. "This looks like as good a spot as any. Drop anchor."

They settled in to do some serious fishing. Mark opened the partition in the windshield and climbed across the bow. There he sat and cast from a sitting position. Over the next fifteen minutes he repeated the process numerous times before he heard the exclamation of victory. "Ha! I win," Bobby shouted. He held the small perch head high and waved it at his sister.

"Now, wait a minute. There has to be a size limit, doesn't there? I've seen bigger fish in a guppy pond."

"We made no such restrictions to the bet. I'm gonna enjoy *my* candy bar."

29

A tug on the line told Mark he had a nibble. He waited patiently, bobbed the line gently, and as the tip of the pole bent he yanked it up, setting the hook. Excited, he reeled it in and as the fourteen-inch Walleye broke the water, he let out a childlike whoop to announce his catch.

"Now, that's a fish!"

"Wow!" Bobby said.

"Way to go, Dad," Becca said. "Bobby, you need to pass that candy bar to Daddy."

Mark climbed down to the deck. Using the needlenose pliers, he reached into the fish's mouth and retracted the hook and ran a stringer through its gill. He set the fish back into the water and climbed back to his fishing spot. He had just completed his first cast when he heard a shout behind him.

"I got one. I got one."

He glanced back in time to see his daughter doing a victory dance. Her perch was twice the size of Bobby's, a fact confirmed by the scowl on his face. To Bobby's amazement, Becca turned to him and held the fish up by the line. With a pout on her face and a baby's voice, she said, "Bobo, would you take the fish off the hook for me?"

"Kiss my—"

"Bobby!" Mark yelled.

Silence. Then, "Please, Bobo; with tartar sauce on top."

Mark's line dipped again. He turned his attention to the pole and heard a victorious laugh from behind him signifying that once again, Becca had gotten her way.

He laughed loudly. "Yep, looks like this is the spot."

For the next forty-five minutes the trio hauled in one fish after another of a wide variety. Before the destruction of civilization, Mark would've instructed his kids to toss the sheephead, carp and other bottom feeders back. Now, they kept them all, regardless of size or species. Food was food. He would smoke the garbage fish and add some flavor to their mushy flesh. They could no longer afford to be that choosy when it came to food.

After he placed another good-sized Walleye on the stringer, Mark was on the bow casting, when a line of small dots on the eastern horizon caught his eye. Squinting he tried to make out what they were. Had they been there all along and he hadn't noticed them, or had they only just come into view? Whatever they were, he kept an eye on them.

Fifteen minutes later, he counted six distinctive shapes on the horizon and thought it might be his imagination, or that he'd been squinting for several hours, but the images looked a little bigger. Mark set the pole down and secured it under the rail, and climbed to the deck. He made a show of stretching, but as Bobby and Becca directed their attention back to their poles, he snatched up the binoculars and went up top.

He trained the glasses in the direction of the shapes. After a slight adjustment, the images came into view: a small armada of various-sized speedboats was heading straight for them. Had they seen this boat or was it a coincidence that they were heading his way? He decided they couldn't take the chance.

He turned and focused the binoculars in the opposite direction to make sure they weren't surrounded. The way back to the marina was still clear as far as he could see. In a long slow arc, Mark scanned the horizon, swinging from Ohio, to Michigan to Canada. Almost halfway back to the line of approaching boats, in the more wide open and deeper shipping lanes, Mark stopped. His grip tightened on the glasses and his heart seemed to freeze mid-beat.

A large freighter had appeared, seemingly from thin air, like a massive ghost ship. Along the sides of the ship rode a line of smaller vessels, like a protective convoy. In a heartbeat, Mark swept the glasses back to the original grouping of boats. Now larger, Mark could make out more details. Each boat rode with its keel exposed, moving fast.

31

A second line of crafts appeared behind the first, raising the total boats to perhaps twenty. On the lead boat, Mark spotted a man with binoculars aimed in his direction. As he watched, the man lifted a hand and gave a mock wave.

"Oh, shit!"

Leaving his pole, Mark ran for the deck and leaped. "Quick! Put down your gear and get the anchor up."

"Wh-what's going on, Dad?" Bobby said.

"We've got company. Lots of company." He started the engine. "Now, stop asking questions and move!"

The deck became a blur of motion as brother and sister went into action. Becca stowed the gear and Bobby handled the anchor. Without waiting for it to come aboard, Mark had the boat turned and heading back the way they'd come as soon as the weight lifted from the lake bottom.

"Becca, take the glasses and give me an estimate on how far away those boats are."

"Boats?" She lifted the glasses to her face and a second later, uttered, "Oh, shit!"

After settling the anchor in its place, Bobby came up behind his sister. "What's 'oh shit!', Sis?"

"There's like a whole navy coming straight for us." She handed him the glasses. A second later Bobby issued his own, "Oh, shit!"

Becca asked, "Can we outrun them?"

"Perhaps not for long, but hopefully long enough to get ashore. If we can get to the SUV before they land, we'll have the advantage."

"You heard him, Bobby, start paddling."

Six

The mist that splashed over the windshield had taken on the added weight of tension. A few large clouds dotted the sky and when one covered the sun, it cast an ominous hue over the water. Bobby pulled out his rifle and knelt at the stern, sighting through the scope. Mark heard him tell Becca, "With all this bouncing, any shot would be nothing more than luck."

Mark shouted back, the wind taking his words, "If you have to shoot, don't worry too much about hitting anything, just try to slow their approach. We need time."

"Daddy, some of them are definitely gaining on us."

Mark didn't respond. Land had made an appearance on the horizon. He hoped he remembered how to get back to the channel into the marina. They flew on and he searched for landmarks. He leaned forward and narrowed his eyes. There! That's the outer channel marker. They were still a long way off.

"Oh, that man is so annoying."

"What's going on?" Mark asked.

"It was bad enough the guy on that first boat kept waving at me, now he's blowing me kisses." More to herself, she added, "Yeah, bring those lips here, lover boy. I'll slice them off your face and feed them to you."

The channel marker inched closer. Mark checked his fuel level. Should be more than enough.

"Ah, Daddy?"

"What?"

"Some of the boats have broken away from the pack. They're spreading out."

Mark thought about what he'd just heard. They were trying to flank him, or perhaps limit the directions he could go. That shouldn't matter though, as long as they could maintain a sufficient lead. "Give me some details. How many boats seem to be gaining on us?"

"I'd say six. Three of those look really long and sleek. They look like those racing boats you see on TV. When we had TV, of course."

"Give me a best guess. How far away are they?"

"I, uh, I—"

"Less than a mile, Dad," Bobby said. "And seriously closing fast."

"Can we make land?"

Pause.

"Yeah, I think so, but it won't be by much."

"Okay, listen. I'm gonna go in hot. Brace yourselves, there might be a collision. Grab the guns and anything else of import and don't wait. Get on the dock and head for the SUV. Becca, come here and get the keys." His daughter appeared at his side. He fished the keys from his pocket and handed them to her, but did not let go. He met her eyes. "Put these in your pocket right now. Do not take them out until you are on land. You understand?"

"Yes, Daddy."

"Get into the car, start it and turn it around. Be ready to move by the time I get there."

"What are you going to do?"

"Buy us some time, if necessary. Tell Bobby to get in the back seat and set up his rifle out the window in case I need cover to get to you." He let go of the keys and Becca stuffed them into her jeans pocket.

Before she could turn. Mark grabbed her arm and held tight. "You listen to this and do what I say. If I go down, you are not to come get me. You get out of here. This is important. If I get shot, you will not be able to do anything to save me. You'll only get yourself captured or killed and after everything you've seen in the past few months, you know capture could be worse than death. Do not argue. You do the smart thing. Use your head, not your heart."

He released her and pushed her away to prevent any argument, relieved when none came.

The channel loomed in front of them. Less than half a mile away the six faster boats were in a position to cut him off from any other option, but to enter the channel. Mark barely slowed as he angled toward the mouth; a dangerous move since he was unfamiliar with the markers and obstacles that lay hidden beneath the surface.

Forced to slow, Mark made the turn into the interior channel. From there, it was a straight path to the back of the marina. They passed the first row of docks and the large sailboat on the right. He thought he saw movement on board the large ship. Their wake had all the vessels rising and falling in rhythm.

"Daddy, the first boat just entered the outer channel."

"We're gonna have to move fast. Gather what you're taking and get ready. Bobby, grab that stanchion on the end of the dock. Pull the boat in tight, but don't bother tying it off." He risked a glance over his shoulder. The first boat turned into the inner channel. Damn! Those boats are fast.

He guided the boat in close, slowing so Bobby wouldn't be ripped from the deck when he grabbed the pylon. "Okay, get ready." He cut the throttle, leaving the engine to idle. Bobby reached for, but missed, the near pylon. Mark turned the wheel hard to get closer to the back one. Bobby snared that one and wrapped his lean but powerful arms

35

around it like a tree-hugger.

"Go," Mark shouted to Becca. She leaped nimbly ashore and raced down the dock, her footsteps thundering on the metal flooring. "Go, Bobby, go!"

"What about you?"

Mark yelled. "Get your ass on that dock. Now!"

Bobby hesitated, but climbed on the gunwale and jumped. His foot slipped and he banged down on his knees. He cursed, regained his feet and sprinted after his sister. Mark throttled up and reversed the boat.

Away from the dock, he turned and aimed straight at the three boats now in the channel. He pushed the throttle to its max, ran for the far side and, rifle in hand, jumped overboard. He landed feet first and struck bottom almost immediately. The water wasn't very deep and the waves lapped at his chest, his head and shoulders clear. His right ankle twisted, catching the sides of the rocks below. He moved with as much speed as he could through the water toward the rocky shoreline at the channel's end. From there it would be a straight run up the slope to the SUV.

The sound of shouts and a loud crash reached him as he scrambled from the water. More shouting, then several shots chipped at the stones around him. Halfway up, Bobby returned fire, his aim much better from a stationary position. Mark was surprised at the closeness of the rounds from the boats.

At the top, Mark ran along the shore until he reached the SUV. Becca had the door open and he jumped into the front passenger seat. As soon as his butt touched the seat, she floored the accelerator. The SUV catapulted forward. The wheels spun, caught and bounced over the uneven ground. A bullet smacked into the rear quarter panel.

Mark turned to see what damage, if any, he'd caused with the boat. He caught one vessel broadside as it turned to evade. Their boat was now embedded amid-ship, splitting the other vessel in half. One body lay over the side while two or three other men were in the water making for shore.

All six chasing boats were in the channel now. One had pulled into an open berth and was off-loading its crew. Unless something bad happened, they should be able to outrun them. His eyes swept back to the boats and he caught sight of two frightened black faces, a man and a woman, in the window of the sailboat. For an instant, the man's eyes locked on Mark's. They seemed to be sending an urgent appeal, "Help us!" Then they were gone, as if he'd imagined them.

The landing party raced for the higher ground. They raised weapons and fired, but by then Becca had made the first turn in the road and the shots flew wide. A collective sigh of relief filled the SUV. They were clear and safe.

Yet even as he sighed, another image opened like a picture-in-picture TV. The face of the frightened man. Mark wondered how safe they would be if the invaders searched the boats.

Becca made another turn and the main road came into view. They had made it. They'd lost some equipment, their fishing gear and the fish, but they were safe. As he settled into his seat a final thought put a period on the episode. Lynn had been right. Again.

Seven

"Here girls," Lynn said, "take the dishes out to the table." She handed over two stacks of plates. The girls went, leaving Caryn and Lynn in the kitchen.

Without raising her head from her task of peeling potatoes, Caryn said, "You know, this past month has been good for me. I don't think I could've survived much longer out in the wilds."

Lynn picked up a bunch of carrots and began chopping them. "You don't give yourself enough credit, Caryn. You're much stronger than you think. I've seen it."

Caryn regrouped her thoughts and tried to approach the topic from a different angle. Lynn had been distracted all morning. The reason was obvious. Her departure had caused a stir amongst the farmhouse community. Many breathed easier when she returned in the morning. "Thank you, but being here, with all of you, has been my salvation. You've been very kind to me, taking me in and making me feel welcome."

"I'm glad we could be here for you. You certainly fit in well. I don't know what I'd do without you."

"I've come to think of you as a friend. Someone I can go to when I have a problem." She paused. "And, I hope you feel the same."

Lynn stopped chopping. Caryn put down the peeler, wiped her hands on a towel, and turned to face Lynn. "I just want you to know that I'm here for you, as you were for me. If you want to talk, you can count on me."

Lynn glanced at Caryn but did not meet her eyes. A flush crept into her cheeks. "I appreciate that, Caryn, I really do." Her tone held a sharp edge of frustration. She must have realized it, because her next words were softer. "I'm not sure there's anything to talk about at this point. At least nothing I'm ready to discuss."

Caryn turned back to her chore. A hand touched her arm. She turned. Now Lynn's eyes met and held hers, an apology written there. "But, if and when I am, you'd be the only one I'd feel comfortable talking to." She offered a sad smile.

Caryn returned it and they went back to their tasks in silence. Two minutes later, Lynn's son, Caleb, came through the door in a hurry, carrying his rifle. "Mom, there's some people walking down the road."

She dropped the knife and wiped her hands. "How many?" Concerned, but all business.

"Five. Three women and two kids."

Lynn turned to Caryn. "I'm sending our girls inside. You know what to do?"

Caryn nodded and Lynn left with Caleb close behind. "How far away?"

"There were a good block and a half when I saw them."

"Were you on watch or did someone report it to you?" That would make a difference as to how close the walkers were now.

"I was on watch."

The community required everyone to take a turn each day on watch. With all the confrontations they'd had since moving there, the watch was the most important task of each day. A regular weekly schedule was posted. Two people worked together on each four-hour shift; one watching the north-south road, the other the east-west.

"Which direction?" She reached a hand back.

"East," Caleb said, handing her his binoculars.

They passed through the long row of pine trees that lined the east-west road, creating a natural barrier between the street and the house. Stopping at the end of the branches, Lynn lifted the glasses and focused the lens. The group of women and children had stopped in the intersection. One woman was looking down the northern road and talking. Perhaps deciding which direction to go. She made a shrugging gesture with her shoulders. Maybe she was the leader.

Another woman looked west toward the house. Lynn looked back over her shoulder but couldn't see past the trees. She imagined rising smoke from their cooking fires could be seen from a distance over the long corn field. Had that been the reason they'd stopped?

"Did you already sound the alarm?"

"Yes."

Lynn just nodded. She studied the women. At first glance, they looked harmless enough. Each woman carried a backpack and were all armed with either a rifle or handgun. The two kids looked about ten years old. One boy, one girl, though with their long wild hair, it was difficult to be sure. Both of them wore small backpacks. One was a teddy bear, the other had pictures of some superhero.

The third woman was short and black and looked pregnant. The woman talking and still looking north looked Latina. She was medium height, but stocky. Her posture gave off a strong confident look. The tallest woman, by at least a head, shifted her rifle from right hand to left and spoke to the Latina woman. The stocky woman turned her head sharply to look in Lynn's direction. Lynn started and backed a step deeper into the branches. *Did they see me?* She hadn't thought she was visible.

She glanced right and discovered what had drawn their attention. One of the daily patrol cars was returning. It turned left at the corner and would come up the driveway any second. "Caleb, quick, go fill in whoever that is and hurry back." Her son left without question.

The Latina woman faced north again and spoke as if she were speaking to someone unseen. She nodded and turned to huddle with the group. After a brief discussion, she walked west. The other two women flanked the sides in a v-formation with the kids in the middle. They looked alert and prepared for battle.

A rustling of branches behind her announced Caleb's return, but the voice startled her. "What've we got?"

She turned to see Lincoln standing there. His presence gave her some reassurance. "Three women and two kids, but ... I don't know, I've got a gut feeling there may be others on the northbound road. Maybe coming through the corn."

Lincoln sucked in one cheek and gnawed on it while he gave that some thought. Caleb came in behind them. "The girls are in the house with Darren," he said. "The others are in the garage or the barn."

Lynn tried to decide what to do. She wished Mark was here. He would know how best to position everyone. But he wasn't and that made her mad. It was up to her now. "Caleb, go get one of the other boys and keep watch on the cornfield. Stay out of sight."

He hesitated and said, "Okay," and ran off.

Lincoln placed a reassuring hand on her shoulder. "That was a good call. Don't worry, I've got your back."

The women approached in a slow but steady pace. As if they'd done it many times before, the lead woman watched forward, the taller woman watched right and behind and the black woman scanned left and forward.

"Should I step out when they get close or just let them pass?"

41

"You should go wait for them at the tables. I'll stay here. If they come through the trees, I'll let them pass, then follow."

Lynn mulled that over, thinking it a sound idea and glad Lincoln had made the call, she handed him the glasses and left him there. She reached the tables and tried to decide how best to wait. She was way too nervous to appear nonchalant. She went to sit, but couldn't make herself settle. Placing one foot on the bench, she felt too posed and paced instead, wringing her hands in front of her. *Damn you, Mark! You should be here to handle this, not off fishing miles away.*

The rear door opened and she jumped at the sound. Caryn walked calmly down the stairs with two coffee cups. She smiled and handed one to Lynn. Lynn took it with grateful but shaking hands. Caryn touched her arm. "Relax. We're all here to support you." She reached behind and pulled out a handgun. "Thought you might want this."

Lynn wanted to hug the woman. She took the gun and tried to slip it in her pants at the small of her back, but couldn't quite manage it. How the hell did the men do it?

"Lynn."

She looked at Caryn who was sitting down.

"Come. Sit, before you fall over."

Embarrassed, Lynn set the cup down and scooted her legs under the picnic table. She set the gun on the bench seat next to her and lifted the cup to her lips. Her hands shook so much the liquid threatened to splash over the rim. Again, Caryn laid a comforting hand on her arm. Lynn gave her a smile as Caryn nodded her head toward the trees. Lynn followed her gaze.

The Latina woman stood there, sweeping a studious gaze across the grounds. She stopped on Lynn and Caryn.

The three women stared at one another for a long moment before Lynn raised a hand and motioned the visitor forward. The leader of the new group took another look around, searching for a trap, said something to someone unseen, and advanced toward the tables.

With the coffee cup in front of her mouth blocking her words, Lynn said, "Is your hand on your gun?"

"Yep."

"If you see the barrel of her rifle swing toward us, don't hesitate, fire. Can you do that?"

"If I have to."

Lynn hoped that was true.

The woman stopped twenty feet from the table and eyed the two women with suspicion. She made a furtive glance toward the cornfield and Lynn was now sure someone was coming that way. Perhaps waiting for a signal from this woman.

"Welcome," Lynn said. "Would you like some coffee?"

The woman seemed to give the offer consideration, before saying, "Yeah, that'd be nice."

"Come, join us. You have nothing to fear here, as long as you haven't come to cause trouble."

The woman hesitated, then moved to the table. Sitting was awkward with the large pack on her back. Lynn thought about telling her it was all right to take it off but refrained. If, and when, the woman felt comfortable enough to take it off, she would.

Caryn stood, left the gun on the bench, and went inside. "I'm Lynn," she said, extending a hand toward her guest.

In slow motion, the woman took her hand and gave it a shake. "Juanita."

"Nice to meet you, Juanita. Welcome to our community. You are welcome to stay as long as you'd like. The only requirement we have is that you do your fair share."

The woman nodded absently. Caryn came back carrying a cup of coffee, the steam rising in the cool morning air. She set it down in front of Juanita with a bowl of sugar, sweetener and creamer packets and a spoon.

"This is Caryn. Caryn, this is Juanita."

43

Caryn sat and said, "Hi," but did not offer a hand.

"I know you don't know us or anything about us, but it's all right to tell the others in your party to sit with us as well. We were just in the process of making breakfast, if you'd like to join us. It's nothing fancy, but it'll fill your bellies."

Juanita nodded in a slow, steady bob as she took in Lynn's words. "You saw us coming?"

"Yes."

Silence.

Juanita said, "How many others are here?"

Lynn paused and studied the woman. "A few. Tell me, Juanita, have you come here to cause trouble?"

Something flashed through her eyes. Lynn stiffened. She didn't like what she saw. Before anything else was said or done, Lynn knew, without a doubt, this woman had brought trouble.

Eight

Juanita tore open two sugar packs and dumped them into the cup. She used her finger to stir then looked up to meet Lynn's gaze. "We're not here to cause trouble, but we will protect ourselves if forced to."

"That's good. As I said, you don't have anything to fear here. We're a peaceful community. Your traveling companions will be safe here if you want them to join us."

Juanita took a drink and closed her eyes, savoring the flavor and the aroma. "Umm! It's been a long time since I've had coffee. I'd forgotten how much I used to enjoy a morning cup."

"How long have you been traveling?" Caryn asked, her voice friendly and light.

Juanita eyed her over the cup. "Seems like forever."

Lynn noted the answer was no real answer.

"I understand. We traveled a while too, before settling here. Where are you from originally?"

"East," she said, and took another quick sip, as if afraid her lack of answers would prevent her from finishing the beverage.

"Understandably, you're very guarded," Lynn said. "That's all right. I can appreciate you wanting to protect yourself and your friends, but we really mean you no harm. Your presence has interrupted our meal time. We would like to continue our preparations and you are welcome to join us, but please, bring everyone to the table. If we're going to be uneasy with each other, it's better to be face-to-face rather than have to keep people on guard watching from a distance."

Juanita drank, watching Lynn with cold, calculating eyes. Lynn wished she would finish her drink and go. She tried to put herself in the woman's shoes. If she was the stranger wouldn't she be just as protective? Yes, but there was something more going on here. Something that made Lynn's skin crawl with unease. She glanced past Juanita toward the corn fields. She couldn't help but think the danger was coming from that direction.

"I will talk to the others," Juanita said, at last. "We'll decide whether to join you or not, or just be on our way."

"All right. Whatever you decide, know you can stay or go … in peace."

Juanita paused with the cup on her lips, then tipped up the cup and drained the contents. She set down the cup hard on the wooden table and stood abruptly. The sharp sound and suddenness of the movement startled Lynn. She jumped in her seat. Juanita's eyes sparkled as if taking joy from the reaction. She stood, nodded once and backed away from the table. Twenty feet away, she spun and trotted through the pine trees.

Both Lynn and Caryn blew out a long audible breath. Lynn stood quickly and stepped over the seat. "Caryn go inside and prepare for breakfast. Send Darren to find Caleb and tell him no matter what, to stay out of sight and watch the cornfields. Hurry." Caryn hurried into the house. A moment later, Darren came bounding down the stairs and ran off behind the garage.

Lynn turned toward the garage and motioned for the occupants to come out. She pointed at the barn and held up a hand like a stop sign, hoping those inside would

46

understand to stay put. She wanted numbers at the table but didn't want to show everyone, just in case.

She looked at the pines searching for Lincoln. Wherever he was, he was well hidden. Caryn came back with Ruth and Alyssa in tow. Lynn did a mental head count. In all, they had more than twenty people in residence on the grounds and across the street in the three houses there. Mark and his children were gone, of course, but they still had the numbers. As the girls worked, she counted off the groups. Three kids under twelve; ten women, eight men. She debated whether or not to send word to the other families off site.

Myron and two other boys came from the garage. Melanie and Debbie came out of the house. She wasn't sure who, but someone was on guard duty watching the north-south road in front of the farmhouse. One of the boys was with Caleb watching the corn. Lincoln was in the trees. She suddenly wished she had more fighters around her.

She grabbed one of the boys. "Devon, you and Debbie take one of the cars and go tell Jarrod about our visitors. Tell him Mark isn't here. Tell a few of the families along the way. Be careful."

Devon ran into the house to get the keys. "Debbie, where's your gun."

The young girl blushed. "Oh, I forgot."

With a touch of anger, Lynn said, "You have to get in the habit of carrying it. You never know when you might need it."

"I-I'm sorry, Lynn. It just scares me."

"I know, honey, but if you get attacked, you're going to wish you had it with you. Now please, go get it so you can protect Devon. Go." She gave her a gentle push.

"Okay everyone, let's get ready for breakfast. Don't stand around. You know what to do. We may or may not have some guests. Let's move." She snagged Myron's arm. He carried his bow and quiver of arrows in one hand. "Go find Caleb and help him guard the fields."

The boy hesitated, nodded and trotted off.

The group broke into a somewhat more subdued version of their daily routine. Soft chatter broke out, but the boisterous talk and laughter that usually started their mornings were absent. Devon and Debbie climbed into one of the community cars and drove off.

Darren came running back from the fields. "I told him," he said.

Lynn nodded and tried to think of what else she should do to protect everyone, but her mind went blank. Her mind kept returning to the look in Juanita's eyes. Had it been merely a defensive look, or had she seen something dangerous there? She looked toward the trees to see Juanita and party coming into the clearing. Guess they would know soon enough.

The guests stepped forward and assumed their marching v-formation. Their weapons were more at ready than before. All eyes moved constantly, like predators searching for prey. Or was that just her overactive imagination? Regardless, Lynn decided to err on the side of caution and leave some of the family hidden. She would never forgive herself if anything happened to any member of the community under her watch. She would never forgive Mark for leaving her in charge.

She missed him, even though it had been less than a day. Lynn missed his strength and his confidence. She hoped Bobby, Becca and he were all right. She hoped they'd had a successful fishing trip. But most of all, she prayed they were on their way back.

Nine

Becca sped toward the main road, where she barely slowed to make the turn. The SUV swayed hard to the left and, for a moment, Mark feared the vehicle would roll. She S-curved back and forth across the road fighting the wheel, before gaining control. As the SUV stabilized, they rocketed forward at better than eighty miles an hour.

Mark looked through the side window at the quickly receding marina entryway but saw no sign of pursuit. An image of the man's face on the boat floated before him. "Pull over, Becca."

"Huh? Why? Are they coming?" She turned and scanned his body, a worried look crossing her face. "Are you hurt?"

"No. Please, just pull over."

Her brows knitted in a question, but she did not ask it. She turned into the parking lot of an old bait shop, braked and shoved the stick into park. "What's up, Daddy?"

"There were people back there on that big sailboat."

His kids looked at him but said nothing. Becca prodded when he didn't continue, "So...?"

"So, we brought those pirates right to them. If they get captured or killed, it's my fault."

"No offense, Dad, but that's crap," Bobby said. "You are

not responsible for every survivor's life. We can't help them all."

"No, but we can help those we can."

"Maybe the pirates won't find them," Becca offered.

Mark nodded absently. "Maybe."

Silence lingered for several long moments. Without further discussion, Becca put the shift in drive, spun the wheel hard and climbed back on the road heading toward the marina.

Bobby said, "What are you doing, sis?"

"What's it look like, Bobo? I'm going back."

"Why?"

"Because it's what Daddy was going to do with or without us. I chose with."

Mark felt the tug of a smile at the corners of his mouth. His daughter knew him well. "Drive past the entrance and park in that copse." He pointed and she did as instructed.

"There's a pretty deep drainage ditch in front of the trees," she said.

"Go in at an angle and no matter what, keep moving. If you take your foot off the gas, we'll either get stuck or tip sideways."

Becca hit the ditch at about a thirty-degree entry. The ditch was dry, which helped with traction. As she hit bottom, the front wheels struck large rocks and bounced. Becca pushed the pedal down a little more and turned head on into the climb. Once free of the bottom, she turned the wheel so they rose on a diagonal up the slope. Twice the wheels spun, digging for purchase, but halfway up the wheels caught and had no problem reaching the top. Becca found a small clearing and drove inside.

"That should be good." He opened the door. "Bobby, tear some branches free and cover the back end." As Bobby got out, Mark stood and stretched. His clothes were drenched. Fortunately, it was not cold, but the slight warm breeze still sent a chill through him. He shuddered like a

50

dog throwing off rain water.

His kids joined him and he said, "Here's what's gonna happen and there is no debate. We'll go through the trees. If I remember right, they'll end about twenty yards from where we were parked. From there we should be able to see the entire marina. If the pirates are gone, we'll turn around and leave. If they are still there, we'll watch and do nothing. However, if we find they discovered the people hiding on the boat, well ... we'll worry about that if it happens."

Without waiting for a response, Mark set off through the trees till they reached the edge of the tree line. He motioned to stop and lowered to one knee. Five boats were in the channel. Two had docked, their crews searching the marina. So far it didn't look as though they'd found the people on the sailboat. The other three boats worked to salvage the wreckage of the two vessels that collided, with some men in the water while others stood ready on their boats holding rope.

Mark reached back without looking. "Glasses," he said, like a doctor asking for a scalpel. Bobby slapped them into his hand.

He did a slow pan from left to right and counted about fifteen men. Too many to go up against. He focused the glasses on the sailboat. Nothing moved, not that he expected anyone to. If he were on board, he'd be hiding somewhere too.

He swept the glasses left. No one on shore was looking through any of the docked boats. One man checked the gas pumps for fuel. Two more men entered the marina store. A crash of glass echoed across the open grounds.

Another man went up the road, following the SUV's flight and vanished from sight. Perhaps, looking to see if they'd really left the marina. "Bobby," Mark whispered. "Cut through and keep an eye on him." Bobby nodded and left without a word.

Mark turned his attention back to the boats in the channel. The man with the binoculars on the first boat chasing them stood on the bow directing glasses in their general direction. He was not large but had a powerful look and military bearing. He panned toward them. Mark said, "Get down."

Mark dropped prone but kept the binoculars trained on the man. He wondered if this was their leader. As Mark's opposite brought his own binoculars in line with him, Mark lowered the glasses and placed his head on the ground. He waited thirty seconds before sneaking a peek. The man had moved on. Though relieved, sweat trickled down Mark's face. Lifting to his elbows, he focused the glasses on the leader.

The man on the boat turned his attention toward the sailboat. He scanned past, did an abrupt reverse and sighted in on a spot. Something must have caught his eye. Had he seen a peeking face, too? From this angle, he saw nothing that would set off an alarm. A voice reached him, though the words were unclear. The leader waved his arm, attracting the attention of someone on shore. A man trotted down the dock to the leader's boat. Given his orders, he turned and ran back down the dock to the shore. There he called his men together, spoke and pointed at the sailboat.

Five men turned and walked to the long dock where the sailboat was moored. Mark's heart froze. Each man carried an assault rifle of some sort. Whoever was on board was in trouble. Unless it was some sort of smuggler's boat, there were few places to hide.

The men boarded, their boots thumped loudly on the wooden deck. The boat rocked beneath their weight. They spread out and searched. Two men remained on deck while the others disappeared below, their weapons leveled and ready, like a trained military entry team. The sight of their professional approach sent a chill through Mark.

Almost as an afterthought, Mark slid his rifle in front of

him without breaking eye contact with the sailboat. A sudden commotion came from within the cabin. He could not see what was happening, but heard several screams, possibly from one or more females, followed by a solo shot, then two short bursts.

Mark lowered the binoculars and lifted the rifle sight to his eye. He made a quick adjustment to the scope and drew a bead on one of the men on deck. He stood several feet back and slightly to the side of the doorway down. The second man climbed above the cabin and pointed his gun downward at the opening.

More shots and screams. Mark tensed. He readied himself, mentally and physically, and spoke in a calm voice. "Becca, switch places with Bobby. Send him here. If you hear me start shooting, take out the man Bobby's shadowing."

Becca didn't say a word. Mark didn't hear her go. He wondered what kind of man sends his daughter off alone to kill someone. Sick was the only word that came to mind, although he was sure Lynn could come up with many more appropriate names.

Activity on the sailboat cleared any other such thoughts from his head.

Moving backward, one of the armed men, came through the doorway. His gun pointed at what looked like a family of three, a woman and two children. A second gunman prodded them up the stairs. The tall, slender, dark-skinned woman had both arms wrapped protectively around the two children.

"Hey, Boss," the top side gunner yelled across the water to the leader. "Look what we found."

The leader said something to the man at the wheel and the boat edged closer and pulled up alongside the sailboat. Mark couldn't hear the exchange, but a loud laugh followed. A moment later another voice drew Mark's attention back to the stairs. The third man appeared, dragging a black man by the shirt collar. The body bounced up the steps and was dumped to the deck. A large blood blossom stained the upper right side of his chest.

A leaf crunched behind him. Mark didn't flinch, nor did he look as his son settled softly on the ground six feet away. "When I start shooting, take the two gunmen on the left. I'll start with the ones on the speed boat. We'll work inward and meet in the middle. We need to clear them away from the family."

His son made no reply, but Mark heard a slight exhalation and knew Bobby was now on target.

On the sailboat, the first gunman ripped the young girl from the woman's arms. "No!" she shouted and reached for the child. The man behind the woman yanked her back by her hair as the girl was lifted and tossed overboard to the waiting arms of the leader. He caught her, turned, took several steps holding her away from his body, like she was a baby with a smelly diaper, and handed her down to the man at the wheel.

"Get ready," Mark said. He moved his sights from the leader to the pilot. With no one to guide the boat, he would have more time to get the leader.

One of the attackers hoisted the black man to the side of the boat and shoved him to his knees. The shooter holding him lifted his gun to the back of the man's head. "Bobby?" Mark said with a touch of concern in his voice.

"Got him."

Mark didn't wait any longer. He exhaled and squeezed the trigger. The pilot pitched forward and flipped over the gunwale into the water. A second shot followed a split second later and the man about to execute the wounded black man fell sideways, a red mist settling over him. The kneeling man, unable to stay upright fell forward and he too dropped to the water.

The men on the sailboat all turned toward Mark and Bobby. Bobby punched a hole through the man on the left.

Mark tracked the fast-moving leader and pulled the trigger, but missed, as the man dove headfirst off the bow onto the deck below.

Damn! He fought to remain calm. He couldn't allow that boat to get away with the child on board.

He scanned across the deck but had no target. With no idea where the child was, and afraid to shoot blindly, he hoped for a lucky shot at the leader. To his left, Bobby shot again. Return fire ripped through the trees overhead. The men hadn't taken long pinpointing the point of attack.

To Mark's dismay, the speed boat pulled away from the sailboat. He focused on the wheel. A hand gripped the bottom, guiding the craft into a turn and down the channel. Mark sighted and fired fast. The bullet passed between the wheel spokes, buried deep into the wood and missed the fingers. The boat swerved, zagged back, kissing off the hull of the sailboat before accelerating away. Mark could not get a clean shot.

A bullet plunked into the ground inches to his right ending any further thought of stopping the boat. He rolled away from the shot as another struck the ground right where he'd been. "Let's move," he said.

"Way ahead of you, Dad." Bobby was already on the move. Mark found his feet and, keeping low, ran an evasive pattern toward a thick tree. He reached it just as a series of bullets carved into the trunk. He leaned against the tree and tried to catch his breath, as well as calm his racing heart. That had been close.

He couldn't see Bobby, but he heard the report of his gun. He peered around the trunk to get a bearing on the shooters' positions and noted there was one less and they were on the move. The two remaining gunmen ran down the dock seeking to reach land. Sporadic shots came from the boats still in the channel, but they weren't on the mark.

Mark and Bobby fired almost simultaneously, but neither found a target. The running men returned random fire. They reached shore and turned toward their boat, however, before they'd gone five steps in that direction, Becca stepped out from behind a porta-potty and fired nearly point-blank. Both men staggered backward. Becca continued firing until they hit the ground and stopped moving.

Ten

"Kendra!" a voice screamed from the sailboat. "Kentae!" That same voice went shrill. Becca reached the dock first and pounded down its length.

"Bobby," Mark said, "Give Becca back up. I'll keep you covered.

His son broke cover on the sprint. Mark kept his sight trained on the receding boats. As the boat raced around the bend in the channel, Mark lowered the rifle. He waited several moments to make sure no one returned before he stepped from cover.

He made his way to the sailboat and was about to climb aboard when Bobby came running from around the cabin. "Gangway, Dad." Mark stepped to the side as Bobby hurdled the gunwale and raced down the metal dock. Though his son was in a hurry, Mark had no sense of threat against him. He stepped to the deck and crossed in front of the cabin. Along the side walkway, a wet Becca, the black woman, and a young boy sat huddled around the wet, wounded man.

The man groaned. Mark set the rifle down and squatted. "Give me some room, son," he said, scooting the boy to the side. Becca had already torn the man's shirt and used a portion of it to wipe away the blood for a better look at the wound. She looked up at Mark and frowned as she pressed the wet cloth against the hole.

Mark turned to the woman. Tears streamed down her face. "Do you have any medical kits or supplies on board" She wiped her face and nodded. "Please, get it," he said, trying to keep his voice soft and calm, but thinking she should have already been moving to get the supplies instead of sitting there crying. She got up and left, the boy trailing behind.

He leaned over the body. "Did you check for an exit wound?"

"Yeah," Becca said. "The bullet's still in there. He needs a doctor."

Mark pinched his lips together in a thin line. That meant transporting him back to the farm. He knelt next to the man. "Hey! Can you hear me?"

He opened his eyes and nodded.

"Let me hear you say it."

"I ... can hear you." His voice was a gasp. He was already losing strength. They might never make it back to the farmhouse in time.

"You need to stay with us. We're going to take you someplace where there's a doctor. It's a long ride. Close to two hours. You have to stay awake and keep strong. You understand?"

He nodded and said, "Yes," in a harsh croak.

The woman came back and having heard Mark's words grabbed his arm. "But what about Kendra? We can't leave her. Those men," she sobbed and covered her mouth. Tears seemed to explode from her eyes. "Oh, my God. Those men will do horrible things to her. We can't leave her."

Mark knew she was right, but what could he do about it? If they transported Kendra to the freighter out on the lake, he'd never be able to get to her unseen. They'd surely have guards posted on the ship, not to mention the small armada of speed boats that served as escort. He'd never get through. Not alive, anyway.

"Please," the woman begged. "We have to save her."

Mark looked from the pleading woman to Becca. His daughter, having taken the small med kit from the woman, was working over the wounded man. While her hands worked, she looked up at him waiting to see what he would decide. She gave a gentle nod, understanding the risk and that it was a suicide mission.

"I won't make any promises, but I'll see what I can do. In the meantime, you have to go with your man and your son to the doctors. My daughter and son will accompany you."

"No, I can't leave without Kendra."

"Hey!" Mark said in a stern voice. "Listen to me. You can't do anything to save her. I'm not sure that I can. If you stay here, they will return and you will be captured too. Save who you can. I know that sounds harsh, but in this new world, it is the reality. Save your man and your child. If you don't go now, he may die. I don't wish to sound heartless, but that's the truth of the matter. If you stay he dies, and you either die or get captured. Go, and you all might live, but Kendra may be lost."

"Ohhh!" she doubled over and wailed. She'd been given an impossible choice. One no mother should ever have to make. Mark knew he'd have to decide for her.

The SUV bounced around the bend in the road and made the turn toward the dock. Bobby braked hard, the tires sliding on the loose gravel as it stopped. He leaped from the cab and ran down the dock carrying the first aid kit. He dropped next to Becca and the two of them worked in feverish teamwork to stem the flow of blood.

The woman pulled the boy into her arms and held him tight to her chest as she continued to weep, every once in a while repeating the same words, "Oh please, Dear Lord, help us."

Mark ran the same request through his mind but knew there'd be no such intercession. The young girl's survival was on his shoulders. He knew, of course, that she would not be killed. She wouldn't be a sacrificial offering. Instead, her body would be offered up, repeatedly, and that thought alone was enough for him to want to try to save her.

"Okay, we've done all we can here," Becca said. "If we're going, we have to go now."

Mark looked at the woman. She rocked, still holding the child. He feared the tightness of the embrace might suffocate the boy. "It's time to go."

She gave her head a violent shake. "No!" she moaned.

"Though your heart is breaking, you know it's the right thing to do." He took her elbow and gently lifted. She resisted, pulling away. "Do you want this brave man to die?"

She looked down at the wounded man through tear-filled eyes. "Oh, Dear Lord, please help me."

Mark nodded to Becca and Bobby. They stood and each took an end, lifting the man. He let out a cry of anguish. As they shuffled away, Mark grabbed the young boy and gently pried him from the woman's grasp. He whined and reached for her, "Vonne!" he cried. "Vonne!"

"It's all right, Toriano. You go with them. You'll be safe. You look after Kentae. I will join you when I get Kendra back. I promise."

"No!" He wailed, but Mark lifted and deposited him over the side onto the dock. "You follow my son and daughter to the SUV, okay? You'll be fine. You have to go before the bad men come back."

The boy cried, but turned and walked after Bobby and Becca. Mark returned to the sobbing woman.

"You really should go with them."

She shook her head again. "No. No. I couldn't live knowing I didn't at least try to get her back."

Mark sighed. He understood but wished he could talk her out of her decision. Having her along would only make things more difficult. He decided to make one more appeal, but this time more forcefully. He grabbed her by the shoulders, gave her a hard shake, and shouted, "Let's get this straight, right now. Having you with me will only slow me down. If you get in the way, I will leave you behind. You're too emotional. If you can't get control of yourself, you'll have no chance of ever saving Kendra. You'll either die or become those men's plaything until they tire of you. Your best option is to go with my kids now. They will get you to safety."

"No! No! No! I'm going to save her, with or without your help. I'm staying."

Mark held her at arm's length.

Her tone softened but her words had metal, "If it were your daughter wouldn't you do all you could to save her?"

His shoulders slumped and he released her. Yes, he would and give his life to do so. "All right! Get control of yourself. We'll leave as soon as my kids take off." Mark went after Bobby and Becca. They already had the man loaded in the back of the SUV. The young boy stood outside crying. Becca squatted next to him and spoke in a quiet tone.

"I should stay with you," Bobby said. "You can't do this alone."

"I agree, but if she stays I need you to go with Becca. I don't want her making the drive alone and unprotected."

Bobby frowned. It was a hard decision to make, but Bobby was smart. He'd see the sense of going with Becca. "Remember to avoid that roadblock. Don't stop for anything. Top off the gas tank with the cans right now, so you don't have to stop along the way."

"Okay. Good luck."

"And to you." They embraced.

"But know this. If I don't see you in a day, I'm bringing reinforcements back."

Mark smiled. He wouldn't expect anything else. The

door closed. They looked over to see Becca had somehow managed to convince Toriano to get inside. She came over and hugged her father. "Be safe, Daddy."

"You too. Get moving while there's still enough daylight."

Bobby finished topping off the gas tank from a spare can and climbed in. Mark watched them go saying a silent prayer for their safety. Once out of sight, he turned to the sailboat and the impossible task ahead.

Eleven

The others at the table picked up on the tension that hovered overhead. Gone was the usual loud talk and sharp-tongued bantering. Lynn tried to engage the three women in conversation, as did Caryn, but all responses were guarded and most came from Juanita. Anytime a question was directed toward one of the other two women, they first looked to her for guidance and unspoken permission to answer.

Dondra, the pregnant woman, looked like a teenage girl in a thirty-year-old body. She rubbed her extended belly in a constant clockwise motion. She'd flopped more than sat when she first arrived.

"So, how far along are you?" Caryn asked.

Dondra gave a quick glance to Juanita. "I don't know. Ain't seen no doctor."

"Oh, yeah, I guess that would be difficult. Do you have a guess? You look like about five months."

"That sounds about right." She turned to the tall lady, Gloria. "When did I sleep with Mikey?"

Gloria's eyes went wide with surprise before they narrowed into a warning look.

"Oh, I, uh ..." she stammered trying to recover.

Juanita put a hand over hers and finished for her. "That

was about five months ago when that animal had you. Unfortunately, we got there too late. The deed was done. Now she's knocked up." She rubbed Dondra's belly as if they hadn't noticed the bulge before.

Lynn watched, trying to keep all emotion in check. Inside she was bursting with angst. It had been nearly twenty minutes since the women sat down to eat. She expected an army to burst into the yard at any moment. The anticipation had the small amount of food she'd consumed doing flips in her stomach.

"I have to go to the bathroom. Is it okay if I use yours?" Dondra nodded to one of the two porta-potties set back behind the garage.

"We can do better than that for you," Lynn said. She covered Caryn's hand. "Caryn, would you show our guest to the bathroom?" She gave the hand a quick squeeze hoping it conveyed for her to stay with the pregnant woman while she was in the house.

"Of course. Come on, Dondra, I'll take you inside."

The short woman stood. "Inside? You got one that works?"

"Absolutely. Follow me."

Juanita watched them go with suspicious eyes. Lynn studied her, her own curious thoughts growing darker by the minute. The two kids sat next to Gloria. They hadn't been introduced nor had they spoken since arriving. They both ate egg packed between homemade biscuits. The eggs came every other day from Jarrod's farm.

Jarrod, a large man, looked more bear than farmer. He had an extension of their community housed at his place. Lynn thought of him now and hoped he was on the way with reinforcements.

"Are you heading anywhere in particular?" Lynn asked Juanita, trying to keep her voice friendly.

"Nope. Just walking right now."

"So, no place in mind? Not trying to find a place to settle

64

down?"

No response. She tried a different tack. "Dondra won't be able to keep up the pace too much longer."

"That's our concern, not yours. She'll be fine."

Lynn fought for control. The tone had said, butt out. A twitch worried at the corner of her mouth. "Not trying to make it my business," she said in a level voice. "Just letting you know, that when she needs a doctor, we have one here."

Juanita's eyebrows lofted. "You have a doctor here?"

Lynn nodded nonchalantly and turned her gaze toward the biscuit on her plate. She broke off a piece and put it in her mouth. As soon as the bread touched her tongue, she realized her mistake. She was trying to give the impression of not caring, but the biscuit was dry in an already arid throat. She struggled to create enough saliva to swallow, but it became a small lump that refused to go down. Before she choked, she picked up her coffee cup and drained it, letting out a small cough.

The other woman, Gloria, looked around the table. Her eyebrows knitted in confusion. "None of them look old enough to be a doctor. Which one is it?"

"She lives off-site. She comes when we call for her."

"Oh. Call her? Don't tell me you have a working phone, too."

"No. We use a walkie-talkie system."

Juanita mulled that over. "Huh! You seem pretty organized here. I see you got windmills. Does that mean you have electricity?"

"Yep." She said but didn't elaborate, refusing to give the woman any more than she'd given up.

"Wow! That's pretty cool. Haven't been in a place with electricity since this shit happened."

Caryn came back leading Dondra. They took their seats. Lynn wondered when the black girl would give her report to Juanita. She didn't have long to wait. The girl leaned behind Juanita and whispered in her ear. Lynn heard, "They have ..." but nothing more.

What had caught Dondra's attention? Lynn created a mental picture of what they passed en route to the bathroom. Other than electricity and running water, the kitchen would be the big draw.

Juanita listened, not breaking eye contact with Lynn. The battle of wills waged. Lynn kept her own gaze unwavering. She heard Caryn say, "Is everyone finished?" A few verbal affirmatives followed. "Let's get things cleaned up. Everyone still has chores to do."

Lynn was aware of movement as other members of the community stood. Caryn stood as well but did not move from Lynn's side. After a long silent stare down, Lynn said, "Whatever you think we have that you want, is staying here. We have welcomed you to our table in peace. You should go the same way."

Juanita took her time before replying. "If there were something here that I wanted, I would just take it. You wouldn't be able to stop me."

"It's good for one of our sakes that you don't want anything. I think it's time for you to go."

"Yeah, maybe, but I'd like Dondra to see your doctor first. Why don't you call her?"

Next to her, Dondra started to object. "Nita, I don't want to see no— Ow!" She bent to rub the foot Juanita stomped on.

"Call her."

"For a guest, you're awful bossy."

"Oh, sorry. Please call the doctor."

"Wow! I bet that hurt."

"Not as bad as what I'm gonna do to you if you don't call her."

"Never was very big at responding to threats."

Juanita leaned forward her eyes boring holes through Lynn's. "I don't threaten."

Gloria stood. "Get up, kids." They did so without comment. Gloria swept them behind her and took two large steps backward.

This is it, thought Lynn. Still, she held Juanita's gaze unflinching. Her gun was on the bench in easy reach. She trusted that Caleb and Lincoln were ready for whatever madness Juanita unleashed.

"Let's put it this way, blondie. You can either call her now or call her later when you're lying there bleeding."

"You've overstayed your welcome. It's time for you to go."

The hard stares became an invisible barrier between the two strong-willed women, built by the tension that emanated from them. A massive test of wills that, for the moment, seemed balanced and equal. That changed in the next second as four men emerged from behind the barn. One held a gun on Myron, another on her son, Caleb.

Twelve

"We're clear, Becca," Bobby said. "No one's following us."

"I don't like this, Bobby. We shouldn't have left him alone." Becca's anxiety showed in the whiteness of her knuckles as she squeezed the wheel.

"I know, sis. I agree, but—"

"But what?"

"I don't know. It's Dad. There's no arguing with him. Besides, this guy will die without our help. We really didn't have much choice."

"When we drop him off, I'm coming back. No one better try to stop me." She glanced in the mirror and caught Bobby looking back.

"I'm with you, sis. Let's get this done first. I've got him as stable as I can. He's patched and out, but still breathing." He climbed over the seat from the storage area and flopped in the back seat. They remained silent for the next few minutes. Toriano sat in front, leaning against the passenger door as if trying to get as much distance from Becca as possible. Bobby leaned forward between the front seats. "Hey, bud, you okay?"

The boy sniffled and wiped his nose with the back of his hand. He shook his head. "Wh-where's Shavonne?"

"She's with our dad. They're trying to rescue your

sister."

"Kendra." Saying the name broke the shaky plug he'd put in the dam of his emotions. He bowed his head, covered his face, and sobbed. Bobby put a comforting hand on his shoulder. "I'm sorry. Our dad's pretty good at finding people though. He'll do the best he can to get her back."

"Yeah, if he doesn't get killed in the process," Becca muttered under her breath.

"Becca!" Bobby said, his voice reprimanding.

His sister frowned but made no further comment.

"My name's Bobby. What's yours?"

He waited several moments before he heard, "Toriano."

"Toriano. Great name. Toriano, you're safe with us. No one will hurt you while we're around."

"Is-is Kentae dead?"

Bobby glanced back at the unconscious man. He thought about his reply then decided it was best to be honest with him. "No. He's still alive, but he won't be for long unless we can get him to the doctor that lives with us. That's where we're going?"

"But, how will Shavonne and Kendra find us?"

"Don't worry. My dad will lead them to us. He knows where we live."

With that Toriano began crying again, softer this time.

"Bobby," Becca said. "We should go back."

"I know how you feel, but we have to trust that Dad can handle the situation. Or at least hold out until we return. With luck, we should be back in less than four hours."

"A lot can happen in four hours."

Her brother didn't answer. She tapped the wheel with the palm of her hand like it had a nervous tic. The situation was unacceptable to her. She was about to make an executive decision and turn around when Bobby said, "Sis, wake up. You seeing this?"

Becca snapped her attention back to the moment.

Bobby's hand was stretched out pointing through the windshield. "We've got company."

Up ahead was a van heading straight for them.

"Shit!" Becca said.

"There's a road," he pointed to the right. "Turn there. Maybe they haven't seen us yet."

"Going broadside will make it more likely that they do."

"What choice do we have? If we keep going, we'll be seen for sure."

"Maybe they're friendly."

"And maybe they're not. Which way do you feel better playing it?"

She made the turn. The street was residential, but the houses were sparse. Becca floored the pedal and the engine roared.

"Turn left at that corner," Bobby instructed.

Becca made a wide turn running up over the side lawn of the corner house. "I don't think they saw us turn. I couldn't see them so ..." he left the thought open. Becca made a right at the next intersection.

"Turn up that driveway on the left," Bobby said.

The driveway was long. A line of pine trees on the left gave them cover. She drove past the house and pulled up behind it, alongside a three-car garage. Bobby climbed out to check the road, while Becca surveyed the property.

The yard was wide and open. Ahead, the grounds stretched about a hundred yards. The back of another house was at the far end of the land. More importantly, no fence divided the two lots. If necessary, they had an escape route to the next street.

"What's going on?" Toriano said, his eyes wide with fright. "Is someone chasing us?"

"Maybe. Stay calm. We'll deal with whatever happens. You're safe with us."

Becca looked through the rear window for her brother but he was not in sight. She felt better being on foot and

70

with room to maneuver, but if they had to leave in a hurry, it was best to stay in the vehicle.

The minutes crept by. A sheen of sweat coated her forehead. She wanted to check on the wounded man but didn't want to risk leaving her seat. She glanced at Toriano to see he was watching her. She tried to give him a reassuring smile but doubted she succeeded.

Several anxious moments later, Bobby came back. He slid in the back seat. "They did follow us down the road, but don't know where we went. The last I saw they were turning on the main road going back the way they came."

"Could they be going to get reinforcements?"

"That's possible. We need to move from this area and find a way around them. Hand me the map."

"Toriano," Becca said, "open the glove box and take out the map." The boy did and handed it to Bobby. Becca put the SUV in gear and drove across the yard. They exited down the driveway onto the next street and checked for moving vehicles. The way was clear. Becca drove a zigzag pattern moving west but keeping away from the main street. Two minutes later, Becca braked.

"What is it?" Bobby looked up from the map, concerned. "Did you see someone?"

"Not someone, something. Look!" She pointed down the street to an old-fashioned neighborhood gas station. Sitting on the lot was a gasoline tanker. "What are the odds there's still gas in it?"

"Man, that would sure come in handy. It's been getting harder to find gas."

Becca said, "Should we risk looking?"

Bobby looked back at Kentae. They didn't have much time for exploring. He gave it a moment's thought before saying, "Let's do it quick. We can always come back."

Becca made the turn. She drove into the gas station and stopped on the far side of the semi. Bobby hopped out and looked at the tanker. He turned to Becca and shrugged.

"How do I check if it's full?"

"How would I know?"

The hose had been attached but the cover over the ground tanks was in place. Either the gas had just been pumped out or the driver hadn't had the chance yet. "I could open the valve, but we'd lose some gas and have it everywhere."

Bobby went to the back of the tanker and climbed the metal ladder. The flat area on top made walking easy. At the hatch he bent, gripped the wheel and tried to spin it, but it was locked in place. He climbed down.

"What about those gauges?"

Bobby bent and studied the series of valves and gauges. He shrugged. "Looks like they're all full." With no other way to check, Bobby picked up the hose and opened the valve. Gas shot out in a thick stream. He fought the hose and struggled to close the valve. It took ten seconds to shut it down. Ten seconds of precious gas was now splashed all over the ground.

He set the hose down took a sniff at his hands, then pressed his face to the door of the station. The shelves were full of assorted products. No one had discovered this treasure trove yet. He got back into the SUV.

"Nice move," Becca said sarcastically.

"Shut up! At least we know there's gas in it. And the building is stocked and looks untouched."

"Now we just have to hope no one else discovers it until we get back."

"Let's get away from here so we don't lead anyone else here."

Becca drove from the lot and turned west.

"Eew! What's that smell?" Toriano said.

"Yeah! Thanks, kid."

Thirteen

Mark guided the small boat out of the channel. So far, the plan consisted of locating the escaping boats, but nothing more. It was hard to decide what to do until they knew what they faced. Entering the lake, Mark increased the throttle and aimed the boat in the direction he'd gone before. The fishing trip seemed like such a bad idea now. Why hadn't he listened to Lynn? They could've just gone to the river to fish. They'd have food, they wouldn't be in this situation and, he'd still have Lynn.

Shavonne stood next to him scanning the water with the binoculars. They hadn't gone far when she pointed. "I think I see something in that direction."

"Like what?"

"It's hard to tell. At this distance, it's just a line of dark dots. But I'm pretty sure they're moving."

He altered course to where she directed. He had no idea what they would do if they found the kidnappers. They were outnumbered, outgunned and outboated. Plus, a nagging fear kept at him that the smaller boats were attached to the larger freighter. If Kendra were transferred to the larger ship, he saw no way they'd be able to get her, let alone get on board without being discovered. Pure and simple, this run was suicide.

If they could spot them, the kidnappers could easily see their approach, as well. It wasn't as though there were places to hide on the open water. No, this was insane. They wouldn't get within a nautical mile of the freighter without attracting a boatload of trouble. He glanced at the tall, slim woman. Her black skin stood out like a beacon against the lighter water, sky, and boat. The glasses were pressed to her face. He understood her determination, but at what cost? He had been just as reckless when trying to rescue his kids. But, that had been on land where he felt more confident and in control. Out here –they had no advantage or surprise, none at all.

"Okay, that's them. We're heading in the right direction."

"But, what are we going to do once we get there? We won't be able to just pry her away from them. There's too many. I want to help you, but how will getting killed save her?"

She lowered the glasses and looked at him. The expression on her face showed that she'd been thinking the same thing. "I know it won't be easy and I have no desire to throw our lives away, but I have to try. Do you understand that?"

"Yes, better than you know."

"I can't just leave her to those animals."

"They won't kill her."

"No, but what they will do is far worse."

Mark nodded. He'd seen what lawless men were capable of; too often. "We have to plan what we're going to do before we get there. My guess is once we're discovered they'll send boats after us. We'll never have a chance to get close."

"What if we let them get close?"

"Yeah, and?" Mark had no intention of letting them get close.

"Trade me for her."

That took him by surprise. "What? No."

"Yes, it's the only way. I'm a grown woman." She hesitated. "I've been through what they are going to do. I can survive it. She's just a child. She shouldn't have to know that kind of fear and abuse for the rest of her life."

Mark stared open-mouthed, unable to speak or take his eyes from this brave woman.

"Say something. You know it's the only way."

"First off, no. Second, if I let them get close enough to take you, they will probably kill me. And third, there's no guarantee that they will make such an exchange. After they kill me, they'll have you both. Oh, and fourth, no!"

"Well, what if we don't mention a trade. What if you tell them you captured me and want to offer me as a gift to whoever is in charge."

"They wouldn't believe I was just willing to give you up for nothing."

"Then ask for something."

Mark rolled the idea over in his mind. He had no doubt she was willing to sacrifice herself for the girl. And sacrifice it would be, because he would have no way of rescuing her and she'd have precious little opportunity to escape. He respected her courage and her determination, but could he allow her to throw her life away with little chance of a positive outcome?

"Shavonne." He sighed. "I understand why you want to do this, but if they get both of you, what was the purpose of giving up your freedom?"

Tears burst from her eyes. "I have to do this. Can't you see that? I will never be able to sleep at night knowing what that little girl is going through. I might as well put a bullet in my brain now. If I'm going to give up my life, it might as well be this way. It's just sex. To me, that's all it is. To her, it's horror and pain and torture and … and confusion, and the never ending, never answered question, why?" She dropped to her knees, clenched at her gut and wailed.

She had made up her mind, but Mark could still save himself. He could turn the boat around, get off and let her do whatever she intended. He'd never forgive himself, but at least he'd be alive to deal with the memories.

"Please, help me. I have to at least try."

Mark fought an internal battle of emotions. He thought of his kids and hoped they were safe. He pictured Lynn. At least if he died this way, she'd be able to say, "See, I told you." He faced the distraught woman, watching the steady stream of tears run down her glistening face. He sighed again and reached a hand to her. "Come on. Let's figure this out."

She grabbed his hand. Hers was moist. He pulled her to her feet; she threw herself at him, wrapping strong arms around his body. "Thank you." She kissed his cheek. "Thank you. God bless you."

Mark thought, *We're gonna need his blessing and a whole lot more.*

Fourteen

Though stunned by the sudden appearance of the men and afraid for her son, Lynn acted without hesitation. To do so might mean everyone's death. "Caryn, get everyone inside now." The tone of her command left no room for discussion.

Caryn said. "Come on ladies, move!"

Juanita snarled, "Sit back down!" She started to rise as well.

Lynn out-yelled her. "Go!"

One of the men shouted from a distance and ran toward them. Juanita lifted her rifle and Lynn burst from her seat, swatting the weapon aside and jamming her own gun under the shocked woman's jaw.

"Drop the gun or I'll drop you," Lynn said.

The running man stopped, moved two steps to the right and aimed his rifle at Lynn.

Juanita froze but did not release her gun. Gloria was slow to react, but after making sure the children were behind her, lifted her weapon. Dondra tried to do the same, but in her panic, dropped the rifle to the ground. She bent to retrieve it.

"Tell them to release the boys or you'll be the first one to die," Lynn said, trying to keep all emotion from her voice.

Her mouth went dry, her heart pounded out a rapid cadence.

"You'll be the next to die," Juanita responded.

"As long as you're first, that's okay."

A large pickup drove up the driveway and stopped. After a moment, a large man with wild black hair covering most of his face and a tall, slim woman stepped out. The woman stayed behind the open truck door. The man advanced carrying a shotgun.

The four men stopped and spread out twenty yards from the picnic tables. Lynn kept her gaze on Juanita's eyes. Any movement would be telegraphed there. She swallowed hard. She hated killing. Had even painted Mark, the man she loved, as a cold-blooded killer, and accused him of looking for opportunities to do so, but at that tense moment, with her son's life on the line, she knew she could pull the trigger with little remorse.

"Hey, Lynn," Jarrod said, stopping about ten feet to her left. He leveled the shot gun in the direction of the men. Two of them swiveled their aim in his direction. If possible, the tension seemed to thicken.

"You better get that gun outta my face, bitch."

Lynn pushed the barrel harder into the woman's flesh. "You'd better let those boys go or you won't have a mouth left to make threats with, *bitch.*"

At the sound of a grunt and a body hitting the ground, Lynn shifted her gaze. "Yo'all need to drop your guns," ordered Lincoln. He stood over the body of one of the four intruders holding the unconscious man's rifle pointed at the gunman who held Myron. Caryn and Darren came from the far side of the house pointing weapons at Gloria and Dondra.

The hayloft doors in the barn swung open revealing two more guns aimed at the remaining gunmen. Four rifles pointed out of the garage windows.

Unaware of the total threat against her group, Juanita

chose that moment to make her move. With blinding speed, she whipped her left hand up and knocked the gun away from her face. At the same time, she lifted the rifle. Lynn lunged and grabbed the woman's hair and yanked her head downward. Her face made contact with the table with a thud. She cried out and the rifle fell from her hands.

A gunshot rang out, but Lynn was too involved to pay it any attention, vaguely aware of other shots being fired. Lynn brought the gun down across the back of Juanita's head, driving her face first into the table again. Blood gushed over the table. She slumped to the bench and Lynn scrambled over the table.

Amazed Gloria hadn't fired at her, Lynn looked up to see Caryn with a gun jammed in the other woman's side. The rifle was no longer in sight. Dondra seemed to be unaware of the situation behind her. She held her rifle loosely waist high but was talking nervously to herself.

"Dondra," Lynn said, trying to remain calm, "no one wants to hurt you. Please, lower your gun. You can keep it, just stop pointing it at me, or Caryn will be forced to shoot you."

The woman glanced behind her. Seeing Caryn armed and Gloria without a weapon, she lowered hers and set it on the bench. "Shu-should I put up my hands or somethin'?"

The comment brought a quick smile to Lynn's lips. "No, hon. Just don't shoot anyone." It was only then that Lynn swung her gaze to the gunmen and her son. Her heart leaped into her throat. Four bodies lay on the ground. Three of the four gunmen and her son.

"Caleb," she screamed and raced around the table, sprinting to her son's body. Lincoln had disarmed the last man and was already kneeling next to Caleb by the time she arrived.

Blood soaked the front of his shirt. Fear ripped at her heart. She reached to cradle the boy in her lap, but Lincoln restrained her. "Let him be until Doc can check his wounds. You don't want to make whatever it might be worse."

On cue, Doc, the woman who'd arrived with Jarrod, knelt next to her and examined Caleb. A moment later she announced, "One GSW from back to front with an exit wound. He's breathing, but I need to operate on him now." The pronouncement made Lynn swoon for an instant. With Lynn out of commission emotionally, Lincoln took charge. His loud voice barked out orders as he kept Lynn from fainting. "We need the stretcher now." People sprang into action. "Get the barn set up for surgery. Caryn, get some of the girls out to the barn in a hurry."

"Myron," he said, "get the prisoners into the garage, tie them up and stand guard over them." He pointed to a girl and boy standing there watching. "You two help him, and don't leave until I come and get you."

Jarrod and Lincoln placed Caleb onto the stretcher and carried him into the barn. In a trance, Lynn followed. The interior of the barn was a bustle of activity. The medical equipment they'd gathered over the past month would get its first test. An operating table stood in the center of the room. Four lights on stands were set up at each corner of the table. Doc, already geared up, scrubbed her hands at a stainless steel sink. Caryn and Doris were dressing, ready to assist.

The men laid Caleb on the table. Doc said, "I know this is hard, but I need all of you to leave, now. The longer I have to delay or deal with interruptions, the harder it will be to save Caleb."

Lynn nodded absently but didn't move. Her mind was too stunned to react or comprehend. Jarrod came over and took her arm. "Come on, Lynn. Let Doc do her thing." He guided her from the barn and the doors closed behind them.

Normally, as a nurse in her previous life, Lynn would

have been in there to assist Doc. But, with her son on the table, the idea never entered her mind. Too numbed by the thought of losing her son, she could barely think at all. Ruth ran to Lynn and wrapped her arms around her mother. The two women cried and comforted each other. The rest of the community stood around in shock.

Two more cars drove up the driveway and disgorged another half dozen members. Lincoln went to meet them giving them guard duty around the property.

"Hey," Alyssa said, "one of these guys is still alive."

Lynn looked her way. One of the men kicked his feet writhing in agony. Something hardened within her. A fire burned, fueling sudden hatred. She untangled from her daughter and walked toward the wounded man.

Behind her Ruth said, "Mom?"

Lynn stopped next to Alyssa and without speaking took the gun from the girl's hand. She lifted the gun and aimed at the man's head. He cried out, "No! Please!"

Someone shouted, "Lynn! Don't!"

She cocked the gun, steadied her hand and glared at the man's face. Her finger tightened on the trigger with enough pressure to make it move. A red haze covered her vision. The barrel hovered over the man, his pleas fell on deaf ears. She felt ready to explode just as the bullet would. Someone pounded closer to her. The gun began to shake in her hand. The man needed to die for what happened to her son, yet she could not add the pressure needed to finish the trigger pull.

Lincoln reached slowly in front of her, his hand sliding down her arm until he reached the gun. "This isn't you, Lynn. If he dies, let him do it from my bullet, not yours."

He took the gun and she released it to him. She turned tear-filled eyes his way. "But, he killed my son."

"Not yet, Lynn. Not yet."

Fifteen

Becca hit the main road and turned west. Bobby had plotted a course that would allow them to avoid the blockade ahead as well as stay off the state route. However, to reach the alternative passage they had to risk driving the main road for four miles.

Their speed reached eighty. Becca kept a white-knuckled grip on the wheel. Bobby kept the binoculars aimed forward. Toriano, perhaps sensing the tension in the SUV kept quiet and slunk down in his seat.

"Okay," Bobby said, "the turn should be coming up."

"You sure about this, Bobo?'

"Unless something changed that doesn't show on the map, we should be good. Shit! I see cars coming."

"Cars? As in plural."

"Yeah, the lead car looks like the van we saw before. They must have gone back for reinforcements."

"What do we do? You want to turn around and run for it?"

"We may have to. No, wait! There's the road we need."

"You want to go for it?"

"If Kentae is to have a chance to survive, we have no choice."

"But is his survival worth our deaths?"

"Hey, two options, run or go."

Becca made the turn, slowing just enough to keep from rolling the SUV. She ran up a driveway and cut across two lawns, before driving back down another driveway to the road. The one-time residential subdivision had houses that once sold for a hundred and fifty to two hundred thousand dollars. Now it was overgrown and looked like a ghost town.

"Turn right here," Bobby said.

Having bled off some speed, Becca made the turn with more success.

"Go four blocks and turn left."

Bobby trained the glasses down each side street as they blew past. At the third one, he said, "Damn! A car just turned on this street."

Becca punched the pedal and the SUV lurched forward. She braked at the corner, making a sharp, but somewhat controlled left.

"We have a decision to make. We're only gonna have a few seconds before that car sees where we turned. We can either try to outrun them or hide while we can."

Becca blew a loud breath out. "Man, why can't anything we do ever be easy."

"We have to stay on this road for a while if we keep going. If we hide, there's no telling how long they'll search for us."

"Gotcha, bro." She kept going. Houses flew by on both sides. After a slight curve in the road, they entered an adjoining subdivision of older, but equally expensive homes.

"I caught a glimpse of the car just before we made that jog. I'm guessing we have about a four- or five-second lead on them."

Becca didn't respond. At the speed they raced through the neighborhood, she kept her attention focused on the road, with only occasional glances in the mirror. She trusted Bobby would keep her updated. "Where do I turn?"

"It should be the next main street."

"I'm going right, right?"

"Yeah."

She started to slow. "What's that elevated road up ahead?"

Bobby spun in his seat and leaned into the front to get a view. "It must be the turnpike."

"Is there a ramp?"

"Not here. The next one is probably twenty miles away. Hey, you missed the turn."

"Baby brother, do you trust me?"

"Oh, man! It's a bad time to ask me that."

"Hold on."

Bobby leaned into the front seat. "Keep your head down, Toriano." In the distance, the overpass grew. He turned to look out the back. He didn't need the binoculars to see the car behind them.

"Buckle up, Bobo." She hoped he had because she knew the ride was about to get very bumpy. She eased the nose to forty-five degrees down a ditch. Feeding gas, the SUV climbed up the opposite side. From there she had to gain enough speed in a short distance to crash through the fence that bordered the side of the overpass.

For a fraction of a second, her heart seemed to stop as the wheels spun and slowed their progress.

"Ah, no pressure, but they are getting close."

She ignored him and kept a steady press on the pedal. They climbed, but she doubted they had enough speed to burst through the fence. She swore under her breath. A whirring sound told her Bobby was lowering the window, getting ready to shoot.

The SUV increased speed with agonizing slowness. The crack of Bobby's rifle startled her, sounding like a bomb had gone off inside the vehicle. As if spurred by the shot, the wheels found purchase at the last second and surged forward. They hit the fence, though not as fast as she would've liked. The SUV hesitated, bowing the fence but not breaking through. Fortunately, it had no crossbar for added support or they wouldn't have stood a chance to get past. Still, the links held stubbornly to the posts.

"Damn it! I need more speed."

The rifle cracked again. "They're backing up. I bought us some time."

Becca threw the gears into reverse and backed down the slope. She reached the bottom of the ditch, shifted and floored it. The wheels spun fast and loud, slipping on the grass. They were stuck.

"They're getting out of the car." He fired again. "If I might make a suggestion. Drive along the slope to gain speed before angling upward."

"Good idea, if I can get out of this ditch."

"Back up again and take it slow. Once out of the ditch," he took another shot, "accelerate steadily."

Becca did as suggested. The SUV began to climb just as return fire began. They escaped the ditch and Becca maneuvered the SUV along the steep slope. Bobby slid to the high side hoping to offset the chance of toppling over.

A round banged into the rear door. Another glanced off the side with a whine. From his position, Bobby had no shot at the pursuers. He could only watch as the shooters got back in the car to give chase.

The SUV increased speed, but another problem arose in front of them. A stand of trees blocked them from going further. "Now or never," Bobby said.

Becca waited until the very last second. Bobby gripped her seat and pulled forward to watch. His short quick breaths blowing on the back of her neck told her he was as nervous about their success as she was.

She whipped the wheel hard, turning upward, aiming for the last chain link section. She pushed the pedal down as they made contact. Again the fence gave, but the SUV slowed. "Go! Go! Go!" Bobby chanted as if cheering for a running back racing for the end zone.

The SUV struggled but continued forward. "Yes," Bobby shouted in her ear. "The post is bending. Keep going." He looked out of the rear window. The pursuit vehicle attempted to follow their path and seemed to be having better luck.

The post leaned over more in the soft ground. One of the connecting links snapped. "They're gaining, sis."

"Keep them off us. We're almost through."

The window behind her descended. In the side mirror, she saw her brother slide out the window and perch precariously on the frame. He reached inside and dragged out his rifle. In the distance, she heard gunfire. She couldn't see the shooters but assumed they were firing from the car, trying to keep Bobby from getting off any rounds.

The post was nearly parallel to the ground. Becca willed the SUV to have enough power to pull it free. Another connector broke. With a sudden heave, the fence gave way, and the SUV broke through with a jolt. "Yeah!" She heard Bobby shout from behind her. She floored the pedal and the SUV ascended toward the elevated roadway.

"Ah," Toriano said, "are you gonna leave him behind?"

Becca snapped a look at the boy, before realizing what he was talking about. Glancing in the mirror she saw Bobby getting to his feet. She braked and backed up. She pulled up next to him. He was on one knee aiming at the car. He pulled the trigger twice, pumped his fist and stood. Reaching through the open window, he unlocked the door and climbed in. Becca looked in the rearview mirror in time to see the car rolling down the slope.

She smiled and met Bobby's glaring eyes. "Ah, sorry, Bobo."

"Yeah. I thought you were gonna leave me."

"Now, baby brother, would I do that to you?" She drove

bouncing along the grass until they reached the pavement. Her brother didn't respond. "Hey! Seriously? You think I'd leave you?"

"I'm thinking about it." He checked to see if Kentae was still breathing. Relieved to find he was, Bobby slumped into his seat.

"You ass. I should have left you."

"Except you needed me."

"Ha! I don't need you for anything."

"Yes, you do."

"No, I don't."

"Okay, I'm taking a nap. Find your own way home." He lay down on the rear seat. Less than a moment later his sister said, "No problem. I know exactly where we are." Moments passed. "I just keep heading straight, right? West? Wait, am I going west?"

Bobby hid his smile and closed his eyes.

"Come on, Bobby. I said I was sorry." She looked over the seat. "Fine, but if we get lost, it's your fault."

Sixteen

Mark throttled back to idle.

"Why are you stopping?"

"Because if we can see them, they can see us. Before we go any farther, we need to have a plan and an understanding."

"I told you my plan, and you'd better be understanding it. I'm going in to get that poor girl, with or without you."

Mark left the wheel and got in Shavonne's face. "Now you understand me. I'm going to do everything I can to save that girl, but if you put my life at risk with no chance of success, I will turn around. And if you don't like that, I will toss you overboard and let you swim." He stared her down until she averted her gaze. He backed away and spoke in a calmer tone. "Now, let's talk about options here."

Her jaw worked back and forth, fighting anger. "Okay. What's your plan?" She snapped the words off in contempt.

"If we wait until dark, we might be able to get close if we run without lights. If we get lucky without being seen and stopped, I have no idea how we're gonna get on the freighter. At this point, I'm only assuming Kendra is on the ship. We don't even know that for sure." He stepped back to the wheel. "Can you understand the dilemma here? I know you want to save her, but we could both be dead before we ever find out where she is. We can't just throw our lives away without gathering as much information as possible. That serves no purpose."

Shavonne flopped down to the deck and cried softly. "I know. But when I think of what might be happening to that poor child, I just can't think straight. It tears me up inside."

"I understand. I do. But, if we're going to make this work we have to be smart. And to be smart, you have to get control of your emotions." He raised the glasses. In the distance he saw the large vessel quite clearly. The smaller boats surrounding the ship were easy to see as well, but not in detail. As he studied the scene before him, sudden movement to the rear of the freighter drew his attention. His jaw slackened in surprise, as the massive anchor splashed into the water. They might have just got their first break.

Maybe they anchored each night to avoid running aground. Perhaps it was to save fuel. He wondered how long they would be able to cruise the lake with gas in short supply. Did they have access to more? If so, they would need a large amount. Mark also pondered on whether they ventured out of the lake, perhaps traveling around the other lakes or back toward New York. They had a great opportunity to make contact with a lot of other survivors. They could be a source of information and a great way to link communities.

However, his first encounter with the members of this group was not encouraging. As with other large gatherings of survivors, they only seemed to be interested in their own goals, with little interest in the advancement of civilization.

He shifted view and caught sight of a patrol boat coming their way. Run or stand? The decision might be life altering, one way or another. He looked down at Shavonne, whose knees were pulled up to her chest and her chin resting on them. For the moment she was quiet. He watched her while he ran the beginnings of a plan through his brain. Anything at this point would be a gamble. How best to protect them if the plan went awry was the big question. They had to have a fallback.

"Shavonne." She lifted her head. Even with the sun setting, he could see the tear tracks on her face. "They're coming."

She perked up, eyes wide, and started to stand.

"No! Stay down and listen to me. I'm going to let them get close. When they do, I'll tell them I've captured you and want to trade you for something, maybe food or water."

Excited, she rose to her knees. Mark motioned with his hand out, palm forward to keep her down. "No! Trade me for Kendra."

Mark shook his head. "I don't think they'll do that. They'd rather have two women than one, even if one is grown and the other a child. My intention is to get you on board. The rest is up to you. It may take a while and you may have to endure some, ah, abuse, first, but hopefully they'll let you roam loose on the ship, or, at the very least, put you in the same holding area as Kendra.

"If they let me, I'll hang out alongside the ship for as long as possible. Once you find her, get to the deck and signal me. If you can't find a rope to climb down, you may have to jump. I'll get to you as fast as I can. From there we'll make a run for land." He sighed. It wasn't much of a plan, but he didn't see any other way. Of course, a lot depended on whether or not they allowed him to live.

"What do you think?"

She wiped her eyes and nodded vigorously. "Yes, I'm willing to try."

"You understand the danger you're placing yourself in?"

"I told you, I'll do anything to save her."

Mark shook his head, knowing what she would have to go through to make this work. She was determined and he saw no other way.

"Okay." He searched through the various cabinets and storage benches until he found some rope that wasn't nautical. He cut two pieces. "I'm going to tie you up so it looks like you're my prisoner. I'll place a gun and a knife near you in case this goes south on us. If shooting starts, duck and use the knife to get free. I might be too busy, or dead, to help you. If this works, they'll escort us to the ship. From there, I don't know. I guess we'll make it up as we go."

"Okay," she said, but her voice was a whisper.

Maybe she just realized the downsides to this plan, but it's what she wanted to do. He stepped forward and tied her hands in front of her, snug but not tight. "Here's the knife and here's the gun. You should be able to reach both. Keep down until you're free then come up shooting. Now, I need you to drop your pants."

She gave him a quizzical look but to her credit, didn't hesitate. He tore a strip from a roll of duct tape, showed her a three-inch blade pocket knife and taped it to the back of her thigh. "If they take you, you won't have a weapon. They'll search you. Hopefully, they won't pat there."

She pulled up her pants. Mark held up a small, one-inch blade pocket knife. "Put this in your shoe."

She nodded and did so. As he stood, she grasped his hands with her bound ones. "Thank you for doing this. I don't want anything to happen to you, but promise me, if it comes down to a choice between Kendra and me, you'll choose her."

"I can't make that—"

She squeezed his hands tighter, nails digging into his flesh, her voice more intense. "Promise me. Please."

Mark met her determined gaze and, grudgingly, nodded. "If that's how you want it. I promise."

Seventeen

Two hours later, Lynn still waited for word on her son's prognosis. Frenzied with worry, she wanted to storm inside the barn and scream for answers, although she understood it would only delay what she craved. Lincoln sat on a picnic table and watched her with an unwavering gaze. Even if she decided to go in, she doubted Lincoln would allow her to get far. She stopped pacing and pressed her palms to the sides of her head hoping to alleviate the pressure within.

"Lynn, please, come sit before you fall down."

She threw her arms to the side. "I don't understand what's taking so long. I should have heard something by now."

"You know Doc is giving him the best care possible. It's gonna take as long as it's gonna take. The fact we haven't heard anything is a good sign. If she's still operating on Caleb, then there's a reason. He's still alive."

Lynn thought of Mark again, wishing he was there to offer support and strength. She knew now that she'd been wrong to be that angry with him. It wasn't that he looked for trouble, it was everywhere, at all times and in all places. She offered up a prayer that he would come back to her, to all of them, safe and loaded with the catch of the day.

As if God had heard her plea and opted to intercede, the SUV whipped into the driveway. Although thankful and relieved, Lynn recognized the speed of the approach for what it was, urgency. Her heart skipped a beat as she searched the windshield for Mark's image. Where was he? She spied Becca and Bobby and the top of another head in the front seat, but Mark was nowhere in sight.

Bobby leaped from the back seat as the SUV pulled to a stop and she broke into a run, vaguely aware of others moving next to her, but she could not take her eyes from the SUV. Where was he? The thought a scream in her mind.

Bobby ran to the rear and opened the tailgate. Becca jumped out, said, "We need help here," and ran to assist Bobby.

At Becca's announcement, Lynn's step faltered for a moment. Her chest heaved, caught on a sob. "Oh God, not Caleb and Mark." The idea of losing both of them was too much to bear. She froze and watched as if no longer attached to her body. Unable to prevent the flood of relief upon seeing the body was that of a black man and not Mark, she almost folded to the ground.

As others joined the sibs in carrying the wounded man, Lynn found the will to press forward. She searched the interior of the vehicle. A small, frightened boy sat in the front seat, but otherwise, it was empty. She collapsed against the SUV, not sure she could take any more bad news.

The human stretcher walked past. Bobby caught her eye but didn't speak. Becca followed the group and said to Lynn, "We'll explain later." Lynn walked around the car and opened the passenger side door.

She helped Toriano down and crouched before him. "Are you hungry?" The boy looked at her and swayed as if he might faint. "Hey," she gripped his shoulders in case he collapsed. "You're safe. I'll look after you. "Come on. I'll take you inside, introduce you to some of the others and get you some food." She stood and offered her hand. Toriano looked from her to the hand, then took it.

* * *

Jarrod stepped up and placed a supportive hand under Lynn's elbow. "You gonna be all right, Lynn."

She leaned her forehead against the big man's chest. "Oh, Jarrod, where is he? I can't take anymore. How can any of us be all right, ever again?"

He put an arm around her shoulders. "Yes, you can, and you will, 'cause unless I'm mistaken, that man's in need of some serious medical attention, and with the Doc and the others working on Caleb, that leaves you to make sure he has a fighting chance to survive."

"Look at me, Jarrod, I'm shaking. I couldn't help anyone. I might kill him."

"Lynn, look at me."

She tilted her head upward, her eyes filled with tears. "You're the rock who holds this community together. It's not any of us and it's not Mark. It's you. Everyone knows it. In times of trouble, everyone turns to you for advice and instructions. You don't freeze up when lives are at stake, and that man's life is surely hanging by a thread. You do nothing, you'll feel worse than you do now."

Jarrod put a large hand on her back and guided her forward, walking toward the barn.

"Whatever's happening to Caleb is in Doc's and God's hands. That man only has God, and although that may be enough, even God needs a helping hand and that's you. Don't let that man die."

She wiped her eyes, slapped a palm on his chest, and said, "Damn you, Jarrod!" She pushed away and jogged toward the barn. She stopped, turned and said, "Thank you." She stepped inside the madness of new world surgery. Someone closed the doors behind her.

There was no way on this planet that she wouldn't glance at the table that held Caleb. None of the four people who surrounded the operating table looked up from what they were doing. The sight of blood, her son's blood, gave her a momentary light-headed feeling. A knee buckled, but she fought off the nausea and forced her feet to take her to the sink. She gowned up and scrubbed her hands.

Someone had dragged a stainless-steel kitchen work table into an open space and was busy disinfecting the surface. Two young women spread a white sheet over the top, while Bobby, Becca and Lincoln lifted the man and set him on top. Everyone was involved. The entire community came together at times like these. They all had a job and contributed in whatever capacity was needed.

She stood beside the table, studied the injured man, and blinked away her indecision and worry. Turning to Bobby, she said, "Bring that light closer and set up another." She looked for Becca, pleased to see she was already dressing. "Alyssa, scrub up. Bobby, while you work, tell me about his wounds."

One of the women wheeled over an IV stand. Lynn said, "Check his blood pressure." To another woman she said, "See if we have any O negative blood." While she listened to Bobby's account of the events leading to the wound, she cut away the patient's clothes. Her hands shook as she tried to insert the needle; she inhaled and breathed out slowly to calm her nerves, found a vein on the third attempt, just as the blood arrived.

They had no way of testing blood type in such a hurry with Doc occupied, so she went with the universal donor. "That's the last of O negative," the woman informed her. Lynn said, "Start asking for donations." The entire camp had taken turns, as they needed to donate pints of plasma for just such emergencies, but they tried not to store too much.

A bag of saline appeared on the stand and a second needle inserted.

Though the equipment they had on hand was limited, it

was much better than a few weeks back, when they had scavenged local doctor's offices, clinics and urgent care centers. Now they could handle all but the most severe of medical emergencies.

"BP's 62 over 28 and dropping."

Lynn made her fingers work faster. "Ready for a crash." She washed the wound and got a better look. *Damn, the bullet is still inside!* Becca and Alyssa stepped around the table. "Becca, put him under."

While Becca handled the anesthetic, Lynn ran a mental list of things she needed and had to do, before she began. She checked the available tools and satisfied, picked up a scalpel.

"Still dropping," the woman announced, a tinge of anxiety in her voice.

Lynn took a deep breath, willed her hand steady, and set the blade against the wound and made her first incision. She made a second and set the scalpel down for a probe. Finding the bullet, she widened the incisions a bit more and slid in the forceps.

"We're losing him."

Before she could react, Doc was at her side. "Give me the scalpel and get the paddles."

Lynn wanted to scream at her, "Go back and work on my son." She risked a quick peek at his body on the other table. One of the women there, she couldn't tell who, caught her eye and nodded. She took that as a good sign and went to get the paddles.

The alarm sounded, announcing the flatline. "Lynn!" Doc called and tore the paddles from her hands. "Clear," and thrust the electric charges onto the man's chest.

The body jumped just as she pulled back.

"He's back," the nurse shouted in excitement.

Doc handed the paddles back and leaned over the body. She looked at the wound and without a word picked up the forceps. In seconds she extracted the bullet and dropped it to the floor. She pulled the light down closer to the table and examined the wound. Satisfied with what she saw, she stepped back and stripped off her gloves. "The bullet broke a rib. Clean, sterilize and sew it up. We'll get him stable before worrying about the bone." She gloved up again and went back to Caleb.

Lynn finished stitching the wound and stepped back from the table, releasing a large breath. She looked at the monitor and saw the blood pressure, though still low, had stabilized. The woman nodded to Lynn. She felt ready to collapse, numb to all around her.

"That should do it," Doc said from the other table. She stepped back, snapped her gloves off and turned to look at Lynn's handiwork. She looked up and caught Lynn's eyes over the mask, the look of desperation clear. She pulled her own mask down and offered a reassuring smile. "I think he's okay, Lynn. It's in God's hands now. He's strong and came through the surgery fine. He needs to rest and heal. I'll know a lot more by tomorrow."

Relief washed over her and her legs did give out this time. Becca was there in a heartbeat, helping her back up and supporting her weight. Alyssa came up on the other side and they walked her out of the door.

Ruth, Lynn's daughter, rushed into her arms and the two women cried. "Doc said he might be okay," Lynn told her. "We have to wait and ... and pray."

Caryn came out of the barn, stretched and gazed upward, allowing the sun to warm and caress her face. Spying the four women huddled together she moved to join them. Lynn released her daughter and embraced the new arrival. "Oh, Caryn, thanks for all you did in there."

"I just assisted. We should all be thankful to have a doctor as good as ours available." She pushed Lynn back a bit. "Hey, there's no time for tears. Caleb will be fine. But, we still have a community to feed."

"I want to wait for Doc."

"She's working on the wounded intruder. She'll be busy for a while. Come on. Let's get to work."

Lynn smiled at her obvious attempt to distract her. "When did you become such a leader?"

Caryn smiled and wrapped an arm around Lynn as they walked toward the house. "From hanging out with you. Besides, you know what they say, 'women's work is never done.'"

"I hear that," said Becca.

The others stopped and looked at her, each with an expression of surprise.

"What? I work. Sometimes."

Lynn said, "Did you catch any fish?"

"Well, that's kind of a long story."

"One you still have to tell. You can start now and continue while you're peeling potatoes."

"Ah, yeah, sure. I guess."

Eighteen

Three boats peeled away from the mother ship and intercepted them about a quarter mile out. One turned broadside across their bow while the other two took up positions on either side, guns pointed. Mark feared they had made a huge mistake.

A fit man wearing an old Cleveland Indian baseball cap, standing in the port side boat said, "Turn your boat away or we'll shoot you and sink it."

"I, uh, I come bearing gifts?" It sounded as strange as he thought it would. "I mean, I wanted to make a trade. You do that right?"

"Sometimes and only with those we know. And that's not you."

"I have a woman. I was hoping to trade her for some food."

"What makes you think we want the woman?"

A man on the boat on the opposite side said, "Yeah, and if we did, we'd just shoot you and take her."

This wasn't going as planned. "Okay, I'm going. Sorry to have bothered you."

Shavonne squirmed on the deck and in a harsh whisper, said, "No, we can't leave." Her eyes held the mixture of a plea and fiery anger.

Mark looked away and stood in front of the wheel. He could see no other option at the moment. He shifted into reverse, but before he moved more than a foot, the man with the cap said, "Wait! Let me see the woman."

Mark shoved the stick into neutral and let the motor idle. He had no down shift for the acceleration of his heart rate. This was the moment of truth. They'd either go for the deal or he'd be dead.

He reached down and hauled Shavonne to her feet. Her bound hands hung in front of her making it look like she was a prisoner. He'd slid a gun in the waist band at the small of her back, his lone chance of defense. He doubted it'd be enough, nor did he think he'd be able to get a shot off before being ripped apart by the numerous guns pointed at him.

They stood and were examined for what felt like an eternity. Mark's hand inched across her back and touched the butt of the gun. He rehearsed his move mentally, knowing it wouldn't matter what he did.

"Okay," the capped man said, "transfer her to this boat and we'll get you some grub."

Mark hesitated. He'd be an easy target once Shavonne was off the boat. "Ah, no offense, but like this other guy said, what's to stop you from shooting me once she's over there? I'd feel better if she stayed here and we made the transfer near the freighter."

The man laughed, as did many of the others. "If I wanted you dead, you'd already be dead. It doesn't matter if it's here or there. You're alive. That should tell you something."

"Okay. What if I wanted to join your, ah, navy?"

The leader tilted his head and studied Mark as he pondered the request. "Follow us to the freighter. We'll make the deal and I'll discuss your offer with the captain. And don't vary from the course or we will sink you."

He said something to the pilot and the boat swung

around to take the lead with the front craft. The opposite boat let Mark pass and took up position in his wake. "Get down," he said and Shavonne did. "Now scoot over here. I need to get that gun before the transfer." After slipping the gun out, he slid it into his belt and covered it with his shirt. He patted down her legs. "Are the knives still in place?"

"Yes."

They might frisk her, but most men would pat down the front and the sides but seldom reached around the leg. He hoped that would be the case, but if that blade were discovered, she had the small pocket knife in her shoe. "Remember to walk so you don't give it away."

"I know."

As the freighter grew ever larger through his windshield, Mark wondered if these might be the last sights and moments of his life. He looked at her. The whites of her eyes shone like porcelain saucers, showing her fear. He understood how she felt. "It's not too late to turn back." He wondered if he'd asked that for her sake or his?

She shook her head in response. He turned his attention to the freighter and thought about Lynn. He hated that the last moments he'd been with her were spent in anger. He wanted the chance to make it up to her.

The leader's boat veered to the side and he motioned Mark onward, before falling in next to him. "Follow him," he pointed to the lead boat, "aft," he shouted to be heard above the engines. "Stop when he does and wait."

Mark waved that he understood. The leader's boat accelerated, pulling away from the convoy. Mark watched as the boat swung about and idled next to a cargo net that hung over the side of the freighter. The leader stretched, caught a loop, and without a pause, the man scaled the massive vessel in less than a minute, and disappeared topside. As Mark slowed his engine to match the lead vessel's speed, he caught sight of the baseball-capped man ascending the steps to the bridge.

A man in the lead boat motioned with a hand, sweeping across his throat for Mark to cut the engine. He did so and his hand hovered above the gun, as he wondered if he'd be quick enough to draw and shoot before he became Swiss Mark.

The trail boat came alongside and the man who'd spoken about shooting and taking what they wanted said, "You wait here. The woman comes with me. Now! This is non-negotiable."

Mark swallowed hard, but it seemed to catch in his throat. He bent to help Shavonne up. "I guess it is too late now. Good luck."

She nodded again, stood and Mark led her to the side. The other boat moved closer. The man and another passenger reached out and snagged Mark's boat, pulling and bumping the two vessels together. The crewman in the rear held fast while the front man held out a hand to Shavonne. Mark heard rather than saw her chest heave as she fought back her fear and a sob.

As she alighted on the other deck, Mark stepped back into the pilot's area near the wheel. It didn't offer much protection, but more than he'd had. He slid the gun free and cocked the hammer, determined to get off at least one shot. He focused hard on the lead man's chest, marking him as his first target.

To his surprise, they didn't treat Shavonne roughly or as a piece of meat. The man in control led her to the rear of the boat and sat her on the bench. He returned and said, "You wait right here. Do not make any attempt to get closer to the freighter. The men haven't had a chance to shoot anyone in a while. I'm sure they're eager for some practice."

He motioned the other boats forward, like a trail master leading a wagon train, and closed in on the freighter. Mark was curious how they were going to get Shavonne on board. As if in answer, a platform, like a window washer's scaffolding, lowered from the deck of the freighter. The leader stepped on it, steadied himself, then reached down for Shavonne. The passenger on the boat helped her up onto the railing and the leader guided her onto the platform. It swayed under the new weight. Shavonne lurched but the man caught and held her and placed her bound hands on the side rope. He leaned back and waved to someone on the freighter and the scaffolding was hauled up.

As the boat rocked gently under the waves rebounding off the freighter, Mark watched Shavonne grow smaller against the huge gray mass of the ship. He wondered if he'd ever see her again. She was a brave woman and he had a lot of respect for her and her willingness to sacrifice her freedom for that of the girl's.

He hoped she hadn't miscalculated, for her sake, and his. For just as she was willing to exchange herself for the girl, Mark knew he'd probably do the same for her. He glanced at the boat still guarding him. If he was still alive to do so, of course.

Nineteen

"Unbelievable!" Lynn exclaimed. "It's just like I told him. Your father can't go anywhere without falling into some dangerous situation. And for what? Fish! And he didn't even bring that back."

"Hey!" Bobby said, "that's kinda unfair. Look what happened here and you sure didn't go looking for it."

Lynn glared at Bobby but knew he was right and let her anger bleed away. "You're right. I'm sorry. I'm a bit stressed."

"The question is," Becca said, "what are we going to do?"

"What can we do?" Lynn replied. "Other than send a team to look for him, of course."

"Well, that's a start," said Bobby.

"We know where he was," added Becca, "and, knowing Daddy, we have a pretty good idea what he planned to do. We'll go to the marina and figure out what to do from there."

"I suppose that's the best place to start," said Lynn.

"It's the only place to start," Becca said, her tone showing signs of impatience.

"It's too dark to start now."

"Lynn," Becca snapped. "time is one thing we don't

have. He could be lying somewhere dying. We have to get to him as fast as we can."

"Becca," Lynn said, forcing a calmness she didn't feel.

"No!" Becca shouted and exploded to her feet. "I'm not going to listen if you plan to delay. Every second we debate, Daddy could be bleeding out. I'm not waiting."

"Becca," Bobby interjected. "Sit down. Lynn has a valid point and we need to talk about it."

She fumed at her brother, but sat down, looking ready to detonate again at any moment.

"Becca, I'm not trying to delay. I'm as worried as you are, believe me. I—"

"Ha! That's why you were so quick to leave my dad and move out, eh? Because of how worried you are!"

Lynn's face flushed. She averted her gaze.

"Becca." Bobby said, his voice stern. "Stop!" She whipped her head in his direction and shot a withering glance at him. Bobby did not back down. "That's between Dad and Lynn. They'll work things out as they see fit. We need to stay focused on one thing, finding Dad. Now, calm down and lose the hostility. It's counterproductive."

Lynn said, "Whatever is or is not happening between your father and me, it doesn't mean I don't care about him. That will never change. I've said and done some things that I regret, but that's for later. What I was about to say is that I'm concerned about sending a rescue mission out in the dark where they might run into their own trouble. You told me about the barricade and the people chasing you. At the marina, you ran into what amounted to modern-day pirates. How will you see well enough to avoid an ambush at either location or, for that matter, anywhere in between?"

Lynn took a deep breath. "I want your father safe. I can't imagine life without him and after almost losing my son, I understand how that feels better than ever, but as the person making the decisions, I can't justify placing other

105

lives in jeopardy to rescue one person, no matter how much I want to … or how much that one person means to me. Can you understand that?"

"Then I'll go myself."

Lynn bit her lip. "I know you can. I can't and won't stop you if that's what you decide to do. But I'm asking you to wait till just before dawn so you don't lead yourself, and others, into an ambush. I hope you can see the sense in that. That will also allow us to gather some people to go with you."

Becca's face crumpled in on itself. She lowered her head to the table to hide the tears. Just as abruptly, her head shot up. "What I know is, if he dies, it will be on you." She got up from the table and walked quickly away.

Bobby let her go without comment. "I'm sorry for that, Lynn. You know how she gets under stress. She really doesn't mean half of what she says."

"I know, Bobby. I've been there before with her. We'll get past it. Do you understand my position?"

"Yes. But I also know my sister. As much as she agrees with you deep inside, she will be unable to wait for long. Even if it's just the two of us, we'll be leaving soon. I won't ask anyone else to come with us, but I hope you will send a team after us in the morning."

"You know I will. And Bobby, just because I won't send people with you, doesn't mean *you* can't ask for volunteers to go with you."

He nodded. "True."

"At any rate, take some time to think and to get prepared, whether or not you leave in the morning or in an hour."

"Of course."

They let a few moments pass before Bobby spoke again. "There's something else you should know." In the firelight, Bobby saw her eyebrow go up in silent question. "We found a gas tanker that I think might be full of fuel."

"Where?"

"Not too far down the road from the marina. It's in a secluded area near a factory and at the end of a small neighborhood. It looks like the driver was ready to empty his load into the underground tank, but got sidetracked. Who knows how long it's been there or for how much longer. Getting that tanker here would be a huge boost to our dwindling gas reserves."

"Yes, it would go a long way. Go find your sister and get ready to leave. I'll call a meeting of those here now to ask for volunteers. Ah, your father is the priority though, of course. Regardless, I'll send a second team out before dawn."

He nodded and left to find his sister.

Lynn sat for a moment, thinking about how cold she must have sounded to Bobby. She'd balked at rescuing his father, the man she supposedly loved but was willing to call a meeting over the possibility of scoring a tanker full of gas. No wonder Becca questioned her feelings for Mark. She must see her as a heartless bitch. Maybe she was.

"Becca," Bobby called. "Where are you?" He stood at the edge of the corn field spinning in a three-sixty. "Don't make me search for you, you twit. Get your butt out here so we can make plans to get dad. We're wasting time and your little temper tantrum isn't helping."

The rustling of stalks made him turn fast and reach for his gun. He relaxed when Becca stepped out.

"Who you calling twit, dweeb?"

"Dweeb? Aren't we all nineties? At least you didn't call me a dork."

"That too, and nerd and dingledorf on top."

He chuckled. "You're such a bitch sometimes."

"So?" she challenged.

"Don't take your worry about dad out in anger against

107

Lynn. She wants us to go find Dad, she's just concerned about the danger in the dark. She doesn't feel right about ordering others to risk their lives against the unseen and unknown."

"I know it's not her fault. She just pisses me off sometimes. I mean she tossed Daddy away like a used, ah, I mean, she just left him. How much can she really care about him?"

"If they're having problems, that's between them, but I don't think you can question that she still cares about him. Come on. She's calling a meeting to ask for volunteers and we have to get ready."

"She is?"

"Of course." He didn't tell her it was only after he mentioned the tanker.

"In that case, I take back what I said about her and half of what I thought."

He smiled. "You're just an emotional and slightly — "

"Hey, don't you say crazy bitch."

"I was gonna say tense, but if the other word fits ..."

She punched him in the shoulder. "Tense I can take, but don't ever call me crazy."

No, he thought, disturbed maybe, but not crazy. At least not to her face.

"You know, little brother, you sounded an awful lot like Daddy back there, when you were reprimanding me for my outburst."

"Yeah? Is that a good thing or bad?"

"I'll let you know. Just don't make a habit of it."

Twenty

Mark waited for more than an hour before the platform lowered again. The man who'd taken Shavonne was the lone figure. A box or crate sat next to him. What had become of Shavonne? Mark knew they wouldn't have killed her, but there were other things as bad.

He thought about the siege they had laid to a compound of men a few weeks back who had abducted some of the women from his commune. They auctioned them off to the highest bidder like so much chattel. Would the same fate await Shavonne?

The scaffold stopped next to the speedboat and the man stepped off. He reached back and dragged the box on board, then the platform was hoisted back up. Mark speculated that his trade had been approved; the contents of the box his payment. He felt like Judas. How much had her body been worth to the men?

The boat pulled away and veered toward him. In minutes he'd know what kind of payment to expect, food or bullets. He fingered the gun in his belt and decided to put it where he could pull it faster, placing it next to the wheel.

The patrol boat slid next to his and the crewman grabbed the side again. "Here's your food. Your trade was approved with the captain's thanks." He held out a cardboard box.

Mark hesitated. If they were going to kill him, what better time than when his arms were full with no way to defend himself?

He glanced at the gun but left it. As much as he wanted the security it offered, the sight of it in his hands would lead to bloodshed for sure. Most of which would be his.

He stepped to the port side, reached out and accepted his reward for exchanging a human life. He tried not to look at the contents, instead keeping his eyes on the man. He knew he should say something, but came up blank. Before the other boat shoved off, he found his voice. "What will happen to her?"

"That's not your concern anymore." The man paused. "Don't worry. We don't abuse women here. She'll be indoctrinated into our society and given a chance to be part of us. She'll be fine."

"What about my request to join the group?"

The man eyed him and said, "That's still under discussion. I wouldn't hold my breath, but if you want to wait for an answer, pull back away from the ship and someone will send word."

"When do you think?"

"How the hell should I know?" The crewman pushed away. "Probably in the morning. Stay back from the ship and away from the patrol boats. My advice, if you don't hear by morning, don't stick around." The engine revved and swung in a wide arc back to its position near the freighter.

Mark set the box down and examined the contents. Shavonne's life had been worth two dozen assorted cans of food and a pack of taco shells. He took the wheel, shifted into gear and moved away from the larger vessel. He stopped and dropped anchor about a hundred yards away.

He stared for a long time at the deck of the freighter, not

sure what he was looking for. He looked down at the box. It'd been a long time since he'd eaten. As long as he was waiting, he might as well take the opportunity. He pulled out a can of chili beans and a can of corn. Below deck, he rummaged through the drawers and found a spoon and a can opener. Taking food to the rear bench he sat down and made a meal, putting some of the beans and corn in a taco shell.

As he ate, he studied the ship for ways to get on board without raising the alarm. Without seeing the other side, his options were limited: the cargo net or the anchor chain. Both would be in view of the many escort vessels alongside. Scaling the ship would be suicide and although he would exchange himself for Shavonne and the girl, giving up his life trying to get aboard would accomplish nothing.

No, he would have to find another way. He made another taco and worked on a plan. Not much of one, but a plan none the less.

The meeting concluded, Becca, Bobby, Lincoln and one of their newest members, Drew Morris, piled into the SUV. Their gear already loaded, Bobby shifted into reverse as Lynn came to the passenger window. Becca hesitated but lowered it.

"Be careful. I'll have a large group following before dawn," Lynn said.

Bobby nodded. Becca looked down, avoiding her eyes.

"You've got your radios, right?"

"Yep, we're all set."

"I know they won't work this far away, but we'll need to contact you when we get there."

He nodded again, anxious to get on the road. He noticed Becca's leg bouncing with nervous energy as well. It was best to get rolling before she said something to exacerbate

111

the already strained situation.

Lynn said, "Okay then." She paused and placed a hand on Becca's arm. "I know it may not seem like it, but I do care for your father. Bring him home safe."

It was the first time Becca looked at Lynn. Whatever she saw there softened her attitude. "We will."

Lynn backed away from the vehicle and Bobby drove away. No one spoke for several long moments till Becca said, "Damn! I can really be a bitch sometimes."

"Sometimes!" Bobby said.

"Hey, it's better than being a dick."

"You're only saying that 'cause you don't have one."

From the back seat, Lincoln said, "I don't know about that, but she's got balls big enough to throw touchdowns."

Silence. Everyone howled with laughter.

"Damn, Linc!" Bobby said.

"That's right, baby brother. I've got bigger balls than you do."

"Yeah, well try not to fumble them."

They reached the turnpike and accelerated. The dire situation called for more speed than Bobby was comfortable with. They had to drive with the headlights on, but as fast as they were going, he'd have little warning if something suddenly appeared in front of them. Not to mention that the headlights might draw unwanted attention.

A while later, Becca said, "Bobby, do you think he's all right?"

Bobby was thinking about that very thing, only in more of a prayer. "He'll be okay." He has to be. "Besides, he's too ornery to get," he hesitated, "get taken by a bunch of pirate wannabes."

"Yeah, that's what I was thinking too." But she clearly hadn't been thinking that. The worry was etched on her face.

Lincoln said, "Don't you be fretting about your dad. He's

a lot smarter and tougher than anyone I know. Besides, he's probably holed up somewhere with his feet up and a beer he discovered someplace, in his hand."

"Bullshit!" said Bobby.

"Double bullshit from me," Becca said. "He's probably neck deep in trouble about now."

"Yeah, well, I can always hope," Lincoln said.

Bobby laughed. "I know what you're hoping for. That he's got an extra beer set aside for you."

"And your point?"

"My point is, as long as you're creating dreams you might as well hope for a keg."

"A keg," Lincoln mulled that over. "Bobby, I like the way you think."

"Like father like son," said Becca.

"And *your* point?"

"Hmm! Yeah, I guess that's a good thing."

Lincoln chuckled.

"What's so funny?" Becca asked.

"I was just thinking. I shoulda known your daddy would get me to go fishing, one way or another."

Twenty-One

Mark finished his meal and took out the binoculars. Though dark, the ship's lights illuminated the deck enough for him to see anyone moving. So far he'd counted eleven different men and three women. The bridge was behind tinted glass which blocked sight of anyone there. He scanned from bow to stern checking for anyone watching him, but if they were there, they were well hidden, unless they were on the bridge.

He didn't want to leave his post in case something happened. If it did, he would have to move fast, but he also knew, working by himself, he'd need equipment, so he took a few moments to do a quick search of the boat.

Setting his findings on the deck at his feet, Mark did another quick scan of the freighter's deck and set about organizing his catch. He had two lifesavers, both of which he tied to long yellow ropes. The flare gun and three extra flares he placed on the bench next to him. The fillet knife he stuck point first into the wood where he'd be able to find it if needed. He'd also discovered the location of the first aid kit. Nothing else was of use, but he had more than he started with.

An image of what Shavonne might be enduring flashed through his mind, but he quickly pushed it aside. Those thoughts would serve no purpose. Instead, he looked at the night sky to fix the time. A slim moon hung in the air to the south, almost even with his position. He estimated it was nearly midnight. Morning was a long way off and he doubted he would sleep. Shavonne and Kendra's lives depended on him remaining vigilant.

He thought about his kids. Had they made it safely back home? *Will I ever see home again?* His children? Lynn? He shook off the thoughts. He had too much to do to allow other things to distract him. But he couldn't shake one idea. Knowing Becca and Bobby, they'd be on their way back to rescue him by now. Lynn would be unable to stop them, even if she tried. He hoped there would be something left of him to rescue.

His name sounded over the water from a distance; he snapped his head up and stood. "Mark!" Again someone called his name. He snatched up the glasses and almost immediately they lined up with Shavonne running on the deck, a young girl held tight to her chest. Several men gave pursuit.

He spun around and hustled to the wheel. The motor roared to life and he shifted into gear, accelerated; the bow threatened to lift from the water. He tried to keep the glasses pressed to his face, but as the craft gained speed, the bouncing made it difficult.

Shavonne ran toward the guard rail along the top deck of the freighter. She reached the end, called for him again, and searched the dark waters for the boat. He steered a path to get underneath her. From where she stood there was no way down unless she jumped. What was her plan? "Oh, dear God!" he said, seeing her climb over the rail. Light swamped the deck as large spotlights on the forecastle ignited and captured Shavonne in their halo.

Mark felt his pulse quicken as an injection of fear-laced adrenaline flooded his veins. Aware of other engines starting around him, he was unable to pull his eyes from Shavonne. At this pace, the men would reach her long before he arrived.

How would she find him in the dark, amidst all these other small craft?

He thought of the flare gun, but he'd left it on the bench across the deck. He gauged the distance, checked the path in front of him, let go of the wheel, and lunged for the flare gun. The wheel turned a few degrees as the boat dropped over a wave. He adjusted the course and back in control and on target, he lifted the gun and fired. A bolt of red flew skyward, bursting into a fiery ball. Shavonne seemed to focus on his boat then.

The men were only steps away. She held Kendra, the name came to him, out away from her and he knew what she was going to do. She pulled the girl back for a quick hug and kiss and released her just as the men arrived. The child plummeted toward the water.

Above, Shavonne struggled with the men, trying to make her own dive. Mark pulled his gun and tried to draw a bead on one of the men, but at this speed over the choppy water, he could just as well hit Shavonne. She broke free for a moment and jumped, but multiple hands reached for and snagged her before she could drop beyond their grasp. They hauled her back, kicking and screaming frantically.

Mark looked to where Kendra hit the water, then judged how much time he had before others got to her first. One boat was closer. With a last look at Shavonne, Mark turned toward Kendra, praying he reached her before the other boat and before she drowned.

He closed the gap in a hurry, but the other boat had already slowed to begin its search. A quick glance around showed he had perhaps a minute to eliminate the competition and get Kendra on board before being surrounded. He advanced on the other vessel, swung the wheel and threw up a gout of water and soaked the enemy crew.

He shifted into neutral and snagged a life preserver on his way to the side. A scream helped him pinpoint the panicked girl. The other boat had to come about to reach her. He flung the life preserver. It arched high in the air and fell a foot from Kendra. Struggling to stay afloat, the girl failed to see the flotation ring. He slowed so as not to swamp her. The competing boat pulled up on the opposite side. They were nearer. One of the men had a pole and extended it toward her. The tip touched her and she screamed.

She spun in the water and found the pole. She grabbed hold and the man pulled her toward the boat. Mark aimed to broadside the boat, climbed on the bow and ran forward, working hard to keep his balance. Just before impact, he took two running steps and leaped. The boats collided just before he made contact with the man with the pole. The boats rose up bringing the deck closer. His opponent went flying backward and over the side. Mark landed in a heap on the deck. His boat veered off toward the freighter, while the one he was on now, bounced deeply, sending water rushing over the sides, the deck slick as he got to his feet. He spied the pole, now hanging on the sidewall, straight up.

As Mark reached for the pole before it slipped beneath the waves, he pulled the gun from his belt. The speed boat's pilot moved to intercept him, but Mark reached the pole first. Wrapping one hand around it, he spun fast and whipped the gun across the other man's face. He staggered and crumpled to the deck.

Mark leaned over the side to find Kendra, all the while pulling the pole in. To his surprise, the young girl still clung to the metal end. He put the gun back in his belt and hauled hand-over-hand. He looked around him. At least half a dozen boats were aimed at his position. Mark leaned across the gunwale and grabbed her slender wrist. He pulled the child up and over the top and dropped her unceremoniously on the deck before racing to the wheel. They had to get to safety.

He paused and looked upward. Shavonne screamed and her voice carried down to him. "Go! You promised!" Several men dragged her away.

Guilt struck deep at his heart, but he recognized the situation was lost for her. He could still save Kendra if he went now. He shoved the stick forward and the boat jumped, sloshing the collected water along the deck. Kendra coughed repeatedly and rolled with the water. He could do nothing for her at the moment, all his attention focused on escape.

He split two boats coming at him. A man on one side swung a long pole at him striking and cracking the windshield, but the force of the impact tore it from his hands and it bounced off the bow and into the water. The boats came about in seconds and joined the other four boats already in pursuit.

The echoes of gunshots flew over the water. He ducked in automatic reflex. He checked the heap that was Kendra. She lay sucking in air in between sobs. He looked back at the freighter. Shavonne was no longer in sight, but he would remember how brave she was and the sacrifice she just made for this girl. He wondered if Kendra would ever fully understand what Shavonne did for her.

Mark turned back to the endless dark water in front of him. Any shore, at this point, was just an extension of the water, blending into the long black surface. Should he try to find the same marina, or just find the closest harbor? In the dark he couldn't make an intelligent decision, so decided to just run until he thought he was close to land and hope he didn't hit anything.

How long until dawn? Did he have the gas needed to run till then? He glanced around. It didn't matter if he had enough gas, they would run him down long before. The pursuit vessels had spread out behind him. To alter course would allow them to flank him. The only path he had was straight ahead and that would only last until he hit land. They didn't have until dawn.

Twenty-Two

"Watch out!" shouted Becca.

Bobby slammed on the brakes. The rear end of the SUV fishtailed toward the center guard rail. A semi-trailer had been set across the two-lane road. Whoever set the barricade had picked the perfect spot. Only a few feet remained between the trailer and the guard rail.

Bobby whipped the wheel from side to side to keep from rolling the SUV. They skidded sideways and for a scary moment thought they would smash into the semi. "Duck!" he shouted. If they hit it, the collision would shear off the roof. He pressed the pedal down and the tires caught, sending them forward, parallel to the trailer, aiming for the shoulder along the right side of the highway. He found little room to maneuver. A car had been backed into the space, between the semi and a cement barrier.

Braking again, the vehicle slid on the loose gravel and crashed into the wall. The impact sent curses and air bags exploding throughout the interior. Bobby was thrown forward, and smacked in the face. Stunned, he was unable to move for long moments.

As his vision and hearing cleared, he heard a multitude of moans within. An acrid chemical smell filled his nose and he sneezed. He fished for his knife, opened the blade and popped the airbag. He turned to his sister as he released the seat belt. "Becca, You all right?"

A hissing told him she had sliced her bag as well. She put a hand to her face and patted it. "Damn! That burns." A thin trickle of blood descended from her nose. He looked in the back seat. Lincoln and Drew were shaking off the effects of the impact but looked fine.

He glanced at the semi. He'd thought they had a few more miles before reaching the barricade. In the dark, he misjudged their position. Bobby rolled his head, his neck cracking in protest. He lifted a hand and rubbed at the soreness before he opened his door. For a moment he feared the door would resist his efforts, but putting a shoulder into the attempt, the door creaked and opened. He put his feet on the ground, stood, but leaned against the SUV for support. He drew in a large breath, but before he could exhale a voice behind him said, "Don't you move. I've got a gun pointed right at your head." Bobby stiffened. "Put your hands on the roof and spread your legs."

Bobby did as commanded, lowering enough to catch Becca's gaze. He motioned to the side with his head. She slid into the well and waited. The voice said, "You others get out of the car. You," he nudged Bobby in the back with something hard, "open the back door." Bobby did. "Both of you slide out this way. Don't try no tricks, 'cause I will shoot you."

Drew exited first. Trying not to be obvious, Bobby kept his body directly in front of the gunman's line of sight hoping to block Becca's exit. He watched the man's eyes but if he was aware of Becca's presence, he didn't show it. Drew moved off to the side and let Lincoln step out. "Now, you two, turn around and put both hands on the roof like this other fella." As they did, the man said, "Hey, wasn't there another one in the front seat?"

"No," Bobby said, "it was just me in front."

Running footsteps pounded toward them. "Hey,

Antone, you got one. Aw, man!"

"Benny, sound the alarm. We gotta let everyone know we got them."

A sudden blare from a trumpet pierced the night, making Bobby cringe. Benny didn't appear to have the skill to play a tune. He blasted out alternating notes. Bobby wondered who was being alerted and how many would answer the call. He craned his neck to find where the responders would come from, looking for an escape, knowing his sister would strike at any second.

Lights to the left gave him one answer. Flashlight beams danced across the ground from the far side of the barricade. They descended from a slope on the right side. Bobby thought he could make out the outline of some buildings above the roadway; perhaps an apartment complex or condos.

"Whatcha'all got in there?" Antone said.

Benny inhaled to blow the horn again. Bobby tensed, ready to spring, hoping the gunman wouldn't notice. The first notes escaped the horn but ended abruptly.

Silence for a moment, then, "Benny? What'd'ya do, swallow that mouthpiece?" Benny didn't reply. Bobby readied, turning his hips. "Benny?"

Bobby sprang. He found his target two steps back and drove his shoulder into the man's midsection. The gun exploded over him. He tackled the man and climbed to his gun hand. Grasping the wrist, he banged it on the ground to dislodge the weapon. A disturbance of air in front of his face gave him pause until he felt the man below him go slack. Bobby looked up to see Becca withdrawing the blade from the man's body. With an icy nonchalance, she wiped the blood from the blade on the man's shirt.

Bobby pushed to his feet. "Hurry! Everyone back inside. There's more coming." He jumped into the front seat and tried to restart the SUV, but found it refused. He hadn't thought the collision or the damage was that extreme.

Drew said, "It might have an automatic shut down after a collision."

Lincoln got out and ran for the parked car. Bobby kept trying to turn the engine over while watching the approaching flashlights. There had to be several dozen, not fifty yards away. The motor started and with relief he put the stick in reverse, but the SUV did not budge. With a sinking feeling, he realized it was the car's engine that started, not the SUV.

He hopped out and called to the others, "Quick, help me push this out of the way." The three of them took up positions near the front. The angle was uphill, but only slight. Between them they got the SUV rolling.

Multiple, excited voices drifted to them. Bobby withdrew his handgun and fired two warning shots over their heads. Lincoln reversed the car just as fire was returned and stopped on the far side of the SUV using it for cover. "Unload the SUV," Bobby said. Becca crouched at the front bumper of the SUV and spread out shots at various distances toward the crowd. A barrage of gunfire came their way, many striking the SUV. In less than a minute, their gear had been transferred to the new vehicle. "Becca! Let's go," Bobby shouted.

Becca laid down her own barrage and as her magazine emptied, bolted for the car. Lincoln backed up before Becca could shut the door. He turned to the left to put the semi between them and the shooters. Spinning the wheel hard, he sent the car in a one-eighty-degree turn, jammed the pedal to the floor and rocketed forward, a hail of bullets pinging off the body.

Becca spun in her seat. "Everyone all right?"

"Fuck!" Lincoln said.

Drew just nodded, but looked dazed. She noticed a dark line on his head. "Lincoln, turn on the dome light." He glanced at her in the mirror like she was crazy. "Just do it, I need to see." The dome light came on and Becca leaned into the back. Drew had a large gash on the side of his head. "Oh, Drew, you're hurt. Why didn't you say something?"

His hand went to his head. He touched the spot and stared at his red fingers as if confused by what he saw. "Drew? Drew! Can you hear me? Bobby check him. I think he's got a concussion."

Bobby leaned across the man, examined the injury, and looked into Drew's eyes. "Hey, buddy, you all right?"

Becca turned and rummaged through the glove box, finding a wad of napkins. "Here," she handed them over the seat. "Press these to the cut."

Drew flinched away at the contact and the pain seemed to snap him from his fugue. "I'll hold them," he said. Bobby released all but one. He poured water from a bottle onto it and said, "Let me wash it."

Drew held still while Bobby wiped the blood away from the cut. The flow was steady. "Yeah, looks deep. He's gonna need stitches to close this."

"I tossed the first aid kit in the back somewhere," Becca said. "Get some butterfly bandages on it to try and stop the bleeding." She leaned into the back seat and rummaged through the equipment. "Here," said Becca.

For the next fifteen minutes, they worked to stop the bleeding, while Lincoln drove. Checks through the rear window showed no sign of pursuit. His mind worked hard to find the alternative route they'd used earlier, as he tried not to think of his father and the added danger their delay might cause.

Where ever you are, Dad, stay safe, we're coming. I promise.

Twenty-Three

Sporadic gunfire chased him in the dark. Few shots came close, leaving Mark to wonder why they wasted the bullets. A thought struck him. He altered course. The immediate response was two rounds fired off, well wide, his suspicions confirmed: they were herding him and wanted Kendra back, and didn't want to risk hitting her.

They obviously knew the lake better than he did and what he faced, but it couldn't be too dangerous, because if he ran aground, Kendra might be hurt. Maybe they hoped he would see the danger before he hit it, but in the dark, how was that a reasonable conclusion? Mark had few options and the longer he ran, the less time he had before land forced him to stop and the pursuit would pen him in.

He narrowed his gaze in a futile attempt to penetrate the dark. Again, he panned the boats, still traveling in a straight line behind him. They'd made no effort to close the gap in the last twenty minutes, intent on keeping him moving in the direction they chose. He had to find an out somehow. Maybe he could use the dark to his advantage.

"Kendra!" The girl did not respond, no longer even whimpering. She lay on the deck curled in the fetal position. "Kendra, please, come here. We have to make a plan or those men will capture you again." Still the girl lay still. "Kendra!" Mark shouted. This time her little body twitched. Without speaking, she got to her feet and moved closer. She seemed zoned out, like some zombie.

"Can you swim?"

She stared at him.

"Look, Kendra, we have to find a way to reach safety. Can you swim?" She managed to stay afloat out on the lake, but she needed to be able to swim for shore.

She tilted her head upward to look at him. Even in the dark, Mark saw the tears well. He softened his tone. "Shavonne went to a lot of trouble to get you away from those men. She did it for you, to get you to safety. I made her a promise that I would take care of you, but I need your help. Can you do this? For Shavonne?"

She nodded and wiped at the tears that now fell.

"Good. I need you to be brave and strong. Okay?"

She nodded again. "Yes."

"Yes what?"

"You asked if I could swim."

"Oh, right. Are you a strong swimmer?"

She shrugged. "I guess."

"Look around the boat and see if you can find any life jackets or other flotation devices. Hurry."

Kendra turned and scampered off. Mark studied the area off to the left. If they hit land, it would come from that direction first. He veered a few degrees away picturing that he was now running more parallel to the shore.

Kendra came back holding two life jackets. Mark saw the problem immediately. They were orange and could be seen in the water, even in the dark. He thought of another potential danger. They had to swim past the last boat in line or risk being seen or run over. He glanced at his gas gauge. The needle pushed E. They didn't have long, one way or another. If they could get over the side without being seen they might be able to buy enough time to reach shore and make their escape.

He had to make sure Kendra was safe in the water. He also had to be able to find her if they got separated. "Okay, here's what we're going to do. Go below and take off your shirt. Get into the vest and put your shirt over it." She stood still. "Go! Hurry! We don't have much time."

Kendra went below deck and once more Mark searched the horizon for any sight of land. He turned another degree to the right and checked the pursuing craft. Picking up their running lights, he noted two of the vessels to the right had edged forward from the rest of the line. They were getting ready to close the trap. He flicked the switch, killing the boat's lights.

Kendra started up the steps, but Mark stopped her. Her shirt barely stretched across the vest. He pulled his shirt off. "Put this on over the top." She did, the shirt hung too low, exposing an orange ring around her neck. It was the best they could do. They'd have to chance it. "Hand me that other vest." Kendra did. Mark hung it from the wheel. Maybe in the dark it would fool his pursuers long enough for them to go past.

He made sure his gun was secured in his belt, with no idea whether it would work after being submerged. He could see nothing else they needed. "You ready?"

She nodded.

"We're going over the side together. Stay close to me and don't make a sound. Swim that way," he pointed, "as fast as you can. If the boats get close, duck and let them pass. Can you hold your breath?"

She nodded again.

"When I say duck, take a deep breath and go under. Stay there as long as you can. Go sit by the side."

He tied the wheel to keep a steady heading, squatted low and joined her. Lifting her, he said, "Put your feet over the gunwale. Hold on." Mark slid his body over and hung next to her. "Ready?" He gripped her hand.

"I'm scared."

"Yeah, me too. But it's better than letting those men get us. We'll be okay. I promise." But even as the words left his mouth he prayed it was a promise he could keep. "Put your feet against the side. I'll count to three. On three, push off the boat as hard as you can. One. Two. Hold your breath. Push." Keeping a strong hold on her small hand, he shoved off the bow. Kendra lagged behind, but as he hit the water, he still held her hand. Mark pulled upward to make sure her head broke the surface. She broke through with a choking cough. He covered her mouth and whispered, "Shh! They'll hear you. I'm going to let go of your hand. Swim fast." He let go and waited for her to swim before stroking toward what he hoped was the shore.

The roar of the boats increased. Had the pirates seen them jump? They'd know soon enough. Kendra's small arms plowed through the water. Mark kept his pace slow. In only a few strokes, he knew they would not get past all the boats before they were upon them.

The approaching engines were thunderous. Estimating they had ten seconds before the line of boats reached them, Mark took three more pulls through the water, stopped and hugged Kendra to his body. He put his back to the boats to help shield her. "Get ready to duck. Okay. Deep breath. Now!"

He dragged her under despite resistance from the preservers, praying she had taken a lungful of air and could hold it. The sound of the engines was amplified underwater. He tried to go down deep enough to miss the propellers, but couldn't be sure. They weren't down ten seconds before Kendra struggled with a desperation that told Mark she was out of air.

Stuck with the choice of surfacing too soon and either being seen or hit by one of the boats or risking Kendra drowning, Mark kicked toward the surface. Kendra became more panicked with each passing second. The boats hadn't passed them yet. Time had run out. Forced to reach air, they broke the surface just as the boats arrived and a dark mass rushed toward them.

Twenty-Four

Mark yanked Kendra beneath the water, not knowing if she'd had the time to suck in air. It sounded like a thunderstorm passing overhead. Kendra's tiny body writhed against him, fighting to reach the surface. He refused to let her go. He thought about pressing his mouth to hers and blow a breath down her throat, but feared, in her panic, she'd swallow water too.

For an agonizing eternity, he waited for the boats to clear. He felt Kendra's body go limp and kicked hard to the surface. Kendra was unresponsive to his whispers and shaking. Shore was too far away. He had to resuscitate her, there.

Turning her, Mark pressed her back to his chest, placed his arms around her and, finding the sternum, put his palms under her rib cage and pulled. Once. Twice. On the third attempt, water expelled from the girl's mouth and nose like projectile vomiting. She coughed and gagged, but this time it was a sound Mark was glad to hear. He feared he'd killed her. Relieved, he slid one arm under hers and around her chest and began side kicking toward shore.

He stopped for a second to get a better grip and checked on the progress of the chase. All the boats were still moving, but the gap between them had closed. It wouldn't be long before they realized their prey was not on board. His wet clothes, coupled with his exhaustion and Kendra's slight, but extra weight, made the going slow. Twice he had to stop to reposition Kendra. He strained to see the coast and refocused all attention to listen for the sound of waves crashing against the rocks.

A sudden flash of light pierced the darkness about fifty yards almost directly in front of them. He skulled the water, holding them afloat but in place, as he stared at the location. Had he imagined it? No, there it was again. Like someone flicking a flashlight on and off. Was someone signaling them? Maybe Bobby and Becca had found him. He kicked in that direction. The light flashed again a minute later.

Halfway to where he'd seen the light, Mark became aware of the sound; or rather, the lack of sound. The boats had stopped. Damn!

He didn't want to take the time to look. Instead, he increased his pace. The light flashed again. They were close. The light was behind them. Confused, he stopped and paddled in a circle. It wasn't the light he had seen before, the source of this light came from the boats pursuing him. Several had turned on spotlights and were shining them around the water. They had discovered his ruse.

He pushed harder toward the land light, but it did not blink again. Perhaps whoever was signaling feared being discovered by the boats.

Three more kicks and pain exploded in his shin. He muffled a yelp but had to stop swimming until it subsided. He held the injured leg bent at the knee and the other foot touched bottom. He set it down on the uneven rocky bottom and put weight on it. Though still in pain, he walked onto the shore.

"Kendra, we found land. I'm going to put you down, but keep hold of my hand."

He set her down and felt the small trembling hand in his. He scanned the shore, but only darkness surrounded them. Like the whispered voice of a siren, someone said, "Here. Take my hand."

Mark jumped and fumbled to reach his gun.

"You're safe, but hurry. Those spotlights are getting closer."

Mark took another step and with both hands lifted Kendra from the water. He held her in front of him. Movement, then two strong hands gripped and took her from his grasp. Stepping from the water, fighting to maintain his balance on the rocks, Mark reached behind him for his gun, but the voice stopped him.

"Leave whatever weapon you're reaching for right where it is. We have three guns pointed at you. We don't want to shoot, but we don't want to get shot either. If we'd wanted you dead, you would be, or we wouldn't have bothered signaling you."

Mark couldn't be sure if what the man said about the guns pointed at him was true, but decided not to take the chance. Besides, what the man said, made sense. Why rescue them if only to kill them? He lifted his arms in case they could see him better than he saw them. An arm took his and pulled and guided him to the safety of the trees. Before he had a chance to move or defend, a hand patted him, found and removed the gun.

"Any other weapons on you?"

Mark hesitated. He had the knife, but could they see it? He chose to take the risk. "No."

"Not even a knife? Come on, everyone carries a knife."

That was true. He insisted that all of his people had one on them at all times. He slid the long knife from its sheath and handed it, handle first, outward. A few seconds later a hand found and took it.

"If you're here to save us, why take my weapons?"

"Trust is not an easy thing to give these days. If we feel

you're no risk to us, they'll be returned."

A beam of light swept and probed the trees. "Get down!" a voice said. Mark ducked but noted it was a different one from the first one. There were at least two of them.

As the light moved on, Mark asked, "Where's the girl?"

"Don't worry," a female said, "I've got her. She's safe."

"Who are you?"

"For the time being," the first man said. "We'll ask the questions. Come. Let's get away from the water to someplace we can talk."

As they walked, Mark inched his right hand into his pants' pocket. He withdrew and palmed his pocket knife. They walked on for several minutes. Every few seconds, whoever was leading turned on the flashlight to illuminate the path. Mark tried to use the quick bursts to size up the number and position of his rescuers.

A short time later, the first voice, said, "Let's stop here for that talk." The light blinked at Mark's feet. The small group circled. He thought he noticed four other sets of legs besides his and Kendra's.

"Why were you being chased by the raiders?"

"Raiders? Is that what you call them?"

"We'll ask the questions. Please answer."

At least his interrogator was polite. He saw no reason not to give them the information. It didn't sound like they were involved with the kidnappers. But, they could be a different group of abductors.

"They kidnapped this girl and another woman. I was rescuing them."

"Liar!" the woman shouted. "We saw you. You traded that woman for food. He's just as bad as they are, Elijah. Worse. He sold her out for his own gain."

Tension constricted his chest. Beads of sweat dribbled down his forehead. He wiped it with the sleeve of his left arm, keeping the right down by his leg where he flicked open the blade.

"That's true. We did see you. You should know, we have reason to hate them and others like them for what they've done to us. If we decide you are one of them, your death will be quick."

"But painful," the woman added.

Mark blew out a long breath and forced himself to relax. If he had to strike, he needed to be fast and fluid.

"I can explain, but not if you've already passed judgment."

"At this point, you're still being treated with courtesy. We always try to be fair. The world may have changed, but that doesn't mean we can't be civilized. Go ahead. Explain."

"My name's Mark."

"Who cares!" the woman was clearly against him.

"Darlene," the leader said in a calm, but stern voice. "Give him his chance."

Mark edged toward the woman. If things went south, she would most likely be first to react. She probably had her weapon aimed at him already. He planned to take her down, use her body as a shield.

"I come from a large community about an hour to the west. I came here with others to fish. We're trying to build up our food stores for the winter."

"Aw Elijah, he is such a liar. He's the only one we saw. It was just him and the black woman in that boat. Let me gut him now." Her anger was so strong Mark could almost touch it.

"Elijah, am I going to get that fair chance you talked about?" He sidestepped again. Judging by the sound of her voice, he thought he was within a step and a lunge from her.

"Darlene, let him talk or leave."

"This is bullshit!"

"Proceed, Mark."

"Like I said, I came here with others. We went out to fish

133

but were approached on the lake by an armada of small craft. We fled back to the marina and hid. However, when a party landed to search for us, they found a family of four: man, woman, boy and girl. The man was shot. My kids took him and the boy back to our home, where there's a doctor."

Quiet muttering swept around the circle at the mention of a doctor.

"We stepped in to rescue them but, although we saved the woman, during the gun fight the raiders escaped with the girl. The woman, Shavonne, refused to leave without her, so she devised a plan where I would appear to trade her for food. If she got onboard the ship, she would search for the girl. Shavonne made me promise that if she saved her, but not herself, I was to get the girl to safety and leave her there." He paused expecting comment. "That's what happened. She found the girl, dropped her overboard, but she was unable to jump. Basically, she sacrificed herself for the child."

"He doesn't even know her name," the woman spat.

She wanted him dead, not caring about the truth of his story. Kendra began crying softly. Someone made comforting sounds.

"Anyway, that's what you saw. I picked up the child and made a run for safety. Oh, and her name's Kendra."

A voice behind him said, "Do you have any way of proving your story?" Unlike the woman, it hadn't been said in anger.

Mark gave the question some thought. "Other than what you saw and what Kendra can confirm, no." He swallowed to steady his voice and not sound nervous. "And trust runs both ways. How do I know you won't just take Kendra and do the same things those pirates would've?"

"You don't, you'll have to take our word for it. But turning the question back around to us does not alter the decision still to be made about you."

"I'll agree to trust you if you at least give me the benefit of doubt."

"Let's vote," the woman said. "I vote to kill him."

The lead man chuckled, which made Mark more nervous. He inched a bit closer and readied the knife. He tried to estimate height and distance, knowing his first strike had to be good.

"Why doesn't that surprise me? Anyone else?"

"I vote to give him a chance," a voice said from behind.

Another voice to the right said, "I'm with Darlene."

"Okay," said the leader. "I'm with Paul. Two-to-two."

"Bullshit!" Darlene exclaimed again. Movement and sound gave Mark the impression she had cocked and leveled her weapon at him. That changed his approach. He would have to duck and dive to the side.

"We need a tie breaker," the voice behind said.

"Why don't we let Kendra decide," the leader suggested. "After all, if anyone knows about this man's intentions, it's her." He paused to let that idea sink in. "Everyone agree?"

Everyone, including Darlene, was willing to let Kendra decide Mark's fate. He tried to think back if he'd done or said anything to sway her against him. Did she understand he saved her life? He wasn't sure. She might see him as the man who handed over Shavonne.

A rustling of clothes and the flicker of a narrow beam of light showed the leader, a light-skinned black man, squatting next to the visibly shaking young girl. "What do you say, Kendra? Did he save you, or is he a bad man?"

The small dark eyes flitted Mark's way, locked on his eyes for a second, then slid back to Elijah's. "He pulled me from the water and kept me away from the bad men."

Mark was relieved, until, "I think he tried to drown me though."

His eyes flew to Elijah. He felt his body moving before he had given it the command. Mark lunged for Darlene. With the light still on, he saw her weapon was aimed low in his direction, but her eyes were on the child.

Everything morphed into slow motion. Darlene's head turned, her eyes widened, and the gun rose. Mark adjusted his height and movement, so he blew past the barrel of her rifle and to the side of her body. With the knife hand, he batted the barrel down, while the other snaked around her body and up to her neck. He slid behind her and pressed the knife to her throat.

"Everyone freeze and stay calm," Mark ordered.

No one moved except Elijah. He stood and studied Mark through casual eyes. "This is not the move of an innocent man."

"To quote our friend here, 'Bullshit!' I've done nothing wrong and to place my fate in your hands seems foolish at best."

"Shoot the bastard!" Darlene yelled.

"I don't want trouble. I still need to find a way to get Shavonne off that ship and you're costing me time."

The other two members of the group spread out and aimed their weapons.

"What's it gonna be, Elijah. Peace or death?"

"I'd say at this point that's entirely up to you. I promise you this, Darlene may be a hothead, but she's one of us. If you hurt her, I will order your death."

Mark thought it was exactly what he would say if the roles were reversed. "I don't want to hurt her, but I'm not ready to die. Walk away and let us go and I'll release her."

"We could do that, but we haven't established any trust. Besides, I'm not sure we should allow Kendra to go with you."

"If I can trust that you won't take advantage of her, I'll let her decide what she wants to do."

"You'd be willing to do that?"

"Yes."

"Why?"

"Why?" It seemed such a strange question. "Her safety

is the most important thing. I gave my word to keep her safe. Besides, I can't do what I need to, to save Shavonne if I have to protect her as well."

Elijah appeared to ponder his words. "And you do plan on trying to rescue Shavonne?"

Mark wondered if that sounded as absurd to them as it now did to him. "I'm not sure I can rescue her, but she deserves my effort."

Elijah raised his voice a bit and issued a command. "Everyone lower your guns." The other two looked at him with surprised expressions. "I'm serious. I trust Mark to not hurt Darlene or us. Go ahead. Show good faith and lower them."

In staccato movements, the guns were aimed downward.

"No," Darlene said, "don't trust him." Mark pulled the knife from her throat. Immediately, Darlene stomped on his foot, spun and threw an elbow at his head. Mark ducked, and the strike glanced off the top of his head. In a flurry of motion, Darlene launched an all-out attack, throwing punches and kicks in a steady and practiced pattern.

Mark was able to block most of them, but the ones that landed, hurt. Not wanting to injure her, but unwilling to take much more abuse, Mark counterpunched one attack with a short jab under the sternum and Darlene collapsed to the ground, gasping for air.

As Mark looked up all three of the others had weapons trained on him again, only now he was without benefit of a human shield.

Twenty-Five

The sun was a hint of color on the eastern horizon as the three-vehicle caravan saw the barricade across the highway ahead. Mel stopped. "What do you think?" she asked Tara. The small, muscular black woman leaned forward and squinted. "Well, it was certainly put there on purpose."

Lynn grabbed the two front seats and pulled herself forward. She pointed. "That's their SUV."

Mel looked where Lynn pointed. "Are you sure?"

"As sure as I can be without taking a closer look."

Tara said, "Looks like it's been in one heck of a battle."

Cold fingers ran up Lynn's spine. Tara was right. Much of the glass had been blown out and bullet holes dotted the body like a deadly form of acne. Tara lifted binoculars to her eyes and studied the area.

"I see legs moving on the far side under the semi. Someone's there, waiting to ambush us. We need to turn around."

"No!" Lynn said. The tension made her voice a higher pitch than normal. "Bobby, Lincoln and the others may be in trouble. We need to take a closer look."

"They may also be dead already and getting us killed isn't the best way to find out," Tara said.

"Please don't say that, Tara. I can't think like that. I have to believe they're all right and need us to rescue them."

Tara looked at Mel. "Not this way, Lynn. We have to retreat to safety and come back on foot." She put the glasses back to her eyes. Mel looked at Lynn. "She's right, Lynn. I'm sorry."

Lynn sighed. "I know, Mel." She lifted the radio and keyed the mic. Before she could speak, Tara grabbed her arm and pulled the radio down. "I'm trying to call them. Maybe they're not even there."

"Or maybe they are and they're hiding. The radio will give away their position. If they are prisoners, whoever has them will be alerted we're with them. They can be used as leverage against us."

Lynn sighed, put a thumb and forefinger to her temples and massaged the building pressure.

"Looks like a group of people coming down the hill to the right from that apartment complex," Mel announced. "They're armed."

Tara said, "Time to go."

Mel made a U-turn and the other two vehicles followed. She drove until the road curved enough that they were no longer in sight of the barricade. She pulled to the side of the road. The three women got out and waited for the other transports to do the same.

In all, they had ten people in their rescue team. The three women rode in Tara's SUV. A minivan carrying four men from the community and the group's equipment followed, and a jeep with three soldiers from the nearby Air National Guard post, brought up the rear.

Tara and the three soldiers joined the group near the minivan. One of the soldiers, Corporal Ward, said, "We can backtrack and take Route 2. It runs right past the marina."

Tara shook her head. "Lynn thinks the shot-up SUV on the side is the one the first group took."

Ward's face seemed to droop. "Aw, shit!"

Private Menke said, "We can bust that barricade up with

139

the .50 cal."

Tara again shook her head. She wore the uniform of a captain and had been Air Force before the apocalypse. "That's a last-resort option. I don't want to get into an all-out war with these people if we can avoid it. I also don't want to use up all of the .50s ammo."

Lynn said, "Let's try to find a less combative way of finding out if our people are prisoners, or — "

"We could send someone with a white flag to talk to them, but I'm not sure who you'd get to volunteer for that," said Mel.

"I'm not willing to risk anyone else's life," Lynn said. "I'll do it."

'Wait! What!" Mel said, her voice raised an octave. "No. I was kidding. That could be suicide."

"We have three choices here," said Lynn. "We can shoot it out with them and hope we don't take any casualties, but one of them is still alive to tell us what we want to know. We can try to talk to them peacefully."

"And pray they don't shoot you," interrupted Mel.

Lynn nodded. "Yes. Or we can turn around and find another route to the marina. I'm open to other suggestions."

Tara said, "We can send a few people back and around to try and flank them. If we can capture them without a fight, that would be best."

"I agree," said Mel.

"But it may take more time than the others have."

"Why?" said Mel. "Do you think they're eating them or something? If they're still alive, they'd be holding them for whatever reason. If they're dead, the time won't matter."

"I vote we do it the safe way," said Tara.

"I second," Mel added.

Lynn said, "All right. But let's see if we can capture one of them to avoid a gunfight. Maybe we can get answers without bloodshed."

"Okay, I'll handle it," said Tara. She moved off to call her troops around her. Lynn leaned against the SUV, shoved her hands into her jeans pockets and stared at the ground. Thinking they might need the extra man and firepower, the idea to call for help from the nearby military camp had been a last-second thought. She hoped it wasn't a mistake.

Lynn couldn't help but think her way was faster, but she had to admit to feeling relief at not having to be the one who tested whether the symbolism of a white flag still held any meaning.

She turned her head to watch as Tara laid out her plan to her men. She should go and take part in the meeting, but in truth wasn't up to the task mentally. Her fear and emotions were running too high. Tara would do a better job.

Her mind wandered back a few short weeks. Bobby and Becca had rescued Tara, Mel and Caryn and brought them into the community. Tara had been severely wounded, but Doc had saved her. Mel had been instrumental in the rescue of some of their community members and Caryn had been a godsend around the house, taking much of the daily grind and burden of running the household upon her shoulders.

Tara and Mel had gone to stay on the base. Although Tara had been military before the event, Mel hadn't. She had never officially enlisted, but General West was so happy to have any bodies, he didn't push her. She trained with everyone else but didn't wear the uniform. How appropriate that those two be present to rescue Bobby and Becca. A shiver ran through her. If they were alive to rescue.

Ten minutes later, Tara and company loaded into their SUV. "I'm leaving Private Ordway to man the .50 cal." All businesslike, Tara talked to Lynn like a subordinate. "Shift one of your people to the jeep to act as driver. Keep your radio close and listen for me to give the word. I'll either say, 'safe,' 'attack,' or 'run.' Do not question or hesitate – just do it. Understood?"

"Yes."

Tara gave a quick salute. Lynn stopped an automatic response to return it. Ready to move, Lynn approached the driver side, patted Mel's arm and said to everyone inside. "Be safe."

"Post a lookout down the road so they don't sneak up on you," Tara said. "I'll call for a report before we make a move. It may take a while to find a route to take us there. Be patient."

Lynn didn't reply. She stepped away and Mel accelerated back the way they came. Lynn rubbed her temples again in an attempt to ease away the tension. Would the danger ever end?

Twenty-Six

"There's the marina," Bobby said, pointing unnecessarily. He slid forward in his seat like an excited child happy to have reached his destination. A few miles back they'd changed seats so Bobby and Becca could focus on the landscape. Lincoln slowed to make the turn, then crept along the dirt road. Bobby's eyes swept the ground but, except for birds, saw nothing moving.

Becca directed Lincoln off the road toward the copse of trees they'd hidden in before. At the tree line, Bobby hopped out and guided him forward until much of the vehicle was out of sight from the road. Becca opened her door and turned to look in the back. Frowning, she looked at Drew. His head was back and his eyes were closed.

"Drew, we're heading out. You want to stay or go?"

He opened his eyes and shook his head. That must have been a mistake because he groaned and closed his eyes again.

"We'll scout out the area," she said. "You stay here and guard the vehicle." She thought his reply was, "Okay." She slid out and joined Lincoln and Bobby.

"Lincoln said, "I haven't been here, so you two lead the way."

Bobby led the way through the trees toward the channel.

A few minutes later they arrived at the northern tree line. They crouched and studied the area. The marina was empty of people. The two boats that collided were still in a pile on one side of the channel, with no bodies or signs of a struggle evident.

Bobby pointed. "Let's make our way around the shore in that direction. That way we can keep to the cover of the trees." He strode off without waiting for a response.

For the next ten minutes, they cut a trail through the dense undergrowth until they reached the rocky shore of Lake Erie. From there they each used binoculars to scan the water. Though the sky was beginning to lighten on the horizon, it was still dark enough to inhibit defining details on the water.

"I can't see a damn thing," Lincoln said.

"Yeah, this isn't getting us anywhere," said Becca. "Maybe we should take a boat out on the lake."

Lincoln hesitated. "Why don't we wait a few more minutes for the sun to come up enough to see? Once we know what's out there, we can decide what to do."

"I hate waiting," said Becca.

"Yeah, but he's right. Let's give it a few more minutes."

Bobby kept his glasses pointed east, while Lincoln scanned west. Becca paced incessantly between the two. In five minutes the difference in the light was evident. "There's nothing at all to the east."

"I think I've got something large to the west." Lincoln pointed. "Out that way. Near the middle of the lake."

Becca and Bobby trained their binoculars on a path with his.

"Yeah," said Bobby. "It's definitely a ship."

"Now what?" queried Becca. "We need a boat to get out there, but it's not like we can sneak up on them in a surprise attack."

"Even if we could surprise them, sis, there's probably so many of them we wouldn't get far. We have to think this through. It won't do Dad any good if we get captured too."

"Now hold on a second, you two. We don't even know for sure he's on that ship. Seems to me the first thing we have to do is determine where he is."

"And how do we do that?" Becca asked, her natural sarcasm coming out full force. "It's not like we can ask anyone, or … or check security cameras, or something."

"Becca, settle down," said Bobby.

"Didn't anyone ever tell you that ordering a woman to settle down when she's upset is like adding fuel to the fire? It's only gonna make me blaze hotter."

Lincoln muttered, "Even I knew that one."

"Let's try to decide our best course of action," Bobby said in an even voice so as not to incite his sister further.

Becca exhaled a loud breath. "Okay. Let's decide. But while you're doing that, let's go find a boat to use so when you come to the obvious conclusion that we have to go out there, we're at least ready."

"You know, Becca," Lincoln said, "I like you. I do. But sometimes your intensity is so severe it impedes intelligent thought and hinders progress."

"Is that like 'be part of the solution and not part of the problem'?"

"Sounds like to me he just told you to calm down," said Bobby.

Lincoln cleared his throat. "Yeah, either thing."

"All right, give me some suggestions I can live with."

"Just in case, let's go find a boat," Lincoln said. Becca threw her arms into the air.

"Kiss ass," Bobby told him.

"Yeah, kiss mine," was his response.

They made their way back to the marina and searched through the boats for one that had keys. They'd made it through about a third before Lincoln said, "This is crazy. No one keeps their keys on board. Don't either one of you hoodlums know how to hot wire a boat?"

"Is it the same as a car?" Becca said.

"Why doesn't it surprise me that you'd be the one to respond?"

"Hey, this one has the keys in the ignition," Bobby shouted.

The engine sputtered but started on the second try. "We've got about half a tank of gas. Anyone know how far that gets us?"

"Isn't there a gauge that tells you how many miles it can go?" Lincoln asked.

"Nope," Bobby answered. "It's not like a car."

"Well, go until the gauge shows one-quarter, then we know we've still got enough gas to get back," said Lincoln.

"Good idea."

Becca said, "Or, we could go to the pump over there and fill up."

They looked where she pointed. Lincoln shrugged. "Or we could go fill up over there."

Bobby shook his head.

"What? When she's right, she's right."

Bobby made kiss lips at him as they cast off.

"Now, you see there? That's the exact reason why I didn't want to go fishing with you guys in the first place. You two are extremely abusive."

"You played football?" Bobby asked sarcastically.

"Yeah, toughen up, pansy," added Becca.

"You're lucky I like your dad. I wouldn't put up with this shit for anyone else."

They reached the gassing dock, but the pump needed encouragement to give up its fuel. They found a generator hooked up to the pump. "Someone's been here," Becca said.

They filled up and rode out onto the lake. The sun was a quarter way up over the horizon, offering enough light to see the shape of the freighter.

"Now that we've gone this far, maybe we should have

some sort of plan before we take on an entire fleet," Lincoln said.

"I'm going to move along the coast parallel to the ship while we think. Maybe, if we stay close and move slow, they won't notice us," said Bobby.

"Do whatever you need to keep the ship in sight, but getting closer is stupid unless we have a plan," Lincoln said.

"Well," Becca said, "stop whining and start thinking."

"Hey, guys," said Bobby, "it looks like there's something going on near the shore ahead of us."

The three crowded together at the wheel. Lincoln and Becca focused their glasses. "Ah, Bobby," Lincoln said. "I think maybe we should pull in someplace before we get spotted."

Bobby scanned the coast ahead and looked behind. The distance for safety in either direction was a toss-up.

"I count eight boats," said Becca. She lowered the glasses and looked at her brother. "You think maybe they're looking for Dad?"

"Don't know, sis. But it'd be just like him to piss them off enough to come after him."

"Yeah."

He aimed toward a small cove.

Twenty-Seven

Elijah tugged on the rope to ensure they were snug around Mark's wrist. "I apologize for this, but it's for everyone's safety until we decide what to do with you. I don't think you're here to do us harm, but ..." he shrugged. "So much has changed over the past few months, we never know who to trust."

A man he had not seen before burst into the small opening. Elijah went to speak with him. Mark's gaze shifted to take in his surroundings. Morning light was trying to force its way through the branches. The man named Paul, stood ten feet away watching Mark, his weapon not aimed, but ready.

Dear Darlene sat on a rock sharpening *his* knife, her eyes boring a hole through his face, right about where he knew she wanted to plunge the blade. The other man stood on the outskirts of the clearing, alternating his gaze from in the circle, to outside it.

Whatever was discussed, the look on Elijah's face said it was serious. "We have to move. The raiders have landed several boats and are searching, I presume for our guests."

Darlene made a sound. "Guests, my ass."

Elijah ignored her.

"Manny, take the lead. Darlene, take Kendra. Paul and

Donny cover our backs. Let's move." The group moved out fast, as though they'd done it many times before. Elijah slid next to Mark, guided his elbow to his spot in line and released him.

"Elijah, they're coming for me. Cut me free."

"No."

"If they attack, I can help defend."

"No."

"Trust your own judgment. I'm not going to hurt you."

"You put a knife to Darlene's throat. If I cut you loose, I'd have an open rebellion on my hands. I can't afford that."

"Let me go to fend for myself. I can lead them away from you."

"We won't have to worry about confronting them if we hurry, and you keep your voice down."

From ahead, Darlene turned and said, "Don't let him talk you into anything."

Elijah gave Mark a look as if to say, "See, told you."

"And if he's making too much noise, I can always cut out his tongue," she offered.

They moved with stealth through the trees and brush. Not more than five minutes later, a gunshot broke the silence. Mark ducked instinctively and turned. The shot had come from behind. After a pause, several other shots followed, shouting reached them from a multitude of directions.

"Go! Go! Go!" Elijah looked at Mark. "If you know what's good for you, you will follow them to safety." With that, he spun to help Donny and Paul protect the rear.

Mark watched the man disappear behind trees and brush, then looked toward the end of the line. Darlene had stopped twenty feet away and stared at him, as if daring him to run. Her hand held a gun, her fingers flexing and tightening on the grip. Mark decided to follow.

The next flurry of shots was closer and more intense. As he walked, Mark tugged on his binds. Whenever Darlene looked to the front, he sank his teeth into the knot and ripped. As the battle heated up behind them, the knot loosened. He worked an end free. The ropes gave, but not quite enough. Running steps behind him made him stop and look, ready to dart away if necessary.

Paul and Elijah came running, dragging Donny's bloody body with them. In the distance, Mark spotted a speck of color moving through the trees. The raiders were in pursuit and close. Mark sank his teeth into the second of the three knots and with determined pulls had it nearly undone by the time Elijah and Paul drew even with him. Mark stepped in front of them and squatted. "Put him over my shoulder."

The men paused. "Hurry! It'll free your hands up to shoot." He crouched. They lifted Donny, who Mark was fairly certain was dead. He extended his arms out for the wounded man's legs to slide inside them. He shouldered the weight and stood erect, clamping his right arm against the back of Donny's thighs to hold him in place. He met Elijah's eyes and nodded. The two defenders looked for defensive positions as Mark turned to follow the line.

Seconds later the gun battle re-engaged.

Though awkward, Mark continued to put the rope to his mouth. Frustration at the slowness of the process left him swearing under his breath. He kept Darlene and Kendra in sight. The second knot gave way. Losing the binds was easy from there. He pulled his hands apart and the rope slid off his wrists, falling to the forest floor.

Gripping the back of Donny's legs with one hand, Mark was able to move faster. Movement to his right showed the pursuit had flanked them. Two men had reached a position level with Darlene, but the woman had yet to see them.

Mark pushed harder closing the gap. "Darlene!" he shouted. The woman spun around glaring, hatred pouring from her eyes. He pointed. "To the right." She either didn't hear him or refused to avert her gaze. "Look!" he insisted.

Her eyes narrowed and she lifted her handgun aiming it straight at his chest. The shot missed; her not him. The two flanking gunmen chose that moment to ambush them.

Mark rushed behind a tree and set Donny down. He risked a quick peek, but Darlene was not in sight. Had she been hit? He needed a weapon. A shot from an unseen location somewhere near the front of the line gave Mark pause while thinking of his next move. Had Manny come back to help or was he under attack as well? Mark glanced around the trees behind him, first looking for other assailants, then searching for an escape route.

If any raiders were there, Mark couldn't see them. He darted away from the fight, running from tree to tree. No shots chased him. Out of sight from the attackers, he circled around. Gunshots filled the woods from left and right. He made his way between the two battles, attempting to get behind the raiders pinning Darlene and Kendra down.

He thought he'd gone undetected. He stopped and crouched to get his bearings. To the right and behind him, only sporadic fire came from Elijah and Paul. To the left, a steady cadence told him the defense was still alive. Moving with more caution, he moved diagonally away from the two shooters to come up behind them. He found them twenty yards farther on. He stopped to analyze their position and his chances of taking them both on without getting shot. They didn't seem good.

One man used hand signals to direct his partner to a new position. Mark moved as that man did, but trying not to make noise slowed him. He had no idea of their condition or rounds available to them, but if he didn't hurry, Manny and Darlene were in trouble.

The moving shooter disappeared. Mark couldn't be sure if he'd ducked into a new firing position or kept going. Regardless, he had to take out one before he could tackle the second. Keeping low, he advanced toward the stationary gunman. He stopped and moved and stopped and moved. The last five yards would be the hardest. If the shooter heard him, he'd have ample warning to turn and shoot him.

Mark got down on all fours to take advantage of the thick foliage that lined the forest floor. The man fired several more times. Mark prayed none of the rounds found his captors. He crawled to within three yards of the shooter, when the man stood and moved to his right.

Damn! Mark scrambled to his feet and ran at the man. His best and perhaps only chance was to move when his prey did.

The man made a sudden drop to the ground, catching Mark by surprise. Unable to cover his pursuit, he launched at the gunman as he spun to face Mark. Shock covered the raider's face seeing Mark, in full animal mode, rushing at him. He brought his gun up and backed away. Mark felt the pain long before the bullet was fired.

The shot roared in his head, as his hands reached the man's throat. To his surprise, he had little to no pain. The force and speed of his attack drove the man back, onto a fallen tree trunk. He bent over the trunk backward, with Mark's full weight curving his body. All the wind driven from his lungs, the man's eyes bugged out and his gun fell to the far side of the log. Mark's momentum carried him over the trunk. He grabbed his opponent's shirt as he went dragging the man with him. They pounded onto the ground. Mark's hand smacked against a rock. He winced but picked it up and cracked the shooter's head with a sickening, wet thud. The man's eyes opened wide, he exhaled and slumped, his eyes rolling up.

Mark stood and stepped away from the body. He did a quick search of the man's belongings, taking the gun and a knife; he looked for the second shooter but for the moment, everything was quiet. He checked the magazine. Five rounds remained. Patting the man down, he found seven more bullets in a pocket. He filled the magazine. Twelve shots. He would have to make them count.

He stood, the weapon aimed forward, and swept the gun in a slow, short arc. Up ahead a lone gunshot broke the peace. The shooter broke cover only a few feet from where Mark stood. Surprised, Mark jerked the trigger and missed. The man dove for the ground. Standing in the open, no cover close, the only thing Mark could do was keep firing.

He stepped and fired at the area he last saw the man. He slipped to the right and fired three more times, before ducking to listen. After several long, nerve-racking minutes, he moved again. He found the body under some pine tree branches, legs protruding. He ducked to see underneath, expecting a bullet any second, but nothing happened. He grabbed a leg and hauled the man out. Mark doubted death had come quick, but it had come. Two of his blind shots had struck him in the back. He blew out a loud breath and spun in a circle. No one else was in sight.

"Darlene!" She didn't answer. "Darlene," he called louder.

"What, asshole?"

"Just making sure you're all right."

"Why don't you step out somewhere I can see you to find out?"

"Somehow I don't think that'd be wise. I'm going back to make sure Elijah is all right. Get Kendra to safety."

He didn't wait for her to respond. It would most likely just be a threat anyway.

Twenty-Eight

"In position," Tara's static-filled voice announced over the radio. Lynn turned down the volume. Though expecting the call, when it came, it surprised her enough to jump.

"Report," she said, motioning with her hand for the others to join her.

"Count at least twenty adults, most armed. Several children. If they're holding our people, I cannot determine where. Setting up ambush now. Will call back when done. Going to radio silence."

Lynn was about to say something to sign off but decided against it. She put the antenna under her lower lip and thought. This was taking too long. She wanted to do something, but what? Her mind returned to her original plan. If she didn't hear something in the next few minutes from the scout team, she would put her own idea into motion.

The wait was intolerable. Patience exhausted, she issued orders. To the driver of the jeep, she said, "Pull up to a position where you can see the barricade, but one that offers the least amount of risk. I want them to know you're there, but not be able to target you. The rest of you, pull the minivan parallel to the trailer and take up shooting positions behind it. I'm going in under a white flag. If they shoot me, I expect you to avenge me." She tried to force a smile, but the effort was too great. "I need something long, like a pole or tree branch, and a white flag."

Someone handed her an old white towel. Minutes later a branch appeared and Private Ordway used his knife to whittle off the nubs and branches. The towel tied to one end, she was ready.

"This is crazy," a tall man named Denver said. "You should wait for word from that officer."

"That may take too long. This way, I'll get an answer one way or another, as well as serve as a diversion for what Tara and her people are doing. If they shoot, return fire. Keep them pinned down so they can't get off any shots. Let's go."

The looks they gave each other spoke to the fact they all thought this was a bad idea, but no one offered any argument. They climbed in and the two vehicles moved out. The jeep stopped first and the machine gun swung toward the barricade. The minivan moved another ten yards before turning broadside. Everyone hopped out and found a shooting station.

Lynn stood on the floor of the van, grabbed the roof and leaned out. Lifting the makeshift white flag, she waved it above her head. After several seconds, with no volley loosed their way, she stepped down and went to the front of the van. There she waved the flag a few more times before she took a deep breath and walked into the open.

She advanced in slow, measured steps, stopping a third of the distance from the barricade. A high-pitched voice shouted, "What do you want?"

"I just want to talk. We're not looking for a fight."

"So talk."

Lynn took another step forward. "We're looking for the people who were in that SUV." She pointed.

After a brief pause, a huskier voice answered. "Yeah, so are we."

That wasn't an answer Lynn expected. Did that mean they didn't have them or had they been captured and escaped? "Are they here?" she said.

"Why are you looking for them?"

Lynn thought about her response. "They took something of ours and we want it back."

An argument broke out behind the trailer, but the words were lost in the distance.

The first voice came back. "We want them too. They killed two of our people."

"So, you don't have them here?"

"No."

"Would you let us look?"

More discussion. "You're close enough right there."

Lynn tried to think of how to phrase her next sentence without making the other group angry enough to shoot. "We really need to know."

The second voice yelled, his tone angrier. A short, squat man in blue jeans and a Cincinnati Reds jersey stepped from the side of the trailer nearest the abandoned SUV. "We don't have to show you shit."

He pointed a menacing finger at her. "We're not afraid of your machine gun. We've got plenty of weapons aimed at all of you. We're telling you we don't have them. If you don't believe that, tough shit. If they were here, all you'd find is bodies anyway. And we'd give those to you. We've got people out searching for them now. If you want them alive, you're too late. When our people find them, they're dead. Now turn away or we'll open fire."

Fear touched Lynn's heart. Though it fought to control her, it was in an all-out battle with her anger. She backed away, thinking it the best course of action before she said or did something that might get her killed. Her radio squawked. She put it to her mouth and said, "Go!"

Tara said, "You're one crazy be-yatch, you know that?"

"What?" Lynn said, as if not hearing her right.

"Never mind. Your bold little walk drew the defenders attention in your direction. We took the apartment complex with no resistance. Our search and subsequent interrogation of a few of the residents leads me to believe our people are not here. They were, but after a confrontation, escaped. These people sent out a posse to pursue. I think it's best to walk away without a fight, while we can."

"Agreed," Lynn responded. She took two more steps back, spun on her heels and hurried to the van. "Let's pack up and move out." To Private Ordway, manning the machine gun, she said, "Keep us covered until we're clear." He gave a quick two-finger salute.

Denver had just shifted into drive when the gunshots started. "Quick," she shouted, "get us out of range."

She lifted the radio, "Tara! Tara, come in."

A few tense seconds later she got a response. "Sorry, I was a little busy for a moment."

"You all right?"

"Yeah, we're good. A few of them came back up the hill as we were leaving. A few shots were exchanged, but no one was hit. We'll join you about a mile back from your position. Out."

"Roger. Out" She sat back and exhaled, releasing her anxiety.

She lifted the radio and stared at it. To call, or not to call. If they were in trouble and she used the radio, it might give them away. But, if they were in a tight spot, wouldn't they have called? If they were out of range, that'd be a moot point, but if silence were of importance, they would have turned the radio off. She decided to try. "Becca! Bobby! Lincoln! Come back." No response. She tried twice more. They were either out of range, had the volume off, or, no … there was no or.

The anxiety was back. She tried to push it aside, to wall it off, thinking there was no sense in worrying about the

157

unknown, but the nagging fear persisted. She stared out of the window and thought about Mark. She missed him, but especially at times like this.

Twenty-Nine

"Sounds like gunshots," Lincoln said, stating the obvious. They had hidden the boat and disembarked, taking up defensive positions along the large boulders that lined the shore.

"Shh!" Becca hissed. She pointed to the left. "That way, on the other side of the marina. In or beyond those trees."

"You think we can get to it on foot, or should we take the car?" said Bobby.

"Let's backtrack to the marina and decide from there," Lincoln said.

They moved, their increased speed and noise justified by their need to get to their father before it was too late. They broke from the trees and ran along the channel shoreline, able to go faster in the open. Reaching the edge of the woods they turned and raced down its length. Lincoln led the way, utilizing the speed he'd once dazzled rival defenses with on the grid iron. Where the tracks were when the car entered the trees, he darted into the space, pulled up short, skidded and dropped to one knee.

Bobby barely avoided running into him, pivoting to the side. Becca stopped in time but shielded from what caused the abrupt stop by Lincoln's body.

"Well, looky what we found, boys." The voice surprised

her, but she recognized trouble. Still out of view from the speaker, Becca retreated two steps and bolted around the trees. "Go get her," the voice shouted behind her. She ducked into the trees before they came into sight, dropped and buried herself under the foliage and behind a tree. She slid her knife free and fought to control her breathing and her revving heartbeat.

Running steps pounded on the ground in front of her. "Where'd she go?" one said.

"Dunno," a deeper voice answered. "But she couldn't have gone far. I'll go around the corner, you cut through the trees. I'll meet you on the other side."

"Shouldn't we stick together?"

"Dude, it's just a girl. If you find her, shout out and drag her ass back to Max."

Becca heard rustling as someone moved cautiously through the undergrowth. She slowed her breathing. The approaching hunter was close. Lying on her stomach, she cursed herself for not stopping in a better striking position, but she dared not change now. She tightened her grip on the knife. Sweat beaded and ran from every pore. Something creepy crawled up her arm. Every fiber in her wanted to swat the thing off, but she bit her lower lip and buried the urge.

Footsteps to the right. Then nothing. Had he seen her? More steps and he stopped again. She imagined him just to the right of the tree she hid behind. How well did the green carpet of vegetation covering much of the ground conceal her? She'd know in a moment. More steps.

Bobby watched helplessly as the two men went in pursuit of his sister. The remaining three men had their weapons trained on Lincoln and him. The leader said, "Armando, take their guns." A tall, lean brown-skinned youth of about eighteen, stepped forward and snatched the weapons. He deposited them on the trunk of the car.

Bobby wondered where Drew was. Was he still in the car, or had he gone looking for them? He didn't see a body, so he didn't think whoever these people were, had spotted him yet.

"What do you want?" Lincoln said, defiance ringing in his voice.

"Payback, asshole. You killed two friends of ours. Now, we gonna take you back to answer for it."

"We only defended ourselves. Your friends attacked us first."

"Don't matter. It also don't matter how many of you we bring back alive. As long as we have one of you to bring to the council, it's all right if we kill the others. So, if I were you, I'd be real calm."

Armando said, "We have to kill at least one of them. We deserve that, don't we?"

The leader laughed. "Oh, we will. Wait till they bring the bitch back. We can have some fun with her then decide who dies."

More constant gunshots came from the trees across the marina to the west. Bobby and Lincoln locked eyes. They knew they had to get away, but how?

"Sounds like someone's having a good time," the third man said. "Think that's too far to be our guys though."

The leader scrunched up his face, either in thought, or he had gas. "Go stand watch in case there's more of them somewhere. We don't want them sneaking up on us."

The third man ran off.

They wouldn't have a better chance, thought Bobby.

As if reading his mind, the leader backed up a step and aimed his weapon, a single-barrel pump shotgun, at his chest.

Two more steps and Becca saw feet inches from her face.

He was directly above her. She closed her eyes expecting an explosion of pain, but nothing happened. The hunter moved on. Becca followed the feet with her eyes. Before he got too far away, she twisted her torso and slashed with the knife. The finely honed edge sliced his Achilles tendon with little effort. The man buckled at the knees, his hand reaching for his foot. A banshee-like wail rose from his mouth filling the forest with his pain.

As his body crumpled, Becca pounced, cutting off the scream by piercing his larynx. Becca dragged the blade left and right, finishing the job, and pushed the still twitching body away. She was on her feet in an instant, going deeper into the woods in the general direction of the car.

Bobby heard the horrific scream at the same time he noticed movement inside the car. Drew sat up, his eyes still looked unfocused. He shook his head once, then gazed out of the window again. Whatever images registered in his brain, the look on his face told Bobby that Drew knew it was serious.

The scream ended as suddenly as it had started. Bobby ignored it for the moment, reassured in the knowledge it was not his sister. His eyes caught Drew's, who nodded. Bobby tried not to tense, but whatever Drew did, he had to be ready to move. Plotting his move, he would go for the leader, hoping Lincoln would adjust and take the second man.

Both men stood near the trunk with their backs to the car. Drew grabbed the window frame and pulled upright. Unable to control it, Bobby's heart rate soared. He glanced at Lincoln to see if the big man gave any signs of whether or not he saw Drew, or was just a good actor; he gave no outward sign.

A hand snaked out of the open window, a gun in his grip. Bobby gulped hard seeing how much Drew's hand shook. If he took a shot, it had just as much chance of hitting him or Lincoln as it did either of the bad guys.

Bobby closed his eyes and waited for the explosion. He didn't have long to wait. Bobby was moving before his eyes opened. He took in the scene in a second. Armando spun around as if he were a top and someone had pulled his string. A mist of blood lifted into the air. The leader turned as well, but seemed to think better of it and spun back.

Not sure he could reach the gunman in time, Bobby dove for Armando's legs. A bullet carved a path through the air just above him. Another shot from Drew was answered by a burst of automatic fire. Bobby ignored all else as he wrapped his arms around the leader's legs, twisted and pulled. The man collapsed on top of him. Bobby kept a tight grip and rolled, pulling the man with him. The gunman fired again. How much longer before he brought the gun in line?

Releasing his grip, Bobby risked everything by diving for the gun. Another bullet was triggered. A searing pain burned Bobby's left forefinger as the bullet whizzed past. Bobby envisioned a bloody stump on his left hand, but could not afford to dwell on the loss. He gripped the gun hand and gun and twisted it hard against the man's wrist.

His opponent fought hard to retain possession, but Bobby felt the advantage swing his way. With the upper position, Bobby applied pressure to the wrist. The pain would either be too much for the man to bear or his wrist would break. Bobby didn't care one way or another as long as he released the gun.

The man pummeled the back of Bobby's head with his opposite fist. The blows weren't hard but still had an effect. Bobby forced the gun arm up over his opponent's head. Bobby crawled higher and his body covered the gunman's face, who sank his teeth into Bobby's belly.

Bobby screamed and pulled away; using the same tactic, he lunged at the gun hand, sinking his teeth into the wrist;

he applied pressure. The other man latched on with his teeth again. It became a battle of who could handle the pain best. Bobby forced the agony from his mind as he bit down harder. Coppery tasting blood leaked into his mouth, as fire spread across his stomach. He tried to lift up and away from the teeth, but the man had a good hold and rose with him.

Snarling, Bobby went berserk, gnashing and tearing and bouncing up and down on the man's face. He twisted with each rise and slammed as much weight down with each descent. The gun fired once more, the blast echoing in his ears before it dropped to the ground. Bobby drove an elbow into his enemy's face. He brought up a knee and dropped with all his weight on the man's gut. The explosion of air signaled the end of the fight. The man doubled up clutching his midsection.

Bobby rose to a sitting position and dropped four straight right-handed power shots to the biter's face and he stopped moving. Bobby growled, stood and howled. A sudden sound behind him smothered the animal cry in his throat. He spun, arms raised, ready to defend, in time to see the third man's gun fall from his hands; a second later, his body fell on top of it. Becca stood behind him, bloody knife in hand. The cold-hard look of the hunter lit her eyes. She lifted her head and imitated Bobby's wolf-like howl. He joined her in unison.

"Jesus Christ, stop that!" Lincoln said.

Brother and sister stopped, looked at each other, then embraced.

A man ran into the clearing, saw the carnage and fled.

Becca laughed and howled again. Bobby laughed. Lincoln covered his ears.

Bobby stopped and he moaned. "Oh, no."

Becca and Lincoln turned to see what he was looking at. "Shit!" Lincoln said. Drew's bullet-torn body hung from the rear window.

Thirty

Mark stopped, crouched and listened. Nothing. After the distant gunshots and strange howling had ceased, even the birds had gone silent. He waited, afraid he would move into someone's line of sight. After two minutes, about to advance to another position, rustling to his left caught his attention. Leaning against a small tree trunk, he brought up his weapon and tracked the movement.

His finger tightened on the trigger as a bush moved twenty feet to the left. As it parted, he breathed out and relaxed the pressure on his finger just before putting a bullet into Elijah. The man struggled to keep a wounded Paul up and moving. Blood covered much of the man's torso and legs, giving no clue where the actual wound was. They moved unaware of what was around them.

Mark scanned for pursuit. If anyone were tracking them, the noise from their movement, coupled with Paul's low moans would have made the job easy. Seeing nothing, Mark stood, about to lend a hand carrying Paul, when two men burst into the small open space. They spied Elijah and Paul and raised their weapons.

Elijah tried to spin to meet the attack, but with Paul in tow, was too slow. Mark fired in a hurry. His first two shots were off target. The two men pivoted and fired back, too surprised to make the shots count. As they fled for cover Mark managed to score a hit in the upper back of the taller man, but both disappeared from sight. With limited ammo, He contemplated following but thought better of it.

Instead, he kept the gun raised and sighted on the spot where the men escaped; he sidestepped toward Elijah and Paul. "Keep moving, I'll cover you."

Elijah didn't speak. Lifting Paul with a grunt, he hauled the man out of the clearing and into cover and used a tree trunk to shield him. If the two gunmen were still there, they weren't making their presence obvious.

Mark caught up to Elijah and wrapped an arm around the opposite side of the wounded man. As they moved faster, Mark fumbled for the handgun Paul wore in a holster on his belt, pulled it free and stuck it in his belt. If Elijah noticed he was not concerned.

After another five minutes with no signs of pursuit, Elijah called for a break; his chest heaved from the exertion. They set Paul down and Elijah doubled over sucking for air and leaned against a tree. Mark scanned the area focusing all his attention on listening for unnatural sounds. As sure as he could be that they were alone, he knelt down to examine Paul.

The man had two wounds. One in the right shoulder, the other in the right chest. He wasn't a doctor, but he'd seen enough wounds to know he needed some medical assistance, and soon.

"We have to go. He needs help."

Elijah nodded. He drew in a deep breath, pushed away from the tree and helped Mark lift Paul. They moved on in silence for a time.

"How far?" Mark asked.

Elijah hesitated. "Not very."

"Do you have someone with medical experience?"

"Limited, but yes."

"Freeze," a voice shouted. Mark closed his eyes and

sighed, knowing the source of the command. Darlene stepped from cover, her gun pointed at Mark. Elijah said, "Darlene, lower the gun."

"No, we can't trust him."

"You can't, but I do. He saved my life. Now, lower the gun."

"Did he shoot Paul?"

"Now you're being ridiculous. You're too emotional for clear thought. Come, help me with Paul."

She stepped closer but refused to lower her gun. Elijah positioned his body between her and Mark. "Darlene, I'm not asking again."

A blur darted from the left, catching Darlene from behind. Gun and body went flying. By the time the picture came into focus, Becca had her down, a knife descending toward her throat.

"Becca. No!" Mark shouted. Almost too late, Becca pulled back. The tip of the blade pierced the skin a micro-fraction away from severing her carotid. The hostility on his daughter's face was enough to make Mark blanch. "Becca," his voice was but a whisper, but it seemed to fill the space.

Still, all but frothing, Becca hissed, "She-she was going to kill you, Daddy!"

Mark forced a calm he did not feel into his words. "She's not going to now. Let her up."

The vision of his daughter's horrifying bloodlust refused to release his mind. "Becca, let her up."

Becca looked from Darlene to her father. Something changed inside her, as though an evil presence had been exorcized. She pulled the knife back and stood, backing away from the woman as Bobby and Lincoln joined them.

"Christ," Lincoln said.

Bobby rushed to his sister, put an arm around her and guided her away from Darlene. The other woman lay on the ground, shock robbing her of anger, unable to move.

Lincoln said, "Man, am I glad to see you."

"Likewise," said Mark.

"I'm getting way too old for this shit," Lincoln said.

"I'm with you."

"Only you could turn a simple fishing trip into a war zone."

"Yeah, thanks, *Lynn*."

"Hey, just saying."

"Give Elijah a hand with Paul, would you?"

He holstered his gun. "Sure." He lifted the wounded man by himself.

Mark stepped to Darlene's side and offered his hand. She stared at him, still breathing hard from her near-death experience. "We're not your enemies, Darlene. Let me help you up."

A spark of fire lit her eyes for a second, then passed away as quickly. With a tentative hand she accepted Mark's. He hauled her to her feet. They stood looking at each other. Mark waited for her to say something, but she didn't. She bent to retrieve her gun. Mark glanced at his daughter. Becca's hand was on her gun, ready to draw and fire if the need arose.

Darlene picked up the gun stared at it for a moment, slid it into a holster hanging from a rope tied around her. She looked at Paul, at Mark, and said, "This way." She led the group into the woods. Five minutes later, she stopped and whistled. It was returned by someone unseen ahead. She strode off again. A minute later they came into a large clearing reminiscent of a small Indian village. Tents and hastily constructed wooden structures had been erected in a circle around a large central fire pit.

A group of about twenty people, men, women and children, came out to greet them. A woman and two men rushed to Paul as Elijah and Lincoln entered the opening. "He's bad. Quick, get him inside." The two new men took Paul to the largest building near the center of the village.

"Welcome to our community," Elijah said. To the gathered group, he added. "These people are our guests and should be treated as such. Some of you bring food and drink for them, please." A few of the small community went off, Mark assumed to take care of his request.

Elijah turned to Mark. "I have to both apologize and thank you. You saved maybe all of our lives. I am burdened by guilt over how we treated you. Please understand, we are a peaceful and welcoming sort of commune, but in our meetings and dealings with others, we've learned to be very careful and quite defensive."

"I do understand. Some of the groups we've met haven't had the same ideas about community and family that we do."

"Yes, it is certainly a strange and harsh new world we live in." He swept an arm toward the central gathering area where several tables sat around the fire pit. "Please, go and refresh yourselves. I have a few things to tend to then I will join you."

Mark watched the man walk off and wondered what his previous role had been in society. He spoke like a politician, or perhaps teacher. He seemed friendly and peaceful enough, but having been fooled before, he remained wary and alert.

Mark turned and moved to join Lincoln, Bobby and Becca at the tables.

The activity in the camp amped up. Everyone was in motion with a job to do. Bowls of some sort of soup were placed in front of them. Fish and what appeared to be seaweed floated in a greenish broth.

Lincoln sniffed at it and made a face. Mark had little interest in food, but Bobby tucked in. "Hey, this is good." Broth dribbled down his chin and he wiped it with a backhand.

Lincoln looked at him like he was being put on.

"No, really. Try it."

169

Lincoln took a tentative slurp and his eyebrows lifted in surprise.

A man sat across from them. "Good?"

Bobby said, "Yeah, what's in it?"

"Yeah," Lincoln said. "What's all these weeds? Looks like something picked up after the grass has been cut. You sure they're edible?"

The man laughed, stood and went into one of the tents. He came back a moment later carrying a book. "It's all in here." He handed the book to Lincoln. He read the title aloud. "Edible Wild Plants by John Kallas, Ph.D."

"It lists all kinds of edible plants and even gives recipes. Found it in a house and thought it would be handy. Added fresh herbs that we grow and fish we caught, and there you go." He waved his hand over the table.

"Hmm!" Lincoln said, "Still looks like weird." But he took another slurp.

Mark glanced around the camp getting an idea of their numbers. His eyes stopped on Darlene. She sat on a tree stump honing her knife. What was more disturbing was the hatred in her eyes. He followed her glare and saw it connected with Becca's eyes. Even more heart-stopping was the eerie smile on his daughter's face.

Thirty-One

"Wait!" Lynn said. "There! Yes," she shouted with more enthusiasm than intended.

"Where?" Denver said.

"That sign up there on the left."

"Remember, you were looking through binoculars."

"Oh yeah, sorry. It's about a mile further." She looked off into the distance at the two apocalyptic-looking stacks of the old Davis-Bessie nuclear power plant, highlighted against an ominous gray sky. Did that get shut down properly or did they have to worry about a meltdown at some point? She wondered if they were far enough away that they wouldn't be affected if that did happen but decided there was no safe distance.

"Here?" Denver asked, disrupting her thoughts.

"Yeah." She picked up the radio and tried to reach the lead group. Still no answer. Lynn wanted to slam the radio down. "Slow down, Denver. We're not sure what we might run in to." She clicked the radio to get the other vehicles' attention and without waiting for them to check in, said, "Everyone be alert."

Not wanting to waste any more time after leaving the barricade, Lynn had stayed in the minivan, rather than transfer back to Tara's SUV. Now she wished she had. Tara could offer more insight as to what to look for or how to position the convoy.

The radios squawked. "Tara to Lynn, come in."

She lifted the radio, depressed the button and spoke. "It's Lynn, Tara."

"There're tire tracks leading into those trees. Did you see the two trucks parked just off the main road?"

"No, I missed them."

"They don't look as though they've been there long. It's not an area anyone would stop unless they had a purpose."

"You thinking it might be the ones the barricade people were talking about?"

"That's my thought. Stop where you are and wait for us. We're gonna check out the tracks."

"Stop here, Denver." Lynn turned in her seat and saw Tara's SUV veer off the dirt road and follow the twin tire lines toward the trees. The jeep stopped on the road, the gunner swiveling the gun to cover the SUV.

"What's going on?" Antwan, a young black man in the back seat, asked.

"Tara's investigating something suspicious."

The car went quiet, adding to the building tension of waiting. Several minutes later, Tara called. "They've been here all right. Signs of a gun fight and a few freshly dead bodies."

Lynn felt her heart pound harder and try to rise up her esophagus. "Any ..." she cleared her suddenly dry throat, "anyone you recognize?" She held her breath waiting for the word.

"One that looks familiar. Mel says his name's Drew." She paused. "He's been shot multiple times. We don't recognize any of the others."

Lynn closed her eyes, picturing Drew. Her heart bounced like an out-of-balance elevator, rising with elation it wasn't Mark, but dropping just as fast at the loss of a family member. Tears welled, her nerves shot, her escalating emotions flew around within her like a bird caught inside a car.

"Lynn?"

"Huh, yeah." She realized she hadn't pressed the button and tried again. "I'm here."

"Leave the car there with a driver," Tara said. "I'm going to have the jeep change positions. Bring your group over here and we'll search the woods."

Lynn, still in shock, nodded her head.

"Lynn! You with me?"

"Yeah, sorry. We're on our way."

"Denver, stay with the car. Keep an eye out for intruders and us. If you see me waving, come in a hurry."

"You got it."

"Everyone else out."

Corporal Ward joined them and suggested they spread out. They approached the tree line and Mel stepped out. "Over here." They followed.

Drew's body had been laid out next to a Malibu. Three other bodies lay on the other side of the car. Sorrow struck her like a bullet at the sight of Drew's corpse. He had only been with them for a little over a week. He was eager to please; always willing to do whatever he was told, and when finished, would ask 'what else do you need done?' He just wanted to fit in, like most of them, he wanted to feel he belonged. She wiped a lone tear away. "Sorry, Drew," she whispered.

"Any ideas where to begin?" she asked Tara.

"There're some tracks leading off that way," she pointed across wide open ground. "They headed that way, anyway, whether they continued on that course is anyone's guess."

Lynn glanced from Drew to the ground they would have to travel, not knowing if that was even the right path. They could be anywhere. If they went that way, had it been of their own accord, or at the insistence of others? Frustrated, she glared at the radio as if daring it to stay silent. She lifted the radio and called for Mark, Bobby or anyone to answer, but before a response came, Tara came running. "We've got four small craft entering the marina."

Damn!

From the main road behind them came the roar of many vehicles approaching.

Double Damn!

"Shit!" Tara exclaimed. "Quick, everyone into the trees." She waved an arm wildly for the jeep to come. Lynn motioned with quick circular movements for Denver to bring the car. The line of cars and trucks appeared long before they were out of sight.

Tara took command issuing orders and assigning duties. "Use the cars as cover. Stay down. I'm sure they saw us, but just in case. Don't move unless necessary. You," she pointed at Antwan, "go in that direction to the end of the trees and keep watch on the water. If they get off the boats and come our way, retreat and tell me. Got that?" He nodded. "Go."

He took off running.

Corporal Ward called out, "That column of vehicles has stopped on the main road. Someone just got out. Looks like he's giving instructions. Yep. They're turning here, coming in a straight line across the open ground."

Tara said, "How many?"

"All of them."

"No, dummy, how many vehicles?"

"Oh, yeah, sorry. Seven."

"Are they fully loaded?"

"Can't tell, but you have to figure there's at least two people to a car otherwise why waste the gas for one person?"

"So we could be dealing with anywhere from fourteen to twenty-eight people," Tara said. "No one shoot till I give the word. There's a slight chance they might pass us. Private Menke, target the nearest two cars. When I give the word, fire until they're no longer a threat, then switch to the farthest car. Shoot not just to kill, but to incapacitate their vehicles. If we need to run, we can outdistance them. The rest of you pick off the closest targets. If you see anyone enter the woods, get our attention."

Ward said, "They're level with us and swinging our way."

The line of cars had performed a complete left turn so that the entire column now faced the woods. Tara eyed the situation and altered the plan. "Menke, take out the vehicles in the center. Everyone else, concentrate fire on the ends."

The group of defenders watched as the line stopped and doors across the line opened. Maybe twenty-five men and women emerged. They hid behind the open doors as the column advanced. Tara called up to Menke, "Target the drivers. On my mark."

She waited a few seconds more. "Fire!" The tree line erupted in a volley of gunfire, a plume of smelly smoke hung cloud-like over their heads. The loud constant chatter of the machine gun created an image of what a real battle was like. The bullets ripped through machine and flesh, leaving little standing in its path.

In less than a minute the attacking force had taken severe casualties and was in retreat. Whatever training they had done to work on advancing formations, they'd obviously not practiced retreating. Chaos ruled, making the scene before them look like a keystone cop routine.

Those vehicles that could move collided with destroyed and moving cars alike. Of the seven vehicles that started, only three drove off and one of them trailed black smoke behind. People scattered everywhere. The lucky ones got away, while others who weren't shot down, were hit by cars, or knocked down by panicked allies. It was a mad scramble to escape.

Tara called a cease fire, if not for humane reasons, to at

least save ammo. They watched as the survivors climbed jumped or clung to the escaping cars. Lynn estimated they'd lost as many as half their numbers in the first, and hopefully last, assault.

She turned away from the carnage and leaned against the minivan. Had Mark and company had to face the same thing? If so, had they been as effective? Running steps coming toward them from behind startled her. Quickly, her gun and everyone else's pointed in the opposite direction. Antwan burst into the small clearing unaware of the danger he had been in.

"Those people in the boats," he sucked in deep gulps of air. "Once the shooting started, they watcha'macalled the boats, and—"

"Do you mean docked?" Mel asked.

He nodded with vigor. "Yeah, and a ho' bunch of them got off. I think they're coming this way."

Lynn looked at Mel and Tara. "It never ends."

Tara went into immediate action. "Ward, get that jeep out of the trees and behind that building." She pointed toward the one-time marina store. "The rest of you load up and move down to the marina." To Mel and Lynn, she said, "I'd rather face them in the open where we can see what we're dealing with."

They moved out just as a few sporadic shots were fired in their direction. Tara had them drive around the trees and down the road to the docks. She got on the radio and called Ward. "Stay out of sight. If anyone comes out of those woods, cut them down. Antwan."

"Yo."

"Which boats are theirs?"

"Down that second river-like thing."

"The second channel."

"Yeah."

"Mel, stop broadside to that dock." She called to the minivan. "Denver, turn so you're broadside to the woods."

With everyone where she wanted them, they dismounted and took up defensive positions in the L-shaped barricade. Using binoculars, she scanned the docks. "We've got two guarding the boats." She spun around and looked behind her. "Mel, go to the building. Get Private Menke and climb up on top of the store."

Mel snorted. "And how do you propose I do that? This body," she swept her hands down her stocky form, "wasn't made for climbing."

"Do I have to do everything here?" Tara said, a little testy. "Use the jeep and have Corporal Ward boost you. You'll have superior position and sighting from up there. If you get a shot, take out those two guarding the boats. Now go, while you still can."

Lynn, who'd been listening, said, "I think we should talk to them first."

"Talk? Sounded like they were willing to let their guns do the talking to me."

"We need information, Tara. We have no idea where Mark and the others are."

Tara studied Lynn's face while she mulled her words. "How do you propose we make contact? If you step out there, you'll get shot. I doubt these people will cease fire because you're holding a white flag."

"I could just wave it from here and see what happens."

"Hey, give it a try. It can't hurt."

"One of the boats is moving," someone called out.

They turned their attention to the docks in time to see one speedboat pull away, do a sharp turn in the channel and head back out to open water.

"What do you make of that?" Lynn asked.

"My guess? They're going for reinforcements," Tara answered.

Lynn sighed and muttered. "Great."

Thirty-Two

Elijah had just sat down to join them when the echo of gunshots reached them. The many questions Mark wanted to ask were put on hold as Elijah sprang to his feet and into command mode. "Who do we have away from the camp?"

Someone responded, "Amos and Mary are on watch to the north and east. Gladys and Arturo are south and west."

"Anyone else unaccounted for?" he said.

A couple walked up to him. "No," the man said. "Everyone is here."

The woman said, "The shots came from the east."

"Send two to check it out."

A sudden thought entered Mark's mind. He spoke to Bobby. "You said Lynn was following you with another group?"

"Yeah."

"Daddy," Becca said, "they could be in trouble.

Mark stood and strode quickly to Elijah. "We'll go look."

"I can't ask you to do that. This is our community. We need to protect it."

"I understand and normally would respect that, but that could be our people out there in trouble. No offense, but we're going."

A flash of anger narrowed Elijah's eyes for a brief moment.

His look turned to a glare. Mark thought perhaps the man wasn't used to being challenged, but he had no interest in the man's job or ego, nor did he have time to argue. To his group, he said, "Let's go see."

The four of them gathered their gear and raced off, leaving the camp in loud chatter. He heard Elijah say, "Follow them," but wasn't sure how many he sent or what that meant. So much for trust. He pushed it aside, replacing the potential problem with thoughts of Lynn. He'd been surprised when his kids told him she was coming on the rescue mission herself. Normally, she would stay and run things at the farmhouse.

He wondered what her presence meant and hoped it was good. If she were in trouble, nothing Elijah said or did would prevent him from getting to her.

They ran on for five minutes before coming to a large swampy area. It seemed to stretch on for quite a distance. Searching for a way across, he noticed three of Elijah's followers leaping over a section further to the left. "Quick! Follow them." He bolted toward the crossing. By the time they reached the area, the three were only occasional blurs between the trees. He found the place where the waterway narrowed and leaped over it. The ground on the other side was soft, his foot sank in, but he drew it with a sucking sound, and sped after the other group, and trusted his party was behind him.

He ran as hard as he could through the trees, dodging and ducking branches. Glimpses of those he followed indicated he was gaining on them. A good fifteen minutes later he reached a clearing. Across the wide open space, he recognized the marina. Elijah's people were nowhere in sight. Lincoln pulled up next to him, followed by Becca and Bobby.

Becca dug out binoculars and scanned the scene before them. "Okay. You can see the jeep behind the building, right?"

"Yeah," Mark said.

"The cars out by the dock? That's where Lynn and Tara and a few others are. I don't see anyone else."

Mark squatted. "The way they're positioned, they're

defending from the trees and the water. Focus on the trees."

"Yeah. Yeah, I see movement there, but can't get a fix on numbers. My guess is maybe five to ten," Becca said.

"Now scan the water, paying attention to the boats."

"I'm not seeing much. Maybe one or two guys in those smaller boats."

"Did any of you see where Elijah's people went?"

"Nope," Lincoln said.

"Not me," said Bobby. "Didn't you see them when you got here?"

"No." He wasn't sure why that bothered him, but it did.

"There," Becca pointed, "over by the lake, along the shoreline. See 'em? They're crawling over those huge rocks." She handed the glasses to her father.

Mark took them, adjusted the focus and found the three immediately, as they crept along the rocks getting behind the jeep. A sudden jolt of panic hit him. Were they observing or going to attack? Maybe they thought the soldiers in the jeep were the enemy. He slapped the glasses back to Becca without looking. "We have to get to them before they do something stupid."

He took off running for the shore. Though less than a quarter mile away, traversing the rocky shore made the journey seem to take forever. The three they pursued dropped from sight and reappeared many times. Each time they went out of sight, another knot formed in Mark's stomach. Pushing harder, he missed his step several times and incurred more bruises, scrapes and pain. However, the worst sensation came when the three ahead of them vanished and did not reappear. They were either in a long low spot, or they were in shooting position. Mark feared which.

Taking a chance, Mark maneuvered to the edge of the rocks and jumped to level ground; though in sight from the woods, he was able to move much faster. In seconds, he discovered the barrels of three rifles across the top row of boulders, aimed at the backs of the two men in the jeep.

Pulling his handgun, Mark crouched and ran on. The shooters were too low to see, so he focused on the guns and hoped he would arrive before the shooting started. Six feet away, he leaped for the rocks, bounced from one to the other and landed in a small cove next to one of Elijah's men. He pointed the gun at his head as the others scrambled to adjust their weapons. "Put them down, or he dies."

The two men and a woman continued to move. With a backhand swipe, Mark pistol whipped the first man and switched targets to the woman. She froze as Lincoln, Becca and Bobby jumped down from the rocks and aimed their guns.

With reluctance and glares of hatred, the other two dropped their guns. Becca and Bobby scooped them up and dropped them over another line of rocks.

"What was your intent?"

"We don't answer to you," spat the woman.

Becca stepped toward her, but Mark put out a restraining arm. "Those people out there are with us. Were you planning on shooting them down from behind?"

Neither of them spoke. The pistol-whipped man sat up holding his bloody face.

"What were Elijah's orders?" Mark said.

"Let me ask the question, Daddy. I'll get an answer from her."

The woman glowered at Becca. Before the situation could go any further, the sound of boat engines bounced off the rocky shore. Lincoln leaped to the top of the rocks and threw himself prone. "Aw shit! We've got major company now." He paused. "Looks like six, no seven speedboats. Each one has three or four people in them. Could be more."

"Raiders," Mark said. "They're your real enemy," he said to the woman. "Not us."

"They're stopping at the mouth of the main channel," Lincoln informed them.

Mark said, "One of you go and tell Elijah." The two uninjured people looked at each other. The man nodded and the woman started to climb. She glanced at her gun. Mark said, "Take it. And take him too," he pointed to the bleeding man. They scampered over the top and dropped to the other side. Mark forgot about them knowing Bobby and Becca had their weapons ready in case of attack. A few moments later he released the breath he'd been holding.

"They're landing on the far end of the marina," Lincoln said. "Looks like we're about to have a war."

"Becca, get that guy's gun," Mark said.

Without a word she climbed over and returned with the rifle. She handed it to Mark and he, in turn, gave it to the other man. "Make sure you know who's on your side." The man held his eyes for a moment, nodded and took the rifle.

"What's our play here?" asked Lincoln.

Mark crawled up the rocks and lay next to him. He studied the landing party then looked to Lynn's group. The building obstructed his view of the cars and where Lynn was. This vantage point allowed only a view of the back of the building, and the western portion of the woods. He did, however, have a full view of the arriving boats and disembarking army.

He assumed the attackers were unaware of the jeep and the .50 caliber machine gun. They also didn't know about his group. From where the raiders landed, they could easily outflank the vehicles and come up behind the jeep and building. Lynn's group would be trapped.

"I think we hold here until we see how they attack. We'll counter whatever moves they make. My guess is a portion will come this way to get behind our people and catch them in a crossfire."

"So, we wait?" Lincoln said.

Mark nodded. "For now."

"Good, cause I gotta piss like a racehorse." He scrambled down the rocks leaving Mark, in spite of the situation, with a smile.

Thirty-Three

"Oh, man!" Mel said into the radio. "Tara, you seeing this?"

"Yeah. Make sure Ward knows. Stay low so they don't know you're there. We'll need the element of surprise."

Mel told Private Menke to crawl to the far edge and tell Ward an army was coming up from the opposite side.

"Mel," Tara said, "One of you cover the trees while the other covers the new group. Don't shoot until I tell you, but keep me posted as things develop. My guess is they'll try to get behind the building for a better firing position. Have Ward turn the gun in the opposite direction. We should be able to hold off those in the woods okay without his support."

"Roger."

"And hey, girlfriend ..."

Mel smiled at that. "Yeah?"

"Be careful."

"And you." She lowered the radio.

Lynn said, "What do you think?"

"About what? Our general situation or your idea of waving the flag?"

"Both, but mainly the flag thing."

Tara shook her head. "I don't know, Lynn. I'd prefer it

worked so that we could avoid an all-out war here. But my gut says there's no chance. Especially now that reinforcements have landed. We might have had a shot when the odds were more even. Now, who knows."

"I guess we won't know till we try." She took the white towel, but the stick had been thrown away. Rising level with the minivan's roof, Lynn lifted the towel above her head and waved it back and forth. Nothing happened. She stood erect and continued the attempt.

Behind them, the landing party took up defensive positions. Where Lynn's group had had the advantage of a superior position, now they were flanked on both sides. They could retreat and flee over the open ground to the west, but there was a good chance they would suffer some casualties. But, maybe that was a fair trade for getting some of them out alive. No, she thought, no loss of life was a fair trade for anyone. They shouldn't be fighting each other at all. If she presented that suggestion to Tara though, would she think it the right move? Isn't some living better than none?

She said a silent prayer that her flag-waving efforts would result in a peaceful solution. The bullet struck the flag, ripping it from her hand.

So much for peaceful solutions.

Tara grabbed her and yanked her behind the van. A barrage of bullets tore into the vehicles. The defenders scrambled to find a safe place between the two groups.

Antwan spun to the side with a yelp and fell to the ground. He writhed, holding his left arm. Denver grabbed and dragged him to cover. Just as he let go of Antwan, he took a bullet in the chest and flew backward, dead.

Lynn looked on in horror. They'd been in gunfights before, but nothing with this kind of intensity. She didn't remember pulling her gun, but it was in her hands now. She feared she would die, not that she feared death, but she didn't want to die without seeing Mark first.

A bullet impacted the minivan above her head. An involuntary squeak escaped her lips and she pulled her body in, shrinking. The gunfire was so intense from the attackers they couldn't even risk shooting back. Behind them, Mel and Private Menke sniped at the two sides. That might keep them from a full-on attack, but for how long?

"We have to get out of here," someone said, their voice on the verge of panic.

Tara said, "We have to pull the cars back to the building, to keep both groups in front of us."

"How?" the unseen person said. "It'd be suicide to get in the driver's seat."

Tara crawled under the SUV to take a look at what was happening. A bullet kicked up dirt to her right. She flinched and looked for the source. The man guarding the boats had climbed on the bow and lined up a second shot. A precognition of death descended down her spine. Even as she backed away, she knew she was too late.

The bullet cracked and she closed her eyes and ducked. No pain registered and she opened her eyes cautiously. The guard was no longer there. Mel's voice squawked over the radio. "Score one for the good guys." Tara barked a mixed laugh and sob, vowing to reward her lover later, if they survived.

As loud as the battle had been previously, it ratcheted up a few notches once the jeep pulled out from behind the building and entered the fight. Part of the landing party broke off on a flanking maneuver and the jeep opened fire, catching them in the open. Six of the eight men went down in an instant. The remaining two reached the shelter of the boulders by the shore.

The sudden appearance of the jeep had a game-changing effect on the battle. A lull settled over the marina. The sudden silence was just as loud as the gunfire had been. Lynn's ears rang. She raised up to get a better view. A haze had settled over their heads, drifting with the breeze in the

185

direction of the lake.

The machine gun rattled again, chewing up the dock where the boats had landed. A few sporadic return shots banged off the building. Silence again, as everyone waited for the other side to make a move.

"Here they come," Lincoln said.

"How many?" said Mark.

"Six, plus the two already there. They're creeping alongside the water with their heads down. I doubt our people even know they're there."

"Okay, let's get ready." He looked at Elijah's man. "You're welcome to join us if you want."

The man looked at Mark, nodded and followed him up the boulders. As soon as the five of them had line-of-sight on the advancing group, Mark said, "Fire!"

The five shots rang out and three of the six dropped from view. "Becca and Bobby, go along the shoreline and fish them out of their hiding spot."

The sibs moved out, scurrying around the boulders and stepping into the cold Lake Erie water. Mark left Lincoln and the other man and changed positions. He aimed at a spot the first two had hidden and waited. A few minutes later gunshots flushed the three from their berth. Lincoln and his partner opened fire. Mark ignored them, keeping his eye down the sight. As the first head popped up behind the rocks he squeezed the trigger. The only sign of a hit was the fine red mist that sprayed the rocks.

"Don't shoot!" a voice called out.

"Toss all your weapons over the rocks," Mark commanded. The rifle flew up and landed well out of reach of the shooter. From another spot to the right, another gun went airborne, clattering among the boulders.

"Now, climb out of there where we can see you."

"How do we know you won't shoot us?"

"Well, you don't, I guess, but know this, if you don't come out, we'll shoot you for sure."

"Okay. Okay." Extended hands stretched above the rocks. "Please don't shoot."

The surviving two men came into view. As they climbed up, Becca and Bobby advanced on them.

"Hey," shouted Lincoln, and a gunshot sparked off the rocks between Bobby and Becca and the two raiders. Mark swung his gun toward the shooter. Lincoln wrested the rifle away from the other man then delivered a savage punch to his head. "You asshole! They surrendered. We don't kill defenseless people."

The man backed away, rubbing his head. "You can't trust them. Elijah says never to take them prisoner 'cause they'll only find a way to hurt you later."

"You're not with Elijah."

"He is now," the voice startled them. They turned to see ten people standing along the rocks, their weapons aimed at them. "You will release my man and surrender your weapons."

"I don't think so," Mark said.

"Then you'll die."

"Then you will."

"Your people will never get here in time to save you or stop us. We'll be back in the woods long before they arrive."

"Is this really how you want this to go?"

"No, but it's for the best. Your presence disrupts the norm and brings us danger."

"Your best bet is to let us go in peace."

"I wish it were that easy."

"It is."

Elijah pondered that for a moment, then shook his head. "Sorry, I just can't trust you. The lives of these people depend on my decisions. I can't risk them by making the wrong choice."

Rage ignited within Mark. About to attack and risk the outcome, a red dot crawled across Elijah's chest. It danced on his chest as if signaling to Mark.

He smiled. "I'll tell you what," he said, raising one hand over his head in slow motion. "You either back away, drop *your* weapons, or die."

A confused look crossed Elijah's face, morphing into a smirk. "Now that's some bravado. Are you going to kill us all with this many guns pointed at you."

Mark smiled back, but with a hard cold glint in his eyes. "No, just you. As soon as my hand comes down, the sniper who has you in his sights will put you down."

"Sniper?"

Mark motioned with his head at Elijah. Elijah lowered his gaze and saw the dancing dot on his chest. His eyes widened, the reality of his situation hit him like a fist. "I, uh, I ..."

"Yeah, I'd be speechless too. Back away while you still can."

Darlene yelled, "No, we've got them."

"Shut up, Darlene." The words snapped like a whip leaving her mouth open. "Everyone lower your guns and back away."

Mark didn't look, but he was aware of an approaching engine. As the jeep's machine gun appeared over the rocks, Elijah's group broke and fled. Mark sat in relief, the anger and fear flooding out of him, leaving him drained.

Thirty-Four

"Looks like the rest of them are cutting and running," Lincoln said.

Mark didn't respond. He stared at the two captives, deciding how best to utilize them. Question them was the obvious choice, but he wondered if these men could somehow get him and others aboard the freighter to find Shavonne. He opened his mouth to ask some questions when someone climbed the land side of the rocks in a hurry. Lynn perched there, staring back at him.

His heart soared and a lump formed in his throat. He cleared it to say something, anything, so as not to look like the fool he now felt, but another lump replaced it. Overwhelmed by emotion, he was unable to move. Lynn would never understand what it meant to him that she had come to rescue him. Never great with words, he doubted he was able to express what he was feeling.

She stared down at him apparently waging her own internal struggle. She looked amazing, poised high above him, the rising sun behind her, a halo highlighting her fair hair with a golden essence. He loved this woman with all his being. He'd been a fool and she was right. His desire to go fishing miles away from home had put them all in danger.

"Oh, for God's sake," Becca shouted, "hug each other before you both explode."

It was enough to break the spell. Mark issued an embarrassed laugh and stepped toward the rock, one hand outstretched to Lynn, intending to help her down. Their fingers touched and lit a fire deep within him. Mark reached up, wrapped his strong hands around her hips and lifted her. He held her there for a few moments staring up into her eyes before setting her gently on the uneven rocks.

Tears welled in her eyes and he brushed hair from the sheen on her face. They threw their faces at each other and kissed, passion exploding around them.

"Aw geez," said Becca, "I said hug, not tongue wrestle. Get a room. You're scaring the little children."

They broke the kiss and it lingered on his lips. Without looking, Mark said, "Becca, go to your room," and he kissed Lynn again. This time when they broke apart, he pulled her close and held her tight. "I'm sorry. You were right."

"Hush, it's over now." She pushed back to look at him. A lone tear streaked down her face. He wiped it away. "And, for the record," she said, "of course I was right." She smiled.

He hugged her again. "Forgive me."

"Let's talk about it later. Let's gather everyone up and go home."

Her statement not only ruined the moment, but he realized what he was about to say would annoy her all over again. "We can't. Not yet."

She studied him, no longer smiling. "Why?"

"We have two things we need to do first. Please, hear me out."

She nodded. "Okay, but I think everyone should hear so they all get a chance to weigh in on it."

"Good idea." He turned to his kids. "I need one of you to stay here and guard them."

190

Becca stood and said, "I caught more fish, Bobby can do it."

"Hey!" he said, jumping to his feet.

"I've got a better idea," Mark said. "You both watch them and I'll fill you in later."

"Now see, that's just wrong," Becca said. "I can think of a ton of qualifiers that Bobby's the one who should stay. I'm older. I'm smarter. I'm obviously way prettier."

"Both."

"But, I could go on."

"I'm sure you could. Feel free to continue after I leave," he said, scaling the rocks.

"Dad, that's just wrong. This is like a double punishment," Bobby whined.

Mark chuckled to himself and jumped to the ground.

Lynn called the entire entourage together near the building. Mark arrived as she finished her statement. "So, you'll have a choice, but wait until you hear what Mark has to say. Mark."

"First, I want to thank you all for coming to our aid. It means a lot and reinforces the bond we've formed as a family and community. Lynn has already told you I want to stay, but regardless of my own feelings on the matter, it's up to you if you want to assist.

"Earlier, yesterday actually, we ran into the group we just fought off. They found a family hiding on that big sailboat, over there." He pointed.

Most of the group turned their heads to look. One person said, "Sweet boat!" Others agreed.

He went on. "Bobby, Becca and I managed to rescue the boy and the man, but as some of you are aware, the man was wounded. Bobby and Becca brought the boy and man to the farm.

"The raiders took the little girl, Kendra, and the woman,

Shavonne, was determined to get her back. I stayed to help. Under the guise of making a trade, Shavonne was able to get on board this huge freighter out on the lake. She somehow managed to grab Kendra and drop her overboard where I picked her up and fled. However, Shavonne was captured before she could jump.

"I have two goals here, one is to get Kendra away from a group who helped us at first, but now I'm not sure if they're friend or foe. The other is to try to get Shavonne back." He paused, waiting for comment.

One of the men said, "Not to sound cruel or anything, but these people aren't part of our community. We'd be risking our lives for people we don't know."

Mark started to speak, but Lynn interrupted. "Whether they're one of us or not shouldn't enter into your decision. At one time, all of us were strangers to the community, me included. Instead, look at them as people, fellow survivors. If it were you, wouldn't you be praying for a rescue from somewhere?

"Look, I'm not trying to talk you into anything. I don't have that right. One of the reasons our community has survived and grown is that we have the freedom to decide. Think of some of those other groups we've encountered that didn't live that way. A few made the decisions and basically ruled the others like kings or dictators. I don't ever want us to be like that. If you want to help, great. If not, no judgment."

Tara said, "I'll stay, but how do you plan on getting on board that freighter? Sounds to me like a suicide mission."

"I don't plan on attacking it," Mark said. "I'm going to pitch the idea of a trade. The two men we have captured for Shavonne."

Tara nodded.

"That way, no one will be in danger, but me. I'll need help making the transfer if they decide to go with it. As far as getting Kendra back, I think that will just take a show of force. I'm not sure what's going on there, but I think we can salvage some sort of relationship. Again, I'm hoping that will be a negotiation."

"I have a suggestion," said Mel. "I think one vehicle should go back and take our wounded. We also have two dead that need to be buried, either here or back at the farm."

"Good suggestion," Mark said.

Lynn added, "They're members of our community. I think they should be buried at the farm where the other members can pay their respects."

After a little more discussion it was decided that Private Menke would take the minivan back with Antwan and the two bodies. Two others went with them, one to look after Antwan and the other to ride shotgun. The remaining members grouped around Mark and Tara.

"I think we should go for Kendra first." Mark swept his gaze slowly from face-to-face. "I'm hoping I can reason with Elijah. I don't know what his agenda is, but we shouldn't be enemies. However, the best form of negotiation is from a superior position. We'll have to surround their encampment, but I don't want anyone shooting. Tara, you take charge of the placement of the group, while I go in to talk to Elijah."

Tara took over. "We won't be able to utilize the machine gun's firing power if this camp is where you say it is. That will cut out a lot of negotiating power. Also, I'll have to leave someone with the gun. We can't afford to lose it. We also have to consider that they will be prepared for us. So, do not go off by yourself, or start shooting blindly. Let me decide when and if that time arrives. Let's get ready to move."

The group dispersed, heading to the two vehicles. Tara turned to Mark. "What are we going to do with our prisoners?"

"We'll have to leave someone to watch them. I hate to do

it, but we'll need them."

"Let's tie them up … less chance of escape. I'd like to have more of an advantage going into the woods. Sounds like we'll be outnumbered."

"We will, but I'm hoping Elijah will be willing to talk and avoid bloodshed. I'll carry my radio with me and leave the channel open so you can hear. I'll see if I can draw him to me, instead of going into their camp."

"That'd be good." She rubbed her face in a thoughtful gesture. "I wish there was a better way. Is this girl that important?"

He shrugged. "I think she will be if we manage to get Shavonne back, but I'm going to leave it up to her. If she wants to stay, I'll walk away."

"What about if we get Shavonne back?"

"I guess we'll cross that bridge when we come to it."

Thirty-Five

They took the main road a mile west thinking they might have a better chance of closing on the camp from a different vantage point. Tara drove her SUV up the dirt driveway of a long abandoned and overgrown house. A portion of the porch had collapsed, and more than half the chimney had crumbled and fallen. Both front windows had been broken at some point.

Tara led them behind the house using it to block their presence from the road. They gathered for final instructions before Mark walked toward the woods behind the house. Lynn caught him before he'd gone three steps. "Hold on a second there, mister. You're not going anywhere without saying goodbye."

He smiled, accepted her embrace and added a kiss. Their eyes held for a long moment before she released him. "Here," she handed him her white towel. "Just in case."

"Might come in handy. Thanks."

"Go. Save that child. We'll talk when you get back."

He nodded and left her there. By the time he reached the trees, Becca had fallen in step. He glanced up but wasn't surprised to see her. He didn't bother trying to convince her to go with the other group. If she was next to him, it meant that was what she decided to do. "Do what I tell you."

"Yes, Daddy." Her voice was too sweet. He had to swallow the chuckle.

They entered the trees and veered to a course Mark projected would bring them to the camp. As he walked, he tried to figure the possible scenarios and how to deal with them. Elijah would either have his group in defensive positions, or they would be gone.

They walked on for nearly thirty minutes before he stopped to get his bearings. The woods weren't necessarily thick, but the undergrowth was dense enough to obscure lines-of-sight. Mark altered course a bit and walked with more caution and in more of a defensive crouch. After another five minutes, he whispered to his daughter, "I'm about to draw attention. Move off to the side a good twenty feet and be ready. I don't know what the response will be."

She did as instructed without a word. Mark keyed the radio. "Position?"

"Close."

"I'm going to announce my presence."

"Roger. Give me sixty."

"Roger."

Mark moved forward for another sixty seconds then stopped behind a tree large enough to offer cover. He looked out around the trunk and did a slow scan of the area in front of him. Nothing moved or looked out of place. Becca, knelt behind a tree thirty feet to his left, her eyes hard, penetrating the foliage.

Taking a deep breath, Mark shouted, "Elijah." He waited and tried again. "Elijah, it's Mark. I want to talk." Still no reply. He looked for another tree and moved low and fast to it. He switched to the left side of the trunk and searched the area. "Elijah, all I want to do is talk."

He moved again, but this time as he pulled behind the tree, a bullet chipped bark inches from his arm. He winced, feeling a splinter embed itself. He heard angry voices.

"Elijah, I don't want a fight, but if you force it, I promise you I will make it bloody. Is that what you want?"

"We don't want a fight, but we're not afraid to do so. The best way to avoid bloodshed is for you to leave."

"And, I will do that, once I see Kendra."

"No," another voice shouted, more to the left.

Mark recognized it as Darlene's. "Elijah, let's talk about this. You and me. No one else. Just talk."

"We can talk just fine from here."

"I want to speak to Kendra to see what she wants."

"She's fine right here."

"If that's her decision, I have no problem with it, but I want to hear that from her and, I want to see her when she says it."

Silence. The low murmur of discussion reached him seconds later.

"I think we should just let it go. Kendra will be all right here. She will not be mistreated. We will treat her like family."

"I'm glad to hear that, but here's the thing. We're gonna attempt to get the woman she lived with back from the raiders. If we do, she is gonna want to see Kendra. Will you be willing to take her in too?"

"Yes, that will not be a problem."

"And what if they decide they want to leave?"

More silence.

"Elijah, that's why we need to talk. I have no problem if they want to stay with you, but I have to know that you'll let them go if they want to leave."

A rustling noise from behind gave him a start. The hairs on the back of his neck stood up. Mark kept watching the woods in front of him but focused his hearing on his immediate vicinity. He was sure he had pinpointed Elijah's position, not more than thirty yards in front and slightly to the right. But if he was there, who was closing in on him?

The crunch of a dried leaf reinforced his belief he wasn't

197

alone. He turned his head in slow, almost imperceptible increments. It wouldn't be Becca. She would've had the sense to give him a signal. Besides, he'd seen her work before. If she was sneaking up on him, he didn't think he'd hear her. He braced, ready to react.

Like an animal pouncing on prey, Darlene burst through the foliage, knife aimed like a spear, bearing down on him. Too late to dodge, he raised his hands to deflect, but before she made contact, a blur streaked in from the side like a guided missile and slammed into her. The ball of limbs rolled across the forest floor, careening off trees and flattening brush. They stopped and separated. The combatants sprang to their feet. Becca faced Darlene, their eyes locked and burning with hate, each wielding a long-bladed knife.

The two warriors circled wary steps to the right, searching for an opening. Mark was about to run to his daughter's aid when he saw movement through the branches. He raised his rifle and drew a bead. Though concerned for his daughter, he knew he could not afford to help her. The chances for them to be overwhelmed were too great. He sneaked glances in her direction but otherwise kept his sights on the trees.

He said a silent prayer, set the rifle down against the tree, and slid out his handgun. Things were about to get close and the rifle would be too slow. Plus, if Darlene got an advantage he'd fire, if only to distract her. His eyes were drawn to the fight.

Becca feigned a lunge. Darlene jumped back and countered with a slash at Becca's wrist. A quick flurry of stabs and slashes from both women had each breathing hard and looking more wary of the other.

Mark brought his eyes back to the trees in time to see another flash of red material dart through the trees. He triggered a round into the tree the figure hid behind. That should give whoever it was pause before trying to get closer. He turned back to the two women.

Darlene feinted left, then did a quick backhand cut. A metallic clang rang out as Becca parried the strike with her blade. Stepping forward, she lashed out with a front kick, catching Darlene in the pelvis. She spun back, but Becca continued the assault. As Darlene tried to stab forward, Becca managed to grab her wrist. Becca stepped inside her defense and stabbed, but just before the knife penetrated the girl's face, she turned her hand and struck the woman with her fist and knife handle.

Darlene cried out and tried to snap her hand free, but Becca held tight and followed the punch with another kick, which landed between her legs. Darlene's body lifted from the ground. Her feet touched down again and her legs folded under her. Becca dropped a knee into her chest, exploding whatever air was left from Darlene's lungs. She pinned Darlene's knife hand to the ground and put her own blade to her throat.

She snarled as if preparing for the kill. From a distance, a tortured voice screamed, "No!"

Mark looked to see Elijah sprinting through the trees. "Please, don't hurt her!" He tossed his own weapon away and ran on, unconcerned about the danger he faced from Mark's gun.

"Becca!" Mark yelled.

His daughter forced her eyes up to meet his as if waging an internal battle. He shook his head violently. "Don't."

Elijah broke into the small clearing and stopped, his hands up, in surrender. "Oh, please, please, please, don't kill her."

Becca glared at the man as if incensed by his intrusion. Breath puffed from her nose like a bull ready to charge. Elijah looked from Becca to Mark and tears filled his eyes. "She's my daughter."

Mark shifted his gaze back to the trees. His radio sparked. He thumbed the button. Tara's voice came over the airwaves. "Go, we've got you covered."

Trusting her words, he lowered the gun and went to his daughter. Becca snarled and leaned forward as if preparing to puncture through the soft flesh of Darlene's throat. "Becca, let her up."

Becca's eyes darted from Mark to Elijah, finally lighting on Darlene. Her opponent had gone white, her eyes wide with fear. "Tell her to let go of the knife," Becca said.

Elijah took a tentative step forward and softened his voice. "Darlene?" His daughter looked at him. "Drop the knife, honey." A sob escaped her lips, racking her body sufficiently to cause the blade to nick her. She winced.

Mark stepped forward too. "Becca."

"Daddy, she has to let go of the knife."

It was obvious to Mark, Darlene was struggling with that as if preferring death to admitting defeat. Elijah dropped to his knees and crawled to his daughter. He reached across her body, in front of Becca and placed his fingers on her hand. He pried Darlene's fingers apart and withdrew the knife. Switching his gaze to Becca, he made a show of placing the knife on the ground a few feet beyond Darlene's head.

Becca gave one more snarl as if declaring victory and pulled her knife away. She sat on Darlene a moment longer, stood and picked up the knife, claiming it as a trophy.

Darlene rolled to a sitting position and cried as Elijah wrapped his arms around her. He looked at Mark as he rocked her. "Thank you."

Thirty-Six

A steady breeze blew off the lake bringing with it a heavy, fishy smell. They sat around the tables in Elijah's camp to talk. Most of his followers stood behind him, watching and listening to the discussion. Lynn sat to Mark's right, Tara to the left. The only other member of their group present in the clearing was Mel. Mark wanted to keep as large a team as possible outside the encampment should a rescue be necessary.

They hadn't planned on sitting with Elijah at all until he commented, "They have three of our people. Two women and a teenage boy."

Mark saw an opportunity. "If we get onboard, do you want us to try to bring them out too?"

Elijah's voice was a whisper. "Yes."

"We need to talk about how best to do that. Will you help us?"

"One of the women is my wife."

Elijah stood and closed his eyes and lifted his head to the wind. He inhaled deeply and turned his attention back to Mark. "Christine is not really my wife in pre-event terms. We came together afterward and have committed to each other in front of our community. Before the deaths, I was a minister with my own congregation and a professor of religion at a small religious-based private college.

"Christine had been one of my students. I found her sitting on the shore out at Maumee Bay Park. We've been together ever since; at least until the raiders swooped in and took her." Elijah faltered, the wounds still tender.

Lynn filled in the silence. "How long ago was that?"

He cleared his throat. "Just over a month. We've been waiting for the right time to make a rescue, but as you see, we have been unable to find a way to sneak through. There are just too many of them."

Mark tapped the table with his fingertips. "I agree an assault would be suicide. Our plan is not to attack. We're hoping to make an exchange. You've been watching them and know them better than we do. Can you offer any ideas on how best to approach using that scenario?"

"We don't have a contact aboard, if that's what you mean. We have studied their movements though, and I think we have their schedule down. They don't stay long in any one area. They anchor, send raiding parties ashore, move on. It usually takes them a month to turn around and sail to the opposite side of the lake."

"That might be helpful."

A man sitting to Elijah's left and introduced as Nathan, said, "Whatever you're planning, it's not a good idea to get on the freighter unless you have superior numbers and fire power, which you don't. No matter what they say, you'll never make it back off the ship ... not alive anyway."

"Yeah," Mark rubbed his face as if the action would wipe away the problem. "That's how I see it too."

Tara leaned forward and looked at Mark. "We might not even get past the patrol boats."

"Yep, thought about that as well. It won't be easy."

"I've got a Browning Automatic Rifle in the back of the SUV. We could put the BAR on one of the boats for added firepower. The only problem is we have fewer than a hundred rounds and the way that gun spits out bullets that won't last long."

"That's still a good idea, Tara. I wish we had more."

"We found some TNT at a construction site," said Elijah. "Don't know if they're any good. Only took it so others wouldn't be able to use it against us."

Mark tightened his lips and nodded. "That might be very helpful."

"They're yours. I think there are six sticks." He looked at Nathan for confirmation.

Nathan nodded. "Yep. Six."

"What about your people? Will they help?"

"I would normally speak for them, but since there is a good chance of losing a lot of lives, I'll let them decide for themselves. You can count me in."

"And me," Nathan said.

Elijah looked around the circle. "You all know what we're planning. If any of you would rather not continue, back away now. No one will think less of you. For me, this decision is a no-brainer, but you do what's right for you. I'm not going to attempt to persuade you in one direction or the other."

"Okay," Mark said, "we need to get moving. It's getting late."

"That might work to our advantage." Tara stood and stretched. "The dark can hide much of our movement."

"A lot of the boats have spotlights," said Nathan.

Mark stood. "Let's get everything and everyone we're taking down to the marina."

"I'll speak with my people and let you know what's decided," Elijah said.

Mark thanked him and they left.

An hour later they were ready to go. They found enough boats to carry them. Some had keys, while others needed to be coaxed to life via hot wiring. The boats were loaded and the plan, for what it was, finalized.

The steady breeze had become stronger sporadic gusts.

A storm headed their way. Mark, Becca and Bobby took the two prisoners on one boat. Tara controlled the BAR, with Corporal Ward as gunner and Mel as pilot. Lynn took the helm of a third boat; Lincoln another. Elijah and his followers had not yet appeared, but Mark could not afford to wait for them any longer. After pinpointing the freighter's location, the seven-craft armada launched. The two end boats broke away from the main battle group. Mark's vessel moved ahead of the remaining line. All had been instructed to keep a safe and consistent distance between them.

With little more than an hour before sunset, Mark raised his glasses to get a more accurate count of the patrol boats. After several attempts, he settled on twelve. But that was on the side of the freighter he could see. He doubled the number of defenders, then glanced at his boats. Twenty-four against seven. A suicide run for people they didn't even know.

His mind recreated the image of Shavonne tossing Kendra overboard and being hauled away. He respected her for her sacrifice to save Kendra, a child not of her blood. If humanity were to be nourished and grow, shouldn't he be willing to do the same? His eyes drifted to his own kids. His only regret was dragging them into this. He doubted he'd ever recover if something happened to them on one of his 'missions.'

His ruefulness was moot though, because he knew, even if he forbade them, they would find a way to get involved somehow.

Too late now. He pushed all thoughts aside and focused on the encounter to come.

Thirty-Seven

Evidenced by the quick defensive alignment of the patrol boats, their presence had not gone unnoticed. Mark allowed his own flotilla to advance for another minute before waving for them to stop. He would go accompanied by the boat with the BAR for support. The others would stay ready for an abstraction under fire. They had debated this for a while, but Mark was afraid a show of force would send the wrong message about their intentions and trigger a war they clearly could not win.

The two boats moved forward, Tara piloting her boat away from Mark's to have a clear shot if needed. Mark tapped the stick to increase speed. So far none of the patrol boats moved to intercept. He imagined they were discussing options. He lifted the white towel over his head. He didn't have to wave it, the air current snapped the material in its flow. He squeezed his hand tighter to prevent the towel from being ripped from his grip.

A line of five defenders jumped forward to meet them. One man stood higher on the deck than the others. He waved his hand at the boats to his right and two of them broke off and aimed at Tara. The other three continued at a speed much faster than his. Mark guessed it was to keep them from getting too close to the mother ship. That was fine by Mark. If the discussion came to an abrupt end the farther from the freighter, the better.

"Dad," Bobby pointed to the right, "look."

Mark swung his gaze from the advancing three boats. From around the stern of the freighter, four more boats emerged.

"They must have some way of communicating with the boats."

Mark agreed. That was bad. If they could coordinate their efforts, escaping would be more difficult. The four new additions continued on in a straight line to the right, an obvious flanking maneuver. Mark knew their play was to prevent his other boats from coming to their rescue. Icy tentacles squeezed his heart. Had he miscalculated their reaction? A nagging alarm pounded in his head to stop before it was too late. If he allowed them to cut him off from the others, his already slim bargaining power would be nil.

He glanced left at Tara. She stood at the wheel looking at him. Clearly she understood their situation as well as he did. He cut the speed. Two seconds later Tara matched him. "Bobby, use the radio and tell Lynn to move the others up and spread them out. But make sure she knows not to initiate a fight."

He was only vaguely aware of Bobby's voice as he scanned the water searching desperately for options. He kept the boat moving, not wanting to have to run from a dead stop. As the three boats in front of him closed, he was forced to slow to a crawl. "Becca get below and cover the prisoners from there. Stay out of sight." Becca moved without comment. She crept down the steps, lay down, and aimed at the men.

The vessel with the tall man moved nose-to-nose with Mark's boat. The other two swept past him and swung behind. Mark caught a glimpse of three men on each craft as they passed. Nine to three. They had no chance if the raiders opened fire.

With the lead vessel in his path, Mark was forced to drop into idle. Bobby crouched next to him, his rifle aimed at the leader.

The tall man said something to the pilot and the boat inched forward at an angle across the bow. They closed to a point Mark could make out who he was speaking to. The tall man had patterned his appearance on some pirate. His head was shaved save for a long braided ponytail down the back. He wore one long earring that looked like a miniature sword; a necklace of what appeared to be bone adorned his chest.

"You will order all your boats to disarm and follow us or we will sink you." The smug cockiness in his voice echoed off the water.

Mark kept his tone even yet firm. "No. We've come here to do business, nothing more."

"This isn't a request or a negotiation. You'll follow my orders, or you will die."

"If that's how you want it, that's your choice, but you'd better be willing to lose a lot of men and boats unnecessarily."

"But, in the end, you will all be dead."

"That may be, but I guarantee, you'll die before I will." He let that sink in, rewarded by the first sign of doubt on the man's face. "We are not here to cause trouble. I propose a simple exchange. The woman I brought before, and two women and a boy you took from the camp in the woods, for two of your men."

"Men? What men?"

Bobby made to get the prisoners on their feet, but Mark stopped him with a quiet, but harsh, "No. Keep your gun on that man." He left the wheel, put his gun to one of the captured men's heads and said, "Stand up. Both of you."

The men looked at each other. "Two for four, that's my offer."

"Not very likely."

"Maybe you need to take this to your boss."

"I don't need to take this anywhere."

"I doubt he would give you permission to make decisions for him."

"If I give the order to open fire on you right now, he won't blink an eye or question that decision."

"It's an easy thing for you to check. If yes, we do the deal, if not, we leave. No fuss, no blood, no death. Nothing lost and no one hurt."

His counterpart leaned to the side and said something to the pilot. Mark saw him reach for something, but couldn't see what. He tensed ready to start shooting. He waited, the angst of their predicament increased as each minute passed. Sweat beaded and ran. "Something's wrong," he said, "be ready. Becca, don't make your presence known until absolutely necessary. We may need the surprise."

The leader finished his discussion and called over. "The captain wants to speak to you."

"Who?"

"The captain of our little navy. I'm to pilot your boat and only your boat to the ship. Everyone else stays back or we will open fire. Understood?"

Mark wasn't sure how to take this new development but damn sure didn't like it. He'd have no leverage and no fallback. But it was a way onto the freighter.

Without moving his eye from the scope, Bobby said, "Dad, you can't seriously be considering this. Once they get you on that ship, you'll never get off."

"You might be right, but it might also be the only way to negotiate a deal, talk to the head man."

"I'm waiting for your answer."

Mark made a snap decision. "Let me offload my people first."

"Leave our men on board."

"Let me rephrase that. I'm going to offload my boat

208

first." Not waiting for a response, Mark reversed. Clear of the others, he shifted the wheel and piloted to Tara's craft. "Bobby, help our friends to the other boat. Becca, stay where you are."

He cut the engine and drifted alongside, where one of Tara's people snagged the gunwale and snuggled them close. "What's happening?" Tara asked.

"The captain of this crew wants to meet with me. I'm offloading so they can take me to him."

"Wait! You're going alone on that ship? How stupid is that?"

"You tell him," Becca's voice came from below.

"It may be the only way to negotiate a deal without everyone getting killed."

"But we don't even know these people. Why risk your life for them?"

Mark sighed. Why indeed? He wasn't sure he could answer that, he just knew he had to try. "Because, even in this lawless world, no one should be held against their will. It's the right thing to do."

"Man, how am I supposed to argue with that? Try to find a way to signal if you need us."

"Keep your eyes open. They may try to circle you. Don't let them."

"Be safe."

Mark nodded as Bobby finished transferring the captives. He turned and Mark said, "You too, Bobby."

"What? No way!"

"Yes, you go too. I'm not going to let them get both of us."

"What about Becca?"

"She's just there as a precaution. They don't know she's here. She's not going aboard. Besides, if things go bad, I'm going to need your sure shots to aid my escape. You're the only one I trust with that."

A swarm of emotions raced across his son's face. Mark

understood his conflict, but he stepped forward, embraced his father and climbed onto the other boat. They pushed off and Mark re-engaged the engine. "Becca, hide someplace where you can still hear. Only come out if you need to. Once we get to the ship, they may board and search it. Stay out of sight until they go, be ready in case I make a quick exit."

"Okay, Daddy. Hope you know what you're doing."

Yeah, me too.

Thirty-Eight

He cut the engine short of the leader's boat, but the choppy waves prevented him from drifting far. Even with his limited time on a boat, he could smell the storm in the wind. The other boat moved close, one of the crew latched on to his. The leader came alongside. "We're not off to a very good start, mate. I told you to leave them aboard."

"I wasn't about to give up my only leverage for getting off that ship."

With an experienced and practiced step, the other man landed on the deck of Mark's boat. He carried no weapon, Mark covered by an automatic rifle held by one of the crew. "Oh, believe me, if I'm ordered to get our men back, it will happen and there won't be much your little navy can do about it 'cept die." A second man followed. He took a quick look around, ducked and peered below decks, but did not go down the stairs. He gave a quick nod to the boss. "Step aside now, and let me have the wheel."

Mark did as instructed. While the gunman watched Mark, the leader moved the stick and the boat shot forward at full speed. Cold water sprayed them. The leader stood tall, the wind blasting full in his face, his long hair trailing like a cape. "Yahoo! We gotta big storm heading our way. Hope you told your captains to batten down the hatches."

A pang of dread struck Mark like a bolt of lightning. Either Tara or Lynn would have enough sense to give that command. He thought of Lynn, picturing her the last time he'd held her, kissed her and wondered once more, if *this* would be the last time he saw her. He could almost hear her voice, "So, this is normal, huh?"

He closed his eyes against the harsh wind. It felt good against his sweaty face. He opened them again, forced to squint, but something seemed different. The mass of the freighter grew before him, blocking anything beyond. But that wasn't it. He glanced to each side. What was it? He squinted harder and ducked low to block the wind. Had his eyes deceived him? No, the other patrol boats were gone.

Panic gripped his heart. He spun fast, almost falling off balance as the boat crested another wave. To his relief, he could not see the armada streaking toward his friends. But if not there, where? He scanned the lake on both sides. Not one boat was in sight.

Their craft launched into the air and slammed into the bottom of another wave. The water getting rougher by the moment, the wind velocity increased. As if reading Mark's mind, the leader yelled, "Don't worry, mate, our boats are still there. Whenever a storm brews, we move to the lee side. The freighter bears the brunt and shelters the smaller vessels. See," he pointed, "we've dropped anchor for the night to wait it out."

The information did little to nullify the fear Mark felt for Lynn and company. Would they know enough to seek shelter before it's too late? He tried to think of those aboard the boats. Did any of them have any boating experience? What had he gotten them all into now?

The leader deftly maneuvered the craft toward the stern where a ten-by-ten foot platform had been lowered to just above the lake surface. The guard reached over the side and grabbed it. The boat pitched, throwing all of them off balance. The guard stumbled and fell over the side landing on the platform. If Mark intended to make a move, now was the time, but as he stepped forward, he glanced to the leader and noted the steady stance and the gun pointed at him. "Easy now, mate. Wouldn't want to have to hurt you before the captain says it's all right."

Mark started to raise his hands then thought better of it.

"You okay over there, Clancy,"

"Aye."

"Well, steady on. Here comes our guest." He motioned with his gun for Mark to climb to the platform.

Mark stepped on the gunwale just as another wave hit. The sudden rise and fall pitched him forward. He bounced on the platform, clutched for the guide rope but missed. The next thing he knew he was underwater. He spluttered and kicked toward the surface. Something strong latched on to his hair and lifted him painfully above the surface. The platform was right in front of him.

He placed both forearms on the metal surface and tried to lever his body high enough to slide a leg up. However, his efforts fell short and drained him. Hands grabbed each arm and lifted him till he could place both feet on the platform. A heavy hand swatted his back; he jolted forward and coughed up water.

"There, ya go. That's the stuff. Get all that nasty Lake Erie water out of your system." The leader patted him hard again. "Don't have very good sea legs, do you? Well, no matter. Once you get on deck you'll think you're on dry land."

Mark wiped water from his face.

"Most days at any rate. The storm will give you pause now and then, but otherwise smooth as a shaved snapper. And I don't mean the fish." He laughed. The platform ascended, again throwing Mark off balance. "Whoa! Best hold on to the rope or we'll be fishing you from the water again." He laughed loud and hard.

The higher they went, the stronger the wind. The

platform swayed and bounced on the ship's side. Mark stumbled from the impact, but a powerful hand grasped his arm to ensure he didn't fall.

The ride seemed to take an eternity. Once they cleared the side guard wires, a large crane swung the platform mid-ship and lowered it to the deck. "Well, now, that wasn't too bad, was it?" The leader slapped Mark on the back once more. "This way, mate." He led the way, the gunman falling in behind them.

Shipping containers lined the deck, two high and set in blocks two by ten. Most of them were closed, but Mark caught enough details to see the containers were being used as accommodations. How many people lived on the freighter? The ship was massive, like a city on water. And that was only what he could see. No telling how many lived below.

The leader came to a set of metal stairs leading to the bridge. He ascended without looking back to make sure Mark was behind him. Mark paused and looked up and the gunman nudged him with the gun. The man probably didn't realize he'd made a huge mistake. With one quick move Mark would have the gun, but then what? He wasn't about to take on an entire ship by himself. But, that did tell him that he wasn't dealing with professionals. They would make other mistakes. He would wait for a time when the odds were better before making a move.

The steps rose in two sections, from both sides of the deck. The first section took them to an open-air bridge. They walked about twenty feet to another set of stairs leading to the enclosed bridge.

Like an old-time horror movie, the first bolt of lightning lit the sky just as his guide opened the sliding door leading inside. For an instant, the large figure midway across the bridge stood haloed in the lightning, but far from giving off an angelic countenance, the eerie glowing eyes gave off a demonic image.

Mark blinked several times, refocused and stepped inside. Heavy rain pelted the bridge. For the first time he was struck by just how vulnerable he was.

"This here's the man, Captain."

The burly man addressed as captain surveyed him with dark, hard eyes. A captain's cap rode high on a shock of black curly hair that framed his round face. Mark was reminded of a pirate or perhaps Captain Nemo from the Jules Verne classic, *20,000 Leagues Under the Sea.* At first, the man's scrutiny made him nervous, but as it continued Mark got angry.

"So, this is the man who has caused us much trouble, eh," he stated. He spoke with a slight accent Mark could not place. Perhaps Greek.

"This is him," the man who brought him said.

"Sir —" Mark said.

A large raised hand silenced him. "So, you kill my men and then want to trade with me." He stepped forward, hands clasped behind his back. "That is very bold. Didn't we make a fair trade with you for the woman? And now you want her back. She must be very special person for you to do this. I think you are more pirate than I." He smiled and the men on the bridge laughed.

He shook a finger. "I think you try to scam me. You offer the woman for food and the woman try to escape. Only this time it not work. Your woman get caught. Now you bring back friends to threaten poor me. I am victim. You try to steal."

He paused; a flash of red ignited in his eyes and his voice rose and crashed like thunder. "From me?" His hand smashed into Mark's face so fast he had no time to dodge or deflect it. It struck with such force it sent him into the wall and to the floor.

Mark lay stunned for a moment, but the desperate survival portion of his brain screamed at him to get up. He staggered to his feet and fought to meld the two images of the captain into one. He tried to lift his arms in defense, but found he lacked the strength to both stand and fight. To his surprise, no further blows landed.

"I wanted very much to meet such a man, but now that I have I see no reason to waste any more time on you. Put him in the brig. We hang him tomorrow so all his friends can see."

The leader said, "What about his friends?"

"If after we hang him, they're stupid enough to still be there, salvage what you can, then kill them."

Two men grabbed Mark and took him through a door leading to the interior of the ship. His legs did not offer much support, but whenever they faltered the men just dragged him. They descended several levels, how many Mark could not recall. Reaching their destination, one man slid back a dead bolt, opened a steel door and they pitched Mark inside.

On the floor, still somewhat dazed, Mark was aware of the solid thud of the closing door and of the deadbolt being thrown. He lay on the cold, hard floor and struggled to clear his thoughts. He had miscalculated. This time, however, it would cost all of them their lives. He'd been such a fool.

Shards of fear invaded his veins. Where was Becca? Did they have her? He prayed his daughter was safe and had sense enough to run, but deep inside, he knew running wasn't in the girl. He had to find a way out, if not off the ship, at least someplace where he could send a warning to Lynn and the others.

He clutched his face between his hands as he realized they would come for him when he didn't return, or when they saw his lifeless body swinging over the deck. They would come and they would all die. This was his fault. He'd risked their lives on another foolish plan. All in the supposed search for normal life.

"No!" he couldn't allow them to die. He had to find a way out. His friends – his family's lives – depended on him.

Thirty-Nine

"How long do we wait?" Mel asked.

Tara shook her head. A trail of water flew in all directions. The heavy rain made staying on the water more difficult. The water kicked up to the extent that the rise and fall of the waves presented major problems for the crews. She picked up the radio. "Tara to Lynn, come in, Lynn."

"It's Lynn, Tara. What's up?"

"I hate to say it, but we risk losing boats and lives by staying out here." Lynn was silent. Tara continued, "We need to get to shore. We can watch from there. Once the weather clears we can come back, but to stay out here might mean the death of all of us." Still no reply. "Lynn!"

"Okay! Okay! I hear you. Let's go."

A minute later they turned around and headed for land. Mel stepped next to Tara and put a hand on her shoulder. "It was a tough decision, but the right call. I want to save him as bad as anyone, but staying out here would be suicide. Even if we survived the storm, we'd be in no condition to rescue Mark, let alone defend ourselves."

"I know," Tara said. "I hope he makes it through the night."

"Yeah."

The ride back to the marina took twice as long as the one

going out. The gusting wind and high waves had the small craft struggling for headway. By the time they reached the marina, they were exhausted. They moved into the building, which at one time had been a convenience and bait store. The shelves had been picked clean, but there was enough room for all of them to lie down. Their meager rations distributed, they ate in silence. Soon more than half their number fell asleep.

Tara crawled to where Lynn sat and stared out of the glass door. Lynn gave her a quick look then shifted her gaze back to the window. "I'm sorry, Lynn, but for the safety of the group, we had to come in."

Lynn turned. "I know, Tara. It was the right call."

"We'll head out again as early as we can."

"I know."

"You okay?"

"I'm as okay as this new world we live in will allow." She offered a weak smile. "I'm fine, Tara. Thank you. And, thanks for staying to help."

"Of course. That's what friends do. Besides, if it weren't for you and the others in the community, I wouldn't be here now."

They shared a silent bond for a moment. Lynn said, "You should get some sleep."

"You too."

Tara crawled back to her floor space leaving Lynn to her thoughts. She prayed Mark would be safe and settled down for a fitful attempt at sleep.

Becca opened the cabinet door where she'd secreted herself. The life jackets she'd burrowed under had concealed her enough that the man rummaging through the cabin in the dim light hadn't noticed her. Peering into the darkness, she couldn't be sure she was alone, but a few minutes earlier a boat had moved off. She waited until she could no longer hear the engine, but in the increasing wind and cracking thunder, she wasn't sure how far that would be.

Stepping out, the deck disappeared from under her as the boat pitched, rising and dropping like a roller coaster. She stumbled and fell and rolled to her knees to defend herself should anyone come to investigate the noise. Slowly, eyes focused on the companionway, Becca climbed to her feet. The boat lurched sideways, but this time she recovered her balance before she fell.

Taking three tentative steps forward she reached the stairs and lay down on them, stretching her lithe frame upward to view the deck. Lightning illuminated the night through a heavy curtain of rain, showing an empty boat and the massive wall that was the freighter in the background. She waited, getting used to the roll of the waves beneath her. Several minutes later another bolt lit the sky. After her eyes adjusted she tried to see as much as she could before it all melted back into blackness.

She crawled up the stairs and across the deck, lifting up on the rear bench and peering over the side. She strained against the rain and wind to see. As far as she could tell, hers was the only boat in sight. Neither the pirates nor Lynn's boats were in sight. Where had they all gone? Maybe they left to seek shelter in some port or marina.

Shifting her gaze to the freighter, she strained her neck back to see the immense structure in front of her. Her father was up there somewhere. He would need her help, but how was she going to get up there? Another wave struck and the boat bounced toward the freighter. A breath caught in her throat as the wall came closer. Something snagged, stopping the progress, as though an invisible hand had pulled her back. The sudden stop threw her into the bench smacking her shoulder. She cried out and grabbed it.

Becca lay down for a minute rubbing the spot then moved to the side nearest the freighter to see what the boat was stuck on. She didn't know much about boats, but there had to be something other than an anchor holding her in place. It took a while, but with the aid of more lightning, she discovered the boat had been moored to the massive chain of the ship's anchor.

Relieved, she sat on the deck to ponder her next move. How to get way up there? And once there, how would she ever find her father? The ship was massive. She glanced over her shoulder. How many people were living on the ship? It was an impossible task. While the rain pelted her, she pulled her knees to her chest, lowered her head and tried to come up with a plan.

Like an internal burst of lightning, an idea struck her. She pushed to her feet and moved to the wheel. Shielding her eyes, she studied the mooring line. It would be thick enough to hold her. She didn't doubt she could reach the chain. But then what? Her eyes drifted up the length of the enormous links. Could she climb it? On a dry day, maybe. In the strong wind and heavy rain ...

She looked down at the water. If she fell, so what – she'd get wet. That wouldn't be so bad. She was drenched already. The real question was whether she had the strength to make it all the way up. She tried to steel herself for the climb. The task was mostly mental; believing that she could do it was half the battle. Besides, her father was on board. Providing she could find him, of course.

Her mind made up, she searched the cabinets for a length of rope. Finding one, she donned a life jacket, slung the rope over one shoulder and checked her weapons. Timing the waves, she stepped on the bow and crawled forward. The mooring line was secured to the forward cleat. It stretched about ten feet to the chain. She tested it, then dangled her legs over the side. Clutching the line with both hands, she looked down at the dark writhing water and took several deep breaths; just as she was about to launch out onto the line, a wave crashed over the bow and washed her overboard.

Forty

Mark paced the cell, testing the steel walls at every turn.
He worked from touch in the pitch black. Echoes of voices
drifted down the passageway. Somewhere, someone was
singing. Were there other prisoners? His door had no
opening or slit to listen through, all sound filtered by the
steel, thus unintelligible.

How was he going to get out? If he couldn't break out,
that left two choices, talk his way out, or jump whoever
came for him and try to overpower them. He doubted the
success of either option but was determined not to let them
lynch him without a fight. He'd rather death be on his
terms.

He sat and thought of his folly. How did he think this
would end? And why had he been so stupid as to believe it
would end the way he wanted? The truth was, he'd been
lucky in his past dealings with other groups. He'd come to
believe he could bend any situation to his will. It was like
the old saying, 'no matter how tough you are, there will
always be someone tougher.' Well, he'd found that
someone tougher, and it would cost him his life.

His mind wandered to thoughts of Lynn and the kids.
He thrust them aside; to start thinking of them now would
be to resign himself to his fate. He pushed to his feet,

determined to survive. How many would come for him? How would they enter? He rehearsed his attack from different positions and against various numbers. Plans never went as expected, but better to work something out than to make it up as you went. Besides, it helped to take his mind off the situation and keep his outlook positive.

* * *

Becca broke the surface gasping, her lungs burning. The wave had caught her unprepared. The rolling waves had moved her ten yards from the boat. Summoning all her strength, she swam against the wind and current. After only a few strokes, Becca knew she was in trouble. Her strength would be spent long before she made it back to the boat.

The rope still coiled around her shoulder, she slid it down, fighting to maintain her position. Treading water, she tied one end around her waist and readied the remainder to throw over the mooring line. The waves lifted and dropped her. She paddled and kicked as hard as she could to close the distance; at the apex of a large wave, she tossed the rope as hard as she could. Without a solid base beneath her, the throw was weak, but as the coil unwound, it opened enough to drop about ten feet over the line.

With a surge of elation and adrenaline, Becca swam hard for the rope. Every time she seemed to be close enough, a wave carried her back. But Becca stayed determined and focused on the rope. Cresting a wave and riding it forward, her hand hit the rope. The wave carried it to her. In desperation, Becca speared at it. She missed and was carried a few feet away. *No! No! No!*

Exhaustion ignited panic. She tried to swallow it and drove her strokes harder. Her fingers brushed the rope again. With all her remaining strength, she lunged and snagged it with a tentative grip. Kicking for all she was worth, she got close enough to grasp lower on the rope with her other hand. She pulled the end, hand over hand, until it drew taut over the guideline. Working as fast as she could, Becca tied the other end around her waist. She clung to the rope, afraid she'd be washed farther away and have to claw her way back. She knew she didn't have the strength to make the effort again.

After long moments sucking in air through the rain, she looked up at the mooring line. It was not that high above her. Perhaps four feet, yet it seemed like a mile. Gathering her reserves, Becca hauled on the two ends of the rope and slowly pulled her body from the roiling water. With a Herculean effort, she reached the line and hooked her arms over. She hung there, her weight drawing the rope down, her legs underwater.

Becca couldn't remember ever being so exhausted. Her chest hurt to draw breath. A glance in each direction told her she was about midway between the chain and the boat. Which way to go? If she returned to the boat, she could lie down and try to recover, but she knew if she did, she might not get back up to try the crossing. She was exhausted enough to sleep until next week.

She stared at the chain, up its length to the deck a long ways off. What was she thinking? How did she think she had the ability to make such a climb? An image of her father drifted before her blurry eyes. "Damn it, Daddy," she said. Sliding her arms along the rope, she made her way to the chain. "Hang on, Daddy, your little girl is coming."

Tara lay awake and stared at the ceiling. An idea had hatched a few minutes before and she worked her way through the possibilities. She decided she had it planned out and thought it a good idea, or at least worth the gamble, and sat up. Lynn was still at the window, her head pressed against the glass. Tara was sure the woman had fallen asleep.

She reached over and nudged Mel. Her friend grumbled and rolled over. Tara crawled till she was directly over Mel and shook her again, one hand poised should Mel wake up and yell. Mel's eyes flew open and she started to move, but Tara clamped a hand across Mel's mouth and put a finger to her own lips. "Shh!"

Mel's eyes flitted around the room searching for the source of concern. Tara waited until she calmed down then released her. "I need to talk to you. I have an idea, but I'm gonna need your help."

"Okay," Mel said, her voice tentative.

"Let's go outside."

As quietly as possible, they stood and crept between the bodies until they reached the rear door. Outside, they moved away from the door along the wall and huddled under the overhang out of the rain.

"What's up?" Mel shivered against the cold.

"Isn't Camp Perry close to here?"

"Ah, yeah, I think so. It's on the other side of the power plant, but I'm not sure how much farther."

"I remember training there and a competition a while back. They don't have an air base, but they do have a heliport."

"Okay?"

"Listen, if I can get to the base and find a helo, it would help us gain an advantage over that ship. I could get a lot closer and fly over so we can see what's going on."

"Are you nuts? What if they have machine guns or missiles or something to shoot you down? You'd be an easy target up there."

"Not if we mounted the BAR. We'd have enough firepower to keep their heads down."

"But, but," Mel searched for another objection. "It's raining. That would hinder visibility and make flying harder, right?"

"To some extent, yes, but they'd have the same

224

problems."

"Except, they wouldn't be in the air. I don't know Tara. It seems awful risky to me."

"What does?"

The new voice made them jump and reach for weapons. Lynn stepped outside and eyed them. "What are you planning?"

Mel answered. "Suicide if you ask me."

"I'm thinking about going to Camp Perry down the road, to see if I can find a helicopter. That might give us enough of an advantage that we could negotiate from a position of power."

Lynn stepped forward. "What are the odds that you'll be able to find and fly one?"

"That depends on if one's there and if someone's protecting it."

"Don't they need a key?"

"Yes, but there are ways around that."

"And you know how to do that?"

"Yes, depending on the bird."

"Lynn, it's dangerous," Mel said.

"Is it any more dangerous than being on the water with all those other boats coming after us?"

"She could get shot down," Mel insisted. "I don't want her to go."

"What do you think, Tara?"

"I think it's worth exploring."

"Don't get me wrong. As much as I like this idea, I do not want to throw your life away on something that's so dangerous that success is slim and your death a high possibility."

"Trust me, I'm not ready to throw my life away. I do think it's worth looking into though. It could make all the difference."

"What will you need?"

"I can't believe this," Mel said.

225

"My vehicle and one other person."

"Okay. Go for it, but don't force it. If you can't do it, don't risk your lives. I'd rather have you back here."

"If she's going, I'm going."

Lynn said, "I'll leave that and the details to you. Good luck."

Forty-One

Becca slid her legs around a link and held on. She'd made it a third of the way up the chain and needed a rest. The iron links were rusted, cold and slick, but she'd made good progress. Enough so her confidence in successfully reaching the top had grown.

She waited about two minutes and scaled the chain once more. To block the daunting task from mentally draining her, Becca allowed her thoughts to wander. She thought about that spoiled girl she'd been in college. That girl would never have contemplated doing anything this crazy.

Truth be told, she'd never felt more alive. Ironic that the feeling only developed after nearly everyone else had died and out of the necessity to survive. Becca despised the person she was back then. In fact, if she ever saw someone as prissy and wimpy as she'd been, she'd most likely beat the snot out of her.

None of her old college friends or sorority sisters would recognize her now. She had become a total bad-ass. How many of them had survived the apocalypse? She pushed that thought away and focused on her metamorphosis from college sorority girl to female action hero. Was she crazy? Well, maybe. After all, she was trying to climb a chain in a storm, in lightning, to assault a ship full of armed people, all by herself. So, yeah, she was a tad crazy, but, so what. Crazy had kept her alive so far.

Another bolt of lightning revealed about twenty yards to go. The diversion of her thoughts had worked. She'd climbed much higher than she expected. Her foot slipped. She threw her arm through the link and squeezed. Her knee banged against the metal, sending a spike of pain through her. She cried out. As she hung there, she turned her face into the rain to see if she'd been discovered. No one came. She air-walked a few steps before finding purchase, took a moment to recover. She risked a glance down. It looked much farther than from the opposite view.

"You've come too far to fall. Now stop being such a wimp. You're bad-ass, remember?" With that, she renewed her efforts. This time, however, she was unable to divert her thoughts. The distance closed. The wind blew harder at this height. Her arms and thighs grew heavy. Still, Becca climbed. To her surprise, the chain links changed direction; she no longer climbed upward, but horizontally. She almost sobbed with relief at seeing the deck.

No longer over water, she tried to slide off the metal but ended up falling with a thud that drove the air from her lungs. Only the rain pelting her face kept her conscious. She rolled onto her stomach and snaked underneath the chain for shelter, lowered her head to her arms and closed her eyes. For now, she was done. This bad-ass needed to rest.

Forty-Two

"I think this is it," Tara said. "Yeah. That's where the obstacle course was. Most of the shooting ranges are in the back. The barracks are in the middle, I think. It's been a while since I was here. The gate is up ahead."

"Were you stationed here?"

"No, I came for marksmen instruction. They run both military and civilian shooting competitions here. The base is home to the 200th Ohio Air National Guard Red Horse Squadron."

"Have you given any thought to what you're gonna do if the base is occupied?" Mel leaned forward in her seat, trying to pierce the rain-streaked darkness.

"Yeah. I'm going to introduce myself and ask to be taken to the base commander."

"Ah, wrong. Bad idea. They are not going to let you walk in there and take a helicopter. And that's if they even have one for you to borrow. Most likely they'll either arrest you, force you to join, or shoot you."

Tara slowed the SUV. "Seriously, that's what you think?" She drove past the gates.

"How can you not think that?"

"Well, because it's a military base. They all operate under the same principles. Authority and discipline."

"In case you haven't noticed, we don't live in normal times. If you're determined to do this, I think it's best done by stealth."

"You mean sneak onto the base and steal a helicopter? And in case you haven't noticed, these are the new normal times."

"Ah, yeah, that's exactly what I mean."

"But, if we get caught, for sure we'll get shot. Did you see anyone at the guard post?"

Mel turned to look through the rear window. "No. It's too dark, but the gates were closed and I assume, locked. Look, there's not a light on anywhere."

"Well, they might not have electricity." Tara didn't sound as certain about her plan now.

"If it's being run like a military base, wouldn't they have an alternative power source?"

"You would think so." Tara pulled to the side of the road at the far end of the camp. They studied the grounds with only the benefit of periodic lightning flashes for illumination. "We do have the rain for cover. No guard is going to patrol the grounds in this weather. Hand me the glasses, would ya?"

Mel passed them and Tara squared up to the window. In the rain-obscured darkness, not even the glasses helped. She lowered them after several minutes. "The only way to know for sure is to go in."

"We're gonna get drenched."

Tara looked at her and smirked. "Aw, poor sugar cube gonna melt?"

"Hey! Stop that. And what if I do?"

Tara laughed. "I doubt it would make much of a puddle."

"What's that supposed to mean? I'm not that sweet?'

"Come on, sweetness, let's do this."

They got out and Tara lifted the hatchback. She rummaged through equipment bags finding two rain parkas and two flashlights. Using duct tape, she created a funnel around each light to narrow the beam and lessen the chance of discovery. Last, she put a small tool kit in a pouch she hooked to her belt.

"Let's stay at the far edge of the base and work our way to the middle once we get past the buildings."

"You da boss. Lead on."

Tara led along the eight-foot high, chain-link fence until they reached a corner. There they scaled the fence. Tara climbed and landed like an expert, while Mel struggled, her wide boots slipping from the links. She fell, dragging the fence with her, landing hard. The rattling sound of the chain-links was loud.

Tara rushed to Mel's side and helped her up. "You okay?" she whispered.

"Yeah, but now I've got a wet ass."

"Keep making all that noise and that'll be the least of your problems."

"Well, sorry, G.I. Jane."

"Come on." She tugged on Mel's arm to get her moving. "I'll use my light, you keep yours off until we need it."

Mel didn't respond. They walked along the fence for a quarter mile. Tara kept her light pointed at the ground. Apart from a few tree roots the way was clear. They got their bearings after a lightning bolt lit the area, and were soon past the barracks and other buildings.

The trees were sparse but offered the best cover. Tara moved inward and led them toward the lake but away from the structures. No lights shone anywhere on the base. They reached a point where they no longer had cover and Tara stopped and crouched. "I'm going to make a dash for the end of that building. You cover me and wait for my signal."

"How am I gonna see your signal?"

"I'll flash the light once. Use it as a beacon. If you get lost, don't keep going. Stop and get low. If I don't see you in a minute, I'll flash it again."

Tara eyed the open space. The darker shape of the building was about forty yards away. She rose slightly, paused, then bolted. Mel watched her progress but after ten yards Tara melted into the night, absorbed by the darkness.

She waited, growing more uneasy. The hairs at the base of her neck stood up. Was it the chill of the rain and cold air, or was someone watching her? She turned her head in both directions without moving her body. It was pointless. She couldn't see anyone in the darkness. She was tempted to turn her light on and swing it in an arc but fought the urge.

In the distance, a light flickered, on and off. Taking one more quick glance around, Mel took off at a hard run in the direction of the light. The run seemed to take forever. She wondered if she missed the mark when she heard, "Mel! Over here."

Mel adjusted her course to the left, the building suddenly right in front of her. If not for Tara stepping out and extending an arm she might have run right into it. She shuddered, although couldn't pinpoint if it was because of the near miss, the cold night, or the nagging feeling that someone had her in their sights.

Tara flicked on the light. The beam displayed the wall of the building. From where they stood, at the rear of the structure, she could not discern its purpose. "Try not to touch the wall, in case someone's inside. They may think it's just the wind, but let's not take a chance." She set off along the side and when they reached the front, she squatted. In the distance to the right, waves crashed on the boulders. They were closer to the lake than she thought.

She wanted to aim her flashlight into the darkness in front of her but feared the risk. Still, she couldn't decide on a direction until she knew what was out there. She weighed the pros and cons, deciding in the end to take the chance.

Aiming the light to the right, she turned it on and swept the beam from right to left for a count of three, before shutting it off.

They waited for signs of alarm and to take in what they'd seen. "I didn't see anything. You?"

Mel said, "Not a damn thing."

"I'll try it straight in front of us now. Get ready."

Mel leaned over Tara's shoulder. The beam flared carving a slim path across the blackness. As before, on three, the light went off. "Anything?"

"I'm not sure, but it looked like maybe a building more to the left, a distance away."

"I didn't see it. I'll aim more to the left this time." She counted and by two, the light found something small. She halted the beam and stared until she said, "It's a jeep. Maybe it's the motor pool." She turned the light off. "I think that's where we should go. This time let's walk and go together."

"Sounds good to me."

Tara moved out. Every ten steps she flicked the light on for a second to make sure they were going the right direction. The crossing felt as though it took forever. To the left, another building took shape. Tara deviated to the side wall and stopped. From there, she used the building to guide her to the front where she stopped again. Ten feet in front of her was a jeep. She flashed the light long enough to see it was the first in a line of vehicles, ranging from jeeps to Humvees to troop and cargo-carrying trucks.

"If they've got a bird, it'll be around here some place."

"I'll take your word for it."

Staying low, Tara moved to the row of vehicles. Using them for cover, they walked to the end of the line. "This is taking forever. I'm gonna take a chance and scan the area with the light on."

"You think that's a good idea? We have no idea if anyone's out there."

"That's true, but searching this way might take all night. Besides, with the rain, I doubt anyone will be outside standing guard. If there is a helicopter, I'd prefer taking it while we still have the night for cover."

"You sure you can fly one of those things?"

"Girl, please."

"Hey, just asking."

Tara tore off a few rows of tape to allow a wider beam. She stood and moved her arm from right to left in a slow pan. She'd gone about a third of the way through the arc when she stopped and reversed. "Oh my God! Mel, does that look like a bird?"

"Hell, if I know. I just see a shape."

"Can't you see the propellers?"

"I can't see shit. You sure you're not seeing it 'cause you want it to be there?"

"Only one way to know for sure." She stepped from cover and followed the light. This time she didn't turn it on and off. As they drew nearer, the shape took on a more recognizable form.

"It is." Her voice was loud and filled with excitement. "It looks like an old MH-60A Black Hawk." Her pace quickened. "Yes, look, four-bladed, twin engines. This'll work, providing I can get it started." They arrived at the dark aircraft and Tara turned off the light. Working by feel, she worked her way to the door. It was not locked. She pulled it open and leaned in. "Yes, I think I can hot wire this if I can't find a key. Go around the other side and climb in. I'll have this baby airborne in a minute."

"I don't think so," the voice said from behind them.

They froze shocked by the sudden intrusion. Their chests tightened, restricting their breathing as the gunshot rocked them.

Forty-Three

Becca had no idea how long she lay there, but if not for an explosive crash of thunder seemingly right above her, she might have slept on till morning. She peered under the chain. Dim lights shone high in the distance, lighting her path to the bridge and the stairs below decks. Crawling out from under the chain, she bear-walked to the first stack of metal shipping containers. As far as she could tell the stacks would offer cover halfway to the bridge, but the open deck would leave her vulnerable to scrutiny and discovery.

She moved with caution along the containers noting all of them had their doors closed against the wind and rain. By the time she reached the last one, she'd decided on a course of action. A lot depended on being seen as one of the inhabitants of the freighter, a fact she hoped to accomplish aided by the night and the rain.

Taking a few quick short breaths, she stepped boldly from cover and walked, head down, against the rain and toward the stairs leading down. No one challenged her approach. Reaching the stairs, Becca ran down them, pulled open the hatch and stepped inside. To her surprise, the passageway was lit. Not brightly, as only every other bulb was on, but enough for her to navigate the labyrinth of intersecting walkways.

Now that she was inside, Becca considered where prisoners would be kept. She guessed her father wasn't being treated as a guest. However, if he were, it made her search all the more difficult.

Deciding her best bet was down, she took the stairs to the lowest level possible. The lower levels were much warmer. Becca welcomed the heat. Soon her body had a glisten of sweat.

Moving to what she thought was the rear of the boat, she came to the engine room. A small, thick portal dotted the center of the door. She crept forward and peered through. She spied a shadow just once but otherwise saw no one. She moved from the door and leaned against the bulkhead, puzzled by how few people there seemed to be. Other than the shadow, she had yet to see a living soul. For whatever reason and despite the warmth, that thought chilled her.

Becca took a different route back. Passageways lined both sides of the ship but none seemed to run through the middle. Fifty feet from the engine room she found another door. This one had no portal. The handle was a lever that pulled up. She gripped it, lifted, held her breath, and yanked it open. It gave with a squeal, its weight straining against the huge hinges.

She waited, but no one came to investigate or sound the alarm. The same caged lights lit the area. The interior was massive. She was in the bottom of one of the holds. Storage containers filled the area, but unlike topside, most of these had their doors open. In the dim light she saw movement within several of the containers. With a sudden start, she realized these were living quarters. She stepped back and swung the door closed, pushing the handle down to seal it.

She backed away until she hit the wall. How many people lived down here? She looked down the passageway. How many holds were there? This was a floating city. With a sudden realization, she understood how truly daunting finding her father would be. *Get a grip, Becca. You're here, you have to check it all out.*

She continued to the next door. Again she opened it to find a larger hold. This time someone called out to her. Without hesitation, she closed the door and hustled away. Panic struck a moment later, as she heard the hatch open behind her. An opening appeared to the right. She ducked inside. A bathroom. What did they call it on a ship? The head.

She noted the wall of urinals. Of course she would choose the men's room. Was there a woman's room on a freighter? She darted into a stall and locked the door. Becca tried to control her breathing, but the harder she tried the louder it seemed to be.

The scuffling of feet came closer. The zip of a fly and running water next. The man hummed to himself. His body odor filled the room. She wanted to gag. A minute later, the feet shuffled away. She allowed her breath to exhale in a long release. This was nuts. She had no idea where to look from here.

Allowing a few more minutes to compose herself and for the man to reenter the living quarters, Becca stepped from the stall and went to the sink. She turned on the water to splash her face, but the tap was dry. That explained the man's foul odor.

A glance in the oily, cracked mirror showed a person on the verge of a breakdown. A fire seemed to ignite in her eyes and an angrier, more determined, person looked back. They had her father. It was time to find him. She pushed away from the sink and went to the doorway. Peering in both directions, Becca found she was alone. She turned to the right and continued her search.

The way in front of her was blocked by a hatch. This one had a portal. It was cloudy, making it difficult to see through. She attempted to wipe the grime away with her hand, but only managed to smear it more. One small spot offered a clearer view. The passageway continued but had a lot more doors. This must be the section beneath the bridge where all the original living quarters were for the crew.

Becca started to open the hatch when she saw blurry movement on the other side. A man left a room midway down the corridor carrying what looked like a plate of food and a mug. He stopped at a door, different from the others in that it had a large deadbolt in the middle of it. Balancing the plate on the mug, he withdrew the bolt and pulled the door open. He said something to whoever was trapped inside, then went in. He stayed inside for at least five minutes before he came out, carrying an empty plate. He closed and locked the door then went back the way he came.

There appeared to be an open area on the right. Becca wondered if that might be the galley. She waited, but the man did not reappear. She tried to count the rooms but could only estimate there were four. If her father were kept anywhere, it would be somewhere locked. She opened the hatch and stepped through.

This door opened more smoothly than the hold hatches. She closed the door and hesitated about locking it, in case she had to make a hasty retreat. But someone might notice if she left it unlatched and go searching. With a sigh, she locked it.

Becca slid along the inner wall, keeping a steady gaze down the corridor until she reached the first door. No window. Indecision froze her. Should she open the door or go deal with the man? What if she discovered there was more than one man? Her fingers drifted to the knife she wore in a sheath hanging from her belt and strapped to her thigh.

If the door made any noise at all he would be alerted. If she was inside the room, she could easily be trapped. No, the best option was to deal with the man first. But what if his body were discovered, or his absence noticed? The argument continued inside her head for another moment before Becca forced herself to move. The longer she stood undecided, the better chance of being revealed.

She slid the knife free and edged closer to the opening. Becca passed the four doors, stopping at one as she heard crying from within. She moved on. At the opening, she noted the doorway was twice as wide as any of the others and though open, had a sliding door rather than a hatch. She lowered her height and peeked in. It was the galley. Six metal benches were bolted to the deck to the left. Kitchen equipment lined the wall to the right. A second exit stood on the opposite wall. The room was currently empty.

Becca moved fast. She ran back to the first door, drew back the bolt and opened it. The room was dark. As her eyes adjusted, she saw the ten-by-ten foot square was empty. Along one wall was a cot. She closed and locked the door and moved in a hurry to the second door, the one the crying came from.

Repeating the process, she stood allowing her eyes to focus. A gasp came from someone inside. She looked toward the galley before entering the room. Inside were two cots, both occupied. One woman sat on the edge of hers, while the other lay in a fetal position crying.

The sitting woman said, "Who are you?"

Becca didn't want to step too far inside the cube for fear of being trapped. "A friend. Are you ready to leave?"

The question sent the crying woman into a panicked frenzy. "Nononono!"

The other woman shushed her. "Stay if you want, Doreen, but I'm going."

She stood. The woman was tall, thin and black. Her dark skin made it difficult for Becca to see her properly. As she came closer the woman said, "I know you."

The statement took Becca by surprise, but not as much as the shock of hearing the voice behind her. "What the hell, is going on here?"

Forty-Four

Mark waited, but no one came. The effort to remain vigilant and ready to spring took its toll both mentally and physically. His mind wandered and his eyes grew heavy. After a while, his efforts to stay awake weakened and the need for sleep grew ever stronger.

At last someone did come to his door; he had to shake sleep from his brain, his actions slow and sluggish. By the time he made it to his feet, the door was already swinging closed. As the last of the dim light faded with the solid contact of door to frame, he spied a metal plate and cup on the floor. The bolt slammed home, a sharp reminder of his predicament. He chastised himself for giving in to sleep. Resigned, he lumbered toward the plate, bent and felt for it. He picked it up and went back to his cot.

Sitting, he probed the plate for what it contained. Bread and water. How appropriate. He weighed up whether he should drink the water, fearing it might be drugged, but shrugged off the notion. They wouldn't feel the need. He doubted they would see him as a threat. Breaking off a piece of the crusty bread he chewed it slowly. It was stale and needed extra mastication to swallow.

His stomach complained. He hadn't eaten in a while. He sipped the water. The warm, somewhat scummy drink made him suspect it had been intentionally fouled by spit or urine. He tried not to think about it since the alternatives were non-existent.

As he ate, he thought over his plan. How many men had he seen before the door shut? He closed his eyes to bring the picture back to mind. One man had entered, set the plate down and backed out. But behind him, obscure for the most part by the first man, was a second. Was there a third? If so, he hadn't been in a position to be seen. He would go with two and hope that was all.

The sparse meal finished, his stomach still protesting, Mark set the plate aside and stood. He put his body through a series of stretches. If they came back for the plate, he wanted to be ready. The time passed and with it his concentration. He paced in a steady rhythm to keep alert. His chances were running out as the dawn approached. He might only get one more. He couldn't afford to sleep through the next one.

He picked up the plate and reflected on its use as a weapon, but the lightweight aluminum would do little damage. He might be able to use the edge, driving it into the man's throat, but if he was going to do that, he might as well use his fingers or the edge of his hand. He renewed his pacing and his plotting.

Was it her imagination, or was the sky getting lighter? Lynn had slept little. Her mind refused to shut down. The rain continued to fall. Most of the thunder and lightning had moved off to the east. She wondered how Mark and Becca were faring. Mel and Tara too. The group had spread out and the lack of knowledge or control ensured her anxiety level remained elevated enough to prevent sleep.

Someone entered through the back door. The silhouette stood and scanned the room. Corporal Ward strode toward her and whispered. "Sorry to disturb you, ma'am, but I have a man out back who wants to speak with you."

"A man?"

"Yes, ma'am. That man you met with earlier in the woods."

Elijah was a distraction she did not need. She debated whether to have Ward send him away. Her mind was too exhausted to reason what he might want, but she forced her body to a standing position amid the collective protests of her muscles.

Ward turned and led. Outside, Elijah stood against the wall under the small coverage of the overhanging roof. Water ran and dripped from the shingles in a steady flow from a multitude of places. The flat roof had no gutters or downspouts.

Ward stepped to the side but stayed close. Lynn appreciated his presence.

"It's Lynn, right?"

She nodded cautiously, waiting for whatever was to come with a feeling of dread.

"I have come to offer my services. Well, mine and that of my followers."

Whatever she had expected, that wasn't on the list. "And what are you volunteering for?"

He studied her for a long moment. "I have nearly twenty fighters. Surely you can use the added firepower against the raiders?"

That was true, but keeping in mind they had been at odds not long ago, she would only allow a "Yes."

"I am here to assist."

"Why?" The word was out of her mouth before she could halt it.

His smile was patronizing. "I realize we've had a somewhat rocky beginning, but, if Mark can risk his life to free our people, I think it's our duty to aid him in that endeavor."

"What is it you are offering?"

"Well, for one, we can man a few boats to give you more firepower on the water. Two, I can keep a small group on shore to offer cover for escapes or retreats."

Lynn mulled over his words. The extra guns would be useful, as long as she could trust they'd be pointed at the raiders and not at them. "Okay. We're happy to have you. Corporal Ward, would you escort Elijah to the docks and help him find suitable boats for his people, please?"

"Yes, ma'am."

Elijah gave a slight bow and flashed a knowing smile. The question was, what was it he knew and how would it affect them? Elijah's followers appeared from nowhere. She watched them disappear again around the building and went inside to pretend she was ready for sleep.

"You," the armed man said, "Why are you in that uniform?"

Tara looked over her shoulder. Her arms were up and all her weapons, save one pocket knife, were on the ground. "What do you mean, why?"

"It's not a hard question. Why are you in uniform?"

"I'm a captain in the 180th National Guard Unit."

"Bullshit! If that's the case why isn't she in uniform? And where's the rest of your squad, or platoon, or anything?"

"We're on a rescue mission. Some of our people have been captured and are on a ship on the lake."

An eerie silence fell over them. "And what does that have to do with you being on this base?"

Tara wondered how much to tell the man. If she admitted they were there to steal the 'copter, he might shoot them. But, on the other hand, how *did* she explain their trespassing? "I didn't know the base was occupied. I'm a pilot. I was hoping to use the bird to fly over the ship."

"You know how to fly this thing?"

"Yes. It's what I did before the Event."

"Ha. The Event is it? Not an act of terrorism by country or countries yet unknown, although I could hazard a few good guesses. This country is at war. What I have to determine is whether you're the enemy or not."

"I serve this country and the people of the community in our area."

"Easy to say when you've got a gun pointed at you."

"Why are you here?" Mel asked.

"I'm assigned to this post. My job is to protect it from all intruders. That would be you. The only reason you're still alive is because of the uniform."

Tara turned slowly to face the man. "What I have told you is the truth. A few miles down the road is a small group of like-minded people who have tried to re-establish civilization. We are not your enemies, nor do we wish you harm. This copter might make the difference between life and death in the rescue of our people. If you let us borrow it, we'd be grateful. If not, allow us to get back to our people."

"Not saying I believe any of this, but if I let you take it, how do I know you'll bring it back?"

"You'll have my word. That's all I've got."

"You could come with us," Mel offered. "That way you can see for yourself we're telling the truth. Besides, we can always use another gun."

The man seemed to think about that. "Is the base you belong to operational?"

"Yes. We're just under fifty in number. You are more than welcome to join us."

He laughed. "And what of my duty to this camp? Who will watch it? Protect it from being looted?"

"I can't answer that. You have to do what you think is right. As do I. Right now, I'm asking you, can I take this copter?"

He motioned with the barrel of the rifle. "Let's go inside and discuss it."

Tara blew out an angry breath. "We don't have time for that. We have to be airborne before dawn."

"Don't see you have much choice in the matter." He leveled the rifle at her midsection. "Now, move, or the next time I pull this trigger, it's gonna result in blood loss."

Forty-Five

"Okay Lynn, I think we're ready," Bobby said.

A small group, consisting of Lynn, Lincoln, Bobby, Corporal Ward, Private Menke, and Elijah, had gathered to review the plan. Each member gave input. Not all were in agreement but agreed to follow Lynn's lead.

Lynn turned her eyes upward. Nothing in sight. She tried to focus her hearing, but even though the rain had eased, no helicopter sounds penetrated. She sighed. Regardless, they had to go now or it would be too light by the time they reached the freighter. She took one more look at the sky and said a silent prayer that Tara and Mel were all right.

She turned to Bobby and the other boat captains. "Let's do this. Remember to keep some distance between the other boats and watch for flanking moves. We still don't know what kind of defensive capabilities they have but assume they're deadly. If we make a run at the freighter's cargo net, the other boats have to keep us covered. If it doesn't look good, I'll call it off. I'm not going to lose people to save a few. Questions?"

"Just for the record," Private Menke said, "we have little chance of getting on board that ship."

Bobby rushed to the plan's defense. "We won't know that until we try."

"Stick to the plan," Corporal Ward said. "They'll send out

their patrol boats. We need to capture as many of them as possible. Trading them is the best way to get our people back without bloodshed."

No one else spoke. "Let's go," Lynn said.

The small group turned and moved toward their boats. Lynn gave one more hopeful look at the gray sky then followed.

Everyone was already on board. No one spoke. The danger of what they were about to do weighed heavily on the groups. One-by-one they pushed off and made their way through the channel. The flotilla rose and fell over the surging waves. In the distance, thunder pounded in a long drum roll. A slim line of light shone upward on the eastern horizon like an accent light, making the sky a lighter shade of gray.

Lynn scanned the outmanned, outgunned armada and wondered how many of them would return to shore. Would she have enough strength and wisdom to turn around and leave Mark to his fate if it was obvious the attack would fail? She prayed she wouldn't be put in the position of having to choose. But, though her heart would break, she knew she would make the right decision.

"How'd you get out of your cell?" the short, burly man asked. He reached out and grabbed Becca's arm. He didn't bother pulling a weapon, evidently thinking his strength alone and the fact that he was a man and she nothing but a woman, would be enough to control Becca. "You," he said to Shavonne, "get your skinny ass back in there before I give you a lash."

Shavonne backed up a step and her cellmate wailed.

"You come with me. Which cell did you escape from? You don't look familiar." He yanked Becca's arm and pulled her into the gangway. She pretended to stumble and bumped up against him as he reached with his free hand to close the cell door. As their bodies collided, Becca withdrew her knife. The guard shoved her away and Becca slashed the blade across his stomach. He flinched and grabbed his belly as if stung by a wasp. Surprise registered on his face. Blood seeped between his fingers. As he looked up, Becca delivered the killing blow, thrusting the knife straight into his throat.

Blood bubbled from his mouth. He gurgled, gripped the knife with both hands and slumped to the floor. The body slid from the blade as he fell. Becca wiped the knife and kicked the door open. She grabbed his feet and dragged him inside, where the other woman screamed. From the darkness, the sound of a slap ended the shrieking.

Shavonne stepped forward and helped Becca place the body in a dark corner. "If you're coming, we have to go now."

She grabbed Becca's arm tight. "Can you tell me about Kendra? Is she safe?"

Becca peeled off Shavonne's fingers. "Yes, my father got her to safety." She turned to leave.

"What about her?"

Becca started for the door. "I don't care if she comes or not, but if so, she has to come now and has to keep her mouth shut." She peered out the door in both directions, noted the blood smear on the floor and frowned. Nothing she could do about it. She stepped out. Behind her, she heard the murmur of discussion. Becca didn't care what they decided; finding her father was the only thing that mattered.

They were marched at gun point into the base HQ. Their captor motioned with his M-16 for them to sit. From down the hall came a voice. "Harold, is that you?"

"Yeah, Ike and I brought some intruders. Told you I saw a light out there."

"You okay, or you need me to come out there?"

"Nah, man, you stay right where you are. I got this."

"What were they trying to steal?"

"Man, you'll never guess. The Black Hawk."

The unseen man snorted. "Seriously? What'd they say they were gonna do with it?"

"Well, one says she can fly it."

"Say what?" A groan and the sound of someone moving on a bed or worn sofa reached them. A few moments and a few more grunts later, a tall, bald black man hobbled down the hall. He stopped and leaned against the corner and studied the two women. "Huh! Two women." His eyes wandered up and down their bodies; as if coming out of a trance, he shook his head and blinked hard.

"I'm Lieutenant Stevens. Right now, I'm in charge of this base." He pushed away from the wall, winced, and limped to a chair, where he lowered his lean frame slowly. Settled, he said, "That there's Corporal Levine. We're the only two remaining members of this once proud base. And you are …?"

As if waiting for a cue, Tara said, "I'm Captain Tara Lewis of the 180th Air National Guard, just west of Toledo, under the command of General Ralph West. This is Mel, civilian."

Stevens steepled his fingers and rested his chin on them. "I'm familiar with the 180th, but not with General West. I once knew Lieutenant Ralph West from down around Fort Campbell, Kentucky."

Tara tried to smile, but with the M-16 still pointed at her, it felt tight on her face. "One and the same."

"He got promoted fast."

"I believe most of it's self-promotion."

"Huh! The West I knew was a pompous ass and full of himself."

"Still is, but he's proved an able leader."

"Is that so? But to raise himself to General ...?" He shrugged his disapproval.

"I think it's what you call a battlefield promotion."

"Battle? What battles could he have fought?"

"It was before I arrived, but it is my understanding that several months back, they were in quite a fierce battle."

This got Stevens' attention. He leaned forward placing his

elbows on his thighs. "The devil you say. Is this real or just one of his stories?"

"General West has never discussed it with me, but the troops that survived the encounter have all told the same story. Although, under intense fire soldiers can exaggerate the event, I do believe the battle happened."

He sat back, his face displayed astonishment. "You hear that, Harold? They had a war and didn't invite us." To Tara, he said, "Does this mean we've been invaded?"

"There is some speculation about that being the case, but we have no proof, as yet." She nodded her head toward the window. "However, if we had a bird to do recon, we'd know a lot more."

Stevens nodded considering her words. "Is that why you were trying to steal the copter?"

Tara hesitated, deciding truth was best. "No. Right now, I need that bird to help rescue some friends."

Stevens eyed her. "And where are these friends?"

"They're prisoners on a freighter on the lake."

Stevens leaned forward again and cast a furtive glance at Levine. "A freighter?"

She nodded, looking from one man to the other. "Why? You know them?"

Stevens sat back. "If it's the same people, they're responsible for the bullet hole in my leg. A group of them came ashore to rob the base. They killed the other two members of our squad. They got away with half our food and water stores."

Sensing an ally with a common foe, Tara said, "If you help us, we'll help you."

Stevens snorted a derisive laugh. "And what can you do for me, other than try to rob me of more of our dwindling supplies?"

"We have a doctor."

Forty-Six

Becca, Shavonne and Doreen made their way down the corridor, checking other doors as they went. In one they found a man and a woman, both skeletal, with little strength to stand. Shavonne helped the man, but Becca discovered the woman was dead.

While Doreen and Shavonne walked the man between them, Becca led the way. They came to stairs leading up and took them. The ship was huge. It would be easy to get lost. Becca feared discovery long before finding her father. The ship's inhabitants were stirring, telling her it was time to go, at least for now. She wanted to get the three to the surface and possibly overboard, before it was too late. With them safe, she could hide and search the ship the next night.

They reached the top deck as the sun was making a move to create day. Becca ran from one shipping bin to another until she reached the massive anchor chain. She helped the three of them scoot underneath the heavy links and out the other side. At least there they had some cover.

The rain slackened, now falling in a steady drizzle. She crawled to the edge of the ship and peered over. To her surprise and relief, the boat was still there. Becca glanced back. Of the three, only Shavonne had a fair chance of climbing down the chains. If Doreen kept her wits about her, she might make it, but the man? No way. She didn't feel good about leaving him, but she didn't want to risk the others, or herself. Becca crawled back and explained the situation.

True to her nature, Doreen went into instant panic mode. The man, though understanding his chances, said, "I'll try anything to get off this ship. Dying in the water is no different than dying in that cell. Dead is dead, no matter which way."

Becca pulled them all in close. "It's like climbing down a big ladder. There are footholds and places for your hands. It will also be slippery and in some places, the rust will abrade your hands. If you fall, don't go crazy and scream. Keep calm and remember, it's only water. It might sting a bit on contact but won't kill you. Just surface and swim to the boat. If you can't climb up, wait, one of us will help you."

She turned to Shavonne. "Maybe you should go first." Shavonne nodded. Doreen whimpered but covered her mouth. Becca ignored her and pulled Shavonne close. She whispered. "I'm not going. I have to find my father." The woman pulled back, her eyes wide with concern. "Take the boat and get them to safety. My friends are on shore. They will help you and get you to Kendra. Tell them I'm here and will try to signal when I need a ride."

The two women locked eyes. Shavonne nodded. She moved toward the chain, but the sound of approaching footsteps came closer. A group of five people emerged from the closest shipping container. Three men and two women. They stretched and chatted. One man walked to within ten feet of the chain and relieved himself overboard. A minute later they walked toward mid-ship.

"Go now!" said Becca.

Shavonne crawled to the chain, put a leg over the side and disappeared from view.

They came for him, expecting trouble. As soon as the door opened, Mark made his move. He slammed the tray into the jailer's face, staggered him backward and cleared the doorway for his escape. But, no sooner had he stepped into the corridor than three men fell on him and pummeled him into submission. The first man recovered and delivered a savage blow to Mark's face sending him into Lights Out Land.

He was jostled awake. As his vision cleared and he no longer saw double, he identified the figure in front of him as the captain. He was on the bridge in daylight. "I'm glad you still alive. We haven't had hanging on board in long time. Should be good show." He nodded at his men, who hauled Mark by his bound hands to his feet.

A team of men escorted him down the stairs to the deck. A short distance away stood a group of about forty spectators. Hanging from somewhere he couldn't see, was a rope. No, not a rope, a noose. His body stiffened and he fought his progress, but the men merely lifted and carried him. At the hanging spot, they widened the noose but instead of placing it around his neck, they slid it under his arms and tightened it. They hoisted him to the top of a storage container, where another group rearranged the rope to its proper location around his neck.

The small boats bounced as the waves struck them in a steady rhythmic pattern. The rain had almost ceased, but the storm's aftermath left the water choppy. Lynn's radio crackled. "Say again."

"There's something happening on deck," Ward reported.

Lynn steadied herself and lifted the glasses to her eyes. A fine mist rose over the bow with each rise and fall of the hull. After a frustrating delay, she managed to keep the lens clear enough to focus. Slowly she swept right to left until she found the source of Ward's call. A second later, what she saw hit her like a punch to the gut. She gasped, and stepped forward as if she could run to the rescue. The boat dipped and Lynn went flying, the binoculars sailing over the side.

Bobby's strong hands lifted her to her feet. The look on her face gave him pause. "Lynn! What?"

She pointed and stammered, "Your-your father – they're going to hang him."

Bobby pivoted and lifted his rifle scope to his eye. He scanned and stopped. "Oh, God!"

An excited, unrecognizable voice, shouted over the radio, "Here they come!" From around both sides of the freighter came a swarm of small, fast-moving boats. They moved with choreographed precision in four lines. A line from each direction swung in their path, forming a blockade. The other two lines ran along each side in a flanking move.

Voices filled the radio asking for direction but though Lynn heard, she was unable to respond, or take her gaze from the scene before her. She felt Bobby take her radio and heard him say, "Follow the plan! I repeat, follow the plan!" He shook Lynn, forcing her to look at him. "Lynn, snap out of it. We can't help him if you freeze up."

She blinked a rapid sequence to clear her mind and vision. She sucked in a deep breath and took the radio. "Move into formation as discussed, but do not get too close or engage yet. Let them close in and think we'll be an easy conquest."

She lowered the radio, gave one last look at the freighter and went to get her rifle.

After a long and strained effort, Shavonne reached the boat and clambered aboard, exhausted. The boat pitched to meet her, the sudden contact with the deck driving the air from her lungs. She lay there unable to move and gasped for breath. She closed her eyes wanting sleep, having never before been so fatigued, but the scream shook her into action.

She climbed back across the bow and searched the water. A head bobbed. Doreen. Quickly, she reversed course and ran to look for a life preserver. In truth, she had expected the woman to fall long ago. Maybe she hadn't given the frightened, whiny woman enough credit.

On hands and knees, fearing she'd get tossed into the water, Shavonne crept to the edge, saw Doreen's struggling form and flung the life preserver toward her. The ring fell short, she hadn't allowed enough of the rope tied to it to play out. She dragged it back, aware that Doreen's struggles were growing weaker.

The sudden roar of engines made her jump. She fumbled the ring and almost lost it overboard. Fearing she had been discovered, Shavonne scampered across the bow and dove to the deck, slamming her knee on the surface. She pulled the injured limb to her chest and bit her lip against the cry of pain that fought to escape. The engine noise rose in volume. Unable to prevent herself from doing so, Shavonne peeked above the side and saw multiple boats speeding past. None of them gave her or their boat any notice. They continued away from the freighter. She wondered where they were going, but, though thankful they were not after them, was well aware that their freedom might be short lived. She rose and made her way back to the bow, hoping Doreen was still afloat.

Tying the rope's end on the guide rail, she gripped the dripping life preserver, rose to her knees and hurled it as far as she could. The ring landed right where Doreen's head had been a second before. However, now, she was no longer in sight.

"Oh, no!" Shavonne said. She thought for a moment, stood to dive in after her, knowing the act may be her last, but before her feet left the boat, Doreen's waterlogged head broke the surface, and her hand snatched the ring in desperation. She clung to it but went under again.

Knowing the woman's strength was long ago on borrowed time, Shavonne snatched up the rope and hauled it in. She hoped that by the time she got it to the boat, Doreen would still be attached.

Forty-Seven

Becca watched as Doreen crawled over the side and after a terrified glance back at the deck, disappeared from sight. Becca hoped the woman had the fortitude to make the descent, but after a second gave her no more thought.

She watched as the frail man extended his legs over the side. Their eyes locked for a moment and he smiled and winked, before letting go of the guideline and sinking below deck level. He didn't look as though he had the strength to climb down, but people could surprise you with their determination and fortitude when their life was on the line.

She surveyed the deck, plotting her next move. The ship was active now. Each passing minute increased the amount of movement. Becca judged stealth was no longer an option, so decided to wait for a large group to move and attempt to blend in with them. Her hand flexed and relaxed wanting the knife to be there, but knowing that might arouse suspicion. Still, she fingered the handle while she watched the ever-growing mob.

She had no idea what, but from the reaction of the crew, something important had happened. Perhaps Lynn and Bobby had launched an attack. Everyone on board began moving faster and toward mid-ship. With their backs to her, she used the distraction to join the rear of the crowd.

Christ! How many people lived on this ship?

Becca moved with the group, acting as though she belonged. However, staying calm amidst the enemy was not easy. Furtive glances told her that as yet, no one had noticed she didn't belong. The crowd narrowed along the outer passageway as they passed the stairs leading to the bridge. She walked side-by-side with another woman. The short dark-haired woman looked at her for a long few seconds but gave no indication of sounding the alarm.

Once around the forecastle, the crowd spread out again then abruptly stopped. Becca glanced around but failed to see a reason for it. She turned to look out over the water. Though the sky was clearing, it was still gray, but through the morning haze and the choppy water, Becca swore she could see dark spots riding the waves. Lynn!

A cheer rose from the crowd, drawing her attention. Spying the source of their excitement, Becca cried out. Standing on top of a storage container, a noose around his head, was her father. Her knees buckled and she started to fall. Reaching out, she grabbed an arm and almost pulled the dark-haired woman down with her.

"Hey!" she cried out. "Watch what the hell you're doing." She pried Becca's fingers from her arm. Becca was just able to get her feet beneath her to keep from falling to the deck. Keeping her head down, she uttered, "Sorry," and moved away from her.

Becca took up another position where she could see her father better. The question was, how to reach him before that noose tightened? Even if she did make it in time to cut him free, they would be surrounded with no hope of escape. Still, it would be better to go down fighting, side-by-side with her father, rather than watch him die, swinging from a rope, with no hope at all.

She looked for a path through the crowd. The audience stood about ten deep in a large circle. The position of the storage bin in the center blocked her view of how many others stood on the opposite side. She craned her neck to see how they got to the top of the container: two metal ladders leaned against the longer side. She had to get to that spot.

She slipped through an opening in the outer row when an arm snagged hers and pulled her back. The short, dark-haired woman stood there. "You don't belong here. Who are you?"

Panic accelerated through her system. Becca shot glances to both sides to see if anyone was watching the exchange, then, an overhead loudspeaker came to life, drowning out the crowd noise and gave her an idea. She mouthed something with no volume. "What?" the woman shouted and leaned closer. Becca spoke again, giving voice to every third word. Her inquisitor shook her. "Speak up, damn you."

Becca forced a frown to her face and motioned for the woman to follow her. Becca headed back toward the outer passageway with the woman trailing but still holding her arm. Once out of sight from the assembly, Becca looked down at the water and made her move. She stopped and faced her opponent. Leaning forward, as if to speak close to her ear, she slid the knife free and punched the blade deep into the soft flesh of her abdomen. The woman's eyes widened in horror. Becca slapped her left hand to the woman's mouth and lifted the blade until the rib cage prevented further progress.

Looking over the other woman's shoulder to make sure they hadn't drawn attention, Becca bent, grabbed a leg and attempted to lift the heavy woman over the rail. Several moments and a lot of effort later, the body plummeted, crashing into the waves. She leaned over the rail and thought she would heave. The exertion had left her weak. She sucked in the sea air and scanned the water. Becca no longer had any doubt that the growing dark specks on the water were approaching boats. Spurred by the knowledge help was on the way, she fortified herself with one more deep breath and went to rejoin the audience preparing to watch the hanging of her father.

Bobby lowered the rifle and turned to Lynn. The look on her

face was both determined and frightened. "Becca's on board." He had to shout to be heard. Lynn cocked her head in an inquisitive manner; her eyes lit with comprehension. She nodded, but although the knowledge might mean hope, the look of fear did not recede.

Bobby turned and focused his scope on the spot where he had discovered his sister. A moment earlier, he'd witnessed the brief encounter with the other woman and the body falling into the water. Now, his sister was gone. Feeling a twinge of angst, he scanned right, then back left toward the crowd. He spied her sliding between two men at the back of the gathering and surmised her plan. She would work her way to the front in hopes of cutting their father free. But he knew how her mind worked. She would know there was no escape, so would stand and fight alongside Dad until they both fell. It would be an end they would both prefer, but one he had to try to prevent.

Lowering the rifle, he tried to think of a way to make that happen. In this rough water, it was impossible to get off an accurate shot. All he could hope for was to aim into the crowd to disperse them, thus decreasing the combatants Becca and Dad faced. Of course, that was only if they fought hand-to-hand. If shooting broke out, they'd be gunned down in an instant. What other choice did he have? None was the only answer that surfaced.

The hull of the freighter loomed ever larger until the order came to slow. All vessels along the line did the same. The plan called for a waiting game approach to lure the enemy boats in closer. However, that plan had not taken into consideration the execution of their father. It wasn't likely he had enough time for their plan to work.

Knowing he could do nothing to affect the outcome of the hanging, he sent a mental message to his sister.

It's all on you now, sis. I love you. Good luck.

"Steady everyone," Lynn warned into the radio. "Back row, go to idle."

All along the back line of boats, the power was cut but they kept advancing. Bobby watched as she spoke, her eyes never leaving the scene on the deck. As if aware of his gaze, Lynn faced him, her eyes an unasked question, his answer a shake of the head. Her eyes glazed and watered; she blinked them clear and went back to staring at the freighter.

Bobby swung his attention in that direction too. There had to be something he could do, if only to delay the inevitable. Yes, he could do something, but not from here. He turned his head. "You have to get me closer." Lynn studied him for a moment and nodded. "Everyone hold your position and follow the plan. We're moving forward. I repeat, hold your positions and follow the plan."

She leaned forward, spoke to the pilot and the boat increased speed, advancing on the freighter and the line of defenders like a one-boat assault team. It was a suicide run to be sure, but living, knowing he hadn't done everything in his power to save his family, would be like death anyway. He sent a smile to Lynn, she nodded and returned it. She knew this was the end. He sighed and sighted through the scope, making some adjustments as the target grew bigger.

Shavonne walked across the bow, using the rope to lead Doreen as if she was landing a sailfish. She brought her around to the stern, opened the gate to the platform and flipped the ladder into the water. Bending, she snared one of Doreen's hands and pulled it toward the ladder until she could grasp a rung. Doreen transferred her other hand and both feet then clung tight.

She scanned the horizon where the armada of boats had taken up a defensive position around the home ship. "Doreen, we don't have much time. You have to get yourself on board while I go help that man." She glanced up and spotted him two-thirds of the way down the chain. "Hurry! We have to get out of here while we still can."

If the other woman offered a response, she didn't hear, nor

did she wait around for one. Shavonne ran across the deck and climbed back onto the bow. Catching her balance as a wave struck, she rode it out as if on a surf board, then slid her feet toward the line. She gripped the wet rope and pulled, dragging the boat closer to the rope. She looked up. The man stopped to check the distance, then resumed the descent.

Shavonne held the rope to keep the boat near the chain. A quick glance showed Doreen lying on the swimming platform, her chest rising and falling in rapid heaves. With less than twenty feet to go, the man looked down, swung his legs off the chain and let go. He plummeted, landing just behind Shavonne. He fell, rolled and almost fell off the bow, but Shavonne released the rope and dove to keep him on board. He, too, sucked in air with audible draws.

Sure he was no longer in danger of dropping into the lake, Shavonne went to the wheel, found the key and studied the dashboard. Certain she could operate the boat, she made the climb to the bow. She reached the cleat where the raiders had tied off the boat and worked at releasing the soaked and tightened knot. Every few seconds she swept a desperate glance along the water, praying they had yet to be discovered.

"Come on," she cried out.

A scraping sound behind her made her gasp and turn. Doreen had taken a tentative step on the bow. Evidently, afraid of losing her balance, she squatted and scraped something on the deck to get Shavonne's attention. She looked and spied the source of the noise. Doreen had found a knife. Relief washed over her. She nodded and Doreen slid it along the surface. The knife slid sideways rocking with a wave. For a moment, Shavonne feared it would slide overboard. She dove for it, catching the blade in her hand.

She sucked on her wounded finger while she applied the blade on the rope. She had no doubt it would be a long process, so removed her finger from her mouth and went to work sawing the rope. She was right. The fibers parted with grudging progress.

Forty-Eight

Becca maneuvered to the front row while the assembled masses listened to the droning of some asshole on the PA. He spouted gibberish that Becca only paid partial attention to, most of it relating to the charges against her father, his attacking navy, and the sentence levied against him.

With the ladders in sight, she considered her options. She thought about making a mad dash to scurry up the ladder, kick the other one over to buy her some time, but decided a slow and casual approach would give her the best chance of reaching the top before bullets chased her. People would see her and wonder what she was doing, but she hoped no one would challenge her until she reached the top. Five armed men stood surrounding her father. In her mind, she envisioned the scene and sequence of events. She'd shoot the executioners, pull her father down, out of sight from shooters below, and cut his hands free.

She'd give him one of the dead men's rifles and she'd use the handgun and knife. They might not last long, but they'd certainly take a bunch with them before they went down. Rehearsing the move several times in her head, she steeled her resolve and stepped from the crowd. With a casual nonchalance she did not feel, she sauntered toward the ladders. No one stopped her, but a murmuring of voices followed her.

Her hand shook as it clasped the ladder. She didn't lift her foot high enough to step on the first rung and kicked it. The second attempt was successful and she scaled the rungs waiting for the bullets to riddle her body. More than halfway up, an inquisitive face looked down over the side of the container. She hesitated, forced a smile and continued to climb.

At the top, she paused to get her bearings. Five men stood atop the metal bin. Two held her father in place, one stood behind him and two stood to the sides holding rifles. One of the riflemen stepped closer to her and although he didn't point the barrel at her, he left no doubt in her mind it was ready to swing her way in a heartbeat.

"What you doing here, girl?" the closest gunman said.

The man standing behind her father, said, "Maybe she come to give him his final blow job." The others thought that funny.

Becca glanced at her father. He watched her. She averted her eyes to avoid displaying any connection to him. She placed a foot on the metal surface, but the gunman stepped forward and prodded with the barrel. "No need for you to be up here. Best you take your skinny butt back down the way you came."

Becca searched for something to say ... some reason for her to be there, but all that came out was, "I, uh, I, umm ..."

That's when the first gunshot rang out. Everyone ducked, including her, but she used the distraction to roll onto the container. There, she scurried behind the gunman as if afraid to get shot and used him as a shield.

From all over the boat, return fire was directed toward one of the boats on the lake. It sat proud of the others, a solo target for the assembled shooters. A second shot came from the boat and one of the men on deck fell back. That caused a new flurry of motion as everyone ran for cover. From somewhere to her right a fiery streak flashed toward the lead boat. Becca swallowed hard, fearing the occupants were about to be incinerated, but the rocket missed, flying across the bow like a warning shot, and exploded in the water, ten yards away.

Becca swept her gaze across the deck, trying to locate the source, but, whoever had fired the explosive was hidden from view. The man in front of her squatted and loosed a short burst at the small craft. The second rifleman moved to the edge of the bin to her left and fired single shots. Becca was ready to take both men out when the voice on the loudspeaker said, "Push him off. Hang that bastard."

Fear-laced adrenaline coursed through her veins, her heart rate spiked and her breaths short, choked gasps. She turned to see the two men beside her father, forcing him toward the edge. Her father bent his legs and dug in his heels. They grunted and swore at him, one man punched him on the side of the head. The third man rushed forward and slammed a shoulder into his back and her father was no longer able to delay the inevitable.

Taking a quick assessment of the five men, Becca pulled her knife and handgun. The three men wrestling her father to his death had their hands full and held no weapons. That gave her seconds to eliminate the main threats before her father went airborne.

She plunged the knife into the back of the shooter in front of her. As she pulled it free, she placed her foot on his butt and pushed. Screaming, he fell off the container. As soon as he was over the edge, Becca turned and fired at the second rifleman. She pulled the trigger until he fell then spun on the other three.

The two men on the sides, fumbled for weapons at their belts. The third man, perhaps unaware of what was happening, continued to push like a defensive lineman working on a blocking sled. The man to the right freed his weapon first, so Becca aimed at him and fired point blank into his chest. Her father kicked a leg out sideways, knocking the second man's gun up and off target. But that altered his balance and left him with little resistance against the man still pushing.

Becca shot the second man as her father reached the edge of the bin. Becca jumped behind the man, pressed the gun to his head and pulled the trigger. However, nothing happened ... the gun was empty. Aware of his situation now, he stopped pushing and turned to face the threat. Becca ran at him her hand punching short jabs with the knife like a piston. Her opponent blocked most of the thrusts, but Becca increased her attack. She saw her father pirouette and balance precariously. His body wobbled: at any second he could go over. The noose had already tightened to a point his face was turning red.

Distracted by her father's perilous plight, she missed the counter attack and took a shot to the face that sent her sprawling. She rolled and came to her knees in time to see the man, clutching his bloody abdomen, walk toward her father. He would reach her father before she could get to him. Panic fueled her thoughts and Becca pushed off like a sprinter, giving it every ounce of strength and effort she possessed.

She slammed into the man just as he lifted her father off his feet. The impact sent him over the edge with her right behind him. As the deck rushed to meet her, she had no idea of her father's fate.

As soon as Bobby fired the first shot, Lynn lifted the radio to her mouth and shouted, "Now! Go! Go!"

All hell broke loose. Like mayflies, a swarm of bullets whizzed through the air, past their heads and cracked into the hull. Lynn ducked. Bobby shot again. Lynn couldn't tell if he'd hit anyone, her eyes focused on the top of a metal container where Mark's life was moments from ending.

She didn't bother looking behind to see if the plan was

being carried out. There was nothing she could do about it now anyway. A streak of fire flew past the boat forcing her to duck. The explosion threw water up in a geyser.

"Lynn," the pilot said. "We have to get out of here. We're too close. It's just a matter of time before they find the range on one of those rockets."

Lynn forced her eyes away from Mark and the fight taking place on the container. *Be strong, Becca,* she willed. As much as she wanted to watch to make sure Mark was safe, risking their lives to do so made no sense. "Let's get out of here."

The pilot needed no encouragement. He swung the wheel so hard and fast Lynn had a sudden fear they would flip. As they righted, she was surprised to see the extent of the naval battle before her. Boats sped in wild, zig-zagging patterns, dodging bullets and each other. A cacophony met her ears from all directions. Someone hurled one of the sticks of dynamite and an enemy boat erupted, showering the water with splintered and fiery debris.

She scanned the watery battlefield. As planned, at the signal, the rear line spun a hundred and eighty degrees and charged the row of boats that had circled behind them. At the same time, six boats manned by Elijah's people left the dock and swept in from astern on the unsuspecting enemy line, catching them in the crossfire.

The plan called for the combined forces to make quick work of the rear line, then join the fight. The remaining force would be outnumbered for a time until that happened. If for some reason the maneuver didn't work, the main force would be hard pressed to survive, let alone do much damage.

As she watched, she noted Elijah's boats joining the battle. The plan seemed to be working, having taken the enemy boats by surprise. But her elation subsided when she scanned the main force and realized it was much smaller than when it started. One of their boats listed and began to sink. Another stick of dynamite arched into the air but missed its mark. Water shot up in the air showering the intended target but otherwise leaving it unharmed.

"We have to hurry and join the others," she said to the man at the helm. He nodded and pushed it to full throttle. A streak from the freighter struck the stern and lifted them into the air. Lynn was catapulted from the vessel. The boat, or what was left of it, crashed upside down in the cold, rough waters of Lake Erie.

Forty-Nine

Mark felt bile rise in his constricted throat after seeing his daughter fly over the edge of the container. He managed to backpedal enough that falling and hanging were not a threat for the moment. Getting free of his predicament was another matter, though.

He looked around for a solution, eyes stopping on one of the bodies where a long knife was strapped to a leg. Did he have enough slack in the rope to reach it? And if he did, how was he going to get it into his hands in a position to free him? Only one way to find out.

Mark walked toward the body near the edge of the bin, testing the length of his lethal leash. The rope tightened with him still six feet from the body. It became difficult to breathe at four feet and gasping at three. He backed up enough to allow air to flow and tried to rethink his actions. He was at a loss, resigned to the chance of hanging himself to gain his freedom, when the thumping first reached his ears above the clamor of the battle below. He turned his head to catch the direction of the familiar sound. He'd heard that *thump-thump* before, someplace far away and a long time ago.

It came back to him in a rush. A helicopter was in the sky somewhere to the east of the boat. He gazed into the rising sun, blinded. Narrowing his eyes against the glare, he searched for the approaching bird. Was it friend or foe? How could it be friend? They had no helicopter. The sounds of the gun battle receded to a degree as others heard the approach.

A small black dot came out of the center of the sun. Seconds later, the chatter of a large caliber machine gun caught everyone's attention. Sparks and pieces of metal licked into the air, followed a second later, by blood and bone. Screams filled the deck and the defending force broke and ran for cover.

Mark savored the feeling of relief and the smile that crept across his face. Tears welled as he thought about rescue. His soaring heart fell as the vision of his daughter plummeting over the edge, arms and legs flailing, replayed.

He was in the middle of a prayer when something changed.

He looked around searching for the cause as the noose slowly tightened, but he stood alone on the container. He turned his gaze upward and noticed the crane that held the rope was moving. As his feet lifted from the surface, newfound panic rose in Mark and he realized rescue would not come in time for him.

"Oh shit! Look!" Mel pointed from the co-pilot seat. "It's Mark. They're hanging him."

"Aw, hell no." Tara swung the copter toward the crane. Mark dangled from the end of a rope, his feet kicking in protest told them he was still alive, at least for the moment. "Lieutenant, that man is one of ours. I need you to take out that crane."

"Aye-aye, Captain."

She angled the 'copter so his .50 cal gun had a line of sight. The gun rattled, a vibration ran through the deck of the bird. Bullets ripped through the machinery. The operator tried to escape but got caught and did a death dance before falling to the deck.

Seeing Mark's kicks falter, Tara shouted, "We have to get someone on the container or he'll die." Tara hovered and lowered as far as she could. They were taking fire, though nothing too severe for the moment.

Corporal Levine moved to the edge of the open hatch on the opposite side of the machine gun. "Get me lower," he shouted over the wash.

Tara obliged but still couldn't get much lower than ten feet. Levine didn't hesitate. He jumped, landed on the container and rolled. He splayed his arms and legs wide to halt his progress, stopping just before his momentum would carry him over the side.

Levine scrabbled to his feet and slid a knife free from a sheath on his harness. He ran to Mark stretched an arm out and snagged Mark's body as it swung toward him. His face had transitioned from fiery red to bulging purple by the time he cut Mark loose. Levine wrapped both arms around Mark's torso and fell backward to prevent the added weight from pulling him down to the deck. With no more pressure on his stretched and raw neck, Mark lay on his back, sucking in air.

"Come on, sir," Levine said, helping Mark to sit. "We have to get out of here." He worked on freeing Mark's hands.

Above them, while Stevens kept up a steady covering fire, Mel had tossed out a rope. "I'm going to tie you to the rope and they'll hoist you up."

Mark rubbed his neck and in a coarse voice, said, "No! I have to get my daughter."

His savior looked perplexed. Mark pointed. "She went over the side. I have to get to her."

Levine nodded. He helped Mark to his feet. After arming himself with a handgun and rifle, Mark crouched at the edge. Below, the inert body of his daughter lay on top of the man she'd attacked. His heart filled his throat and he fought back a sob. "I have to get down there." He moved to the one ladder still standing, swung his legs over the side and descended while Levine covered him.

No longer able to hover safely, the helicopter lifted higher and took up position over the water. Someone launched a missile at it, but the shooter missed by ten yards, the white plume it left playing across the Black Hawk's windshield like a scar in the sky.

"Lieutenant," Tara shouted, "that missile launcher needs to disappear."

"Roger that." Stevens directed his barrage toward the launcher.

Mark reached the deck and ran to his daughter. He crouched over her and felt for a pulse. To his relief, he found one. He looked up to see the position of the copter. Above him, Levine looked down and raised a thumb. Mark understood it was a question and nodded. Levine motioned for the 'copter then climbed down.

The rope still dangled as the helicopter returned. Quickly the two men tied the rope around Becca's legs and under her arms. As her body lifted, the freighter crew launched a more concerted counterattack at both the copter and them, forcing Tara to move to safety over the water. Mark watched helplessly as Becca's limp body ascended like a soul toward heaven. Someone attempted to haul her aboard, but the progress was slow.

"They won't be able to come back for us," Levine said. "We're gonna have to find another way off this tub."

Mark nodded. The only other way was over the side. Boat or not, the safest place was in the water. "We're gonna have to jump. Can you swim?"

"Like a fucking walleye." Levine fired left and right to suppress return fire before he broke toward the rail. Mark followed suit. As Levine reached the rail and leaped up, two men stepped from a container and opened fire on him. He arched backward as the round struck home. Mark emptied his rifle into the two men, dropping both, tossed the gun away, placed one hand on the rail and swung his legs over the top. He fell for what felt like an hour, before plunging into the cold dark water.

Immediately, he spread his hands and feet to stop his descent and propelled himself back to the surface. The shock revived him. As he cleared the depths, he scanned for his rescuer. On a wave forty feet away, the body of the man rose and fell like a surfer. He swam toward the body using the remaining strength he had. No other boats were near, as far as he could tell. Even if he reached the man in time, the chances of their surviving were slim. Still, whatever death awaited him, was better than hanging.

He stroked onward, trying to keep track of the soldier's body, thankful that at least Becca was safe.

"Did you see that?" Doreen said.

Shavonne had not seen whatever the woman was ranting about now. She had only just managed to cut through the mooring line and crawl back to the deck. "No."

"A helicopter lifted a woman off the boat, two men just jumped into the water."

Shavonne didn't care about anyone from the ship. She just wanted to get away from there and on dry land. A thought struck her. "A woman?" Could it be?

"What?"

Shavonne gave her a look of annoyance. "You said a woman was lifted off the ship. Did it come to attack the ship or do you think it belongs to them?"

"I think it was rescuing them … whoever is in the helicopter was shooting at the people on the ship."

Shavonne rummaged through the small boat's compartment until she found binoculars. She aimed them at the copter, and frustrated, adjusted the lens. The body of a woman was being hauled upward. It was difficult to see, but it could be the woman who had saved them from the cell. To her dismay, whoever it was did not move.

She lowered the glasses and searched the water. On a

falling wave she spied a body, face down. It took a while to find the other man. He was swimming toward the first man. She exhaled and glanced up at the ship. No one appeared to be looking down. She made her decision and stepped to the wheel. The engine turned over. She hesitated as she put the boat in gear, ready to change her mind. No, people had risked their lives to get her free. She would do the same for them.

Shavonne throttled up and spun the wheel. Doreen cried out from behind her. "Wh-what are you doing? You're going the wrong way."

"We're going to rescue those men."

"Are you crazy? You'll get us killed."

Shavonne whirled on the woman. "Shut up, you ungrateful, bitch. Have you forgotten that others risked their lives for you? I'm not leaving them to die. If you don't like it, jump."

Doreen stepped back, stunned, as though she'd been slapped.

Shavonne looked down at the weakened man lying on the deck. It had taken his last bit of energy to crawl off the bow. He'd be no help. As Shavonne maneuvered closer to the swimming man, she called to Doreen. "Grab that life saver I used for you and get ready to toss it to that man." Shavonne glanced back once to make sure Doreen was doing that. Satisfied, she directed her attention to getting close to the swimmer without running him over.

She idled back and said, "Now."

Doreen threw the ring, but her aim and arm strength left much to be desired. Shavonne stepped to the stern and hauled it back in. As she had done for Doreen, she flung it with all her might. The white ring landed three feet and one wave in front of the man. He stopped and looked around as if surprised this miracle had fallen from the sky. Seeing the boat, he motioned toward the second man. Shavonne nodded. She recognized him now. It was the man who saved

Kendra, father of the woman who saved them.

The wave brought the ring right to him. He latched on and Shavonne began drawing the rope in. The boat lurched forward and she stumbled, almost pitching over the side. Regaining her balance, she looked to see Doreen had taken the wheel. In a flash, Shavonne was at her side. She ripped the woman away from the wheel and delivered a bone-jarring punch to her face. Doreen's eyes rolled up and she fell to the deck.

Shavonne stepped over the unconscious woman, took control of the boat and brought it back on course. To her surprise, the man still held onto the ring. The task of landing the man took time, but once he was on board, they quickly retrieved the second man. He was wounded and didn't look alive.

Bullets whined past the boat. Someone had noticed them. The man said, "Get us out of here. I'll see to him." Shavonne returned to the wheel as a bullet found its mark and bored into the deck. She turned the boat around but not before getting swamped by a large broadside wave. The boat recovered from its sluggish start and jumped across the next wave, riding it parallel to the ship.

Clear of the freighter, Shavonne turned to take in the scene on the deck. To her surprise, the father sat, with his hands propped on the bench. He breathed hard and had his head back and eyes closed. The other man lay on his back, with no sign of life. Her gaze lifted and the father opened his eyes. They locked for a moment and he nodded his head, confirming what she already suspected.

"Where should we go?"

He pulled up high enough to see over the side. The battle was subsiding. The helicopter flashed over the raider's boats, ripping them apart with its machine gun. Most of them were fleeing. "Head for shore," he said.

Shavonne aimed the bow landward.

Fifty

Ward pulled Lynn from the water. He laid her on the deck where she coughed, gagged and spat up some of the water she'd swallowed. She tried to sit up, but a pain in her head forced her back down. "You've got a nasty cut on your head, Lynn. You may have a concussion. Stay put and try not to move around. It looks like they're running. We'll get you ashore soon."

She closed her eyes, flashed on the boat and her two companions. She sat up fast and groaned. "I told you to lie still."

She grabbed his arm. "What about Bobby and Eddie? They were with me. Did anyone pick them up?"

"I don't know. We didn't, but other boats have been circling looking for survivors."

The implication of that word struck home. "Survivors? How many did we lose?"

Ward shook his head. "Don't know for sure. Probably won't till we get ashore. I suspect we lost a few though."

She lay back and closed her eyes, tears welling. What a price to pay ... losing lives to save lives. Was it worth it? Was any of this worth it, anymore? She'd been lucky to survive, but what about Eddie and Bobby ... and Becca ... and who else? How many deaths were justified to save one person? Her thoughts turned to Mark. What would he say? She knew. He would've told them not to risk lives to save him. Yet, he would've been the first one to risk his life to save someone else.

But what of her motivation – had her decisions been selfish, born from the love she felt for Mark? Did she have the right to lead others into battle to save the man she loved? It felt wrong. True they had all volunteered, and in so doing, accepted the risks. But the loss was too great and the gain too personal.

It dawned on her that she had no idea if Mark was even alive. The picture of his body dangling at the end of the rope, swaying with the waves and lake breeze, taunted her. She tried to sit up. She had to look; to know for sure, but the effort and the pain prevented her. Or was it fear of what she might see?

Lynn rolled on her side, ignoring the aches and pain, and wept.

"I saw him go overboard," Stevens said. "He took a running leap, but I lost him when he hit the water."

"We can't stay here," Tara said. "We're taking fire. If one of the missiles locks on us, we're done."

Stevens made no response. He leaned out the hatch searching the water. He spied a boat.

Two men and two women, and the man was pulling a body from the water. "I think I found him." He pointed though no one could see.

"Good. We have to cover the boats' retreat. We're leaving, so get back on that gun."

"Yes, sir."

Tara wasn't sure if his reply was sarcastic or not, but if he was ready to fight again, it didn't matter. She turned the bird and sent it into a dive. The machine gun strafed a row of boats taking the fight out of their crews. Four of them turned and fled back to the freighter. Two others were incapable of doing so.

"Mel, how's our guest?"

"Still out. I can't see any wounds, other than some scrapes and cuts, but her left arm might be broken. I'm guessing she has a head injury but can't be sure of whether she's just unconscious or if her brain's been scrambled. Hell, she might have a broken back for all I know."

"Shit!" Tara said.

They stayed over the water watching their own fleets retreat to shore, before following and setting down on the open ground to the west of the docks. Stevens sat on the deck of the copter and hung his head, exhausted from the killing. Tara got out and leaned inside the cabin to look at Becca.

"What should we do?" Mel asked.

Tara frowned and shook her head. "Until we know for sure, we can't move her. We need to find a board to strap her on and something to prevent her head from moving." She glanced around as if expecting one to appear. Mel's hand grabbed hers and gave a squeeze. Tara looked at her. "You all right?"

"I guess. That was pretty hairy for a while. Especially when that rocket blew past. I thought we were dead for sure."

Tara nodded but didn't speak. She found it too difficult at the moment. She had thought the same thing. Somehow her training had kicked in just in time, as she juked and dodged the deadly blow.

"I can see why you love it though," said Mel. "The flying, not the shooting. The feeling of being up in the air is exhilarating. We'll have to try it again during more peaceful times."

Tara squeezed her hand back. "It's a date." She released Mel's hand. "I need to go and check on things."

"Okay."

Tara trotted toward the docks where the boats were already disembarking. Elijah's group huddled in a circle, hands joined, offering up prayers for their losses. Tara stopped on a dock, put a shielding hand to her forehead against the rising sun and scanned the other boats searching for Lynn. She shifted her gaze to the boats still entering the marina. A knot formed in her stomach.

Ward's boat came in and he jumped to the dock to tie off. He motioned Tara over. "Captain, Lynn's here. I think she's concussed."

Tara looked into the boat. Lynn lay curled in a loose fetal position. Tara thought the woman looked rather pathetic and the only thing missing from the picture was a thumb in her mouth. "What happened?"

Ward said, "Her boat got blown up. It flipped and landed upside down, I think with her inside. I didn't see the other two after they hit the water, but Lynn came floating right to the surface, so we pulled her in and left."

"Has she spoken?"

"Yeah, she asked about Bobby and Eddie, the other two on her boat." Ward pointed to a dock two away from where they stood. "There's Bobby. He's walking without help, so that's a good sign. I don't see Eddie anywhere."

"See if she's awake and if we can move her."

Ward stepped back on board and bent down to Lynn. She stirred and answered whatever Ward had asked. He slid an arm behind her head and guided her to a sitting position. Lynn sat massaging her temples. After a moment she extended a hand and Ward pulled her erect. She wobbled and leaned into him for support.

Tara squatted and called down to her. "Lynn, can you walk?"

Lynn seemed startled by the voice. She grabbed Ward and held on, before turning her head to view Tara. "I can walk, but my head hurts."

"Let's get you ashore to assess the situation. We can go

from there."

They got her to the dock and between the two of them managed to get Lynn to the helicopter and sat her on the ground. Tara found a towel inside the helicopter and pressed it against Lynn's wound. She took the towel from Tara and lay down. Ward went back to collect the others. He led the wounded to one area and the rest to the helicopter. Several of the group administered to the injured.

Lynn forced herself to sit up and scan the faces of the survivors. With one boat just docking, she said, "Does anyone know how many boats we lost?"

Everyone began talking at once. The noise made her head pound harder. She winced and Tara stepped forward. "Hey! Hey! Quiet down. We had eight boats out there, not counting Elijah's. I need the captains of those boats and only the captains to speak."

After a roll call, they discovered three crews had sustained serious injuries. Three were dead, four more wounded.

"Did anyone pick up Eddie?" Lynn asked.

No one spoke. She deflated. "He could still be in the water. We have to look for him." She fought to control her emotions.

"We'll take the copter back up for a look as soon as we decide what we're doing," Tara said.

A buzz of voices drew their attention. The group parted and Mark stepped through.

"Mark!" Lynn said, all control lost. Tears erupted from her eyes. "Oh, God, Mark." She tried to stand, but was unable to. He bent to her and wrapped his arms around her. They clung together for several long moments before he attempted to pull back, but she refused to release him.

Mark looked over her shoulder and said to Tara. "My daughter?"

"She's in the bird. She's unconscious, but we can't tell

any more than that."

Lynn pushed him away. "Go. Go to her." She wiped at her eyes. Mark planted a kiss on her forehead, stood and followed Tara. Bobby and Mel were inside, checking for obvious wounds.

"Dad!" Bobby shouted and flung himself into his father's arms. The two embraced. "I'm so glad you're ..." he paused, " ... all right."

Mark smiled. "Ditto." He looked at Becca. "What's the story on your sister?"

"Not sure. I think her left arm is broken. I can't find any signs of a head injury, like a bump or depression, but she might have spinal damage."

The statement rocked Mark back on his heels. Tara stepped forward. "My recommendation is to air lift the wounded back to the compound where the doctor can check them out. The sooner the better."

Mark nodded. "Yes, that's a good idea. Would you see to it and get going?"

"Right away."

"Hey!" a stern voice called.

Mark turned to face Stevens. "What about Corporal Levine? The man who jumped to save you?"

Mark blew out a breath and shook his head. "He didn't make it. He got shot when we jumped overboard. I don't know if he was alive when we hit the water, but by the time I got pulled out and we got to him, he was gone. I'm sorry. He was a brave man. I wouldn't be here now if not for him."

"Got that right."

Mark wanted to avoid a scene and possible fight with the man. He was obviously mourning the loss of his comrade. "I'm sorry," Mark repeated. "His body is in the boat. Didn't want to leave him in the water."

Stevens nodded and walked away. Mark went back to Lynn.

Fifty-One

The helicopter lifted off with Becca, Lynn, Stevens, Mel and four others with bullet wounds crammed on board. The remaining members loaded into vehicles for the return trip home.

Mark approached Elijah and company. Mark extended his hand and the other man shook it. Elijah's body sagged with exhaustion and sorrow. They'd lost five people in the battle and their loss weighed heavily on the man.

"Thank you for your help. I'm sorry it came at such a cost."

"I could've stayed hidden and not offered to help. If I did, those people would be alive. It's a decision I'll have to live with. To do nothing though, would've been to turn our back on humankind and allow those that prefer chaos and slavery to freedom and civilization to gain a stronger foothold. The only bright side is the return of one of our captured members. Doreen had been a prisoner for several months. Unfortunately, my wife is still aboard. The boy as well. I fear they are lost to us at this point."

Mark didn't know what to say, if any words could ever help. He let the silence grow before he said, "What will you do now? I'm sure the captain of that freighter will not allow the attack to go unpunished. He won't find us, but you'll always be in danger."

"I've thought about that. We discussed moving. We just don't know where."

"You're welcome to come with us. You can set up your own community, but you'll have friends close by. It might prove beneficial to both groups."

Elijah eyed him. "You'll allow us to live as we choose?"

"Of course. Live where you want, how you want. We have more than enough fresh vegetables and game is still abundant enough, for the time being, to have meat. If you're not happy you can always move on."

"Hey," Ward shouted. "We should get moving. They must have seen the helicopter take off. There's about twenty boats heading our way."

"Whatever you're going to do, it better be now. Jump in some of those extra vehicles and follow us."

Elijah issued orders and the group hustled into cars. Mark turned to his son. "Bobby, ride with them in case they get separated." He tossed him Lynn's radio.

Bobby slid out of the SUV and ran toward the first car in Elijah's convoy. Ward's Jeep drove to the rear of the line to cover their retreat. Mark slid into the lead car with Lincoln at the wheel and the small army moved out. They made it to the main road and accelerated west.

Not a mile down the road, the radio chirped at him. Bobby spoke, "Dad, Elijah wants to go to his camp to gather their belongings."

"Negative. We need to all stay together."

"He's rather insistent about it. In fact, we're turning off now."

Mark turned his body to see out the back window. The last four vehicles turned off the road.

"Bobby, get that old fool to get back on the road, now."

"Dad, some of their people are still at the camp. Including Kendra."

"Shit!" He motioned for the driver to pull over. "Bobby,

281

we'll wait here, but he has to hurry."

"He promises to be as fast as possible and says you don't have to wait if you want to get down the road."

If it weren't for Bobby being with them, that's exactly what he'd do. "We'll wait ... for now."

The remote location of the camp meant they could not drive all the way there. That left a little more than a half mile hike through the woods. Bobby frowned, knowing the trip would take much longer than Elijah had said.

Darlene walked next to him. "Thank you for doing this for us."

"Yeah," Bobby said, unable to hide his annoyance.

"I know you're angry, but this is important to our people and my father. It's all we have left of our loved ones. Can you understand that?"

Bobby softened a bit. "Yes, I understand that. At any other time I'd be all for this, but with killers chasing us, I'm worried about getting trapped."

"I promise we'll hurry."

At the camp, the members dispersed in many directions. In a flurry of activity they gathered what they wanted, packed up the camp's meager food stores and were back on the path to the vehicles within fifteen minutes.

Darlene jogged up next to Bobby, a large, overstuffed backpack attached to her. It bore so much weight she had to lean forward to keep balanced. Bobby almost offered to carry it for her. Almost. They trudged on until they reached the cars. Once loaded, Bobby contacted his father. "We're on the way back."

"Okay, we're pulling out. We'll keep the speed down a bit so you can catch up."

Back at the main road, Bobby got out of the car and directed binoculars down the road. No sign of pursuit.

"Let's roll," he said. Elijah fed gas and the car leaped

forward. Darlene sat in the back with Kendra and the woman rescued from the ship, Doreen.

They drove at high speed for nearly twenty minutes. The steady thrumming of the engine and the tires on the pavement soon lulled the exhausted passengers to sleep. A sudden change in the rhythm woke Bobby with a start. He sat up and looked around. "What's going on?"

"Look," Elijah said.

To the left, set back from the road was what had once been a medical facility attached to the Cleveland Clinic group. The two-story brick building occupied a large parcel of land. A fence had been erected around the facility with a gate and guard tower protecting the driveway. The property was set so far back from the road he'd never noticed it before. What drew Elijah's and his attention was the ambulance entering the premises.

Two armed guards stood outside watching the emergency vehicle drive past. The gate was already in motion, closing to prevent further access.

"Doreen," Elijah said, "isn't that where you used to work?"

"Yeah. But it was shut down after the event. There was no one alive."

Bobby's curiosity piqued. "What did you do there?"

"It's a combination hospital and urgent care facility. I worked admissions."

"Something's sure going on there now," Darlene said.

Elijah said, "I wonder if it's medical or just another group setting up camp."

"We could go up and find out," Bobby said.

At that moment, the guards took notice of their interest. They lowered their weapons and pointed them at the convoy. Two more armed men came out of the guardhouse, taking up positions next to the first two. One of the first guards raised a finger and wagged it back and forth, shaking his head. A clear signal that they were not invited to enter.

"We should move on," Bobby said. "We can't afford to get caught between them and our pursuers."

Elijah fed gas and they drove away. Almost to herself, Doreen said, "I wonder if it has anything to do with the research facility in the basement?"

Bobby turned and studied the woman. "Research?"

"We didn't know too much about what they did. There was always speculation, that because they were so secretive, it was something dangerous, but you know how people talk about the unknown."

Bobby looked out of the rear window at the receding building, marking the location and thinking it might be something to check out in the future. At the very least, he would mention it to Doc. It might be nothing. Most likely it was some group laying claim to the building and letting everyone know it was theirs. It wasn't the first time they'd come across groups that had done the same thing. But what was the ambulance for? If you were trying to keep your presence a secret, driving around in an ambulance was not the best way to do it.

Bobby mulled over several possibilities, but he always returned to one. What if they were responsible for releasing whatever had killed the majority of the population? That might explain their need for such an elevated level of security. If people found out their loved ones died because of something that group had done, there'd be riots and an armed assault.

The ambulance was intriguing though. Why use an ambulance? To carry supplies? Sure, that made sense. Why else? Bobby was tired. He leaned back and closed his eyes. Maybe they were transporting sick people. It was a hospital too, not just a research facility. Research.

He spun in his seat to look through the rear window. He'd make a point of coming back to discover exactly what they were protecting.

Fifty-Two

The wide open spaces of the countryside filled with more houses and another memory returned to Bobby. He sat forward and looked for familiar landmarks. "Elijah, I need to make a side trip."

The older man looked at him knitting his brows.

"Down one of these streets is a small gas station and mini carryout which didn't look like it had been touched. A fuel tanker sat in the parking lot, but we couldn't tell how much, if any, of its load was emptied. If it's full, that would be an awesome addition to our stores. Gas will get harder and harder to find as time goes on. And who knows what else we might find inside the building."

"Do you think we have the time?" Elijah asked.

"I don't know."

"Maybe the better question is whether what we find is worth the risk."

Darlene grabbed the back of Bobby's seat and pulled forward. "We could send the other cars ahead and check it out ourselves." She sounded as excited by the proposition as Bobby did.

"I think that's the street we turned on. It leads through a residential neighborhood."

Elijah pulled over. The column followed. "Darlene, go

find Mitch. He used to drive trucks. Doreen, take Kendra and go with her and switch seats with Mitch."

Darlene jumped out of the car and went running. Doreen hesitated but followed. Less than a minute later, a burly man with a long mangy beard came to the driver's window. "Mitch," Elijah said, "Bobby thinks he knows where a fuel tanker is that might be full. Two questions for you: One, can you tell if it's full, and two, can you drive it if it is?"

"I can tell if it's got a load, but I'd need the keys to drive it."

"We won't know that until we get there," Bobby said.

"Well, let's find out." He climbed in and Darlene ran up and jumped in the back with him.

Elijah turned. "Darlene, you should go with the others."

"Not a chance. Just drive, Dad."

Bobby turned to look at her. She sounded a lot like Becca. He smiled and faced the front.

Elijah motioned the others on. As the last car went by, he pulled forward and turned right into the side street, lined with brick- and aluminum-sided ranch and one-and-a-half story bungalows. Other than long grass, the area looked untouched by the devastation and break-ins that plagued the city and more populated suburbs.

"Drive all the way to the end," directed Bobby.

They reached the end and arrows pointed both ways on a yellow sign. "I think we go left. The road curves and around the bend is the gas station."

Elijah turned. Two blocks later, the small gas station came into view.

"Yes!" Bobby said. "And it still looks untouched."

Elijah stopped the car and they studied the area. They saw no movement and nothing to suggest anyone had been there.

"Wait here," said Bobby. "I'll go check it out." He got out and closed the door quietly. Pulling a handgun, he advanced on the small building, sweeping his gaze across the grounds and beyond. He doubted anyone was lying in ambush. If someone had discovered the goldmine that was the station, they would have stripped it bare by now. Unless someone lived on the premises.

Bobby stopped behind a car parked on the side of the building and looked down the side street. The road was clear all the way to the main street. He glanced around, then, in a crouch, moved toward the building. The front of the structure had concrete block walls halfway up and glass almost to the roof. The door was glass as well. Bobby ducked below the glass wall and peeked through the door. A decomposing, insect-infested body lay near the back wall in front of a door marked restroom.

He changed position to see to either side, but shelves and counters blocked his view. He grabbed the door handle and pulled. It opened. He stepped forward but quickly retreated as the stench of death assaulted his nostrils. He turned and squatted, fighting the urge to vomit. Sucking in quick breaths, he pushed the nausea aside. Drawing in as much air as his lungs could hold, he entered fast, latched on to the dead man's feet and dragged him from the room. Bobby kept going until he had the body around the back of the building.

Back at the door, he exhaled in a burst and motioned Elijah forward while he caught his breath. Elijah parked in front of the door and they got out of the car.

"Are there any other bodies?" Elijah said.

"Not that I could see. The store looks untouched though. I didn't have much time to check it out, but I think there's a lot we can use."

Darlene's eyes lit with excitement, like a child at Christmas. "Well, let's go look." She led the way and the four of them entered the space. Bobby propped the door open to let in fresh air. Darlene squealed with delight. "Chocolate. Look at all these candy bars." She tore one open, but the melted mess made it difficult to eat. It did not prevent her from enjoying it though.

Bobby watched as she licked the wrapper clean, then her fingers. A chocolate smear stretched across her face made Bobby laugh. He found a stack of napkins and wiped her face. Darlene backed away at first, stood still and allowed him to wipe her face. Her expressive eyes watched his face as he worked. Finished he looked into her eyes and felt a rush of heat ascend his cheeks. Her face reddened and they looked away at the same time.

"Ah, I think I got it all. You might want to wait until we can refrigerate them before trying another one."

She giggled, "I'll try." She started gathering the assorted bars.

"You have refrigeration at this camp?" Elijah asked.

"Yeah, we have power and quite a few amenities. It'll be a step up from where you were living."

Elijah turned to Mitch. "Why don't you check out the tanker? See if we can move it."

"If the keys aren't in it, they might be in the dead man's pockets," Bobby said, without offering to retrieve them himself. Mitch left and Bobby said, "Let's find something to collect all of this with."

"Here's some garbage bags," Darlene said. She handed a large black bag to each of them.

The room had shelves lining the walls and one shelving unit down the center. Much of the space held fluids and parts for vehicles, like oil, transmission oil and brake fluids and wipers, but one row had assorted snacks.

"Other than food items, what should we take?" Darlene said.

Bobby replied, "Take it all. We'll sort it out when we get home." He placed an arm behind a row of potato chips and swept them into the bag. Row-by-row they advanced clearing the items and depositing the bags in the trunk and back seat.

"We're going to run out of room," Elijah said. "We may have to leave some of it."

"If he gets the tanker running," Bobby said, "two can ride there. But, if he can't, you're right. It's gonna be tight. We may have to rethink what we take."

As if on cue, the diesel engine fired, coughed and roared to life. Darlene, Elijah and Bobby stood watching as Mitch jumped from the cab. Wiping his hands on a rag, he said, "It runs and it looks like the driver never got around to emptying his load."

"That's great!" said Bobby. "Let's finish and get out of here before someone finds us."

With the four of them working, the job went fast. The trunk was jammed and the back seat full to the ceiling. Elijah moved the car to the pump, but with no power, could not get them to dispense. "Too bad," he said. He settled for a half-full old metal gas can they found in a back room. He put it on the floor of the passenger's side. "Let's get moving. Bobby, do you know how to drive one of these?"

"No."

He frowned. "One of us should go with Mitch and learn what he's doing in case we need a backup." He looked from his daughter to Bobby. "I guess that's me. At least I've driven a stick shift before." He tossed the car keys to Bobby. "Be careful." Bobby understood he meant take care of his daughter. They moved to their vehicles and froze. A large red SUV stopped at the corner.

Fifty-Three

Mark kept a constant watch behind them, searching for Bobby's caravan. He cursed under his breath. They should've waited longer for them, but a vehicle had been spotted ahead and he didn't want to be sitting still if they returned with a larger party. He'd ordered them to head out, remembering the roadblock not too far in front of them.

Damn that Elijah. They were too spread out and couldn't give the support that might be needed.

He spied the street they had turned down before to avoid the blockade. The convoy turned and as far as he could tell, they were unobserved. They made it the two blocks before the road turned right, but as his vehicle made the turn, Lincoln slammed on the brakes. The following cars all did the same, but one didn't stop in time to avoid bumping into the one in front.

To Mark's surprise and annoyance, a new barricade had been constructed, perhaps in response to their escape on their prior pass. Whatever the reason, trucks and cars had been placed across the street and the lawns of the houses, barring their path.

The heads of several people could be seen above the roofs of the blocking vehicles.

"Now what?" Lincoln said.

Good question, thought Mark. Fight or retreat? Fighting could be costly and waste valuable time. However, if they reversed directions, they ran the risk of running headlong into any pursuit from the raiders. Ahead, the choice was obvious. Behind, was only a possibility. He lifted the radio and said, "Turn around. Let's get out of here."

No sooner had Mark's car rounded the corner than Ward called over the radio. "We've got company here. Looks like four assorted vehicles."

"Can we run through them?" Mark said.

"They're pulling across the road to block us in."

"Can you shoot your way through?"

"I can certainly entice them to move on."

"Get to it before we get trapped." To Lincoln, he said, "Get us to the front."

"To the front, with you it's always to the front. Remind me not to drive with you anymore." He pulled up a driveway and turned across the front lawn carving trenches through the soft wet ground. Ahead, the .50 cal tore large holes through the blockade. The cars bounced from the contact. The defenders fled the carnage, seeking shelter behind the houses.

Lincoln braked and Mark opened the passenger door. He rested his rifle across the frame and picked off one of the shooters. Before he could sight on a second target, the attackers broke and ran. Mark had clear shots at several retreating forms, but chose not to fire. He slid inside and said, "Lead the way around the barricade."

Lincoln was forced to nudge one car sideways to allow passage. With the convoy back on the road, he said, "Where to from here?"

Mark pondered that question. The only unknown was back the way they came. With all these obstacles, it would be better to rejoin Bobby's group anyway. "Turn right. We'll find Bobby and figure out a way around all this insanity."

"Works for me."

For the longest time no one moved. Bobby slid his gun free, ready to shoot at the first hint of trouble.

"Get in the car," he said to Darlene. Not wanting to take his eyes from the potential threat, he heard the door open and close.

The SUV shot forward, rounding the corner on screeching tires, went down the street and disappeared around the next corner.

"We have to get out of here, now," Bobby said. He jumped into the driver's seat grazing the top of his head on the frame in his haste. He started the car and raced from the lot. The tanker accelerated slowly, but Bobby didn't wait for it. He wanted to get to the main street and see which direction the SUV went.

The car lurched forward; three blocks of houses flew by in a blur. He braked hard and the car shook as the tires gripped for purchase. The car stopped part way into the intersection, but the SUV had passed in front of them. He knew where they were heading. They didn't belong to the pursuers, but to the group they'd run into before, blocking the route ahead. Damn!

Bobby paused, deciding which direction to go. Any pursuit surely would've caught up to them by now. Maybe they weren't coming. He could head east and take an alternative path around the blockade, as they'd done before. To the west, he knew there would be opposition; however, by now, his father's convoy had already passed through. Or had they? Did they make it or were they in need of assistance? What would his dad tell Bobby to do? He'd want Bobby to get the tanker to safety.

Bobby turned east. The tanker made a very wide turn and followed, gaining speed at a frustratingly slow pace. If he remembered right, the turnoff was not too far. He drove slower than he wanted to make sure he didn't miss the turn.

With relief, he spotted the sign, then heard, "Uh-oh!" He looked at Darlene, who had binoculars pressed to her eyes. "There's a group of cars heading our way."

"When you say group, what are we talking here?"

"I can't really tell, but my guess is at least four."

"Shit!" Bobby reached the road and made the turn. He sped forward thirty yards and pulled to the side of the road, precariously close to a drainage ditch.

"What are you doing?"

"We have to give the tanker a chance to get a head start. That means we're going to have to delay our pursuers for as long as we can." He reached out the window and motioned the tanker forward. The chase cars were less than two hundred yards away and Bobby now saw there were six vehicles in all.

"Keep going," Bobby shouted. "Turn west where the road ends. We'll catch up to you." Mitch shifted into a higher gear and the tanker jumped. Once they passed, Bobby angled the car across the road. "You drive." He jumped out.

"Wait, what are you going to do?"

"I'm going to create a diversion. We have to slow them down."

"Stop treating me like a girl and tell me the plan."

Bobby ran around the car and opened the passenger door. He didn't have time to explain but rattled off the basics as fast as he could. "I'm going to pour gas across the road and light it." He lifted the gas can from the car and ripped open one of the garbage bags. The contents poured out while he rummaged through it. "Ah!" he pulled his hand free holding a lighter. "Get ready to drive."

He ran toward the drainage ditch to use as cover in case they arrived before he set his plan in motion. It was deep and his feet slipped. He fell and rolled once and regained his feet. Running toward the main street, he poked his head up to see where the convoy was. He had maybe a hundred yards to do the job.

Opening the can, he climbed from the ditch and poured the entire contents in a line across the road. He tossed the can aside, pulled his gun and climbed back into the ditch, lying near the top. He flicked the lighter several times and adjusted the flame to its highest setting.

The first car reached the street and made the turn. Bobby flicked the lighter and reached his hand toward the gas, but nothing happened. He looked at the lighter, no flame. The first car flew past. He shook the lighter, adjusted the flame size to its highest setting and flicked it again. It fired as the second drove past. He touched the flame to the ground. The gas ignited in a whoosh and raced across the road catching the third car. The fire singed his left hand. The sedan made it through.

With the last three cars trapped behind the wall of flame, Bobby ran at the burning car and as the men jumped out, he shot them. First the two on the driver's side, then around the trunk for the opposite two.

Without stopping, Bobby ran on. The occupants of the second car had already exited and either hid behind it, firing at Darlene, or scattered to the drainage ditch to outflank her. A gunfight had broken out near the first car. Bobby assumed Darlene had engaged them.

Knowing the firewall would not last long, Bobby ignored the cars on the opposite side and ran toward the two cars that got through. Both cars stopped as Darlene shot at them. He came up behind the two men at the trunk of the second car and fired one round into the back of each head, then picked up their guns. The two men on the flanking maneuver were too far ahead to get a shot at. He hopped inside the car and put it in drive. Leaving the door open, he revved the engine and rolled out as the car moved. Pain shot through his shoulder as he made contact with the black top. The car collided with the lead vehicle. The impact caused a man to run like a startled rabbit. Coming to one knee, Bobby aimed his gun and shot him, his body rolling down the side of the drainage ditch.

He scrambled to his feet and ran toward Darlene's car. A quick glance inside the first car showed two slumped bodies in the front seat. Darlene was evidently a good shot. He ran to the car and found it empty. So much for her staying with the car. She followed directions about as well as Becca. Darlene popped up from the opposite side and aimed her gun at him. He froze, shocked by how close he came to being shot. Bobby's mouth went dry.

He reached the driver's door and yanked it open. Tossing the extra guns on the passenger seat, he slid in striking his head again. He swore and reached to close the door. Bullets smacked into the car all around him. He left the door open and shoved the stick into drive as Darlene emptied her gun. She dove through the open passenger door, her head landing across his lap. He pressed the pedal to the floor and the car leaped forward.

Bobby worked the wheel hard to prevent the car from rolling down the ditch. Bullets continued to strike them. As he swung the car back up to the road, the rear window exploded. "Keep your head down." He grabbed her head and pulled her down into his lap.

"Yeah, you wish."

Involved in escaping, the comment flew by him. He checked the mirror. So far no pursuit. If they chose to continue, it might take a few minutes to clear the road. He had to take advantage of the time they had.

Darlene's head poked up. She looked over Bobby's shoulder. Her face was inches from his. "Well, that was fun."

He snorted. Her comment sounded like something Becca would say. She kissed his cheek. Startled, he blinked and pulled his head back to look at her. "Sorry. Seemed like the thing to do. Especially if you're going to insist on me keeping my head down."

With sudden clarity, Bobby caught the previous reference and blushed. His awkwardness made her laugh. She gave him another quick peck and sat up. "Last one, I promise. Oh!" She reached beneath her and extracted one of the guns Bobby had tossed there. "Goose. Goose."

The car reached the end of the road and Bobby swung right. He wondered how far the tanker had gone.

"How many did you get?"

He glanced at her. She had dropped the magazine and counted rounds. "Back there. How many did you shoot?"

"Ah, I don't know. I just shot whoever was in front of me."

"Can't you guess? I killed three in that first car."

"Is it important? I mean, it's not like we're keeping score."

"Is that what you think? Silly man. I asked because it would give me an idea of how many were left, if there were enough to feel confident about pursuing us."

Bobby pondered that for a moment. He'd misjudged her. "Six or seven, I think."

"So, that's two and a half cars, if we figure four to a car and six cars. They might have fourteen or fifteen shooters left."

"Would you keep up the chase with that number?"

"Not against us, I wouldn't. We're a pretty good team, don't you think?" She gave him a playful punch in the arm and he felt the flush to his cheeks again. "Well, aren't we?"

"Ah, yeah, I guess we are."

Fifty-Four

"Yep!" Lincoln said. "Bobby's been through here all right. Although usually I'd be saying that about Becca."

Mark didn't respond. Worried, he looked at the burning hulks and assorted wrecks along the road. Backtracking, they'd joined with Elijah's people and learned of Bobby's side trip. To his relief, Bobby's car was not among them. "Go around them."

"Well, sure, boss. Let me do that for you?"

"What are you pissed about?"

"Oh, nothing, other than driving Mr. Crazy. Not only do I get sent into dangerous situations, I get ordered to do so as if I didn't have any choice in the matter."

Mark gazed at his friend, anger getting the better of him. "I'm sorry if I've offended you, but I hope you know me well enough by now to understand there's nothing personal in what I say. If you'd rather give the directions and let me drive, I've got no problem with that."

Lincoln met his gaze with his own growing resentment. "I'm just tired of being shot at and chased. Every time I'm with you, we get into trouble. You had to go fishing, even after Lynn tried to tell you, you were just asking for trouble. And now, here were are, in trouble. Again. Sorry if I sound pissed, man, but I'm a little concerned about getting shot. If we get out of this one, I'm going to have to rethink being a part of your community. It's too dangerous living near you."

Mark let his rage bleed away. Lincoln's words hit home. This was his fault. First Lynn moved away, now Lincoln. It didn't take a genius to see that he was the common denominator in the equation. "You're right, Lincoln. I'm sorry. We'll talk about it when we get back."

"Yeah, whatever, man. Let's just make sure we get back." He maneuvered around the disabled cars and the convoy drove down the street. Twenty minutes and several wrong turns later, they heard gunfire. Lincoln looked at Mark and frowned. He didn't speak, but his expression said, "See what I'm talking about?"

Mark ignored the look. Lincoln had a right to feel the way he did, but at the moment, Bobby's safety was more important than dealing with Lincoln's grievances. "Stop here." Before the car came to a stop, Mark was out of the car, running toward the battle sounds. He rounded a corner and hid behind a tree.

Up ahead a firefight was in full swing. He sighted through the scope. One set of vehicles lined up across the road, fired at a second set twenty yards beyond them. A tanker was parked behind Bobby's group. He recognized the car Bobby had been in but could not find his son. He prayed he was still alive.

Mark swept his gaze from left to right along the attackers' defense. He counted twelve combatants. The road on the far side of Bobby's group appeared to be a dead end. They had no way out other than on foot. To the right were four houses. On the left was a hill that ran the entire length of the street. At the top of the hill was a partially flattened fence. Mark guessed beyond the fence was the expressway. He ran back to the car and motioned for the others to join him.

"Bobby's group is pinned down. The attackers have their

backs to us. We can get to them through the backyards of the houses and from above," he pointed at the hill, "along the expressway. We should be able to end this fight fast. Corporal Ward, will you take a group through the yards?" Ward nodded, pointed to three people and they ran off behind the corner house. "I'll go up the hill and snipe from there. The rest of you take up positions behind your cars in case they escape this way."

"What do you want me to do?" Lincoln said.

Mark eyed the man for a moment. "Just stay here."

"Oh, fuck you!"

The vehemence of the statement struck Mark like a punch. "Then do what you want." Mark turned and jogged toward the hill. He was halfway up when he became aware of another presence. He glanced left to see Lincoln running past him. At the top, the two men ran far enough not to be seen from below and swung toward the gunfight.

Judging the distance, Mark veered toward the downward slope and dropped to his knees. From there they crawled to the edge of the slope. He'd cut the approach too short and backed away. He moved another ten yards. Satisfied with this new position, he lay prone, his elbows on the ground and lined up his first shot. Lincoln took up a shooting stance two yards away.

As soon as he had a target, Mark squeezed the trigger. A man on the end of the barrier pitched forward and slumped to the ground. Lincoln's first shot followed with the same success. Ward's team started shooting and the crossfire was complete.

The defenders were quick to realize they were in serious trouble. The surviving attackers fled in whatever direction they could. In the heat of battle, Mark only saw one man escape.

"Cover me," Mark said, fully aware he was giving Lincoln orders again, but the need to see if his son was all right outweighed any other concerns. He didn't wait for his friend's response. He stood and ran down the slope toward the defenders' position.

The quiet was unnerving. The smell of the battle rose to meet him. He ran between the two lines and called, "Bobby! Elijah!" He stopped to avoid being taken for an enemy.

"Dad?" Bobby's voice made him go weak in the knees. The intensity of his relief watered his eyes and constricted his throat. Unable to speak, he walked forward. He had a moment to compose himself before Bobby jumped over the car to embrace him. "Wow! I'm glad to see you."

Mark cleared his throat. "You okay? Anyone hurt?"

"Yeah, we lost a few and Elijah is down."

"Let's go take a look."

They reached Elijah. Darlene had his head cradled in her lap. Tears streamed down her face. Blood spread across his chest. In pain, he was awake and alert. Mark crouched next to him and examined the wound. "Bobby, find something absorbent and some tape."

"Mark," Elijah reached for his arm. "Promise me you'll look after my people and, and my daughter."

Darlene moaned. "Daddy!"

"I won't have to. You'll take care of them yourself. We need to get you to our doctor. She'll get you fixed up. You just hang in there."

Bobby came back with a roll of gauze and duct tape. The two men lifted and wrapped Elijah and carried him to one of the cars, placing him in the back seat. Darlene knelt on the floor facing him.

"We have to get going in case anyone else shows up."

"Dad, we took a detour and found that tanker full of gas."

Mark nodded. "Okay, but we have to get moving."

"The only two who knew how to drive the tanker are either dead or wounded."

"If we can't figure it out, we'll have to leave it. We can't risk any more lives. Get your people loaded and up that hill. Use one of the abandoned cars to run through the fence. Get going now."

Mark trotted back to his own group. "Does anyone know how to drive a semi?"

Private Menke said, "I can."

"We need that tanker moving like now."

Menke looked to Ward who nodded, and he ran toward the semi.

"Someone should ride shotgun," Ward said.

"I'll go," Lincoln said. He left without looking back.

Mark felt a pang of sadness but shoved it aside. "Let's get everyone back in their cars and get out of here."

"You heard the man," Ward shouted. "Let's roll."

The defenders had propped up the fence but it wasn't nearly as strong as the first time they'd busted through. It took Bobby several attempts but the fence went down. One-by-one, the cars ascended the hill and took up positions on the expressway. The tanker took some maneuvering to get into position to get up enough speed to make the climb. The jeep brought up the rear. With the convoy on the road, they drove in pairs at a steady seventy miles per hour, exiting at the ramp closest to the farmhouse.

From there, it was a twenty-minute drive home. With so many vehicles they were forced to park along the street. They backed up the tanker on the far side of the property, near the garage and the two gas storage tanks.

The entire community had gathered, waiting for the return of their loved ones. The surgery in the barn was in full function. Doc and the assorted nurses and assistants were all busy. The six wounded were brought in and prioritized. Elijah was first.

Mark entered the recovery room to find Becca and Lynn, surprised to see the number of recovering patients. Stricken by guilt again, the sight was a reminder of the folly of his actions. Had he not been so set on his fishing trip, none of these people would be hurt and the dead would still be here. The burden of his decisions weighed on him like the anchor on the freighter. It took all his will to make his feet move.

He stood between the beds where Becca and Lynn lay. Both were asleep, though only Becca had an IV in. He looked from one face to the other. He loved them both, yet he was responsible for their pain. He touched his daughter's cheek and slid his fingers around her hand. Her left arm wore a cast. Too numb for emotion, he stared blankly at her serene face.

A soft touch on his arm made him turn. Lynn was awake and watching him.

He broke, gazing deeply into her eyes. His head bent and the tears came. He tried to speak, but could not form the words. Lynn pulled him close. She placed his head on her chest and let him cry for a moment. Gripping his head with both hands, she lifted him so she could see his face. "Shh! Shh!"

"I'm so, so sorry, Lynn. This is all my fault."

She shushed him and ran a hand through his hair, but offered no comment. After a while, his tears ran dry and he regained his composure. He forced his way through the guilt to look at her. Knowing what had to be done, his decision made, he kissed her forehead. "Forgive me."

"We'll talk about it later." Her voice was soft, but a hard edge shone in her eyes.

No, he thought. There's nothing left to discuss. He nodded. "I'll let you rest." He pushed away, leaned over his daughter, planted a kiss on her forehead, and left the room.

Fifty-Five

Exhausted physically, Mark's mind denied him sleep. He sat at the picnic tables. How many were there? Eight, he counted, butted end to end like a rural version of a royal dining room table. How many would never again sit at this table to share fellowship, because of stupid, selfish, decisions he had made?

"Mark, would you like some coffee, or are you getting ready to crash?" He looked up to see Lynn's daughter, Ruth. "You look like you could sleep for a week."

He reached out and took her hand. "I'm so sorry about your mother. It's all my fault."

Ruth eyed him, uncertainty playing across her face. "I don't think that's true. She didn't have to go after you. You certainly made her mad enough not to, but that's not how she is. If someone's in trouble, she's going to help. You're the same way, only —"

"Only what?"

"Well, sometimes it seems you go looking for trouble. I don't really think you mean to, but regardless, it finds you."

How old was Ruth now, sixteen? Seventeen? Yet, despite her lack of worldly experience, she could read people pretty well. But, how much of it was insight and how much was from her mother? It didn't matter, the analysis was right on. He had a strange, almost constant urge to keep moving, like a pioneer explorer. Only his wanderings brought death and pain to those he cared about.

"She loves you, you know!"

"Yes, and I love her."

"But, is it enough for you? I think that's what worries her. That one day you'll just up and go and leave her. Or worse, go off on one of your adventures and get killed, your body never discovered."

Yes, smart. That's exactly what he'd been contemplating. Leaving for the sake of all those in the community.

"I think that's why she's pulled away recently ... or had you even noticed? I know that's why she moved out of the house. She doesn't want to get hurt."

Mark didn't know what to say and Ruth seemed to understand that. "So, anyway, back to the original question ... coffee or sleep?"

He smiled. "Coffee, please. And Ruth, thank you."

"Hey, no problem. That's what Dr. Ruth is for."

He laughed to himself, wondering if she had any idea who Dr. Ruth was.

As Mark sipped his coffee, he watched the camp work. Crews went about their daily chores. Bobby supervised the distribution of the newly acquired food and gas to some of the community members. Everyone was doing something of importance, except for him.

He glanced across the street and saw Lincoln sitting on the steps of his porch. A six-pack of beer, probably from Bobby's haul, sat next to him, one can open in his hand. Mark thought the beer had to be really warm, perhaps even skunked after all this time on the shelf of a hot building. Lincoln didn't seem to mind and bottomed up the can. He tossed the empty behind him on the porch, pulled another free from its plastic holder and stared back at Mark.

His heart weighed heavily. He'd not only been responsible for, God, how many deaths? But also for the loss of the woman he loved and his best friend. Even though it would make Ruth's words come true, he believed leaving was the best for everyone. The only question remaining was when to go. Now would be best. With everyone busy, no one would notice he was gone.

But he couldn't leave without knowing for sure his daughter was all right.

He walked inside the house, poured another cup of coffee, and went to his room, the room he had once shared with Lynn, and filled a backpack. Ready, he took his cup outside leaving the bag and walked to the barn. Looking at the outside of the building, no one would know the transformation that took place inside. What had once been a dirt floor now had poured concrete. Four walls had been erected to make an operating room and a drop ceiling had been added for lighting and to create a more sterile environment.

Except for the poured floor, the second section, now utilized as a recovery room, had been left as it was. They'd hung sheets for privacy, but that was as far as they'd gotten with the renovation. The space had never been intended to handle this many patients. A situation Mark was well aware he'd created. The unfinished space added to the already great sense of guilt he carried. He hoped someone would complete the job after he was gone.

He stood outside the operating room wondering about Elijah. How long had he been in there? Doc must be exhausted working nonstop on the patients he'd sent her. He turned to enter the recovery room, when the operating room door opened and Doc came out.

She pulled off her mask and flopped into a chair outside the door. She looked as Mark expected, about ready to collapse. Doc looked up and her eyes locked on the mug. "Is that coffee?"

"Yeah."

She held out her hand. Mark gave her the mug. Doc sniffed at the steam, absorbed the aroma; without testing the heat, she drank half of it down. She moaned with pleasure, wiped her mouth with the back of her gloved hand, closed her eyes and leaned her head back. "Please, tell me I'm done."

"I think so."

"What the hell happened out there?" she raised a hand, "No, don't tell me."

"What's the toll?"

She shrugged. "Final count is still unknown. We lost a few, but most will make it. The one I just finished will be touch-and-go. He could go either way. All the bullet-wound patients, barring runaway infection, should recover. Lynn has a concussion; she just needs rest. Your daughter has some broken bones that should heal in time. She's young and strong, I'm not too worried about those."

Mark's internal alarms went off. "But?"

"Well, I can't see if there's any internal damage. She also took a nasty blow to the head. She could have pressure building inside that I won't know about for a while in this primitive setting. I might have to go in to relieve the pressure and any time you're dealing with opening up the skull, you could create problems. But, even if she does heal, it might be a long time before we know the extent of any brain damage."

She opened her eyes and gazed at Mark. "I'm sorry, but I can't tell you any more than that."

Mark swayed, feeling light-headed. He took an unsteady step but regained his balance. Doc said something else, but Mark didn't hear. His stomach knotted at the thought of his active and vibrant daughter perhaps being a vegetable or a ghost of her former self. That changed everything, or did it? He couldn't leave with his daughter's survival still in limbo, yet knowing he was the one responsible for her condition made the need to run even stronger.

He whirled around and hastened from the barn. Outside, he pressed his hands to his face and tried to think. Everything ran through his head, jumbled together in one long unending ball of stress. He walked without knowing where he was going. Soon, he was on the street, running alongside the property, his mind blank, his movements robotic and automatic, with no reference to time or distance.

A car horn startled him from his trance.

Mark turned to find a pickup truck bearing down on him. He blinked away his confusion. He stood in the middle of the road. The house and property were nowhere in sight. He stepped to the side of the road as the truck bore down on him. He reached for his gun, suddenly aware of how vulnerable he was, only to find he'd walked off without it. He didn't even have the pocket knife, Darlene still had it.

He backed up and crouched, ready to spring as the truck pulled up and stopped. Lincoln looked back at him through the open window. They stared at each other in silence for a long uncomfortable minute. "You're not getting off that easy."

"Huh?"

"You can't run from this. You caused it, now you deal with it. If I'm staying, you have to, too. Face the problem like a man and maybe we'll all get through this and be better for it."

Mark was dumbstruck.

"Don't give me that space cadet look. Get your ass in the truck."

Mark walked around the front and for a moment thought Lincoln might run him down. He opened the passenger door and climbed in. They eyed each other again without speaking.

Lincoln shook his head and drove. "I'm still upset with

you, but you're my friend, I'll deal with it. You never intend for things to work out as they do, but for the good of everyone here, you need to think things through. The solution is not to run from your problems but to face them, correct the flaws that cause the problems and become better. These people need you, God help them all, but they do."

"I don't know about that."

"Oh, shut the fuck up. You ain't going nowhere. You're the one everyone looks to for strength and advice. If you go bananas, how's anyone supposed to survive? Just stop doing stupid things, like cross country fishing trips."

"Can they forgive me? Can you?"

"It'll all pass in time. The question is can you forgive yourself? These people will need to heal. To do that, they need leadership they can rely on. They need routine and consistency. The past few months have shown us we'll never know what to expect or what dangers might come our way. We'll deal with them as they come. But in between those traumatic events, they have to know peace. They have to believe this world is still a place worth living in and that, given time, civilization will have a rebirth."

He slapped a can of beer against Mark's chest. "Here, drink this. Nothing like a warm beer to make everything better."

Mark opened the can and took a sip. Instantly he spat it out. "That's horrid. How can you drink this piss?"

"I pretend it's the best beer I've ever had at a better time in my life, and don't let the taste distract me from that memory."

Mark tried again, making a nasty face as he swallowed. "Man, I don't know if I've ever been happy enough to drink this."

"Don't you waste my good beer, now. Drink up. When we finish this six-pack, I've got another case."

Mark's stomach twisted at the thought.

"I also have a bottle of tequila, but you don't get any of that until the beer's gone."

"Shit!"

"Oh," Lincoln laughed, "I have no doubt there'll be plenty of that after drinking this."

Lincoln parked in his driveway across from the farmhouse. "This ain't perfect. You ain't perfect. Hell, even I'm not perfect, but I'm more perfect than you. What I'm saying here is, we've been dealt this new hand and are still learning the rules of the game. Bad things are gonna happen and we'll face them, but we've got enough to deal with here, just trying to survive. We don't need to go looking for more problems. After a while, the burden is too great for the best of us, which means me."

He smiled. "I snapped back there at the lake and said some things in the heat of the moment that maybe I shouldn't have. I'm sorry about the tone, but not about the words. You needed to hear them."

Lincoln took a long drink, emptying the can. He crushed it in his hand. "I thought about packing up and leaving. I'd had enough. A lot of the community has had enough of the constant battles. Fortunately, Jenny is the voice of reason. Anyway, I'm not going anywhere, and if I'm not," he poked Mark in the chest, "you're not. Got it?"

"Got it." He finished his beer and opened the door.

"Give me the can. We're recycling."

Mark laughed and handed it over. "Linc, thanks."

"For what? Not kicking your ass?"

"For your friendship. For being there for me, for us. For always having my back, and … for not leaving."

Lincoln extended a fist and Mark bumped it. "Yeah, but no more stupid shit, right?"

Fifty-Six

Mark found his son sitting next to his sister in the recovery room. Darlene sat next to him and her father, who'd been placed in the cot next to Rebecca. The two leaned close to each other talking in low tones. He stopped to watch them for a while and realized he'd never seen his son spend much time with the other girls in the community. The young had been deprived of so much in their short lives, but even in this new world, nature had to take its course.

Doc came up and stood at his side. She sipped from a mug of coffee and gazed over the wounded. "It was a long night and day. We won more than we lost, but the cost was still too dear."

Another shard of guilt pierced his heart. He cleared his throat. "How many did we lose?"

"The battle claimed four of ours, five of the new group's, that I know of." She frowned. "And maybe one or two more from this group." She nodded at the recovery room inhabitants. "It's still too early to tell."

She rolled her head in a circle and moaned as her neck cracked. "I'll say this though, considering the circumstances, the medical team we've assembled and trained does an awesome job. We'd have lost a lot more had it not been for them."

"That's all on you, Doc. It's your team and your training."

"True. But it goes to show what people can do when they band together for a common goal. However, that brings to mind a problem. A lot of the supplies we gathered a few months back have been depleted. If these situations continue to arise, we'll have to hunt up some more, and the sooner the better. I'd rather be prepared than have something come up I can't handle because of lack of basic supplies. We'll probably have to do a blood drive too, although storing it could be a problem."

"I'll leave that to you. I'm sure you'll get plenty of volunteers. Let me know what you need and maybe some of us can build it or find it. We'll figure something out."

They stood in silence for a moment until Doc said, "Your son told me they discovered a medical facility out along route two. He said it was under guard like a military installation, but was on the grounds of a Cleveland Clinic compound. They saw an ambulance pull up to the gate and pass through, like maybe it was carrying a patient."

Mark waited for her to finish, knowing she brought it up for a reason.

"It might be good to send a delegation out there to see what they're about. If they have doctors or more complete and operational facilities, it could be a beneficial alliance."

Mark thought that over for a moment, wondering about what Lynn would say about another excursion. "Okay, we'll talk it over."

Bobby stood up and leaned over his sister. He said a few words, looked up, excitement flashing through his eyes. Doc and Mark moved at the same time. They reached the bed and Doc handed her mug to Mark. Becca turned her head toward them.

"How do you feel, Becca?"

She croaked, cleared her throat and tried again. "Hurt."

"Where's the pain?"

"Everywhere."

Doc examined her.

"What happened?"

Mark said, "You fell. Do you remember that?"

Her eyes looked up to the right as she tried to recall the memory. "Yes. They tried to hang you."

"That's right. And you saved my life."

Becca winced as Doc probed her side with her finger.

"Did that hurt?" Doc asked.

"Yeah!" she replied, with an unspoken, "Duh!"

Doc moved down her body poking at her.

Becca looked to the side and saw Lynn. "Is Lynn all right?"

"She's gonna be fine. She's just sleeping."

"Becca," Doc said, "did you feel that?"

"Feel what?"

Doc shot Mark a worried look.

"This. Anything?"

Becca shook her head.

"Can you feel me touching your feet?"

Again Becca shook her head.

"Give me your knife," Doc demanded of Mark. Worry left him immobile. "Mark!"

He snapped from his concern and reached for his knife, confused at not finding it. A hand stretched in front of him holding his knife. He glanced up. Darlene shrugged and handed it to the doctor. "Concentrate now." She poked the tip of the knife in the sole of Becca's foot. Seeing no reaction, she repeated the poke on the other foot. Becca felt neither.

Doc straightened up, patted Becca's legs and smiled. "Okay, honey, we'll try again tomorrow after you've had some time to rest and recover."

"Wait!" she cried out, on the verge of panic. "Wh-what does that mean?"

Doc sighed. "It's nothing to be concerned about right

now."

"Tell me!"

Doc glanced at her other recovering patients as both Bobby and Mark shushed her.

"It may be nothing and it may only be temporary, but for the moment, it appears you're paralyzed from the waist down."

The shock of the statement hung like a mushroom cloud over the room.

"Bobby gasped, "Oh, sis. Oh no!"

Mark felt the earth shift under him and for the moment thought he might fall.

Doc looked from face to face as she spoke. "No one should be too concerned yet. It could just be from the trauma. It could resolve itself at any time. The important thing is not to panic and allow the healing process to take its course. We'll know more in a few days."

Becca turned her head from the others and cried silently. Doc walked away and when she returned had a syringe. In a quick, fluid motion, she jabbed the needle into Becca's arm.

"What the hell was that?" Becca shouted, rubbing her arm.

"Just a sedative, to help you sleep."

"You stupid bitch, you had no right."

"Becca," Mark chided. "That's no way to talk—"

"Shut up! Just shut up all of you. You're not the ones who'll never be able to walk again. Get out. All of you get out and leave me alone." She covered her face and cried.

Doc motioned for them to leave. "Let's leave and let her rest. I don't want her to get too emotional and wake the others."

The group left and Doc drew a sheet across their view. "The sedative will take effect quickly. Hopefully, she'll sleep till morning. Don't worry, one of us will be here all night. We'll keep checking on her."

Bobby and Darlene left the barn, but Mark lingered. "Doc?"

He didn't have to finish his question. "I can't say for sure, Mark. I didn't see any obvious signs of trauma to her spine, but I also don't have the equipment to see something like that. It very well might be temporary, maybe something pinching off the nerves."

She shrugged. "I really don't know at this point. I'll do some reading and find out what I can, but for now, all we can do is wait and see. I know I say that a lot, but it's the reality of our situation. I wish I could tell you something more reassuring, but ..."

He nodded. There was nothing more to say. He would have to wait, and pray to a God he was no longer sure he believed in. He found a chair and sat, his weight feeling heavier all of a sudden.

"You should rest, Mark. From the bits I've heard, you've had a trying few days."

"It's my daughter. I wouldn't be able to sleep anyway."

She nodded and put a comforting hand on his shoulder. "I understand. You'll forgive me though, if I try to get a few hours of sleep. I have a feeling I'm going to need it tomorrow."

"Of course, and Doc, thanks."

Fifty-Seven

Lynn woke and glanced around wide-eyed until she remembered where she was. Becca lay to her left. She wondered about the young woman; she'd been unconscious on the helicopter, but Lynn knew little of her condition. Soft snoring made her look to the other side of her cot. To her surprise, Mark sat asleep in a folding chair set up next to her, his long frame barely supported by the metal chair.

She smiled at seeing him, a warm sensation flowed through her making her feel better. Lynn wanted to wake him and tell him she was sorry; tell him that she had been wrong about his desire to find trouble. Well, to a certain degree, anyway. If they were ever going to find peace and get any semblance of civilization back on track, they had to start living their lives as they had done before the apocalyptic event that destroyed so many lives.

She knew a complete return to normal was unrealistic, if not impossible, but how could she fault Mark for trying to recapture those times, even if they did lead them into danger. Well, that was a problem they would have to talk about, but moving out on him was a mistake. She loved him, and whatever came their way, they would face together.

He stirred and Lynn could no longer help herself. She reached out and touched his arm. He woke with a start, ready to take on more trouble. As their eyes met, the hard edges disappeared from his face. Relief, morphed into joy and the watery eyes showed the love he seldom talked about.

He stood and leaned over her. "Hi," he said.

Lynn touched his cheek and wiped a fallen tear. The fact that he cried choked her up. Her words refused to come. She reached up with both arms and took him into an embrace. Lynn felt him holding back, but she wrapped her arms around further and pulled tight. For a few glorious moments they held that position, melding into each other.

"I'm sorry, Lynn."

"No, I'm sorry."

"No, you were right. I was only thinking about myself. I just wanted to do one thing that made me feel normal again."

"Don't you see Mark? This is our normal. We can't go back, we can only make the best of what we have now. Who knows how long it will be before now changes. For us, the best source of normal is to have our family, friends and community around us."

"You're right. I'm sorry. I ..."

"Shut up and just hold me."

"I will, forever."

"Mark—"

"I love you, Lynn."

His words made her forget her own. She sobbed into his shoulder, confident that no matter what came their way, they would get through it ... together.

Acknowledgements

I enjoy writing post-apocalyptic stories because there is an 'anything is possible' feel to them. There are no rules, no authority, just common sense and the struggle to hold onto to humanity. If you've been reading this series, you know that's been a central theme throughout. How we treat each other when faced with adversity is in direct relationship to how we treat each other during more normal times. Will we help each other in times of need or will we turn on each other in an everyone-for-themselves way?

I'd like to think civilization will continue, that we will all work together to rebuild a new, more accepting world. There will be those who chose a more communal approach to survival, but there will also be those who fend for themselves. We see that in today's world. The hatred we have, the lack of control over urges to attack and kill. The loss of caring and compassion for our fellow man. Perhaps that is why the popularity of the genre continues to grow. We can see the possibility of an apocalyptic event and fear we are heading in that direction.

I do a lot of shows and have met thousands of people this year. I appreciate the positive comments and continued support. I love talking to fans of the genre and listening to their ideas of how they see the world in apocalyptic times. Keep reading, I'll write more.

I'd like to thank all those who have supported the first three volumes. Thank you to my family and friends who leave me alone when I'm in a meeting with the voices in my head, and who try not to let their eyes glaze over when I start talking about weird stuff.

The sites I used in this story do exist although I may have altered a few to fit the story. Camp Perry is real and is part of the Ohio National Guard and run by the Adjutant General's office. The camp houses the Civilian

Marksmanship Program Office, which hosts shooting competitions and National matches.

The Davis-Besse Nuclear power plant is also real and off Lake Erie. The marina is real too, but I took liberties with its grounds.

Thanks to my daughter, April, for the press kits, the marketing and the great work on the website.

Thank you to Jodi McDermmit for the help with the newsletter, your support and help making the stories better.

Thanks to John Kallas, PhD. for his book Edible Wild Plants. Check it out. It's very educational, especially for you survivalists.

Thanks again, to Rebel E Publishers especially EJ and Jayne, for your continued interest and support.

Check my website raywenck.com for current news, a list of appearances, my blog and what's coming next.

About the Author

Ohio native Ray Wenck took up writing upon retiring from teaching. He also owned DeSimone's Italian Restaurant in Toledo for twenty-five years. In recent years, he has proven to be a prolific novelist with a range of action-adventure novels to his credit. After retiring, he became a lead cook for Hollywood Casinos and the kitchen manager for the Toledo Mud Hens AAA baseball team. Now he spends most of his time writing, doing book tours and meeting old and new fans and friends around the country.

Ray is the author of eleven novels including the post-apocalyptic, Random Survival series and the mystery/suspense Danny Roth series and a YA novel, The Warriors. Ray hikes, cooks and plays harmonica with whatever band will let him sit in – or watches baseball – when not writing.

Facebook: https://www.facebook.com/authorraywenck/
Twitter: @RayWenck
Website: http://www.raywenck.com/

Also by this author …

The Danny Roth series: *Teammates, Teamwork, Home Team, Stealing Home, Group Therapy, Double Play*

The Random Survival series: *Random Survival, The Long Search For Home, The Endless Struggle*

Warriors of the Court

Made in the USA
Coppell, TX
01 July 2022